MW00912875

I Believe

Lost at the North Pole

Carol

Enjoy The Book
"I Believe"

Lonnie Brinkley

2009

I Believe
Lost at the North Pole

Lonnie R. Brinkley

Big Bear Publishing US
Ronks, Pennsylvania

This book is a work of fiction. Names, characters, places, and events
are products of the author's imagination or are used fictitiously.
Any resemblance to actual events, locations or persons, living or
deceased, is purely coincidental. We assume no responsibility
for errors, inaccuracies, omissions, or any inconsistency herein.

1st printing 2008 • 2nd printing 2008

ISBN 978-0-9801215-3-7

LCCN 2007908725

**ATTENTION CORPORATIONS, UNIVERSITIES, COLLEGES, AND
PROFESSIONAL ORGANIZATIONS:** Quantity discounts are available on
bulk purchases of this book for educational, gift purposes, or as premiums for
increasing magazine subscriptions or renewals. Special books or book excerpts
can also be created to fit specific needs. For information, please contact
Big Bear Publishing US, P.O. Box 191, Ronks, PA 17572; 717-768-4644.

I dedicate this book to
Wilma Lavern Brinkley Harris.
Thank you for your encouragement over my lifetime.
You're the best, "Lady Laverne."

Acknowledgments

I want to thank my daughter Tiffany Joanne Brinkley for encouraging me to write, for your many hours of typing, and for your input. I also want to thank my daughter Stefanie Joanne Brinkley for your fast typing and for contributing your ideas. Thank you for all the fun we had, girls!

I want to thank Joanne R. Brinkley for the many hours you devoted to working on the manuscript and for proofreading. I want to thank Andrew Knight for your endless hours of fabulous artwork. I want to thank Kate Deubert for your tremendous edit. I'm glad you jumped in with both feet like Bubbles would have. I want to thank Cathy Bowman for your outstanding interior design and cover work.

To all my friends and family for all their encouragement, and to anyone else who has worked on this project, all of us brought this novel together—"I believe!"

Contents

Chapter One
The Expedition

Polar Ice Cap No. 12 Base Camp.

It was getting close to Christmastime and all the children—including me—were getting super-excited thinking about the bright and shiny packages that soon would be piled up under the Christmas tree. There were sure to be clothes and toys, but this year I really wanted something special, a unique gift that I'd kept secret from everybody. Lots of family members were visiting together, talking and laughing, but I sat all by myself contemplating my hoped-for gift. My Grandfather Lon passed by the study door and saw me in there. He came in, sat down next to me, and put his arm around me, saying, "What seems to be on your mind, Tony?"

I knew I could trust Grandfather Lon not to give it away, so I whispered my wish in his ear. He pondered my secret and took a deep breath, then looked me straight in the eye and said, "Grandson,

I have a story I would like to share with you that I have never told a single soul before." I was so curious I thought I'd burst. "What is it, Grandfather?" I said. A smile lit up his face as he asked, "Are you ready to go around the world?" With butterflies in my stomach I immediately answered, "Yes...yes, Grandfather. Tell me...tell me!" He then told me the most amazing story I have ever heard....

❋ ❋ ❋ ❋ ❋

A long time ago, when I was a scientist working at the Lincoln Vanderbilt Science Technology Center, I was sent on an expedition along with eight other scientists. We trekked to the North Ridge near the North Hills to study the polar ice caps.

We were all experts in our fields, the best of the best gathered from around the world for this particular research project. Each scientist's specialty would be key to the expedition, and our collective results would finally fit together like some fabulous puzzle to create a complete picture, and hopefully, a solution.

We all met at the Crystal Resort and Convention Center in Rome and stayed there for a few days prior to boarding a ship to Greenland. The trip lasted eleven days during which we spotted all types of marine wildlife, including white dolphins and a variety of huge whales. The scenery was gorgeous. None of us really knew the correct names of the different creatures: We studied currents, ice, movements, and so on, not marine biology. One member of our group, Leo, liked to make up names for the different mammals. Of course, we could tell he was kidding, but we were having too much fun. The names he thought of were imaginative and they made us all laugh. He really made our trip a pleasure, and the time passed quickly.

When we landed in Greenland, we loaded our gear and possessions onto horses and carriages to be taken to the train station. We had brought so much equipment, it took us a few trips to transfer everything from the ship, then we were going to have to transfer everything again when we reached the train that would take us to Kremaska and the North Ridge. All this lifting and loading had its advantages though. Besides keeping us fit, it gave us a chance to get to know each other. We exchanged information about our professions and discussed what we wanted to accomplish on the project. Our destination was Polar Ice Cap No. 12 where our research base and living quarters were located. We would call it "home" for almost three months.

Tom was the first scientist I met. He was from Romania and studied the thickness of ice. His job was to take measurements in different areas of the region. The process involved drilling holes approximately forty feet down through the ice, then lowering a reado-size meter into the hole to record the depth of the ice. A laser beam would touch the top of the seawater and read back the measurement to the master computer then store the reading into the reado-size meter. After the computer registered the data, it recorded it on a map. Once all the points were noted on the map, Tom would have a map of readings for the entire area.

Sim was a scientist from Spain. He studied the molecules, compounds, and minerals that make up ice. He brought with him various types of microscopes and digital microgram machines that detect the smallest particles in ice to determine how long it has existed. Like Tom, he also needed to drill a deep hole in the ice to bring up small ice samples from forty feet below. To save time and to alter the environment as little as possible, Sim and Tom would be working together.

Then there was Leo, a scientist from Brazil affectionately known as the "master of wind." Besides making up amusing names for sea creatures, Leo's main job was studying wind, and air patterns and currents. He brought along a spectrogram that could show not only one, but four different wind patterns at one time. Many years before, there had been a major disturbance in the North Ridge, and we hoped to discover what had happened. Leo's primary objective on this expedition was to log all the information about wind, air, and temperatures of that area into the master computer.

Sonny was from Canada, and he studied glaciers and other ice formations. His machinery tracked the flow of wind as it shaped the ice and snow. Sonny would be working closely with Leo since their fields of study were similar. Sonny's major piece of equipment was a projectogram that registered information from wind currents and could project a picture of ice formations at Polar Ice Cap No. 12. After he got the information fed into the computer it would be added to the map.

Fred was from Costa Rica, and his specialty was water currents and temperature. He had traveled all around the Earth studying seawater and other bodies of water. He felt that everything in the world had to do with temperature. His hair stuck out in every direction in kind of a wacky way, but don't let that fool you…he had a brilliant mind. Even on the ship, Fred worked gathering water samples to test. Everyone else used the journey as a welcome break and thought Fred should unwind and enjoy life a little. But to Fred, science in general was fascinating fun; it was his kind of recreation. Not surprisingly, he seemed to have the most equipment in his room.

Marie was a scientist from Australia and a wiz at using computers and other electronics. With a master's degree in languages, she was also the interpreter for the expedition and translated our conversations with ease. She was highly organized, checked and double-checked her equipment, and was more than ready to fulfill requests for duplicate printouts and regional data. Marie was our communications lifeline in more ways than one.

Arlie was a scientist from Russia who studied the splitting of ice caps. He would be sinking lots of small tracking devices thirty inches below the snow and ice to detect changes. He would also be placing trimmer devices into the snow and ice to detect different degrees of movement going on. These trimmer devices were called "arlies," named after Arlie. He had invented them specifically for this purpose.

Pat was a scientist from France who would be working double duty. First, she was to assist Marie with computer data input, coordination, and readouts. But also, since she had graduated from one of the top culinary arts schools in Europe, she was to prepare all of our meals. Words cannot express how fortunate we felt to have a cordon bleu chef along on the trip. We knew her computer skills would help keep the information current for everyone. But just as necessary, her special dishes would help to keep away the boredom and the blues that can creep up on you when you're isolated for months in a cold

and distant place. Pat had packed her special herbs and cooking utensils to make the food interesting for us.

Last was me, Lon. I was brought over from the United States to
head up the expedition. My job assignment was to study the temperature and weather, which were strange and unpredictable at the
North Ridge. It was always very cold, around twenty below zero, and
the wind and air currents would shift dramatically and then go back
to normal within just a few hours. I was to keep a daily chart and
record all of my research and conclusions.

The train ride to Kremaska would take three days. The closer we
got, the colder it got, and the excitement built for our little interna-
tional group. This expedition was going to be great! We couldn't wait
to get started on our research.

Spotting wildlife from the train became a great sport. Marie spied
an eagle and a snow fox and pointed them out to the rest of us. We
also saw moose, rabbits, a couple of bears, caribou—the list went on
and on. The animals in this area were amazing!

To the right side of the train there was nothing but snow, and a
few mountains. Sonny, Arlie, and I got to wondering about this and
asked the train conductor, who was called Dana. "Why is there so
much life on the left side of the train, but on the right there seems to
be nothing at all?" Dana answered, "Well boys, I've been traveling
these train tracks for over forty years, from my youth up, and I'm here
to tell you there is nothing—and I mean nothing—on the right side
of the train toward the north. I've never seen a single sign of life over
there, only on the left toward the south." We all looked at each other
in disbelief because *we* were headed for the right side of the tracks
toward the north!

While Sonny and Arlie went back to the group to tell them what
Dana had said, I stayed behind to get more details. Now everyone
was talking excitedly about the trip. We were headed to a very cold
place with nothing in sight except for a few mountains, glaciers, and
snow, snow, and more snow.

When we arrived at Kremaska, nine dogsled teams were waiting
patiently to take us along the final leg of our journey to the research
base. We had changed to heavier clothing and snowsuits before leav-

ing the train. It was going to be a challenge to stay warm in one of the coldest places on Earth. The temperature was twenty-seven degrees below zero, but it seemed much colder. We loaded our belongings onto the sleds and took roll call. Sim, Marie, Tom, Fred, Leo, Sonny, Arlie, Pat, and I were all situated and ready to go.

I settled in to enjoy the ride. I thought about what the train conductor, Dana, had told me: "Lon, I'm the fourth generation in my family to be a train conductor and I'm going to tell you a story. A long time ago, when my great-great grandfather was the train conductor, he brought six people with deer to the North Ridge. They said they were headed to the North Hills, which is on the right side of the train tracks toward the far north. Over the next two years, many small people came and got off at that same stop and headed in the same direction. Those were the only people who had ever gone out that way, and no one ever heard from them again. Therefore, I advise you and your friends to take precautions and be careful; no one knows what's out there.

"We do know of one man who lives in that area. He goes by the name of 'Buddy.' Every so often he has visitors come to see him, but it's mostly in the beginning of the year." I asked Dana if he'd ever seen Buddy. He replied, "No, but my father did. I've heard stories about him riding around in a sleigh pulled by deer. It seems pretty odd to me, but that's the way he gets around, so I hear." Dana showed me a wooden whistle and said, "My father gave me this whistle. It's called a 'train whistle.' It was given to him by Buddy, and when I became a train conductor my father passed it on to me. When you blow through this opening here, it makes the sound of a real train whistle. I don't know if all these stories I've heard are real, but I do know my father always spoke the truth."

Two days later we reached our base camp on Polar Ice Cap No. 12. We were all happy to finally arrive. Pat started the generators so we could have power for lights and all of our equipment in the compound, while the rest of us unloaded our equipment and gear. Leo built a nice fire to keep us warm, and Marie helped Pat cook dinner. After we settled in and enjoyed a delicious meal, everyone was ready for a good night's rest.

The next morning the owners of the dogsled teams joined us for breakfast and got ready to leave. They were to return in ten-to-twelve weeks to pick us up, depending on the weather. We waved goodbye and wished them a safe trip back to town. We had no time to waste, so we set up our equipment, turned on the computers, and got to work right away. We had only so much time to finish our research before the dogsled teams returned to transport us off the ice cap.

Each one of us had a copy of the latest data that had been documented from the area. This data would prepare us somewhat for what we could expect. Our first job was to make sure the ice caps were still increasing in size. The larger the ice caps, the more water there would be on the surface of the Earth. We knew that favorable air temperatures and the right amount of moisture were necessary for the ice caps to continue growing. And ever since the mysterious disturbance that had disrupted the area, Polar Ice Cap No. 12 had gotten smaller and smaller. This was not at all good.

Tom got to work drilling holes all over the ice cap, and his findings were automatically transferred to the master computer. Everyone got copies. Already, Marie had to refill ink cartridges for two of the printers. We were all working really hard. When she wasn't assisting Marie, Pat was busy making lunch. Arlie went over to Polar Ice Cap No. 9 to track an ice split. Each of us had a snowmobile that could go approximately twenty-five miles an hour, so we could all get around the camp on our own. These were some of the first snowmobiles ever made, and they were showing their age.

After nine weeks at base camp, we were all feeling at home, but we were also aware that our time was running out. I knew the territory pretty well by now and ventured farther and farther away from the base camp. Besides, there was too much going on in the compound. The generators were running, the fireplace was going, there were too many fumes, and I needed to get in the open to get the best readings.

I used one of the two tracking machines that could travel seventy-five miles around the base camp, and I made sure to put on all my winter gear—my snowsuit, coat, gloves, and boots. All of our clothing was double-insulated and specially designed for temperatures down to thirty degrees below zero.

Before leaving I double-checked my equipment. I'd packed snow-shoes, a walking stick, and my metrometer, and I'd put extra food and tools in my backpack. In the event that anything went wrong, I was ready. Normally we would never travel alone, always in twos, but everyone was busy and I needed to get my readings. Besides, it was a beautiful day—no wind, no snowfall, perfect weather for taking readings.

I headed toward the North Hills. About two hours out, I stopped near a huge cluster of mountains. I thought if I hiked up a bit I would get better readings than on the low ground. I put on my snowshoes and backpack, and grabbed my equipment and walking stick.

I was hiking for about ten minutes before I noticed the weather changing. The north wind started picking up and snow began to fall. A few minutes later I was in the middle of a snowstorm, so I turned around and headed back down to the tracking machine. The snow got thicker, the wind picked up speed, and it was getting hard to see. At this point I knew I was in big trouble. In the distance I could just see the shape of a large forest that could shelter me, so I began making my way in that direction. It took me the longest time to get there. The closer I got to the forest, the worse the storm got. I could barely see my hand in front of my face, and the going really got rough. Finally, I had no choice. I had to leave the tracking machine behind.

At last I made it to the Black Hills Forest. In the middle of a blizzard I dug out a small igloo as shelter from the wind and snow. Even though it was beyond cold outside, it was warm inside the igloo. I was exhausted and hungry after my hard work, so I snuggled up, had a bite to eat, and tried to sleep. The north wind raged as though it were angry. When the storm died down, I scooped out a small opening in the wall of my shelter so I could check on the outside world. The igloo was completely buried in snow, and I was amazed at what I was seeing through my frosty little peephole.

Chapter Two

What I Saw

What Lon saw through the opening in his igloo.

Peering through my window, I could see it was quiet inside the forest. The snow had tapered off to almost nothing. But beyond the woods the storm still raged.

An enormous white bird swooped down across my line of vision. It was like an eagle, only bigger, with a wingspan six or seven feet wide. Its beak was orange, its eyes were silver, and its feathers glistened as though they'd been rubbed with oil. There were five claws on each foot, three in front and two in the back. It looked to be a very powerful bird, yet the feathers on its chest were soft and plush. Later, I found out it was called a "Wakashinda bird" and was nearly extinct. Just a few were left on Earth, and those could be found only at the North Ridge. In all my travels, I'd never seen a bird like it. It looked magical, but it was quite real.

I panned my narrow range of vision and saw a small herd of deer. They were very muscular, weighing maybe four hundred pounds each. Their broad antlers spread to about four feet wide and swept up and over their backs. There had to be at least fourteen to twenty points on them. The deer were a ruddy brown and white, and their midsection was barrel-shaped and larger than usual. A black nose and blue eyes studded a broad head. They were well kept and groomed, odd for a wild animal. These creatures were gorgeous, like no deer I'd ever seen before. I thought one turned and looked up at me, so I kept still and didn't make a peep.

The deer moved around, and I was surprised to see a small man standing in the middle of them. I had all I could do to stay calm as I watched the strange scene outside my window; my mind was racing wildly. What was this man doing out here and in middle of nowhere? The deer seemed to be friendly to him, as if they knew him. The deer shifted, and I could see the man a little better. He had a thin face with wrinkles, was bald with a little hair on the back of his head, and his skin was tan colored. He wore a long coat that touched his feet, and it flapped open as he moved so that I could see a colorful sweater, green pants, and sturdy boots. A clear glass case lay at his feet, but there was nothing inside.

The man fed the glorious white bird from his hand, picking through its feathers as the bird ate. He explored the bird's feathers as though he was looking for something. Suddenly my leg slipped, and I made a small noise. The animals turned, looked toward my direction, and froze. They didn't move and neither did I. Even though I was well concealed, I suspected the animals might have detected me with their amazing eyesight and hearing. The man, however, kept looking through the feathers, and all of a sudden he plucked one from the bird. I wiped my eyes, stunned by the man's curious actions. What was he doing and why was he doing it? He then placed the feather into the glass case and locked it. I squinted and stared, trying not to miss a thing.

The bird finished eating and flew away, and the little man started walking in the direction of my igloo with the deer at his side. As he got closer I saw he had a long beard that he tucked into his coat. He stopped for a moment and put down the glass case so he could slip on his gloves. This gave me a chance to get a better look at the feather in the case. The feather was a glittery silver color and I wasn't sure, but I thought I saw it move. I was amazed at what was all happening right in front of me. What would he possibly do with this feather? I guessed it must be very special.

The man probably thought he was the only one in the Black Hills Forest. The blizzard had buried my igloo and wiped out my footprints. I held my breath as he walked directly toward me and right up over the igloo. My eyes grew big as man and beast stepped above my head. Then with a whomp! my igloo caved in. The man fell down right in front of me and my heart jumped, as I'm sure his did too. We stared at each other in total shock. Then I noticed the glass case had opened and the feather had fallen out. On instinct, I reached to pick up the feather for him, but before I could he shouted, "No, no, don't touch! This is a Shimatta feather; no one can touch it but me! Thank you, but if you touch this feather it will wither away and vanish." I apologized, saying, "Oh, I'm sorry. So…what is your name?" He replied, "My name is Wrinkles. What is yours?" I replied, "Lon."

The Shimatta feather that Lon saw lying on the ground.

Wrinkles picked up the Shimatta feather and placed it back inside the glass case. That's when he told me about the Wakashinda bird, that it was seriously endangered, that there were only a few left in the entire world, and that all of them were here at the North Ridge. As we sat in the middle of my squashed igloo discussing the

Wakashinda bird, we heard a noise above us. Four deer were leaning over the top of the igloo and looking down at the two of us. We both broke out in laughter. I noticed the deer seemed to be watching over Wrinkles. I asked him, "What is the feather for?" He answered, "After a full day, the Shimatta feather will come to life and I will use it to wake up the other elves." I said, "Other *elves*?" Before I could say more, he said, "Yes, I am one of Santa's elves." Not for the first time that day, I felt overwhelmed. I remembered the stories I'd heard about Santa Claus and the elves at the North Pole—could they be true?

Wrinkles asked me why I was here in the Black Hills Forest. I told him I was on an expedition with other scientists and our base camp was on Polar Ice Cap No. 12. I was surprised when he said he already knew we were staying there. He said, "This entire area is the North Pole. Kris and my son Happy named it. To the east is the North Ridge, and to the west are the twenty-two polar ice caps. That's where you came from. Heading north are the North Hills, and that's where we are. If you travel south you reach Jemdaza, one of the closest towns to us. There are a couple other towns but they're near Kremaska. The North Wind told Ivy there were scientists doing research on Polar Ice Cap No. 12." This was all sounding very mysterious to me.

Wrinkles asked, "But what are you doing way over here in the Black Hills Forest?" I told him, "Well, all of the scientists were busy doing their research and the weather was so good at the time, so I thought I'd get some good, clear air and moisture readings. I had all of my equipment set up taking measurements when out of nowhere snow started to fall and in no time I was in the middle of a blizzard. I took my instruments apart and packed them up because the snow was falling faster and the wind was picking up, and I knew I was going to be in trouble very soon."

Wrinkles wanted to know where my tracking machine was. I told him it was about a mile away, between us and some little mountains. You couldn't see them from where we were. "It's only about a forty-five minute walk, but I imagine it's buried in snow," I said. Wrinkles said, "The little mountains you were talking about are called the Twin Peaks, and you can see them on a clear day. The third mountain is smaller, and it isn't visible until you get closer. The Twin Peaks were named by Buddy, one of Santa's helpers. Lon, you won't make it out of here alone. Follow me; I'm going to help you. I'll take you to my home until the weather clears."

We climbed out of the igloo, and Wrinkles led me through the forest since the trees would provide better protection from the wind and snow. The deer followed wherever Wrinkles would go. I said, "These deer are beautiful. They look very strong." Wrinkles smiled as he told me, "These are called 'raindeer.' Santa named them after the rain. And yes, they are beautiful animals."

He started talking about the raindeer and how they were all different in certain ways. "Do you see the one in front?" he said. "That is Flasher. Someday he will be an important leader of the group. He shows the way and is very strong. The one to the left of us is Veben. He's always looking around, and we call him the protector. To the right of us is Bonner, the defender of all the raindeer. Anyone who picks on the other raindeer usually has to deal with him. He looks after not only the other raindeer but the elves as well. Behind us is Blitzer, one of the strongest raindeer. Blitzer can pull anything. He's the 'bad boy' of the bunch and usually hangs out at the back of the pack."

Wrinkles told me all the raindeer pull trees out from the forest, and that is how they build muscle and strength. The raindeer flanked us on each side as we walked, shielding us from the weather and possible danger. I had asked Wrinkles about the feather but I never asked why he was in this part of the North Pole. "What are you doing way out here?" I said. With a grin on his face and eyebrows raised, he said, "Did you see the Wakashinda bird?" I said, "Yes, that was a very unique bird." Wrinkles said, "Very few people have seen a Wakashinda bird because it is very shy. It is comfortable around me though and allows me to come close enough to feed it. If it had seen you, I never would have gotten the feather, which I absolutely had to have. The elves sleep in what we call the 'Sleeping Chamber' for a solid three months. When the Shimatta feather comes fully to life, in about a day, it will be used to wake them up. Every year in March, Santa wakes me up and I prepare to find the Wakashinda bird so I can bring back this special feather. Usually the bird is near the Twin Peaks. This year I found it in the Black Hills Forest, where I found you, Lon.

I was beginning to feel as though I had traveled to a different world. I asked Wrinkles, "How much longer do we have to walk before reaching your home?" Wrinkles replied, "It's not too far, about another two or three hours." I wondered out loud, "Don't you have anything to ride on?" Wrinkles said, "Yes, but I don't want to startle the Wakashinda bird. One year I had a really rough time trying to get the Shimatta feather. The bird saw Buddy and me with the sleigh and raindeer coming toward the Twin Peaks and it startled him. Buddy had to take the raindeer and sleigh away. He left me with Veben, the protector. It took me the longest time, and I did get the Shimatta feather, but this is the reason why I go by myself and walk slowly with the raindeer."

Wrinkles added, "Once a polar bear started coming toward me. I wasn't sure what to do. I can tell you I was pretty scared. The raindeer surrounded me and held their ground. They were ready to defend me from the polar bear if it made any false moves. When the polar bear stood up on his hind legs and came closer, Veben veered in front of me to block him. The polar bear reached out to swipe down at Veben, and Veben tilted his sharp antlers toward the bear's paw as a warning. Now that the polar bear could see what the raindeer could do, he ran away very fast." After this story I said, "Wow, the raindeer are much more powerful than I thought. It's a good thing they're here with us." Wrinkles said, "I don't like traveling without the raindeer. In fact no one leaves the village unless they have the raindeer along with them."

Wrinkles' polar bear story gave me pause. I began to get skeptical about our safety. As we were leaving the Black Hills Forest I asked him, "Have you seen any polar bears on this trip so far?" He answered, "No, but you probably wouldn't even notice them because they're white and they blend in with the snow. The raindeer can spot polar bears from miles away. Still, we don't get many polar bears at the North Pole. They usually stay in regions where there's food. Every so often they will roam around here, but that is rare."

Walking continued to be difficult. I said, "The weather is still bad, Wrinkles." Wrinkles said, "Yes, Lon, here is the problem...Ivy told Kris, and Kris told me that six climbers got off the train at Jemdaza. They were hiking toward the Twin Peaks to climb the mountains there, which I don't understand; I guess they really like to climb. The North Wind is really putting it to them. Right now they have dug into the snow and are safe in their tents. The storm will progress until they are out of food, then it will die off and the climbers will turn around and go back in the direction they came from. The North Wind protects us from intruders here at the North Pole. We are catching the tail end of a storm that will continue for about six to eight days. After it's over, the climbers will head back to Jemdaza and you will be on your way back to your research base on Polar Ice Cap No. 12. Until then, we'll just have to wait out the storm. Trust me."

"Wrinkles, has anyone from the outside made it to the North Pole?" Wrinkles answered, "No, not when the North and South winds came into power. Well, no one unless we bring them in—like you. You were a surprise. We are completely protected by the North Wind. Even the animals don't seem to stick around in this area of the North Pole. I assume they know how miserable the weather gets in these parts." We both laughed, since we were feeling miserable ourselves. It was a slow process walking through the snow and storm, but we had the raindeer around us to protect us from the wind. On our long walk we talked about all sorts of things.

Wrinkles asked me, "Do you have any children, Lon?" That brought a smile to my face. "Yes, two daughters, Tiffany my oldest, and Stefanie the younger one." I asked Wrinkles the same question; he chuckled and said, "Yes I do, two sons, Happy and Slim. Those two boys can keep you busy. My wife, she works in the Sewing Department. Her name is Joy." Wrinkles asked me about my job again. I think he wanted me to talk for a while, so I accommodated him. "The Lincoln Vanderbilt Science Technology Center sent us scientists on an expedition to study the ice caps and do some research. Our base is on one of the massive blocks of ice, Polar Ice Cap No. 12, and the ice cap is shrinking in size. It seems to me there was a big disturbance in this area many years ago." Wrinkles reacted, and I wondered if he knew what the disturbance was about, but he didn't say anything. Instead, he continued listening. "We scientists do much studying about the environment. We try to find the best scientific answers to certain difficult problems. I'm pretty sure that after our ten or twelve weeks at the North Ridge, we will have some of those questions answered." Wrinkles asked, "Where are you scientists from?" I told him, "We're an elite team gathered from different countries around the world. I'm in charge of the expedition." I figured if he wanted to know more, he'd ask.

After a while, Wrinkles spoke again. "When I wake up the elves for the start of this year, I will introduce you to our team of engineers. Maybe they can help you with your research. They are really great at what they do. They might come up with a few answers for you. Plus, we've been here at the North Pole for a hundred years." I thought, a hundred years? But I didn't say anything because I didn't want Wrinkles to stop talking. He was a very intriguing little guy.

Wrinkles was carrying the glass case with the Shimatta feather inside. I glanced down at it and asked him, "Why did you put a lock on the case?" He said, "It protects the feather, since no one is to touch it but me. There is a special room we keep the feather in called the 'Quiet Room.' This room is totally silent and the Shimatta feather won't be disturbed." I told him, "I knew the feather was special, but a special room all by itself? I guess it is a very important feather." Wrinkles said, "I have many jobs but because I am the oldest elf I also take on the responsibility of finding and guarding the Shimatta feather. I will use the feather on March 31st to wake up the elves. The feather is also used to put the elves into a deep sleep. When the rest of the elves are sleeping, Kris touches my nose with the feather to put me to sleep, and then the feather starts to wither away. Kris is able to use it one more time to wake me up before the feather vanishes. That is why no one besides me is to touch the feather. It would disappear too quickly."

Wrinkles and I continued to have quite a conversation. I was curious about his children's names so I asked him, "What made you decide to name your two sons Happy and Slim?" Wrinkles answered, "Well, when Joy and I had our first son, he was so thin we called him Slim. Years later we had our other son, and he was always smiling and laughing so we called him Happy. These are actually nicknames; their real names are too long for everyday use." I said, "Not to change the subject or anything, but you said the elves sleep for three months. Why is that?" Wrinkles replied, "They work so hard throughout the year that they need to recover, so they sleep from January 1st to March 31st. Kris wakes me up approximately two weeks prior, so I can have enough time to get the Shimatta feather," said Wrinkles.

Wrinkles had a question for me. "About your two daughters, what are they going to do in life?" I said, "My daughters are still in school studying, but soon they will know for sure. Right now they're excited about being out of school for the summer, during the months of June, July, and August." I joked with Wrinkles. "I actually wanted three more lovely girls, but I have only two." Wrinkles chuckled and said, "You wanted five girls, oh my. I bet you're glad you only have two now, huh?" I smiled and said, "Yes, children take a lot of care. I'm happy with just having the two." Wrinkles asked, "Where do you live, Lon?" I answered, "I've been living in Pennsylvania for about three years. I grew up in Michigan then lived in Indiana for a time. I've always lived in the United States." Wrinkles replied, "I've never been there, but I've heard a lot about it. Well, right now you are a long way from home." I agreed with Wrinkles. "Yes, a long way from home."

"Where do you live, Wrinkles?" He said, "I live in a huge complex." I asked him how big it was. "Just wait; you'll see it soon. It contains Santa's home—we call that the castle—plus more than two hundred homes for the elves and their families, stables for the raindeer, a kitchen, a dining hall, the Paint Department, the work facility, the Sleeping Chamber, the Wrapping Department, the candle barn, the garden, the Mail Room, many eateries, and lots more. When I wake up the elves, they will get together with their families and return to their homes It's a time for family and getting their houses in order. On April 2nd we start making gifts for children all around the world and fill requests that have been sent to us. By the way, we are almost there."

I will never forget our walk; it took hours and hours. I was glad that Veben, Flasher, Bonner, and Blitzer were with us. They protected us from the weather—and bears. I noticed we were in a forest again, and I thought we must have farther to go when Wrinkles said, "Here it is. This is home." The woods led us to a mountain. We entered through a door that opened onto the production facility, and Wrinkles announced, "Welcome to the North Pole, Santa's Christmas Village!"

Chapter Three
The Christmas Village and Complex

The Shimatta feather rests on its pedestal in the Quiet Room.

I stood looking through the open door at Santa's Complex. It was incredible! The raindeer seemed to know just where to go. They were carefully weaving their way to the stables, where they would get brushed down and fed. Otherwise, there was no movement of any kind. The elves were still in a deep sleep in the Sleeping Chamber.

The assembly work facility was huge with many buildings and production areas. The entire complex was covered with a gigantic dome that protected it from the weather. From where I was standing I could see saws, cutting machines, paint booths, toy assembly booths, and conveyor belts designed to move toys along from one work station to the next, everywhere throughout the production floor.

Wrinkles noticed my astonishment and said, "See, I told you it was huge. Follow me while I put the Shimatta feather in a secure place." Wrinkles led me to the Quiet Room. There was a glass window in the door and I could see inside. In the middle of the room was a pedestal. I watched as Wrinkles took the feather out of the glass case, ever so gently, and placed it on the pedestal. He made it very clear how crucial it was for the Shimatta feather to rest. Wrinkles secured the door and said, "No one besides me is to be in this room. Santa has a key but he never uses it during the year, only when he comes to wake me up."

Now that his important task was completed, Wrinkles relaxed and opened up. He said, "Here comes Buddy. Let me introduce you. Buddy, this is Lon. He will be our guest for a while." Buddy was quiet but Wrinkles told me Buddy knew everything that went on in the complex. Buddy stood six feet tall and was tan, thin, and rather handsome. For certain, he seemed too tall to be an elf. He looked like an executive in some big corporation, so I was astonished when he gave me a hug. All I could think of to say was, "Buddy, you dress very sharp." Buddy replied, "Thank you. There was a time my appearance was kind of on the rough side. That was when I was just a kid. Now I make it a point to always look nice." I said, "It's a great pleasure to meet you." Buddy offered, "Wrinkles, I can get Lon something to eat and later show him around." Wrinkles said, "That's fine, I need to see Santa and brief him on my trip to the Twin Peaks. I'll see you a little later, Lon." With that, he gave me a quick hug and left. Hugs seemed to be the custom at the North Pole.

I followed Buddy to the kitchen where we sat and ate together. We had a hoagie sandwich with a glass of milk and a juicy pear. The food was fresh and tasty. I told Buddy how Wrinkles saved me in the Black Hills Forest. He erupted with laughter when I got to the part about Wrinkles falling through my igloo. Buddy was a wonderful host and asked if I'd had enough to eat. I said, "Thanks, I could take some more milk if you don't mind," and Buddy got me some. I mentioned that Wrinkles had said he'd been at the North Pole for a hundred years. I hoped Buddy would explain. He said, "Yes, the polar ice caps melt into the J'Yakaboo River, which gives us our drinking water. It is known to stop the aging process. Every four of your years is equal to one of ours. Most of our elves came here when they were in their twenties and thirties. That's why we still look so young." I was taking a drink when he said this and I started to choke. My eyes grew big, and Buddy tried to help by slapping me on the back. "Are you okay, Lon?" Recovering, I laughed and said, "Yes, I'm okay, it just went down the wrong way, that's all." Could the North Pole be the real Fountain of Youth? Since I was a scientist I would have to have proof of this statement but I didn't say anything.

Buddy took care of our dishes and offered to show me around, saying, "I bet you're excited about seeing more of this place." We went to the production facility first. He said, "All the departments work off the production floor. It's empty and quiet right now, but soon it will be bustling with activity. Here is the Lumber Department. Our lumberjack elves cut trees out of the forest with the help of the raindeer. Then the raindeer pull the trees into the lumber room, and the lumberjack elves cut the trees into lumber and logs." It sounded like the raindeer really earned their keep. Buddy continued, "The wood is then stacked in the lumber room from floor to ceiling. The lumberjacks have helpers that renew the forest by planting more trees. In fact, even with all the lumber we use, the forest has gotten larger over the years. Our motto is 'Cut one, plant two.' It is quite time-consuming, but this way we will always have trees to build toys for children. The carpenter elves work in this room too. They have thousands of finely detailed patterns and create beautiful wooden toys."

Touring Santa's workshop was such an unbelievable experience. I couldn't wait to see the next room. Buddy explained everything as he showed me around. "This is the Mail Room," he said. "All the request letters we get from children are entered into the Wiz computer, and all the computers are connected to each other so that any elf can look up any child's name and see what they have requested. It's a fabulous network." I asked Buddy, "What is the process from the child's request to the actual toy being made?" Buddy answered, "Let's say, Johnny from Akron, Ohio, asked for a red wooden fire truck. It would first be put into the computer. The elves in charge of picking would pick a truck off the shelf in the finished toy room, then send it to packing and wrapping, then on to shrinking—our newest innovation, and then to storage. It may sound like a long process but it goes pretty fast. After all, we've been doing it for over a hundred years and we've got it down pat."

I looked around trying to imagine the elves working in this cavernous space. Buddy continued, "The elves who are in charge of picking the toys off the shelf keep track of those toys. Each toy that is taken off the shelf is recorded for the carpenters so they can make more, thanks to the Wiz computer." "How many toys do you stock on the shelves?" I asked. Buddy said, "The carpenters make one hundred of each toy, including toys that are unusual or not very popular. All children deserve to get their wish fulfilled, plus you never know when a trend will take hold."

Next we went to the elf day care. Buddy explained, "Peace is in charge of the day care, Lon. The young elves play here with the baby elves and care for them while their mothers and fathers work in the complex. The younger elves and the baby elves try out all the toys to see how they hold up." I thought this was a smart idea, actually testing the toys before putting them into production. Buddy then took me to see the sewing room where all the clothes were made. "Any and all clothing comes from this room—Santa's clothes, Mrs. Claus's clothes, the elves' clothes, and all the dolls' clothes, plus clothing requests from children. You'll find Mrs. Claus working in here all year long."

Our next stop was the raindeer stables and the garage where they keep the sleighs. I observed the garden and the J'Yakaboo River. I asked Buddy, "Do you mind if I take some water samples?" He said, "Sure, Lon." From my backpack I pulled out my portable case of sterilized bottles and took a few samples. The garden was beautiful, filled to overflowing with every possible vegetable and fruit. I couldn't wait to see the next place that Buddy would take me to. It turned out to be the highest point in the complex. From here you could see all the elves' homes. Buddy said, "We have a total of two hundred homes for the elves." This place looked like nothing I'd ever seen before. It was huge and magnificent. Everything was engineered to run like clockwork. All I could say was "Wow!"

Buddy led the way to the Sleeping Chamber. We didn't go inside since the elves were still sleeping and the vault door was sealed. There wasn't a window to peek through, but I didn't mind because I'd had so many breathtaking experiences already. Buddy said, "Just one more day and Wrinkles will be waking up all the elves."

The last place we went was the castle. Buddy said, "This is where Santa and Mrs. Claus live." The thought of meeting them made me excited to the tips of my toes. The front entrance was outlined with blue lights that went all the way up the stairs to the door. I felt so lucky to be here. Buddy started up the steps, and I asked him, "Are we going to be able to go inside?" He smiled warmly and replied, "Let's go find out."

I was thinking what I would say if I did meet Santa and Mrs. Claus. Sweat beaded on my forehead and butterflies raced around the pit of my stomach as we got closer to the door. All these emotions were running through me when the doors of the castle opened. Kris Kringle, known to all as Santa Claus, stepped out to greet us. Wrinkles was with him. Kris said, "Hello, Buddy." He then walked up to me and shook hands, saying, "Hello, Lon. It's nice to meet you." I gripped his hand with both of mine and replied, "It's an honor to meet you, Santa Claus."

Santa had long white hair and a mustache and beard. He wore a green, red, and white shirt with a Christmas wreath pattern all over it. His pants were black with suspenders. He had on a woolen hat and leather boots. After we greeted each other, Santa said, "Wrinkles briefed me on your situation. I'm glad you're here and safe." Buddy excused himself to go take care of the raindeer, and Wrinkles wanted to give Santa and me some time alone, so he went off to get a bite to eat.

We walked down to the village and sat by the J'Yakaboo River. "I'm glad you're all right," said Santa. "You have to be careful out here in the North Pole, especially by yourself. You never know what kind of danger you'll come across. I hope you feel welcome here because you are. If there is anything you need, just let me know." I replied, "Yes, I feel very welcome, thank you." I told Santa what a beautiful place the complex was, and he said, "Yes, yes it is, though there was a time we had our doubts, ho-ho! But today, we are home to hundreds of people and we deliver gifts to children all over the world."

I asked Santa, "What made you decide to do what you do?" He said, "Lon, let me tell you a little about myself. I grew up in Kaskinen, one of the smallest towns in the country of Finland. People knew me there as Kris Kringle. My father was a carpenter and my mother was a seamstress. We didn't have much of anything but we stood strong together and there was always plenty of love in our home. My mother enjoyed quilting, knitting, sewing, weaving, crocheting, and embroidering for us and for friends and neighbors in our town. She didn't earn much, but the extra money she made came in handy. My father made a living for us, but you could say we were poor. I was an only child with not many friends and I often felt lonely, but I never showed these feelings. I was taught to look on the optimistic side of situations; I was thankful for life and what I had. I treated people with respect and kindness because that's the way I wanted to be treated. I was an all-around good student who listened to my teachers.

"We always did things as a family and I feel very lucky that I can say that. Many families nowadays don't seem to take enough time to do things together. In the evenings when my father got home from work, he'd always sit down and play a game with me. We'd play backgammon, cards, and other games, but his favorite was checkers. We would sit and talk about our day, and sometimes my father would have a story to tell me. I really enjoyed that, and that's why I read to the little elves at our day care. My father taught me: If you see someone in need, give them a helping hand. At Christmas, my family always tried to give more than we received. My father was a carpenter and we spent many evenings together making toys from scraps of wood left over from his job. That's how I learned the trade of carpentry, by watching my father build toys. He let me help him make the toys, and afterward I would paint them. At the same time, my mother made dolls for little girls and sewed pretty dresses for them. We couldn't afford store-bought wrapping paper, so my mother and I would wrap the toys in old newspapers.

"My parents wanted to teach me to give openly and generously, so at Christmas I was the one who gave out the gifts. When my parents saw I'd signed the first gifts with 'From: Kris Kringle,' they explained to me that signing my name on the presents might seem a little boastful to others. My mother softened the blow. She kneeled down to face me eye to eye and said, 'You know, Kris, in a different language your name translates to Santa Claus. Since people in this area know you as Kris Kringle, Santa or Santa Claus would be okay for you to write.' From that moment on I signed the gifts 'From: Santa' or 'From: Santa Claus.' Late on Christmas Eve my father would help me gather the presents in a big green bag, and we'd go around to the homes and place them on the doorsteps. Mostly, I gave presents to children in need, like me. It was important to my parents and me that we did all we could for others.

"Throughout the year I would help my father make toys just for that one night, Christmas Eve. I didn't expect to get much on Christmas morning because I knew we were poor, but just being together and having my parents' love was enough. That was the big gift they gave me all year long. For Christmas I would usually get one or two presents and maybe something in my stocking, but you would have thought I'd been given the moon. The smallest present put the biggest smile on my face. I got so excited and hurried to open it. This made me think there might be children out there without a single gift for Christmas. My desire to make others as happy as I was grew as I grew, until now I'm able to make so many children happy throughout the world, and that brings me so much joy.

"When the Christmas holiday was over and everyone went back to school, we all talked about the gifts we'd received. This was a hard time for me because I didn't have much to say. The other children would brag about their gifts, but I just felt lucky to get whatever small present I got. A few would make fun of my gifts, but it was okay because I knew my mother and father had put a lot of time into my gifts, and that made them very special. So I learned to hold my temper, be kind and caring, and to still show love. This was difficult to do when I was being teased by others, but it built character in me and I always thought about the saying, 'What goes around, comes around.' I still have the gifts my parents gave me.

"Even as a child I loved animals, but I knew we were too poor to keep any. So, for my birthday and holidays my father would always carve me an animal figurine. Over the years I've kept all of my father's carved animals. They remind me where I came from. I am grateful for the gifts of spirit my parents gave me, and I'll always love them.

"The first year my father and I gave presents away for Christmas was thrilling for me. When I returned to school, my classmates were all excited about the neat and colorful presents they'd received from Santa. 'Who is Santa? they wondered. No one knew it was me! I stayed quiet in my seat listening to everyone discuss their Christmas Day. From that day on, word spread from home to home, town to town, country to country, and now I'm known all around the world.

"In those days we had to set our priorities. We had only enough wood scraps to make toys for children less fortunate, like I was. Now I give to all the children whether they're poor, wealthy, or in between. Over the years it has given me great joy to be a blessing to so many children all over the world, and the elves have helped me make that dream a reality. Just as every child deserves a gift for Christmas, everyone—young and old alike—can use the light of hope that has come to be known as Santa Claus.

"After my father passed away, it was up to me to take care of my mother, and I was honored to do so. I continued working as a carpenter like my father, and many friends who knew about my Christmas children's project gave me their leftover lumber. Throughout the year I continued to make trucks, trains, dolls, cradles for dolls, music boxes, whistles, and other toys. The house got rather crowded after just a few months, but somehow we were able to store the toys until Christmas Eve. During the month of December my mother would make chocolate mints for other families in our town of

Kaskinen. As Christmas drew closer, everyone got into the jolly holiday spirit. It is easy to see why my favorite holiday has always been Christmas. It's a time of giving, and so much love goes around.

"I always gave presents away on December 24th, Christmas Eve, because I didn't want to be seen going through the town. It's so much more fun when presents are a surprise. Now, instead of on the doorsteps, I'd slip my gifts in among the other gifts under the children's Christmas trees. Still, some homes didn't have a Christmas tree, so I'd leave the gifts just inside their front entrance since no one locked their doors back then. People all over Finland learned about my Santa's Christmas Eve gifts, and they were amazed that someone would be so generous to give away so many presents out of the kindness of their heart. Over the years more and more people offered to help. Gradually, the little local effort that began in my parents' humble home grew into a global cause. Years later, with the help of Johnathan Andrew Witherspoon, I started the Kris Kringle Foundation. People who give to the foundation enable us to give even more to the children of the world."

I was enthralled by Kris's story of how Santa came to be. Then suddenly Mrs. Kringle, also known as Mrs. Claus, broke the magical mood with "Gentlemen, supper is ready." I noticed her apron matched Santa's shirt. My stomach gurgled, reminding me how hungry I was. Mrs. Claus went on ahead, and Santa said, "Enough of my talking. Let's go get some dinner." I was pleased Santa had spent so much time visiting with me, sitting by the J'Yakaboo River. I had heard stories about Santa all my life, and here I was at his complex visiting with him. It was an enjoyable day I'd never forget.

Santa and I approached the splendid castle and entered. When we reached the dining hall, Buddy and Wrinkles were already sitting at a table, and Mrs. Claus was bringing out the food. I chose a place and sat down. After everything was served, Santa introduced me to Mrs. Claus. She gave me a warm hug and said, "It's very nice to meet you, Lon. I prepared a room for you tonight. I think Buddy will show you that a little later. Enjoy your stay." I said, "Thank you, I really appreciate it. This food looks delicious." We ate heartily and talked over dinner.

The great topic of conversation was how I met Wrinkles when he fell through the roof of my igloo. I said, "I wish you could have been there; it was too funny." Everyone had a good laugh over it. Santa's "ho-ho" echoed through the room. Mrs. Claus, also known as Susie, said, "Lon, I hope you make yourself feel at home while you're here." Santa said, "I spoke to Ivy and he let me know that the mountain climbers are still in their tents. I'm sure they are running out of food, getting uncomfortable, and will probably turn back soon. Their heating systems will run out of fuel and then they will have to leave. We have to keep them away from the Twin Peaks here at the North Pole, Lon, because under no circumstances should the Wakashinda birds be disturbed." I said, "How many Wakashinda birds are there at the Twin Peaks?" Santa said, "Wrinkles, how many do you think?" Wrinkles replied, "There may be three or four families, very few." I asked, "Why is this bird so rare?" Mrs. Claus said, "Over the years many animals in the world have been hunted. The same goes for the Wakashinda bird. That's why the bird relocated to the Twin Peaks here at the North Pole; it was driven here for survival. At the top of the Twin Peaks is a cave where the Wakashinda bird lives. That is why we must keep all climbers off the mountain and out of that area, so the birds aren't disturbed. And the North Wind helps us protect them." I asked, "What do these birds eat out here?" This time Wrinkles answered, "There is food for the birds in the mountain region, but sometimes I make a trip up that way and feed them. I wish they would reproduce so there would be more of them in the North Pole area. It is so very important we have a Shimatta feather every year to wake up the elves and put them to sleep again."

When dinner was over I thanked Mrs. Claus for a delicious meal, and Buddy said, "I will show Lon his room now." On the way, Buddy introduced me to Sir King and Lady Queen, the two white Great Pyrenees dogs of the house. Their pups were named Rosie, Runner, and Sharon. All of them had soft, shiny coats and the puppies seemed to be almost completely grown. Each dog had a collar engraved with its name, which made my life easier since I could then tell them apart. I soon discovered they weren't the only animals in the castle. In the corridor I heard a high-pitched voice say, "Hello Buddy!" I looked around but didn't see anyone. "Who said that?" I asked Buddy. "Let me introduce you to our talking parrots, Lon. This is Goober and that's Sammie, and these are their four offspring, Courtney, Brittany, Whitney, and Bloober. That was mama Sammie you heard. The four little parrots are still learning to talk." Buddy and I continued on our way, and Goober said, "Bye, Lon. Bye. Lon." Pretty neat, I thought. It's not every day you get to talk to an animal—or an animal talks to you.

We stepped into an elevator. It puzzled me that there were no buttons to press. Then Buddy said, "Twenty-third floor, please." The elevator doors snapped shut and we glided upward. Then the elevator opened its doors and said, "Here you are, twenty-third floor," and we stepped out into a long hallway lined with private rooms.

Above the doors were the names of famous people and I asked Buddy about it. He replied, "All the rooms were donated by corporate presidents, CEOs, celebrities, and others. The Kringles have always received gifts from benefactors but they usually end up giving them away for Christmas. The people who donate wanted to give the Kringles a gift they wouldn't be able to give away. So they built onto this mountain we call Lady Laverne and have made it into a castle for Kris and his wife Susie. The donors were pleased as punch to tell the Kringles, 'Here's something you can't give away.' It was generous and funny at the same time. Santa and Mrs. Claus thanked them, and ever since, the complex has continued to grow."

I asked Buddy, "I've noticed that Kris Kringle is known as Santa Claus and his wife Susie is known as Mrs. Claus, but what do you and the elves call them?" Buddy replied, "The elves and I call Kris, Santa, and Susie, Mrs. Claus, only because we know how much they love those names. It reminds them of the joy they give each Christmas, since all the children know them as Santa and Mrs. Claus. Certain times though we do call them Kris and Susie, and they don't mind at all. But they feel they were put on Earth to give to others, and they have a special fondness for their Claus identities."

At last we arrived, and Buddy said, "This will be your room while you're here, and there's a full bath for you as well. If there's anything else you need, just let me know. Please make yourself at home, and I will be seeing you tomorrow. Have a good night." I thanked Buddy with "Goodnight! Till tomorrow then." After a hug, Buddy was gone.

Alone for the first time in hours, I looked around my room. The walls were painted burgundy with gold trim, very elegant. Everything was posh and put together tastefully. Someone had placed a fresh fruit basket on the red oak dresser for me, in case I wanted an evening snack, I figured. The room was bigger than any other room I've ever stayed in, and the bed could easily have accommodated four people. The bathroom had a sleekly designed shower, and the bathtub was equipped with whirlpool jets. The entire layout was fit for a king and sure made me feel like royalty.

I got cleaned up and was grateful to be able to stretch out on a comfy bed after a long, hard, overwhelming day. Never in a million years would I think I'd be staying at Santa Claus's Complex, where he lived and worked! All the stories I'd heard about Santa, and now I actually got the chance to meet him! I was so excited. In a short time the elves would be awakened and Santa's Christmas Village and Complex would be pulsing with activity. The entire day had been amazing. Even though I was a grown man, I felt like a kid again. My head sank into a cushiony pillow, and the stories told to me by Wrinkles, Bubbles, and, yes, Santa Claus himself, encircled my head. Everything I'd heard about Santa was true. My eyes closed in the friendly darkness, and I fell asleep.

Chapter Four
Santa's Raindeer

Santa and the raindeer.

That night I slept like a Christmas log. When I woke up, Buddy was at the door with pants and a shirt for me. "Mrs. Claus thought you might need these," he said. I smiled and asked, "Will they fit?" Buddy replied, "They should. Try them on." Buddy was right; they fit perfectly. I got ready for the day and followed Buddy downstairs for breakfast.

Mrs. Claus greeted us with hugs and a cheery "Good morning! Have a seat and make yourselves comfortable." I thanked her for making me the shirt and pants. I really appreciated them. "Oh, it was nothing," she replied. "I thought you could use some extra clothes so I sewed them up after dinner last night." I asked how she knew my size. A sweet smile glowed on her face. She said, "Lon, I've been a seamstress most of my life and let me tell you, I can usually judge a person's size by just looking at them." I should have known. With a chuckle I said, "Well, they fit great."

Wrinkles came into the dining room and joined us, and Mrs. Claus got busy serving us drinks. Just then Santa stepped off the elevator and joined us with open arms. "Greetings! How is everyone doing on this beautiful morning?" Santa and Mrs. Claus were dressed to match again. Her apron had a Christmas tree with lights that actually lit up, and the same design appeared on Santa's sweatshirt. That made two days in a row, and I imagined they must wear matching clothes every day.

Breakfast was as sumptuous as dinner. The dining room table was covered from edge to edge with a variety of meats, eggs, hash browns, muffins, breads, jams, and baked oatmeal. We had our choice of milk, orange juice, coffee, tea, or hot cocoa with marshmallows. Even with delicious food and great company, this was still a planning session for Santa, for soon it would be time to wake up the elves. "Buddy, Wrinkles, let's make sure the kitchen is fully stocked with food because the elves will be hungry when they awake from their long sleep. Buddy, did you make sure there is a fruit basket at all the elves' homes?" Buddy replied, "Yes, Santa, I double-checked this morning, just in case I missed any. Every basket has blueberries, apples, oranges, strawberries, and bananas." Santa said, "That's great! The elves are going to enjoy that. Mrs. Claus, are you going to do flowers in every house?" Mrs. Claus said, "Yes, I'm almost finished." Santa said, "Wonderful, dear! Mrs. Claus and I have gifts for everyone at their doorsteps. We want this to be a great time for all the elves." Santa preferred to call the elves "elves" instead of "little people." Buddy had told me Santa always treated the elves with respect, never talked down to them, and that whenever he spoke to them he addressed them by name.

After breakfast Santa said, "I need to feed and brush down the raindeer. Lon, would you like to give me a hand?" I was quick to reply, "Absolutely!" We all took our dishes to the kitchen. It seemed to me that everyone helped each other out. The more hands you have doing a job, the faster the job gets done, and that seemed to be the credo of Santa's Complex.

Santa and I left for the stables. He said, "Three cups of feed per raindeer." I scooped the grain into each bucket with all the raindeer watching. Their heads hung over the stalls, and they were more than ready for breakfast. The raindeer seemed to feel comfortable taking food from me. I think Santa's presence helped. As I gave them their rations, Santa brushed them down one by one. They really enjoyed that.

Even before they were brushed, the raindeer looked beautifully groomed. Santa taught me to talk to each raindeer as we brushed. I felt honored just to take part; it still blew my mind that I was here at the North Pole with Santa.

Santa had something special to say to each raindeer. He started with Prancer. "How's your leg? How you feeling, old boy? You know you're the father of these beautiful raindeer? You're so handsome. Dancer, you are such a beautiful girl. You know you're the mother of all these raindeer? You must be so proud." I thought Santa might be going overboard. But the more I watched and thought about it, I realized how much he loved the raindeer, and I think they loved hearing his voice. "Dasher, you're the fastest. You stay strong and swift. I'm glad you're part of the team. Flasher, you're going to be one of my main leaders someday. You're a very smart raindeer and very beautiful like your mother. Veben, even though you are the smallest raindeer you are a great protector. All of us are glad you are here. You're a sharp little raindeer. You help keep the other raindeer from danger. Cupid, we are glad that you are on our side. Bonner, you're our defender. You're always on the alert to make sure we're all safe. Blitzer, old boy, you're the greatest puller. Your muscles ripple as your strength draws us forward. Vixen, you've been with me a long time. Comet, Donner, Blitzen, did Lon brush all of you okay? He's our newest friend, and I know he was trying very hard to take good care of you."

All brushed and fed, the raindeer relaxed in their stalls. Santa sat down on a wooden bench and said, "Lon, join me and let's talk." I was to hear a story about his raindeer.

Santa said, "When I was a boy I never asked my parents to keep animals since I was well aware we couldn't afford them. But I've always loved the outdoors, and when I became older I enjoyed hiking along the mountainous trails in Finland.

"One day, I came across a large cave and entered it to find out what might be inside. The cave had very beautiful, unique rock formations. I heard running water and wanted to explore. So, I gathered up firewood from the surrounding brush and built a fire inside the cave to see by. Right there in front of me was a deer. It was lying down and seemed to lack strength. I didn't want to startle or scare it, so I walked up to it slowly, speaking in a calm voice.

"I tried to give the deer food and water, but it wouldn't eat or drink. Gradually, however, it allowed me to pet it, and I noticed its leg seemed to be broken. I wanted to help, so I explored the deer's leg, ever so delicately. As I gently manipulated it I heard a loud pop. The bone had slipped back into place. Thank goodness, the broken bone hadn't come through the skin. I knew that was a big plus for the animal's healing. I tore off a piece of my shirt and wrapped the leg tightly to keep it clean and in place. Bacteria wouldn't be able to get in now, and the animal's leg could mend properly.

"The fire was keeping the both of us warm. I could tell the animal was feeling better even though his leg was still very sore. The deer slept for a few hours. When he woke I again tried giving him some water, and this time he took it from me. The deer was starting to trust me, so I decided to have another try at giving him food. He ate right from the palm of my hand.

"Over the next few weeks I would take the long hike back to the cave to give the deer food and water, change his bandage, and check on his progress. I always took enough food for several days so I could stay and care for him awhile. The underground stream that ran through the cave supplied the deer with plenty of fresh water to drink.

After a few weeks I could see the deer's leg was healing well and he was getting his strength back. I applied a special medicinal plant to his leg. It's called the garbonzo root, from a rare plant in Finland. It stimulated the circulation in his leg and helped it heal faster. The deer and I became friends, and I named him Prancer because I imagined him prancing around again someday. I could just see how happy he would be!

"Weeks went by, and I made another trip to go see Prancer. This time I found him standing and drinking from the little stream in the cave. I called out to him, 'Prancer!' He looked up, saw me, and started jumping and prancing around just as I had imagined. We were so happy to see each other. Then, out of the corner of my eye, I spied another deer. I turned quickly and came face-to-face with Prancer's mate. Ho-ho, she was beautiful. I named her Dancer, because she seemed to enjoy moving and jumping around as much as Prancer. I tried to get Prancer to calm down so I could look at his leg, but without success. I decided it must be totally healed or he wouldn't have been so frisky.

"Prancer and Dancer accepted me and wanted to be close to me, so I took them to my home where I could look after them. They became big and strong and sinewy. Their antlers grew larger than any I had ever seen. I then realized these weren't like any other deer; they had to be some special breed of deer no one had ever seen before. One day I was watching them standing in the rain with streams of water pouring off their backs. Like a flash it hit me. I would call them 'raindeer.' Over the years I've named each one and the herd has grown because of Prancer and Dancer."

Santa explained that because he spent time with Prancer and saved his life, they bonded and Prancer wanted to give back to Santa. Prancer and Dancer had a secret they wanted to share with him, but the time wasn't yet right They were excited to have a permanent home with their friend, Santa, and over the years sets of raindeer twins were born: Dasher and Flasher, Veben and Vixen, Donner and Bonner, Comet and Cupid, and Blitzen and Blitzer.

Santa continued, "When we moved here to the North Pole we had only six raindeer but now there are a total of twelve. The rest of the herd was born here. On December 24th, we use eight of the raindeer for pulling the sleigh. Buddy uses four of the raindeer to pick up supplies in Jemdaza and Kremaska. All the raindeer have been a big help to us here at the North Pole. They have become a big part of our home, and the trust between us has grown strong.

"One evening when I was feeding the raindeer, I let them all out into the stable area. It was an open space, and I thought they'd enjoy running around and playing together for a bit. This turned out to be a wonderful idea on my part, because the raindeer decided to show their secret to me. The fully grown raindeer at that time, namely Dancer, Prancer, Dasher, Flasher, Vixen, Veben, Comet, and Cupid all unfolded their wings. Yes, raindeer can fly! Ho-ho, I stood there amazed. My mind was racing with possibilities. I knew they weighed a lot and their antlers were huge, but I wondered if they might be able to lift up me and my sleigh.

"Mrs. Claus, Wrinkles, Joy, Slim, and Happy didn't know what to think when I dragged them out into the yard. All of us just stood and watched the raindeer. No one said a word but you could feel the excitement in the air. I wondered out loud, 'If raindeer could pull my sleigh and lift it into the air as they fly, do you realize how many gifts I could deliver to children?' I would be able to cover a much larger distance on Christmas Eve than ever before.

"We began experimenting with the raindeer and sleigh. Four raindeer weren't enough, six would work, but eight were just right. I observed that the raindeer could only fly at nighttime. It had to be dark outside. I also noticed it took several months for the raindeer's wings to recover from their flight. It took me many months to figure out how it could all work, but the raindeer would become a big part of my dream to get gifts to children all around the world. I would use the raindeer for flying only on December 24th and 25th. They would need the remainder of the year to recover. That way, all the gifts could be delivered at the same time throughout the world.

"We've been here for over one hundred years, Lon, and those raindeer have helped me fly around the world for most of that time. They've made my job so much easier. I couldn't begin to count up all the children we have made happy. I wish you could see how far we've come since our early beginnings. We used to be pretty small. We only had six people when we came here, and that was myself, Susie, Wrinkles, Joy, Slim, and Happy, plus my two parrots Goober and Sammie, and the original six raindeer.

"When we first arrived we stayed in the mountain we called Lady Laverne. We built a log home for Wrinkles and Joy, stables for the raindeer, a modest home for me and Mrs. Claus, and a garden area. But now we've expanded each year to what you see here. I never dreamed it would ever grow to this. Oh sure, I've dreamed, but look at this. It's wonderful. My dream has come true and it's so much more than I even imagined. It's amazing, but it takes all of us to make it work: my wife Susie, all the elves, the raindeer, all of our friends who give to the Kris Kringle Foundation, and people all around the world who lend their support. That's what enables us to purchase so many materials so we can create gifts that make children happy. It seems the more we give, the more we get. It's uncanny how that happens, but that's the way it is. I live to make children happy, to change their lives even if it is only for one day out of the year. And I know we have this effect because each year after Christmas I get letters from so many children thanking me for bringing them presents. Some of them say if it weren't for me, they wouldn't have gotten anything at all for Christmas. Well, I'm getting all teary eyed, and it's time for lunch, so why don't we go get some of Mrs. Claus's good cooking?"

Santa and I left the raindeer stables and headed toward the castle, and there was Mrs. Claus returning from the village. She had just finished up arranging flowers in all the elves' homes. Mrs. Claus said, "Well, that job is done, dear!" That put the twinkle back in Santa's eyes.

Indeed, preparations for the elves' reawakening were in full swing. Buddy had picked up supplies in Jemdaza the day before, and he and Wrinkles were almost finished putting them away. The music system was quite advanced, crystal clear in fact. Santa enjoyed Christmas music most all the time. He said it keeps him and the entire staff in the spirit of the holiday and focused on completing their work. Filling children's requests is their number one job.

Santa's parrots flew by and Goober said, "Lunchtime, lunchtime!" Since it was clear they knew what time it was, Santa and I fed the parrots first. Then we washed up and were ready for our meal. Tomorrow was the day—March 31st at noon—the scheduled time for the elves' reawakening, and Santa, Mrs. Claus, Buddy, and Wrinkles were getting ready for it and talking about it. Excitement was building with every meal. Santa said all the raindeer were squared away. Mrs. Claus had placed flowers in the elves' homes. Santa and Mrs. Claus's special gifts were sitting on the elves' doorsteps. And Wrinkles had brought back the Shimatta feather.

Wrinkles said, "The supplies are put away in their proper places. We are all set and ready to go." Buddy explained for my sake, "I put the mail in the Mail Room. The first six months of the year that's usually thank-you letters to Santa. However, July 1st through December 24th is when the requests for presents start coming in, so as of now the Mail Room is in great shape. I also finished up stocking the pantry in the kitchen and wiping down the tables and chairs. I think we're ready for tomorrow."

I was so glad I was able to be here during this time to see the inner workings of Santa's Christmas Village. The timing was perfect. So much had happened in just a couple of days. As expected, lunch was great. We had salad, spaghetti, fresh fruit, and a drink. Santa said, "Well it seems like we're in great shape. Is there anything I'm forgetting?" Buddy asked to be excused since he still had some work to do for the next day. This was Mrs. Claus's cue to say, "You know, Kris, we always like to do something for Buddy's birthday. It was last week and you've been delaying. What should we do about it?" Santa had a solution. He said, "We will celebrate Buddy's birthday this evening. Let's do something low-key since Buddy likes his birthday to be pretty quiet. Goober, did you say something?" Goober said, "No, no." Santa added, "We really want this to be a surprise for Buddy." Goober repeated, "No, no." Sammie didn't say a word. It was her way to bob her head a few times to show she understood.

Later that day, Buddy sought me out to play a game of pool. The recreation room at the castle had a great table and we set up for some eight ball. "Buddy, you're a pretty good player," I said. "You can really shoot some pool." Santa was in his office taking care of business, and we had time to spare, so we played till we had our fill. It was still early afternoon when we finished, so Buddy, Wrinkles, and I thought we'd take a refreshing dip in the swimming pool. This time Santa joined us. He said, "It's always nice to relax a bit before we get back to our Christmas push. We'd better play a little now while we have the time. Starting tomorrow, we're going to be very busy till the end of the year. How about some water basketball, boys?" Santa always enjoyed a little competition. He teamed up with Wrinkles against Buddy and me. I won't go into details, but we smoked Santa and Wrinkles. We didn't want to rub it in their faces, so we just said, "Good game."

Santa pulled me aside and asked me to keep Buddy occupied while his surprise birthday party was being set up. Luckily, Buddy was up for doing some laps. After a long workout, we had pushed to our limit and were turning into prunes, so we hopped out of the pool, dried off, and got dressed. I then suggested bowling, so we grabbed a couple of strawberry slushes and headed on over to the bowling alley. They sure hit the spot. By now I was wearing out, but I was on a mission. I was determined to delay Buddy long enough so Santa, Mrs. Claus, and Wrinkles could get ready for his special party. Buddy and I looked to be about the same age, but he still was raring to go. It must have been the hardy life he led at the North Pole. He wound up beating me in all three games.

By now it was getting close to five o'clock, and by six o'clock we were cleaned up and on our way to the dining hall. Now came the big reveal. Mrs. Claus had decorated the dining room with streamers and glitz, and cheery Christmas music filled the air. Buddy kind of ducked his head and mumbled a sincere thank you. He didn't show much but I think he was pleased. We ate salad, a fruit compote, fish, vegetables, and baked potatoes. A very nice supper it was. After dinner Mrs. Claus brought out the cake and we sang "Happy Birthday" to Buddy. Santa presented his gift and said, "I made this for you, Buddy." It was a portrait of Buddy with the parrots and dogs. Santa said, "I painted it for you last month. I hope you enjoy it." Buddy was obviously touched and very grateful. He said, "Thanks, Santa. I know just where I'll hang this." Mrs. Claus said, "Buddy, I have a gift for you too. I made three new suits for you—one with gray pinstripes, one solid black, and one with blue pinstripes. I made matching shirts for them as well." Buddy enjoyed getting new suits, since he always needed them.

Wrinkles stood up and said, "In the last week Santa was good enough to hold off on your birthday celebration. Well, I want you to know he wasn't ignoring you. It was because I needed more time to finish your gift. It's taken me six months, and I slept three of those. Here are three pairs of shoes—one gray pair, one black pair, and one blue pair—to match your new suits. What took the longest was dyeing the leather, but I hope you like them." Buddy said, "Oh, you shouldn't have. I can see how much time and effort you've put into making these for me." Buddy tried a pair on and said, "These shoes are going to be some of my new favorites. I like them very much! Thank you, Wrinkles."

Buddy then turned to me. I felt put on the spot. "Well, Buddy, my gift is…I was in charge of keeping you busy today." Everyone laughed out loud. Buddy said, "Well thanks, Lon. I enjoyed your company and getting to know you better." Then I said, "However, there's more. At dinner the other night I saw you liked raspberries and desserts, so I thought I would put the two together for you. Earlier today, I made some time to bake you a raspberry mousse soufflé." I handed him the dessert. "I hope you enjoy it. Happy birthday, Buddy!" Buddy tasted the soufflé. "Mmmm. Delicious, Lon. I didn't know you could bake! It is really scrumptious. Hopefully, later you can write down the recipe for me."

Buddy's birthday party was a great success and had distracted all of us from our excited impatience about the next day. Now it was time to have hugs all around, go to bed, and try to sleep, since tomorrow we would wake the elves.

Chapter Five
The Sleeping Chamber

Wrinkles wakes up Dallas at the start of a new year.

The next morning, Wrinkles had still more wondrous things to tell Lon. "Back when Santa's Christmas Village first started, we noticed that the crystal clear water from the J'Yakaboo River and the food from our garden gave the elves amazing energy. At first this was enjoyable and a wonderful advantage. But then problems set in. The continual buildup of energy was causing the elves to become more and more tired, and they were yawning all day long. Everyone was concerned they would get worn out. Santa had noticed the problem early on and had started investigating the elves' family histories. He recorded his observations in a journal, in hopes he might come across a pattern that would help him find a solution. Santa sure had his work cut out for him, and he seemed to be stumped.

"This is where it gets exciting, Lon. I happened to remember a story my grandfather had told me. He shared so many stories with me over the years, but this one in particular seemed like it might help solve our tired elf problem. I ran to find Santa; I couldn't wait to share it with him. 'Santa, I have a story of the utmost importance to tell you! Please listen carefully, because I think it holds some parallels with what is happening to our elves. Maybe, just maybe, this story will help us find the right answers.'

"Santa ate his lunch while I talked. 'Ever since I can remember, my grandfather and I have always shared a close bond. He liked to tell me stories, some of which have been handed down through many generations in my family. There was one story about a very rare bird called the "Wakashinda bird." Grandfather said this bird was not only rare, but almost impossible to find because it lived high in the mountains. The bird was very shy around tall people, but little people could get close enough to feed it. Also, I distinctly remember something very special about the feathers on this bird. Grandfather said there was one feather on the bird that was different from all the rest. He called it the "Shimatta feather." Once you plucked this feather, it would come to life in about a day. He said the feather must be placed in a totally silent room because it needs its rest, and it requires complete silence to come to life. Grandfather said this feather had the power to put someone to sleep. It also had the power to wake someone up. There was one warning: No more than two people could touch the feather, because once the second person touched it, in ninety days the feather would vanish.' Santa's face lit up and he asked, 'Wrinkles, do you think we can find this bird?' I said, 'I will give it my best try,' and I immediately set out on my hunt for the elusive Wakashinda bird.

"After three years of searching, just when I was about ready to give up hope, high in the north at the Twin Peaks, there it was, the solution to our elf energy problems—the miraculous Wakashinda bird. I approached it, and it waited for me to come as though it wanted to help me. It must have known I would do it no harm. It was a thrilling moment!

"I gently stroked its lustrous feathers and saw the Shimatta feather right away. Ever so carefully, I plucked it. The Wakashinda bird didn't react; it didn't seem to feel a thing. I then secured the precious feather by placing it into a special glass case I had packed with me.

"It took Santa and me a few years to figure out how the feather worked, but finally the process was a success. As it turned out, first I use the Shimatta feather to put all the elves to sleep. Then Santa takes the feather from me, puts me to sleep, and places the feather on the pedestal in the Quiet Room. Next, he seals up the elves in the Sleeping Room vault. The vault temperature stays at a comfortable sixty-three degrees. Since Santa and I have now both touched the Shimatta feather, it starts to wilt. Ten weeks later, Santa retrieves the feather and uses it to wake me up. After I awaken, the Shimatta feather vanishes. Then the cycle starts all over again as I go searching for the Wakashinda bird and another Shimatta feather, so that I can wake up the rest of the elves for another year.

"I have only two weeks to return with the feather. Luckily, I now know where to find the birds, and the odds have been improving. Over the years I've noticed there are a few more families of Wakashinda birds making their home at the Twin Peaks. When we first ironed out this whole process, it was glorious. Finally, the elves got their much needed rest during their few months of sleep, and when they were awakened, they all felt so refreshed and raring to go. For nearly one hundred years the entire routine has worked great. But I can tell you, that first year, the anticipation was unbearable as 12:01 P.M. on March 31st drew near. What relief and joy we all felt when the system worked perfectly.

"Along the way, Santa also discovered that if the elves slept for these three months out of the year, they would only need a one or two hour nap in the afternoon, and an hour or two nap in the evening. Other than that, they could work all the time. Obviously, this was a great boon. The elves would have plenty of time to accomplish their work and fill children's request by Christmas. Santa's grand plan was really working out great.

"Now Lon, during the elves' three months of sleep, Santa, Mrs. Claus, and Buddy had their time all to themselves. During these months they'd invite guests to the castle. These were usually generous benefactors to the Kris Kringle Foundation or people who gave of themselves to others. Financial donors wanted to come visit Santa to see what their donations were used for. Each year, Santa, Mrs. Claus, and Buddy looked forward to welcoming people from the outside world. They had so much fun with their guests, it was like a vacation for them. It gave them a relaxing and refreshing break from the routine.

"Let's go find Santa, Lon, and check with him to see if it's time for the elves' reawakening." We found Santa tending to the raindeer, talking softly to them as if they were human. Santa spotted us and said, "It's time! Let's get Buddy and Mrs. Claus and meet at the Sleeping Chamber."

We stood in front of the vault door with high expectations. Santa put his finger to his lips and whispered, "Be very quiet now." You could have heard a pin drop. Slowly and carefully, Santa opened the doors to the Sleeping Chamber. There were rows and rows of little beds that seemed to go on forever. Some of them were covered with a small glass dome. I asked Santa about them, and he said, "That's an invention dreamed up by the Design Department. The domes are soundproof so the snoring elves don't wake up the others." What a bright idea, I thought. These elves thought of everything.

Wrinkles let me tag along with him to the Quiet Room to retrieve the Shimatta feather. He spoke to the feather and it began to flutter like a butterfly. "It's now time to wake up the other elves," he said. I noticed how tightly Wrinkles clutched the priceless feather. We returned to the Sleeping Chamber and Wrinkles entered. I watched him go down the aisles touching each elf individually with the feather. One by one, he tickled their noses till they sneezed, and called out their names till they opened their eyes. Wrinkles would say, "Hello, Shooter," and Shooter would smile and answer, "Hello, Wrinkles." "Hello, Torch...Hello, Blue Eyes..." All the elves were waking up and greeting each other. They were all so happy to see their moms, dads, sons, daughters, grandfathers, grandmothers, aunts, uncles, nieces, nephews, brothers, sisters, and all their friends. Everyone was so excited, including me. So much positive energy was in the air, knowing that another year was beginning here at Santa's Christmas Village. There were many tears of joy. I was brand-new to their world, but their mood was infectious; I couldn't help share in their happiness.

The waking, stretching elves were like a sea of white foam—they wore soft white flannel sleeping gowns that reached to the floor and fleecy white sleeping caps embroidered with their names. Not only did they match, but they looked so very delicate to me. What a delightful picture they made.

The whole procedure was done with the utmost care. Wrinkles was so gentle with each elf, just as he was with the Wakashinda bird. This made me think, perhaps that was why Santa had chosen him for this honor each year. It was important that he didn't scare the elves as he woke them up so that no one but Wrinkles would touch the Shimatta feather. It wouldn't do to have it disappear before everybody was awakened. The elves knew it was important that to give him a wide berth as he worked his way up and down the rows of beds.

Wrinkles continued his mission. "Hello, Bottoms." "Good to see you, Wrinkles." "Hello, Sugar…Hello, Petunia." The elves were rubbing their eyes and blowing their noses. There was some prolonged sneezing. The room was abuzz with talking and laughing as they picked up where they had left off three months earlier. I laughed too; it was a fun, fun day. Everyone hugged and kissed and chatted for hours. I could hear them saying things like, "You look taller," and, "Your hair has grown." They were getting reacquainted. Some danced and sang together to the piped-in Christmas music. And they were obviously thrilled to be starting another year of work in the Christmas Village. They all shared the same goal: taking care of each other, and making children happy all over the world.

The elves woke up burning with new ideas and ambitions for the coming work year, and they were animated as they shared them with their family and friends. Some were planning on new machinery, equipment, designs, and work projects. Others were looking forward to school. It turns out all elves go to school until they're eighteen—similar to our kindergarten through twelfth grade. For them, it is important to be as educated and well rounded as possible. They study math, history, hands-on science, a variety of languages, building techniques, design trades, sewing, tailoring, exercise techniques, and many other disciplines. They work at making learning interesting and fun. It's a wonderful approach to education.

Wrinkles saved his family for last. We watched as he woke up his elder son first. Wrinkles lightly brushed the Shimatta feather across Slim's nose, and he awoke. He said, "I'm so glad to see you, Dad!" And he hugged him and kissed him on the cheek. Then Wrinkles woke up his younger son. "Hello, Happy." Happy sneezed and said, "Dad! I'm so happy to see you!" He hugged his dad tightly around the neck, and Wrinkles swung him around in a circle. Happy said, "I love you, Dad." Wrinkles then woke up his wife, Joy. He had saved the most "joy" for last, for she was truly the joy of his life. Wrinkles silently gazed into her eyes as she came out of a deep sleep. She sneezed, then smiled and gave him a big hug. They cooed all the words they longed to hear: how dearly they loved one another, how glad they were to see each other, how happy they were that they were both safe, how much they had missed each other. Joy then turned to her boys and told them how much she loved them and had missed them too. Theirs was a close-knit family and I was deeply moved.

A crash of canine fervor burst through the doors of the Sleeping Chamber, and in came Sir King and Lady Queen, and their pups Rosie, Runner, and Sharon. They jumped and licked and nearly toppled the elves in their enthusiasm. They were followed by the parrots, Goober, Sammie, Courtney, Brittany, Whitney, and Bloober who flew overhead in circles and spirals and chattered with delight. All the inhabitants of the North Pole were in a festive spirit. I stuck with Buddy. He introduced me to his friends, who treated me like they'd known me forever. All the while, Santa and Mrs. Claus were dispensing hugs and kisses to the elves. Santa's favorite Christmas music was playing throughout the entire village, and this big affectionate happy family was together once again.

Santa said, "My dear friends, Mrs. Claus, Buddy, and I have a surprise for you. Last year I made notes of what all of you wished for and, while all of you were sleeping, the three of us went to work making your wishes come true. You'll find our gifts on your doorsteps, and we hope you'll enjoy them as much as we had fun making them. Oh, and one last thing…You'll also see a bonus gift on your doorstep. Our generous benefactors brought you tokens of their appreciation for all your hard work." A wave of glee rose throughout the Sleeping Chamber. The elves were very touched and thankful for all their gifts. As everybody left for their homes, the raindeer stood outside to greet them. The elves flowed out as one into the street like a joyful white parade, with Sir King and Lady Queen following right behind.

Wrinkles performed his final duty for the day. Solemnly and alone, he placed the tired Shimatta feather back on its pillow and set it on the pedestal in the Quiet Room. He sealed up the room, and the Shimatta was at rest once again. Wrinkles left for home to be with his family as Santa cheered him on with, "Thank you, Wrinkles, for another great reawakening!" Wrinkles replied, "Thank *you*, Santa, for allowing me to have this wonderful honor each year." They relived the day's events for a few minutes, hugged, and parted. Goober flew by, talking up a storm, "They're up for the year. They're up for the year," and Wrinkles and I laughed.

Santa invited me to join him, Mrs. Claus, and Buddy at the castle dining room. On our walk over, I told Buddy how grateful I was to be here at this special time, how amazing it was to share in the experience of the great reawakening with him and everyone. The raindeer were making their way back to the stables to rest. I thought how in a day or two, the entire facility would be up and running. I couldn't wait to see all the action.

Santa, Mrs. Claus, Buddy, and I sat down for what Santa called "a snack." Actually, our meal consisted of a huge, delicious salad put together by Mrs. Claus and a hefty slice of Buddy's leftover birthday cake. Santa said, "That was something to see, wasn't it, Lon? Ho-ho!" I replied, "Yes, absolutely! The elves, Buddy, Mrs. Claus, and you, Santa, really seem like one big happy family!" Mrs. Claus said, "You're exactly right, Lon!"

Buddy said, "After we're done here, some of the elves thought they would join us. Are you up to it, Lon?" I said, "Count me in! So, what are we going to do, Buddy?" He said, "First, the elves want to go home for a bit, open up their gifts, and catch a bite to eat—their first food in three months, mind you. They should be ready to join us in a couple of hours. The ladies always enjoy a nice round of miniature golf. Then all the single elves will be gathering over at the bowling alley." I said, "Sounds like fun, Buddy. Let's do it!"

Santa said, "Well, Mrs. Claus and I are headed to bed. Lon, be careful or the elves will keep you up all night—I promise they will!" Buddy and I took our dishes to the kitchen and then went to play a few games of pool to pass the time. "What does Santa do for recreation?" I wanted to know. Buddy said, "You'll never guess, so I'll tell you. Santa loves to walk the dogs—or maybe 'run' is a better word. All five of them." I asked him where. "Well, on a clear day, Santa takes his golf clubs and hits golf balls." Now I was puzzled by a couple of things. I said, "With white balls and white snow, isn't it hard to see the golf balls?" Buddy laughed. "Well, the Design Department paints Santa's golf balls a bright green." "But—" I started to say, but Buddy cut me off with, "Have a little patience, Lon. It will all come clear in a moment. So, they paint the golf balls green, but they also place a small radio beacon inside each ball. This serves as a tracking device. Wherever the golf ball lands, Santa presses a button on his portable computer to activate the beacon so the dogs can hear the signal, and they fetch the balls back to him. Of course, the dogs can also see the bright green balls when they get closer too. It's really hilarious. Santa knocks the balls in every direction. Anyway, this is how the dogs and Santa get their exercise." I said, "Buddy, leave it to Santa, huh?" Buddy said, "Here at the North Pole, the design staff think of everything. You know, Santa has never, ever played a real game of golf. One of our financial donors is the head of a golf ball company, and he's trying to get Santa hooked on the game. For now, Santa just gets a good workout with the dogs. Although, he does have a small putting green in his office.

"Another thing Santa enjoys is playing chess," Buddy continued. "Be careful if you play him though; he's very good at it. I don't think I've ever beaten him. Did I mention Santa is very competitive? Well, it bears repeating, and he sure loves to win at chess. Another thing he likes to do, Lon, is paint. You saw the painting he did for me. Santa always says, 'You must enjoy life as you go. You can't just work all the time. You have to take time for your family and friends every day, before life passes you by, because it passes so quickly.' This is one of Santa's most important statements. He says it's nice to know you can count on your family when you need them. We all have to work to make a living in this world, but parents need to spend quality time with their children. And, if you don't have children of your own, you can always find a way to help some children."

Buddy said, "Lon, we have all learned so much from Santa and Mrs. Claus. That's why we feel like one big happy family here. By the way, are you going to beat me at eight ball this time?" I said, "Man, I'm trying. Three up, three down. Well, Buddy, you sure are a good pool player, but now I'm ready to beat you at golf." Buddy said, "Let's go!"

The single elves had beat us to the Miniature Jungle Safari Golf Course, and Buddy introduced me around. "This is Bottles. He collects all kinds of glass in his leisure time. Then he melts the glass down and makes marbles for the little elves. Watch out for him, Lon. He's a great marble player. Then, meet Willy. He's clever at out-thinking his opponent. This is Sox. He designs his own sox, and tells everyone he likes to set the trend." I chuckled and said, "Hey, that's a great idea." Buddy continued, "Meet Glider. He's light as a feather and a great dancer. This is Space. He especially enjoys stargazing. Here's Bloom. She loves the garden and flowers. She picks flowers for us when they're in bloom Say hello to Sassy. She has attitude, and she really enjoys beating us guys in all the games. She's a great golfer too."

I didn't know if I'd be able to remember all their names, but I was really pleased to meet everybody. Buddy continued on down the line, "Say hi to Yawn. We're always telling her to take a break. She works until she yawns. Meet Peace. She keeps peace between the little ones in the day care. This is Rain. She has learned that if you drink a lot of water each day, your body will stay a lot healthier. She enjoys healthy foods too. Meet Stitches. He thinks stitches in his clothes and hats looks really cool. He's got every stitch pattern you can think of all over his clothes. It actually does look quite sharp. He's sure that someday his style is going to catch on and then he'll be a big wheel in the world of design." I said, "I think you're right, Stitches." Buddy laughed. "Last, but not at all least, is Spring. She loves light-colored clothing. She says it makes her feel bright and cheerful."

Now that the introductions had been taken care of, we were ready to play golf. As the new guy in town, I was very popular. Everybody wanted to play before or after me. Consequently, it took a while to start the game. I remarked how beautiful the course was, and Buddy said, "The president of Miniature Golf World was a board member of the Kris Kringle Foundation. He donated this eighteen hole course in honor of all the work we do for the children of the world."

The course was full of trees and animals, challenging ins and outs, and fun ups and downs. We had to maneuver the ball through little buildings, water features, and daffy sections that dipped and swung from side to side. The guys were laughing and the girls were giggling, and we talked each other's ears off the entire time. Buddy and I and the single elves all had such a great time together—all fourteen of us. We headed on over to the bowling alley to keep up our momentum.

The alley was already jumping with noise and fun. I met more new friends—the chefs, Diamond, Ruby, Munch, and Crunch. Munch and Crunch were twins. They grabbed an open lane and went for it. The elves who weren't bowling served up all kinds of snacks and drinks. I learned that to elves, serving was just another way to enjoy socializing.

I was getting tired, but I pushed myself because I wanted to make the most of my limited time with the elves and Buddy. I would soon be leaving this magical place, and I was starting to think that was going to be hard. Then Santa walked in and made me realize I had good reason to be tired. "Good morning, everyone. It's 9:00 A.M." We had played well past dawn! Santa managed to talk to everybody. He laid his hand on my shoulder and said, "See, Lon, I told you they'd keep you up all night." I said, "Santa, you were right, but I enjoyed myself tremendously. I don't know where all the time went!" It was a sure thing that I had spent a night to remember.

I was really getting to appreciate Santa's wardrobe. Today he was wearing a shirt with Christmas teddy bears all over it. He announced,

"All the raindeer are fed and brushed down for the day." Mrs. Claus entered and said, "I have pancakes for anyone who wants them." And yes, her apron matched Santa's shirt, as expected.

At this point, we had all worked up a big appetite, so it was a race to see who'd get to the dining room first. Of course, there were plenty of Mrs. Claus's famous breakfast pancakes to go around, and Santa loved catching up with his dear friends, the elves, on this pancake day. While we ate, the dogs lay calmly in front of the fireplace, and Goober and Sammie concentrated on teaching their babies how to talk. Begging for food wasn't an issue. All the animals had perfect manners.

What a beautiful place this North Pole was, in endless ways, but I still had a lot to learn. And who better than Santa to teach me? After pancakes, of course.

Chapter Six
The Move to the North Hills

Map that Johnathan Andrew Witherspoon gave to Kris Kringle.

Things were starting to stir around the Christmas Village. The production floor was showing life again. Santa and Mrs. Claus were both so jolly, such a delight. Then Santa said, "Lon, let me tell you how all of this started." I was all ears. "I told you the other day how my dad taught me carpentry and, even more significantly, how to give from the heart. I'd like to continue that story now.

"As I said, we lived in a little town called Kaskinen, in Finland, and we were very poor. My dad would see an old broken chair sitting on the side of the road and he'd say to me, 'Isn't that a beautiful piece of furniture?' To me it looked like junk, but I'd just nod because I knew Dad saw the inner beauty in the chair, and I wanted to see what he would do with it. Sure enough, after replacing a few rungs and with a lot of sanding, it actually started to look like something. Mom refurbished the cushions. Then Dad restained the wood. Now he had a beautiful piece.

"Every stick of furniture in our house was rebuilt by Dad. That is, until he noticed that someone else needed a piece of furniture. Then he'd give it away. The coming and going of furniture in our home got to be a real common occurrence. But his actions showed me the value of giving. Dad taught me many worthwhile lessons; he taught me everything he knew.

"Dad trained me so well, I started looking for scrap wood everywhere I went I wanted it to make toys. Dad noticed, and to encourage me, he taught me how to make a whistle. He showed me how to whittle an opening so it would sound like a train passing by. Sure enough, it did. I ended up making lots of whistles that Christmas. Children all over town were blowing their new whistles. It turned out to be a real success. Some sat in groups playing one after the other or in unison. Each whistle had a little different pitch, and when they were played together, they made great harmony. The adults may have gotten a little tired of hearing whistles that year, but it was music to my ears because I knew I was the one who had made all that fun possible.

"I loved everything about working with wood, Lon. I enjoyed creating with my hands, shaping the wood, how it felt in my hand, the smell of the wood, repairing furniture with my dad, and carving animals and dolls. My mom would make dresses and hats for the dolls. Our whole family enjoyed participating in the giving. It was all fun, especially the smiles on the faces of the children.

"Stories about my gifts from Santa got around town. Soon, many of the professional people caught on to what I was doing for the less fortunate children in our community. When I worked on a job with my dad, those who could afford it began intentionally ordering too much wood, just so I could have the scraps to make toys. They knew I was Santa, but they never betrayed my secret. They just wanted to be a part of the giving process. I was so blessed by these generous benefactors. They gave me leftover paint, nails, screws, glue, and sometimes new materials. Some even gave me a little money for the cause.

"After Mom and Dad passed away, I still made gifts for children. Early on, I had decided I would do my best to continue the dream my family was making real, giving to others. I wanted to leave my mark in the world primarily as a giver.

"Mom had always made and mended my clothes. After she passed, I needed to find a seamstress. One day I took some trousers to Susie's Sewing Shop for repair. Everyone knew if you wanted your clothes to look good, Susie's was the place to go. Besides being a consummate professional, Susie had a kind heart. She knew what I did for the children in our town, and therefore she would never charge me Miss Susie even made me shirts. In return, I did repairs for her. Looking back, I think she sometimes broke things on purpose, just so I would come over to fix them for her. We enjoyed each other's company.

"Of course, Miss Susie is now Mrs. Claus. But back then she was a smart, clever, beautiful, kind-hearted, energetic, and eligible young woman. I don't think I flatter myself, Lon, when I say she seemed taken with me. One day, when I was fixing her shutters, she told me she had always heard nothing but good things about me. She admired how generous to others I was, even though I was poor. She complimented me on my great disposition. She said I was gentle, kind, and had a reputation around town as a very good worker. I was feeling a little embarrassed by all her praise, but I just smiled and said thank you. I was shy in those days and didn't tell her, but I really liked her too. I hate to think I might have lost out on her if she hadn't taken the initiative that day. It was really very brave of her.

"Well, one thing led to another, and we fell in love and got married. Susie became Mrs. Kringle and a big help to me. She's always been wonderful at detail work. She helped me paint toys and she particularly liked painting dolls' faces. She made purses, dresses, and hats for the dolls. We really were a great team. She was always right there, eager to give me a hand. Over the years we've made a lot of children happy. Susie and I never had children of our own, so the children in our town—and now, all the children of the world—were our comfort and joy.

"Do you remember those first few years of marriage, Susie?" Susie chuckled softly. "Santa would say, 'Oh yes, dear,' all the time. And he still does."

Santa twinkled a smile at her and picked up the story. "We had very little money back then and always seemed to be playing catch-up with our bills. A lot of times they were paid late, sometimes very late, but we somehow seemed to scrape the money together. We were great friends with a family that lived just a few blocks away. Their company meant a lot to us. You'll recognize their names: Wrinkles, Joy, Happy, and Slim. They were small people. Happy and Slim were Wrinkles and Joy's sons. The boys were teased all the time because they were short in stature. But Susie and I just fell in love with this family. They were tall in spirit and big of heart. They became very good friends of ours. It seemed like we were always over to their house, or they were always over to ours. We shared sugar, salt, eggs, food of all kinds, and anything else we could. In those days we were all just trying to get by.

"Wrinkles wanted to learn everything I knew about wood. So I taught him carpentry. He was a natural. With Wrinkles working with me, we made twice as many wooden toys as I could by myself, and the Santa legend spread even further. We were all so poor, and talking didn't cost anything, so that was one of our main sources of entertainment. I told Wrinkles and his family all about my dream to reach as many children as possible. That's all I talked about most of the time. I went on and on about how I wanted to touch children's lives and make them happy, that I just wanted to help make this world a better place. I'd talk while we worked. I told Wrinkles that I wanted to teach people to give and be more kind to one another. Good ole Wrinkles, he would always listen. He knew my heart. I was so thankful. He would tell Joy and their boys about our conversations. None of them minded, because they had a strong desire to be a part of it all. All six of us were like one happy family.

"I remember this one day…Johnathan Andrew Witherspoon sent me a letter to come to his home. I didn't know him; I figured he wanted me to do some work. I said to Wrinkles, 'I think we may have a really big job here. The wealthiest man in town wants to see me.' I went to see Mr. Witherspoon on the day and time he requested. I didn't want to be late for an appointment with such an important businessman.

"I had butterflies just a-churnin' in my stomach as I knocked on the door. Could I do this? I tried to appear calm, but I was really shaking inside. As soon as he opened the door, I said, 'Hello, Mr. Johnathan Andrew Witherspoon. I'm Kris Kringle.' He replied, 'I'm so glad you could come, Kris. Please call me Johnathan.' What a relief! I thought. He seemed friendly, so maybe he was just human after all.

"I followed him into the living room. I tried not to stare at the surroundings and décor, but it must have been obvious that I was quite overwhelmed. If nothing else, my open mouth and eyes as big as silver dollars would have given me away. I had never been in a house that looked like a million bucks before, and I couldn't hide my astonishment.

"After we sat down, he had some ice cold lemonade poured for the two of us. He said, 'First of all, I want to thank you again for taking the time from your busy schedule to come see me, Kris. I know all about the fine things you do for the children in our town. I know how much happiness you have placed in so many children's hearts. I want to confess something to you. I have been a scrooge most of my life. I haven't had a thought about other people or cared about them. I devoted myself to my business, and that was that. I have no family left. I don't even have anyone I can call a friend. Honestly, I think people call me 'Scrooge.' I sat there quietly, in shock, trying to take all of this in.

"Johnathan continued. 'Everywhere I go, the bank, the grocery, the cleaners, the shops, well, just everywhere, you seem to be on everyone's lips. You have this impeccable reputation following you. To be honest with you, Kris, I finally had enough of this talk and I decided I was going to dig up the real truth about you. What I found out is that you're poor, kind, generous, creative, a hard worker, a loving husband, and your impeccable reputation is well deserved, which is exactly why I asked you here.

"'I am tired, and I don't have very many years left in me, Kris. I've thought this out completely, and I'm naming you as my sole heir. When I pass away, everything I own will be sold, and the proceeds will be placed in a bank account in the name of Kris and Susie Kringle. All of it. Each and every penny. Now, I know you don't have a bank account, so I opened one for you and deposited one thousand dollars into it. The money is yours to do with whatever you choose, for I know I can trust you to use it wisely.'

"Johnathan handed me the savings book and I was speechless. I even felt a little light-headed and thought I might faint, but I didn't. This was more money than I'd ever seen in one place. It was almost too much for me to handle. I tried to talk, but nothing came out. Then Johnathan said, 'On the first day of every year, I will put another thousand dollars into your account, and I will continue to do that each January 1st until I pass away. At that time, all this property and all my investments will immediately be transferred over into your account. Once again, Kris, I know you're poor. I only hope you don't let this go to your head, and I have every confidence that you won't. I do have one request. I want to be a part of what you do, your great dream. I really want to change, Kris, and I see in you a worthy cause, a golden opportunity, if you will, to do some good on this Earth during my lifetime. Won't you let me help?'

"I was pretty choked up, but finally I was able to say, 'I give you my word, Johnathan. This money will most definitely be used to build a great dream, one that I have been wanting for a long, long time. It's only because of you now that we will see it all come true.' Johnathan had brunch brought in and we continued to discuss our common future. I kept wanting to pinch myself to prove it was all real.

"There were two parrots in the room, and they chattered the whole time I was there. Their names were Goober and Sammie. Every now and then, Goober liked to say, 'I'm rich. I'm rich,' and Johnathan would tell him to calm down. 'Oh Kris, I just can't take care of these parrots anymore,' said Johnathan. 'It's getting to be too much for me. Do you think you'd be able to care for them? I love them so, and I would miss them, but I also want them in good hands. Would you please do this for me?' I didn't want to take away the only creatures he had left to love, but he was so insistent, and I was very grateful for his kindness. It was the least I could do. Besides, they really were wonderful birds. So I said, 'Yes, of course I will. I would be honored to do this for you, Johnathan. I would love to! Thank you for letting me have them. You are doing me a favor. So now I had two parrots, with cages and stands. I really hit the jackpot that day, Lon—a new bank account, the pledge of even more money to finance my dream for children, a wonderful new friend in Johnathan, and two gorgeous parrots with their own cages and stands. As a young boy, I had always wanted talking parrots, and now I had been given them as a gift. It was a day of surprises and dreams come true.

"But Johnathan wasn't finished yet. 'Kris,' he said, 'this isn't all I want to share with you. I want to tell you how I made my wealth. I've never told anyone this before.' As he talked, I listened closely, hardly breathing so as not to break the spell. 'On my twenty-first birthday, my grandfather gave me a treasure map. He had come upon it years before behind the walls of his home. There had been a fire, and the old house had gone up in flames like a tinderbox. It was being torn down when Grandfather found the map. He never got around to exploring the map himself, but had kept it safe in a strongbox. Now he was quite ill and he wanted me to have it. He said, "Johnathan, I guess it was meant for you to find instead of me."

"'Not long after, my grandfather passed away. The map had me curious, and I pulled it out to have a look. It was brittle and creased and brown with age. Carefully, I unfolded it, spread it out on the table, and squinted at it for clues. It soon became apparent that it was directing me to the North Hills, a vast no-man's-land at the top of the world. Not a soul lived within hundreds of miles, and the temperatures there were far colder than any winters I'd ever experienced. But something pushed me to find out what it was all about. I was fearless back then, as only youth can be, and determined to get to the bottom of the mystery.

"'Well, Kris, I traveled to Jemdaza first. It took quite some time, but I wanted to follow my dream. When I arrived, I purchased a warm goose-down ski suit, fishing gear, and some other odds and ends. I kept it light so as not to weigh down my sled. I was going to the North Hills. It was exhilarating.

"'The locals were anything but encouraging. They told me there was nothing in the North Hills but the East Wind, a few mountains, and some trees, that nobody—not a single creature—lived there, that I wouldn't survive even one night out there in the wilderness. They thought I was crazy. But my mind was made up. I thanked them, wished them well, and set out with my map in hand.

"'The locals were right. I didn't see any sign of life as I headed for a steep forest slope in the distance. But a warm fire within kept me going. I trusted my grandfather and was determined to prove him right. I stopped to build myself an igloo before dark so I could stay warm that first night. The next morning I was well rested and ready for another day of travel. For weeks, I pursued my course like a pioneer edging toward a great unknown mountain for the first time as the North Hills waited patiently for me in the distance. Each day, I built a new igloo before sunset and restored my strength at night. I kept a journal of my adventures, which I would very much like to share with you sometime, Kris.' I told Johnathan I looked forward to that.

"Johnathan continued. 'After a few weeks of solitary traveling, I came to the mountain surrounded by forest. "This has to be it!" I shouted to no one. I was crying and laughing at the same time because I realized I had actually made it. It took me a couple more days of exploring, but suddenly, there it was—the entrance to the cave drawn on Grandfather's map.

"'The folks in Jemdaza were so right. There was nothing here. I took my lantern to scout out the cave, then gathered some wood and built a fire. It made the space warm and toasty, and welcoming. I thought I heard water running in the distance, but I was too tired to explore right now. For the first time in weeks I didn't have to build my shelter. I lay down and slept, a happy lad.

"'Morning came very quickly. A bright ray of sunshine pierced the opening of the cave and woke me up. I was still wearing the "best of the best" cold weather gear the salesman had recommended I buy: my goose-down ski suit, padded gloves, the warmest hat, and the finest insulated boots. I was happy I'd listened to him. These had protected me from the cold the entire trip. I closed my eyes for a brief time, basking in the warmth of the sun on my face. I was thrilled to be alive! I grabbed some jerky for breakfast and got right to work, making doors for the mouth of the cave. I didn't want to waste any time.

"'The sunlight lit up a trickle of water at the base of the cave wall. It sparkled crystal clear. So I *had* heard a stream last night! Clear, clean water purified by the mountain. And I was the only one here to enjoy it. Only me. Wow! At that moment, a feeling of divine thankfulness came over me because I knew I alone had the freshest water in the world to drink! I went deeper into the cave. The stream widened and I saw fish swimming and jumping in the water. They were plentiful and would sustain me forever. I could eat and drink to my heart's content. A calm fell over me, as though I hadn't a care in the world.

"'Close by this stream I spotted what looked to be an overgrown garden. The plants were in perfect rows, as though someone had once taken very good care of them. Obviously, somebody—or somebodies—had been here long before me. But when and how? Would I ever find out? I had so many questions now, but I knew they would have to wait. Right now I had a garden to tend. It must have been quite prosperous at one time. It looked like it would have fed about ten people with no problem. Optimistically, I had brought seeds and starter plants with me, and I began to revive the garden right away. I had my work cut out for me; it would need lots of attention. Until it could start producing food, I would rely exclusively on catching fish in the stream. Guess what, Kris…I was there for six years. I wouldn't recommend it to just anyone, but my knowledge about winter survival saved me, and made it a wonderful adventure.

"'The cave turned out to be a real fisherman's paradise. The polar ice caps kept the stream fresh and clear, and I had plenty of fish to eat, even several different types. They were tasty and nutritious and sustained me while my garden grew. It wasn't a month or so later when I had fresh vegetables to eat. I didn't understand why they grew so fast, but I wasn't about to question my good fortune.

"'You must be wondering by now if the map actually led me to a treasure. Yes, it did! I found gold in the cave. I scraped it out of a vein in the wall and panned for nuggets in the stream, storing my fortune in empty flour and sugar sacks as I used up their contents. At the end of six years, I hauled it out of the North Hills and back to Jemdaza. The inhabitants were extremely surprised to see me, but kept their curiosity to themselves. And I didn't feel a need to talk either. I took my precious cargo back to Switzerland, then home to Kaskinen. Then I bought the most expensive house in town. The rest I invested in banks and businesses. So you see, I have lived in comfort and luxury most of my adult life.'

"Johnathan opened an old rusty metal box and handed me a well-used piece of paper. 'Kris, here is the map. I am telling you the truth. Please take it and use it for the good of the world. In my last days, I want to help make your dream come true.' I was in awe. I held the valuable artifact in my hand. It had been Johnathan's ticket to personal wealth, and now it would help spread joy throughout the world.

"Our business was concluded. Johnathan walked me to the door, shook my hand with an earnest grip then pulled me to him in a fatherly hug. I sensed he didn't really want me to leave, as though I were his son and we wouldn't be seeing each other for a long, long while. We had developed a strong bond in a short time. I guess it was because he had opened his heart to me and began a new direction for his life. We were now committed to each other and to a good cause. Ours was a very special friendship.

"When I left Johnathan, I took a walk to the only bank in our small town. I showed the teller my bankbook and she confirmed what Johnathan had told me. 'Yes, Mr. Kringle, you and your wife have one thousand dollars in your account. Do you want any of it today?' I didn't. What I did want was to run home to share my exciting news with Susie and our friends. I got there in a flash. I was bursting to tell them all about it. With two parrots, two cages, and two stands on my back, I must have looked like a traveling caravan. But I didn't care."

Susie interrupted Kris's saga of how Santa's North Pole began, just long enough to get a word in. "I remember when I saw him that day. What a sight to behold!" We all laughed thinking about it. Susie added, "Kris, do you remember when I asked you how your meeting went? I just knew it had to be great because your face was glowing with happiness. I had to calm him down, Lon, just so I could make out what he was talking about. He was beside himself."

Santa continued. "Yes, dear. Well, that evening, I told Susie, Wrinkles, Joy, Happy, and Slim the entire story of Johnathan Andrew Witherspoon. Poor Goober was looking all around our house and repeating, 'We're poor. We're poor. Sammie, we're poor.' Ho-ho! Sammie would just say, 'Calm down, Goober, calm down. Everything will be all right.'" Santa, Mrs. Claus, and I just cracked up over this.

Susie picked up the story. "I remember when Kris handed me the savings book and said, 'I went to the bank, and your name and my name are the only names on this account. We have one thousand dollars in the bank!' I was stunned. We were all stunned and speechless. Happy and Slim had a grand time playing with Goober and Sammie. Goober kept on saying, 'We're poor, we're poor,' while Kris was shouting, 'We're rich! We're rich!' This was a day that changed our lives. We could now start on a much bigger scale to help many more children. We were all giddy with laughter.

"Our new good fortune also brought up many questions. What should we do with all the money? What would we buy? Kris finally spoke up and said, 'Let's all just think about it for a while. Wrinkles and Joy, you're a part of our family. Whatever decision we make, let's make it together.'"

"That's right, dear," said Santa. "A week went by before I came up with a plan. 'Hear me out, first,' I said. 'Everyone will get a chance to talk. Now Prancer, Dancer, Vixen, Veben, Dasher, and Flasher all agree with me.' To this, everyone laughed. 'Okay, here is what I'm thinking. If all of us moved to the North Hills, the mountain could be our home. We have the stream that will provide plenty of water and fish, and we can cultivate the garden. The woods will give us lumber to make toys and build our homes. The raindeer will have lots of room to run around in, and we have Jemdaza nearby for supplies. We could turn the area into our home. We could ask scores of little people to join us in creating one big happy community, and make toys for many more children. We have the money now. What is there to stop us?

"'The raindeer can pull the sleigh to deliver the gifts. We can build a beautiful village with good people. I have strong faith that this dream could really grow.' Wrinkles said, 'How could we get others to join us, Kris?' I said, 'We can run ads all over the world,' and Wrinkles said, 'Well, you can count on me to help.' Susie said, 'I'm with you, dear,' and Joy said, 'I'm with you, Wrinkles.' Happy and Slim said, 'We agree with all of you!' Wrinkles said, 'We'll be with our own kind of people.' I said, 'Okay then, that settles it! Let's move to the North Hills! Ho-ho!' and everyone agreed, 'We're moving!'

"If our project was to be a success, we had to get organized. I said, 'Now we must prepare. We need to build a sleigh so the raindeer can pull us through the snow. We will need tools and very warm blankets and clothes, because it's very cold there. We'll bring seeds to plant and starter fruit trees for the garden. We can build new furniture when we get there. We will need to put all our heads together and think of the most practical ways to get food.' Everyone was brimming with ideas as to how everything would fit together. All of our plans were working out very smoothly. We were now ready for the big move to the North Hills.

"The first job Wrinkles and I took on was building a heavy-duty sleigh big enough to hold our possessions. We were all so thrilled, just as though someone had given us the world—and in one sense they had.

"With all that was going on, I saw Mr. Witherspoon only a couple more times before we left. He seemed sad on our last visit, but he knew he was the one who made it possible for me to leave. He was the reason my dream was coming true. This made him proud of all of us. I wrote often to keep him up-to-date on everything that was happening. Our correspondence kept us close in spirit, right up until his passing, years later."

With that, tears filled Santa's eyes. I knew Johnathan's death had been a great loss for him. I felt honored that Santa had shared his personal story with me, and I told him so. I wanted to go home and share it with my friends and family too. Right about now I was missing them terribly.

Chapter Seven

The Castle

Steps lead up to the main castle entrance.

On my way over to the cozy creek I bumped into Slim. We ate pizza, a favorite among the young ones, and talked about many things. It was great fun. These elves really had the best life. Slim said, "You know, Lon, the greatest thing we do here is make dreams come true. All of us work really hard to get finished by December 24th. We've never failed. And we still make time to study, learn, read, and have fun. Santa always says that's what life is all about. Always be kind to each other, and always be helpful. Santa says, 'Have fun...we will get the work done.' It's because we listen to Santa that every year we make more toys. Every year, Santa delivers more and more gifts. It really is amazing, but it works."

I said, "Slim, I'm a very lucky man because I'm able to see Santa's wonderland here at the North Pole and visit with Santa, Mrs. Claus, Buddy, the elves, and the raindeer. I've been so amazed at what I have seen. Every day has been such a special treat for me. I really have enjoyed meeting all of you. Everyone always takes time to answer my questions. Slim, can you tell me about the castle?"

Slim thought a moment and said, "Let me tell you what I remember of how it was when we first came here. The main mountain went straight up about twenty-two hundred feet. There were two smaller mountains beside it, but they couldn't be seen from far off. When Santa first saw it, he said the mountain looked like a pole shooting straight up into the air. That's when my brother Happy said 'pole…North Pole' and Santa said, 'Yes, Happy, that's it! North Pole! We will call it the North Pole.' Well, the forest went all the way around the mountain. We were all glad to come here, but I'll be honest, it really was in the middle of nowhere. Still, we were thankful to have a place to call our very own.

"I remember riding through the woods on the sleigh. The woods were huge, and there were no signs of life out here. There was just cold, around twenty degrees below zero. The mountain itself was dimly lit. There was a small stream with fresh crystal clear water. A waterfall a few hundred feet high emptied into the stream before it disappeared under the mountain.

"When Johnathan Witherspoon had been here many years before us, he sectioned off one big room in the cave as his living quarters and garden area. On the sides of this room were a few tunnel openings. When we arrived and unloaded our big sleigh, there was a place to put everything. Johnathan had made it easy for us. The kitchen area was a bit tight. We would all stand around to eat until Santa and Dad got time to build a table and chairs. Our sleeping quarters were also small. But I'll tell you, Lon, although in many ways we were roughing it, I never, ever heard anyone complain. I guess we just all knew why we were here, and we also knew it would get better as the days went by.

"Remnants of an old wooden door were scattered at the entrance to the cave. Santa and Dad cut and assembled a new door to close off the cave and keep the wind out. Until much later, our bathroom was the great outdoors.

"Amazingly, the garden was overgrown but still here. Mrs. Claus and Mom had their work cut out for them. Slim and I were little at that time, but we helped out with what we could. Dad and Santa kept occupied cutting down trees. They were planning to build a real home outside the mountain.

"We kept a fire going constantly, of course, to stay warm. We piled up sticks and brush nearby to fuel the flames. All of us would take turns pulling our own load and doing our share of chores. Happy and I turned over the soil in the garden and planted the seeds we had brought with us. With everybody pitching in, it was only a short while before we had the garden producing again.

"Once the door was up, our nice fire inside provided constant heat. As the ground warmed up inside the cave, the trees started coming out of their dormant stage, and in only a few days they began to bud. The garden was also going through a growth spurt. We tended it every day and watered it every other day. Everything we'd planted was growing fast and looking lush—onions, carrots, lettuce, turnips, just about any kind of vegetable you can think of.

"At the same time, we were building log homes outside and stables, and making the cave more comfortable. Soon everything was beginning to take shape. When more elves began arriving, that's when things really started to pop. We now had hundreds of hands, and you know what they say—many hands make light work. All the jobs were getting done much, much faster. We relocated the garden to where the village was being built. The little stream broke out of the mountain and surfaced alongside the village and garden. Finally, we were in our homes, and we sealed up the cave. The Bubble Dome and the Twin Prop Electric Wind Tunnels came much later, but it still felt like luxury to be out of the cave and into our own homes.

"After ten years Santa had made friends with many generous benefactors. They would give gifts to him and Mrs. Claus, and Santa would always give them away. That's when the donors started the Kris Kringle Foundation and turned the side of the mountain into a castle. They knew this was something Santa could use, and he wouldn't be able to give it away.

"Only the best materials were used. The backers brought in master carpenters, stonecutters, and welders. The elves had a lot of fun coming up with designs for the castle, and the builders were delighted with their ideas. They used the glass that Bubbles made out of the vita ore stone. They put windows in the sides of the mountain. They had tons of marble to work with, since we found a humongous vein in the cave. They ended up digging it out and cutting it up into all different shapes and sizes. They were able to use marble for the stairway and many of the floors and walls. The result was breathtaking, as you can see.

"The building was done January through March. This was the best time to work because all of the elves were asleep in the Sleeping Chamber. When they would wake up, the first thing they did was head toward the castle to see how progress was coming. The craftsmen built many fireplaces throughout the castle, but it was our own interior designers who did the decorating during their waking months. Then when it was time for the elves to go to sleep, designers from the outside world would come and help out. Needless to say, every room at the castle is now decorated, and very impressively too. I'm proud to say our silversmiths and glassmakers made all the chandeliers.

"It took fifty years to get the castle to where it is today. And we still add to it every year. It has more than fifty bedrooms for all the guests. The game room is awesome. The theater is magnificent. The soda bar is huge. The front doors of the castle face out into the village, which is now enormous, as is the garden.

"Santa's and Mrs. Claus's offices are beautiful and well equipped for small meetings, as well as for their private use. They have their own library too. What they can't find there, they can find in the school library, which all the elves have access to.

"The kitchen is modern, with marble floors throughout. The dining room is large and spectacular. Honestly, Lon, we certainly have been blessed over the years. We never would have thought all this would happen to us. Santa and our family were the poorest of the poor. The irony, Lon, is that here at the North Pole we have no need for money. We are self-sufficient. We grow all of our own food. We enjoy fish, shrimp, lobster, and the benefit of the dairy farm, to name a few things. Our dream has come true. Just like Santa said, if you can help people and give, it will come back to you. If you give, you will receive. We are all so thankful." I had to agree with Slim; this was a good life. I thanked him for the time he'd spent with me, and left to catch up with Buddy.

Buddy spent a lot of time with me. He seemed to like my company, and the feeling was mutual. We played many challenging games of pool. I even won a few. As we played, he would talk to me about life at the North Pole.

Buddy asked me if I wanted a personal tour of the castle. He knew I would jump at the chance. He started by telling me the entire outside looked just like it did when they first arrived more than a hundred years ago. He explained that the castle was built right into the mountain.

He explained how the castle changed with the light. During the daytime it had a yellow cast. In the evening, it had a bluish tint as the lights shone on it. The lights reflected on the snow and bounced off the windows, and the whole castle glistened. Apparently, it was a magnificent sight. Of course, I hadn't had the pleasure yet, because of the blizzard. But I could imagine the effect.

Buddy led me from room to room, and I noticed the unique designs, many one of a kind. They had used rich jewel colors—very regal. I asked Buddy about the paintings on many of the walls and ceilings, and he told me about a very famous painter from Germany, named Meschbach. "Herr Meschbach was a guest here at Santa's castle, January through March. He did most all of the painting throughout the rooms, including the elaborate paintings you see here. He was one of the finest artists I have ever seen, and very fast."

We arrived at the front entrance of the castle and looked out through tall windows. Lo and behold, we saw the entire village! Buddy said Bubbles and his crew had made the hundreds of windows all over the castle from this same vita ore stone. He also told me the castle had huge pillars to support it. The front doors were hand-carved from thick planks of wood. An abundance of first-rate craftsmanship went into the making of the castle.

Not only the inside steps, but the outside steps as well were cut from solid marble. Of course, this all came about through many years of hard work by master stone masons. And it was well worth it. The stairways would certainly last for many lifetimes to come—even the unusually long elf lifetimes.

"The grounds are meticulously landscaped," I said. "I can tell the elves take great pride in how they live." "They absolutely do," said Buddy. "Let me mention something about the Bubble Dome. It is built up to one-third the height of the castle, so the grounds are protected and kept warm. The castle was designed to overlook the elves' homes and the many other buildings on the property." I can tell you it was so clean and well maintained, it looked as though it had been built yesterday.

"When Santa shared his dream with us," said Buddy, "we all were in this together to make it come true. We never lost hope. Every year his dream became more real, more alive, and more fulfilled. It's because we all worked together as a team from the very beginning, and that's how we got to where we are today.

"I often think about all the things we've learned from Santa. He's read his books to us so many times. All the lessons he teaches us are so true. It's because of him that we have become better people. He never grows weary of spending quality time with us and teaching us how to improve our character. Now you see, Lon, why no one has ever left here. Together we make a great family. And we love to give to children, just as much as Santa does."

Mrs. Claus was making us a snack while Buddy led me through the castle rooms and corridors. At the moment, getting my questions answered was more important than food. What I knew for sure, and fully understood, was how much Santa, Mrs. Claus, Buddy, and the elves cared about children. The more time I spent with them, the more I realized how much they wanted to bring joy to as many children as they could.

All of a sudden Goober flew by with Bloober. Those two parrots were something! Bloober landed on my shoulder and Goober perched on Buddy's shoulder. Buddy said, "Hi, Goober," and Goober started talking. "Where did you go? You left me behind. Why didn't you take me? Who is that with you? What are the elves doing?" Buddy said, "Calm down, Goober. Lon and I are just touring the castle. Now, will you calm down? You met Lon before. Don't you remember?" "Ah yes," said Goober. Buddy said, "Sometimes I think you talk so fast, all your questions run into each other. Everything's okay, Goober." Bloober never said a word, but he seemed at ease on my shoulder. These were Amazon bright split-tail parrots with red, orange, yellow, green, and blue plumage. Like the Wakashinda bird, this species was nearly extinct. I enjoyed their conversation immensely. "Bloober, you stay on Lon's shoulder. Goober, stay with me. Now, let's continue on." With that, Buddy led the way.

We passed the game room again, and Buddy said, "Lon, you know all about the game room." I replied, "Yes, you beat me up pretty good at pool." He continued. "Well, it also has a ping-pong table, chess-boards, checkerboards, and many other games. There's a great soda fountain and ice cream bar too. The overhead lights have a neat artsy motif to match the room. Everyone can't help but have fun in this room. Mrs. Claus and Ice whip up some of the best drinks in here. The kids love the slushes and smoothies. Santa likes to hang out here with his guests in the afternoons. He and Mrs. Claus schedule our once-a-month singles parties here too. If you're single, this is the place to come on the third Thursday of every month. We dance to music on the old-fashioned jukebox donated by one of Santa's friends. It's a great time.

"By the way, Mrs. Claus's favorite drink is a coconut-pineapple frosty with chocolate shavings and a cherry on top. Sounds refreshing, doesn't it?" I had to agree. "Sure does, Buddy." Buddy said maybe she'd make one for us a little later. That was okay by me!

Down the hall a short way, we reached the library. I had to tell Buddy how beautiful it was. Buddy agreed with me. "People have donated books to Santa's library and also to the elves' school library. Let's go in and look." We sank into the ultrasoft couch. The chairs looked plush too. I imagined this was a comfortable place to hang out. "This is the quiet zone," said Goober. "Shhh, Goober," Buddy whispered. "I don't even talk in this room. We all know this room is dedicated to reading, meditating, and being totally quiet. This is where you go if you want private time. As you can see, the cherrywood bookcases are built from floor to ceiling, and all the way around the room. There are books on every subject." "I really like the exotic motifs in the rugs too," I said.

Buddy said, "There are separate bathrooms, his and hers, with smaller facilities for the elves. The designers have thought of everything. They're all marble, and very nice."

Next we entered the movie room. Buddy said, "When guests arrive, Santa and Mrs. Claus love to spend as much time with them as they can, so they can get to know them on a personal level. But after they leave, and when he's tired, this is one of Santa's favorite chill-out rooms. The young elves use this room as often as they can too. Every Tuesday night is movie night, and they like to hang out together. Munch, Crunch, Diamond, and Ruby are always in charge of food and drinks. It's a ton of fun when those four are around. When the movie's over and everybody leaves, you wouldn't know anyone had been here. We all pitch in to clean up. That's why we're pretty liberal about letting the young elves come in here. Everyone pulls their weight because they want to be invited back. Plus, Munch, Crunch, Diamond, and Ruby are a huge help. We all know it's a privilege to come to the movie room." I told Buddy I marveled at how immaculate the place was. Buddy smiled and said, "We don't look at cleaning up as work. It's just another chance to visit with each other. We work together, and that way we get done faster."

I was curious about what might be behind the closed door. Buddy said, "Open it." I saw rows and rows of movies. "Where did Santa get all these movies and DVDs?" "One of the presidents of a movie production company gives funds to the Kris Kringle Foundation, and they gave thousands of movies to us. Now, whenever guests visit, they're always bringing Santa movies. Over the years it's grown to what you see here." It was an impressive collection. Buddy said, "Many of Santa's friends know how hard everyone works, and they want us to enjoy our private time. They figure we've more than earned it." I said, "This seems to me like another case of the more you give, the more you get back." Buddy said, "That really is the truth. Over the many years, Santa's friends have helped build this home and the Christmas Village. Lon, you will hear us say this many times. It takes all of us and our friends to make all of this work, and as you know by now, we all fell in love with Santa's dream."

We made our way to Santa's office and found Sir King and Lady Queen relaxing on their fluffy rugs. Santa's desk was big and ornate, with satellite phones. It suited him. The computer ran constantly, so Santa could check at any moment what toys were being made and what might be needed. He also kept in close personal touch with all who contributed to the Kris Kringle Foundation. Santa always wanted them to know how much they were appreciated.

Santa's putting green was rolled out along the office floor. Buddy said, "Santa sure does enjoy knocking those balls around." I just smiled.

Next we went to Mrs. Claus's office. She was on the phone talking to one of the contributors, and we didn't want to be in the way, so we stood at the door and peeked in. Everything, including her desk, was nicely done with a soft Victorian charm. There was a large colorful Persian rug and some marble-topped side tables. Buddy said, "All of the marble you see was cut out of the mountain. One of our elves is a masonry expert. He is also a gemologist. He does all kinds of amazing work with his hands. His crew helped him lay all the marble on the floors, stairs, and walls. It is beautiful, isn't it?" Indeed, the various patterns and colors of marble were breathtaking. Buddy explained there were many different-colored veins of marble in the mountain. We stood admiring the masons' handiwork.

Buddy said, "Lon, you remember the Sleeping Chamber?" I said, "Of course." Buddy continued. "Well, no one but us has ever seen the elves sleeping in there. Even the people who give to the foundation have never seen the inside of that room. It is totally off-limits." I told him how honored I felt to have witnessed the reawakening. Mrs. Claus cut in, "I have a snack on the counter for you two." We thanked her and sat at the kitchen table to enjoy another of her delicious treats. The dining room and kitchen area were combined, because Mrs. Claus didn't want to miss any conversation when she was serving meals—

to guests or elves. I had spent quite a bit of time here since I'd been at the North Pole, and the entire area was as immaculate as always.

Goober and Bloober were still with us when we went to the pool. Those parrots didn't want to miss a thing, and that included scraps of our food. The room just off of the pool had his and hers changing rooms. Buddy said, "No one comes in here, or the pool, unless I'm in the room. That's the rule! We almost had an accident here many years ago, but I arrived just in time. So everyone knows, 'No Buddy, no pool!' If anyone comes in and I'm not here, they know enough to leave or wait till I arrive. The elves took to calling me 'lifeguard,' since my pool duty was to guard their lives. In fact, they invented the term. After Santa shared the story with some friends from the outside world, the word 'lifeguard' spread around the world. That's a little known fact. By the way, we keep the pool at seventy-six degrees. Wanna go for a swim?" Buddy didn't have to twist my arm. We took time out for a relaxing half hour in the pool.

Dried and dressed, we rode the talking elevator up to view the bedrooms. Each room was different. One was decorated like an African safari. Another had Victorian décor. Still another looked like the Australian outback. Then there was one with architectural and modern design. Each room had its own theme. All of them contained a bed, dresser, mirror, beautiful rugs, knickknacks, and other items in keeping with the prevailing style. All the bedroom windows overlooked the village. On the higher floors, you could see what the weather was up to. It wasn't good today, since the blizzard was still in full force. Buddy told me that Santa and Mrs. Claus's bedrooms were off-limits. Everyone happily gave them their privacy.

We went back to the elevator, and Buddy humored me by riding up and down with me for a bit as the elevator announced our location. At last, I took pity on him and we exited on the main floor of the castle. Two big hands made of glass dominated the entryway. One hand listed the names of the elves who worked at the North Pole. The other was inscribed with the names of contributors to the Kris Kringle Foundation. Buddy told me that these were built by Bubbles and the elves as a present to Santa and Mrs. Claus. They were outstanding works of art. Sparkling chandeliers adorned the entrance, as striking as any we'd seen today. Everything in the castle had been made by the elves, even the items that appeared to be rare antiques. Truly, they were gifted artisans.

Buddy said, "Lon, we are all very proud of our home here at the North Pole. I must tell you what changed Santa's mind about accepting gifts for himself. Santa finally realized that people wanted to give to him because that was what he was doing. The more you give, the more you get. They had learned their lesson well, and Santa didn't want to deprive them of that pleasure." I hadn't realized it until we were done, but Buddy had answered many of my questions along the way.

Goober and Bloober had finished their tour too. They flew over to their stands to get a drink of water then got to playing with Sir King and Lady Queen.

"Do you see how the castle is built into the mountain?" said Buddy. I told him how impressed I was with the design and engineering of everything in the castle. It was a beautiful achievement. "You'd better put on your winter gear now. We're going to go through the sealed door in back of the castle and into the cave. I want you to see where some of us lived before we built our homes and the castle." This sounded exciting, for we were going into the same cave that Johnathan Andrew Witherspoon had originally discovered.

Buddy and I bundled up and headed for the back door. It must have been a foot thick. We opened it and stepped into the cave. We walked along a well-worn path and Buddy said, "Be careful. Stay close, Lon. Let me show you how Kris, Susie, Wrinkles, Joy, Slim, Happy, the six raindeer, and the two parrots lived, when they first arrived here. Over there is the cave door into the mountain from the woods. I don't want to open those doors since they insulate the cave from the cold. The raindeer had their own area over here. It was shielded from the living quarters with partitions. Over on the opposite end were the living quarters."

To the side of the path was the river that ran through the mountain and the village, and finally the ocean. "Here...You can see where the vita ore stone was taken from to make our glass," said Buddy. "Bubbles is still in charge of this area if we ever need to mine ore again."

"Do you see these tunnels through here? That's where we found the veins of beautiful marble that was used throughout the castle and the village. Over here is the cookstove built out of stone. The big stove in the center the main room was used to keep everyone warm.

"Come over here, Lon. This path will take us over to the garden area. You can understand now why there are no windows on the back of the castle, since they would look down into this mountain. That's why it's all closed off." I gazed around trying to absorb all this information. I said, "So this is where Santa's life started here at the North Pole." Buddy said, "Yes…and we sure have come a mighty long way.

"When I first arrived here, the elves' log homes were just being built. It wouldn't be long till they all had privacy and comfort. By the way, Santa keeps this area closed off to everyone. Someday he may do something with it, but for now he just doesn't want the raindeer or anyone to get hurt back in here. See the tunnel over here? Wrinkles is the only one who comes in here. He picks the mushrooms that grow in the moist darkness.

"This beautiful mountain has given us a lot over the years—shelter, warmth, food, marble, water, vita ore stone, and stone for the fireplaces. We call the mountain Lady Laverne. She just keeps giving and never asks for anything in return. Santa says there's life inside the mountain. You can see where we have replanted all the trees from the mountain over to the master garden area.

"I think Santa likes to share how the village started. For a long time, it wasn't all glitz and glitter. When we first came we were poor. But we learned a lot about the mountain and the area, and we worked hard to build our community with our ultimate goal in mind: bringing joy to children everywhere. We're so thankful how our lives have turned out, but none of us will ever forget where we come from.

"Ah, here is where Santa, Wrinkles, and their families made toys for children at Christmastime. Santa left the workbenches right where they stood as a remembrance. He comes out here from time to time to reminisce about those days and to reflect on how far we've come from those humble beginnings. Santa's newspaper ads seeking elves to come join him here said it all: 'Come dream a dream with me.'"

Buddy seemed pulled out of his reverie. He looked around and laughed. "What is so funny?" I asked. He looked at me and said, "Have you seen the parrots lately?" "Well, no," I said. "I don't think they ever come in this cave, Lon. The story is, Goober says he remembers the 'dungeon' and never wants to go back there." Thinking of Goober, I had to laugh too. The cave was definitely on the rustic side. We were finished here. We went back into the castle and secured the door.

Buddy said, "Tonight is Carnivale night here at the village. Slim and Happy told me they'd help you with your costume. Everyone participates. It's our big celebration to kick off the work year. Tomorrow the production floor will be in full operation." I said, "Buddy, what is Carnivale like?" He said it was a surprise. He couldn't tell me about it, but he promised I would really have a fun time. Buddy wanted to take another swim before the evening got started. Who was I to object? It sounded like a great idea to me.

A blizzard still raged outside the village. The wind was blowing the snow horizontally, and it was bitter cold. I suspected I would be staying at the castle for at least a few more days.

I remembered how I had written Santa every year as a young boy, and how he had always come through with wonderful gifts. One particular Christmas, I wanted a crane that could move sand in my sandbox. Of course, I got the crane. I played with it for years. I saw that very crane on the production floor. Many of the gifts I'd received over the years were still being made here. What fond memories! I was reminded of how much Santa loved and cared for me.

My trip to the North Pole made me realize I wanted to give more. I promised myself I would do just that whenever I got home. Like the mountain Lady Laverne. Like the many elves. Many people from all over the world were learning to give. Santa kept spreading the word: Give, and you will receive. I was going to make changes in my life. I decided to be more of a giver than a receiver, to give more than I ever had before.

Buddy said, "Let's get ready for Carnivale!" So, I let him take me to Slim and Happy, my tailors for the evening.

Chapter Eight
Carnivale

I was surrounded by Slim, Happy, and Buddy, all working on my costume for Carnivale. As the sons of Wrinkles and Joy, Slim and Happy had been among the first people to arrive at the North Pole. Slim had told me some of what he remembered about his early days here, but this was the first chance I was able to spend time with Happy. Both boys did their best to make me comfortable around them. They were concerned that I shouldn't feel out of place or lonely. That was very considerate and showed they had kind hearts, and it made me feel kinda special. I think I was benefiting from another of Santa's lessons: Spend good quality time with your family and anyone else you meet along life's way.

Happy told me the "Carnivale" was the first big event after the annual reawakening. First, the elves spent time with their families and friends, and opened Santa and Mrs. Claus's gifts Then they prepared for Carnivale. Today was a day for gathering fresh fruits and vegetables, and for making wonderful dishes for the evening's festivities. We headed over to the garden to help. Already, the heavenly aroma of homemade breads and pies filled the air.

The big protective dome that covered the entire village allowed the garden to flourish. The four of us dug in and picked all different kinds of fruit and vegetables for Joy, who was waiting for us to return with armfuls of choice produce so she could begin her baking and cooking. Slim pointed out several types of trees to me. "Just to name a few, we have apple trees, peach, plum, pear, coconut, banana, and nut trees. Over there we have red and deep purple raspberry bushes. Then behind you, Lon, is a large variety of vegetables." This garden had anything and everything you could ever want in the way of fresh and tasty produce.

I noticed something curious. As we strolled through the garden, the temperature changed to accommodate the plants in that area. The soil was rich and dark and fragrant. Happy said, "There's no other place on Earth where you can grow all these fruits and vegetables in the same location. We're very proud of our garden." Regrowth was much quicker here too. The elves were meticulous in organizing their garden. How lush and beautifully picturesque it was. Buddy explained that the river ran down from inside the mountain and right out through the growing area continuously. The cold and ice never interfered. That was one more reason why the area prospered so well.

Happy said, "There are many advantages to our garden, Lon. There is always just enough sun, shade, moisture, or dryness, depending on where things are planted. It is an absolutely perfect paradise for growing things, that's for sure!" Happy plucked a ripe plum tomato from the vine. It was deep red and perfect in shape and texture. "This is one of my favorites. Take a bite, Lon," he said. I bit into the juicy, sweet fruit and swooned with delight. Everything grown here was extra delicious.

When we had all we needed for Joy's purposes, we left the garden and made for Wrinkles and Joy's home. Scores of elves were still gathering produce in bushel baskets, promising a huge, tasty spread for the evening's celebration. There were elves in the streets all along the way, tacking up lights and garlands, decorating clubs, homes, lampposts, and the main square. It seemed everyone wanted to be included in doing *something* for Carnivale. Much excitement was in the air as everybody anticipated the festivities. Buddy reminded me this was the first time the elves would be getting together in one place since the reawakening. It was kind of a New Year's celebration for them. I realized elves enjoyed parties too.

We saw the Golden Wiskers band warming up for the Carnivale parade, right near the platform where Santa and Mrs. Claus would be sitting. Buddy, Slim, and Happy were putting the final touches on my costume. I still didn't know what I was going to be dressed as, but they told me to relax and everything would work out. I was in their hands, so I decided to trust them.

The elves had a team for everything. Some were sectioning off the streets. Others were working on floats or laying down a dance floor close to the band. Another team was finishing up stringing sparkling lights. The elves were so organized that preparations for the parade had come together quickly and smoothly. Also, nothing was wasted. They even lined the parade route with Mrs. Claus's "welcome home" flowers, making the streets fragrant and breathtaking.

I heard that the floats were now out of storage and lined up for the start of the parade. I knew how much pride the float elves took in making them. Happy told me the raindeer would be pulling them. All the while, the musically talented elves were tuning up their instruments for the parade march. Everything was coming together. I helped out as much as I could, even though I was a bit of a distraction. Many of the elves were curious about me, and understandably so. They wanted to know how I had arrived at Santa's Christmas Village, way out here in the middle of nowhere. It seemed everyone in the village had a story to tell. I was beginning to feel like a native now, because I had a story too.

Fabulous dishes were being laid out on the table, and we would be eating after the parade. I gave the elves the short version of my scientific adventure at Polar Ice Cap No. 12, getting lost in the blizzard, and being rescued by Wrinkles. I explained everything as fast as I could. Everybody listened attentively then told me they were thrilled to have me here. What a nice welcome for a complete stranger. These were very special people.

Wrinkles announced that Carnivale would be starting in thirty minutes. The Golden Wiskers started to play. There was dancing and snacking and just plain visiting. It was the North Pole version of a fun block party! Buddy, Slim, and Happy hurried me into my costume. Oh, what a hoot that was! I joined the other merrymakers in the streets and sought out my float. It was the first one in the parade.

The raindeer were getting hooked up to the floats. They were all decked out. Some of their antlers sported colors to match their float.

Some of the raindeer were even in costume—that was hilarious. Everyone got a kick out of it.

I caught a glimpse of Santa and Mrs. Claus in their Carnivale attire. Santa wore a white shirt with colorful little Christmas trees printed in an overall pattern, black dress pants with a shimmering wavy texture, and sparkly red suspenders. Small Christmas trees on the suspenders matched his shirt. His belt buckle was in the shape of a large decorated Christmas tree, and his black boots shinned like mirrors. His white hair and snowy beard stood out strikingly against his brilliant outfit. Santa was really steppin' out for this. You could tell he wanted to put his best foot forward and have as much fun as everyone else.

Mrs. Claus looked just as splendid as her husband. Her dress was a deep red silk moiré with puffy sleeves and a full skirt. Five-inch-deep Battenburg lace adorned the neckline and cuffs. She wore a coordinating cushiony red velvet hat. Her apron was dotted with sequins and beads so that it sparkled like jewels—and it matched Santa's shirt. She was radiant as she nodded to and greeted all the elves.

The parade was starting up, Santa and Mrs. Claus were revving up their Carnivale spirit, that's for sure. As grand marshals of the parade, they were the center of attention. The happy couple worked their way over toward the band and stopped for a dance. They were light on their feet and quite cheery, and we all clapped for them. All the while, the Golden Wiskers never stopped playing. When someone got tired, another musician would step in to replace them. The music would be continued throughout the night. I had experienced firsthand how the elves liked to enjoy themselves from dusk till dawn, and here was another opportunity.

Watching the band was entertainment in itself. The air pump organ was particularly funny. An elf named Hats pumped the organ while another elf, Tops, played the keyboard. It sounded just like an electric organ, but it ran on elf power. The drums were loaded. They consisted of twelve pieces, with cymbals and chimes. Their pianist was called K2. When he got tired, Hy-Rise took a turn playing. The percussionist was the multitalented Miss Sassy. She played several handheld instruments—blocks of different sizes and shapes, a few tambourines, maracas, the cabasa, and a few other pieces I didn't recognize. Socks played spoons on a washboard. That was something to see! Quicken played the flute, and Crunch and Munch played the saxophone. These elves were really cuttin' up and having fun. They played their instruments with heart and soul. They threw themselves into the rhythm, swaying and fidgeting as though they wanted to get out of their chairs, but that was all part of the show.

As grand marshals, Santa and Mrs. Claus took their seats on the viewing platform. The floats were approaching in the distance. They were decorated with an array of glorious flowers. Elves in Eskimo costumes walked along the perimeter tossing candy to the kids and kids at heart. Mrs. Claus poked Santa. "Here comes the first float, dear. Look at Blitzen pulling it!" It was the Lollipop Float, shaped

like a mountain. It was decorated with so many colorful lollipops you couldn't count them all. Big bright lights lit up the lollipops as they spun around. Even the elves on the float were dressed like lollipops. And there were more lollipop elves in the street handing out brand-new lollipop flavors created by Lavender. Thanks to the machine Chuckles had developed, everyone was enjoying a lollipop—even Santa and Mrs. Claus.

Clever elves dressed as clowns walked alongside the floats and circled round and round. In and out they wove, wearing stilts to great comic effect. "Here comes Lon," said Mrs. Claus. "He's on small stilts and dressed like a clown too!" At the sight of me, Mrs. Claus giggled till she cried and Santa had a deep belly laugh. Usually, I towered over all the elves. But today, we were at eye level because their stilts

The Safari float being pulled by Donner.

were much taller than mine. Who knew stilts could become the great leveler? Mrs. Claus said to Santa, "With their outrageous hats, the elves are even taller than you!" And they laughed again.

Our part was over, so we hurried the float back into storage and put the raindeer in the stables. Then we went to watch the rest of the parade with Santa and Mrs. Claus, where a big team of jump ropers were putting on a show. Santa introduced them as "The Energetic Hoppers." They performed some fancy footwork, and everyone was clapping and cheering.

The next float to appear was the Safari Float. Santa said, "This is the second float, and it's being pulled by Donner. Oh, look, dear! Donner looks like a enormous elephant! Ho-ho!" This was a new theme this year, and Donner made it memorable; it would probably become a favorite. All the elves on the float were dressed like Safari animals. Santa pointed and said, "Look at the giraffe! Look at the big ape—that's new too." Sir King, Lady Queen, Rosie, Runner, and Sharon were all on the Safari Float. Mrs. Claus chuckled and said, "Look, Santa, there's Goober and Sammie in a small tree. And there's Bloober, Brittany, Courtney, and Whitney too!" Goober was repeating, "Look at me, look at me!" loud enough for everyone to hear. The float passed out of sight and was stored away. The elves put Donner back in the stall. Then Goober and Sammie were free to fly over the stands by Santa and Mrs. Claus. They weren't going to miss any part of this Carnivale.

Santa and Mrs. Claus ran a running commentary as we watched the parade together. Santa said, "Here is our dance team, Lon, in front of the next float." They put on a whimsical show. The girl and boy elves were all in fanciful costumes. Their bodies moved fluidly as they performed a variety of dances—tap, jazz, and the big surprise, a ballet. This year they had added a graceful rendition of the famous Christmas ballet, *The Nutcracker*. Three different songs, three varieties of dances. Wow! They were so good, they practically put us in a trance.

Seeing a ship coming down the street woke us all up. "That's the Pirate Float, with Comet pulling it," said Mrs. Claus. Everyone on this float was decked out with an eye patch and a wooden leg, just like a pirate. They were singing old pirate songs, but out of tune. It was pretty hilarious. We all laughed, and the pirates laughed at us laughing, and then we laughed all the harder. Bloober, Brittany, Courtney, and Whitney were perched on the shoulders of the pirates, playing pirate parrots. Real typecasting. I was tickled to hear the parrots laughing too. They were singing along in high-pitched voices. Goober's voice rose above all the noise. He said, "Santa and Mrs. Claus, there's my kids! There's my kids!" This float had my vote for the funniest.

Wiping tears of laughter from his eyes, Santa said, "Here comes our fourth float, the Garden Float pulled by Bonner, our defender." Everyone on that float was dressed like a piece of fruit or a vegetable, and their faces were painted to blend in. All you could see were the whites of their eyes. There were apples, strawberries, peaches, plums, tomatoes, green beans, and corn, to name a few. They were kind of adorable. The band played funny Christmas songs for them, and this garden came to life, giggling and dancing and singing. What a trip!

Mrs. Claus spoke up, "This is our fifth float, the Castle Float, put together by the day care elves." Cupid was pulling this float. All the little ones were dressed like grown-ups, and their faces were painted to resemble their parents. They were practically swimming in their clothes. Their sleeves were way too long, the shoes were way too big, and the gloves were attached with clothespins because they were too big too. They were darling. As they rode by us, their infectious laughter got us going too, especially Santa and Mrs. Claus. These little ones were putting on a super show. Blinking lights were reflected in glitter sprinkled all over the float. As was his way, Goober shouted, "Glitz and glitter. Glitz and glitter. Glitter and glitz. Glitter and glitz." Mrs. Claus said to Santa, "Goober is showing off." then they put their heads together and laughed again. Goober heard this and said, "I'm showing off. I'm showing off," in his screechy little voice. Goober kept me in stitches too. Mrs. Claus especially appreciated the little kings and queens on the float. They were dressed in impeccably tailored tuxes and high-fashion ballroom gowns made by the Sewing Department. Their fine handiwork spoke to her seamstress's soul.

Santa said, "Here comes our sixth float, the Circus Float, pulled by our Blitzer. Look how his muscles ripple! Elves were jumping on trampolines and flying up into the air, doing flips, and walking on tight ropes. The music was very lively and catchy. The Golden Wiskers played in perfect sync with all the different acrobatics. You could tell these kids had practiced diligently to be able to perform such professional feats. They showed no fear. They even did some juggling.

Mrs. Claus was excited to see their six original raindeer pulling the next float. "Look at Buddy leading Dancer, Prancer, Dasher, Flasher, Vixen, and Veben. It's the Under the Sea Float." The elves here were brightly dressed as tropical fish, sea turtles, lobster, dolphins, sea horses, whales, octopuses, and some I couldn't identify. Waves painted on the side of the float hid their feet. As the float went by the grandstand it slowed down, and the fish elves spritzed us with a fine mist to complete the illusion. Once again, Goober had an apt remark. "Don't get wet. Don't get wet. I'm hiding behind Santa. I'm hiding behind Santa." Santa loved the float. He called it "too cool."

Goober announced the next float. "Here comes our eighth float. One two, three, four, five, six, seven, eight." Mrs. Claus laughed and said, "Thank you, Goober, for being so attentive." Santa said, "It's the Big Band Float. And I see Wrinkles is pulling it. Ho-ho, a great excuse to ride a golf cart!" This was by far the loudest float. Anyone and everyone who played an instrument could be on this float if they wanted. It was decorated with blankets of exquisite white flowers and the elves looked like toy soldiers. Their suits were navy with gold trim. Their lively Christmas songs gave us a very joyous feeling, and we whistled and cheered. I don't think they heard us though; they were playing so loud. Mrs. Claus said, "Goober, do you have anything more to say about this float?" Goober whistled and said, "I'm a goody soldier too. Goody soldier. Goody soldier." Goober could always make her laugh, and she had a way of goading him on just for fun.

Mrs. Claus said, "Here comes our last float, being pulled by another golf cart. Joy's driving! It's the Ice Skating Float." The elves on this float were skating and ice dancing. Their costumes were sleek to show the line of the body as they moved, and their skates were enviable. They had several blades so it was almost impossible to fall down. An innovative suspension device created an even balance that helped make their performance flawless. There were even lights on their skates.

We all clapped as the last float left. Santa said, "Well, Lon, that ends this year's parade, ho-ho! And it sure was an extra-special treat to share it with you. I thank you." Then Mrs. Claus said, "Lon, having you here with us this year has given us so much happiness." "The feeling is definitely mutual," I said. "Buddy, Slim, and Happy really made me feel welcome today. They're the ones who dressed me up as a clown and had me walk on stilts…we had a blast. It was sweet of them to want to include me. I'm grateful to all of you and I'll always treasure my memories of today." Santa and Mrs. Claus said, "We will too, Lon."

Santa addressed the crowd. "Can I have everyone's attention? Before we eat all this delicious food and visit with our friends and families, let's give the raindeer, the dogs, and the parrots a big hand. Didn't they do a great job?" The elves burst into gleeful applause. Santa continued. "Also, to anyone else who was in the parade, and to everyone who helped in any way to make this year's Carnivale a big success, Mrs. Claus and I can't thank you enough! Now let's all eat some of this wonderful food prepared for us. Enjoy!" The elves laughed and cheered and chatted as they made their way to the food. They exchanged funny stories about floats in previous years and took turns playing with the band so there could be uninterrupted music all evening long.

One more day, and the production floor would be in full operation. But tonight was party time. One thing I learned, the elves played as hard as they worked. And they included me. I felt right at home, as though I was part of the family. I can't say enough how overwhelmed with thankfulness I was just to be here.

Before it got too late, Buddy and I went over to the stables to see if the raindeer had been fed. Someone had taken care of them. They even had fresh straw to lie down on. Everyone knew how important it was to see to the raindeer's needs, and this time somebody had beaten us to the punch.

On the way back, Buddy and I joined up with Tapper, Ice, Blue Eyes, and some other elves who were heading for the Whispering Pines Club. It looked like this was going to be another all-nighter of fun and games. Buddy announced that he was opening up the pool. The design team, composed of Bubbles, Shadow, Snickers, Ish, and Shooter, was in the library talking about new concepts and equipment. Santa saw them and said, "Listen guys, you should be celebrating. Tomorrow starts our first work day and this is your last chance till next year." Santa gave me a twinkly glance, then he, Mrs. Claus, and I scooped up all five of them, and to the pool we went. Santa had Bubbles and Shadow, one in each hand. I had Snickers and Shooter. And Mrs. Claus had Ish. We tossed them into the water and they didn't really protest. It was all good-natured fun. Then Santa and Mrs. Claus headed out for another slice of pie. That sounded too tempting, so I joined them.

Santa said, "Boy, Lon, you sure looked great in your clown costume! I didn't even know it was you until Goober spilled the beans. Did you hear him? He said, 'That's Lon clowning around…big feet, big feet. Tweet, tweet, smell my feet.' Ho-ho, I sincerely hope you've had a great time with us since you have been here, Lon." I said, "Most certainly I have, over and over again!"

On my way to give Buddy a hand at the pool, I peeked in Santa's office. All the dogs were sacked out on their rugs. They were worn out after the excitement of the day. This was their favorite place, except whenever Mrs. Claus went to her office, Lady Queen and Rosie would follow to be near her. The parrots flew everywhere, but they also liked to buzz the dogs. Goober would lead the way, and Sammie would tell him, "Calm down, Goober. Calm down!"

In the short time I was at Santa's Christmas Village, I realized this was the way a family should be. Everyone had fun working together. Everything got done. No one was left out. If an elf went to get something to drink, they would always ask someone to join them. I found myself picking up their habits and rhythms. When I went to get a scoop of ice cream, I asked Bear and Scars to join me. No one ever did anything by themselves. Everyone was included. I loved that.

After we finished our ice cream, all my energy went straight to my stomach and I got really tired, so I said my goodnights and headed to my room. The Carnivale celebration went on into the night. These elves had all kinds of energy, but I needed to rest since tomorrow was a workday.

Chapter Nine
The Elves

The ad Kris ran in newspapers throughout the world.

Morning came early, and I headed toward the Baker's Dozen for a light breakfast. I asked Slim to join me and we talked as we ate. "Slim, why doesn't Santa refer to the elves as 'little people'?" He said, "That's easy. It's because Santa doesn't want us to feel small. We really like his idea and it makes us feel genuinely accepted. It's a compliment to us. We are his helpers and he gives us total respect.

"Lon, let me tell you a story my father told me. Santa has a strong bond with my father, Wrinkles. He is one of Santa's best friends. When Santa and Dad lived in Kaskinen, Finland, Santa noticed my Dad's family was always looked down upon because of their small stature. Santa thought, just because you're smaller, it doesn't mean you should be looked down upon. He noticed that Dad's friends were also looked down upon. To Santa, their difference actually made them special. Story goes, Lon, they became great friends. In fact, my parents eventually moved so they could live only six streets away from Santa and Mrs. Claus. That's when Santa taught Dad how to make wooden toys. Dad became not only a great carpenter, but also a first-class assistant to Santa. But I'm getting ahead of myself.

"When Dad met mom, they soon fell in love and got engaged. Santa and Mrs. Claus, then known as Kris and Susie Kringle, were by Mom and Dad's side for their wedding.

"My mom was a seamstress, and so was Mrs. Claus. They spent a lot of time together sewing clothes for people in need. As they worked side by side, they became great friends, and are still great friends to this day.

"When my brother, Happy, and I were born, Santa and Mrs. Claus were so glad for my mom and dad. Santa and Mrs. Claus loved us so much, it was as though we had two sets of parents. We spent a lot of time together, like one big happy family. Happy and I were so lucky; it was a good life. Then when Santa asked all of us to move to the North Hills with him, it just seemed natural that we would go along.

"When I was a small boy, Santa would often talk about his big dream with my dad. Happy and I didn't pay much attention to their grown-up talk. We were just kids. School and play were our big concerns. But when Dad told us we would be moving to the North Hills, we were ready. We didn't like being picked on because of our size, and we just wanted outta there! Wherever Santa and Mrs. Claus wanted us to go was just fine with us.

"Once we arrived at the North Hills and got settled, Dad read to us the ad that Santa was running in newspapers all over the world. Santa, Mrs. Claus, Mom, and Dad had taken pains to word it carefully. Here's what it said:

EMPLOYMENT: I WANT YOU!

Under 48 inches tall. Must relocate. Will give food and housing. Looking for great people willing to come dream a dream with me. Contact Kris Kringle at Jemdaza, North Hills. Directions to the North Hills: Upon arriving at Jemdaza, go north one hundred miles. Bring tools of your trade. Dress warm; it's cold here. Start the walk and we will meet you. Let's build together!—Kris.

"All the little people we knew thought this was a great idea. Once we got to where we were going, we knew we would be among people of our own stature, and we all loved the idea! For the first time in our lives, we would be able to have friends our own size. This was a way Santa could protect us. We all thought, what a great dream!

"I remember the day we arrived at the North Hills. I don't want to dwell on it, but boy, was it rough going back then. That was the day Happy renamed the North Hills the North Pole, and Santa was delighted.

Little people kept arriving in response to Santa's ad, and we'd go to meet them. Buddy was the only tall person who came. All the rest were under forty-eight inches. I remember, Mom, Dad, Santa, Mrs. Claus, Happy, and I would try to put all the other elves at ease. Buddy would pick them up. Whether alone or with a family, it seemed like the little people felt at home right away. Of course, we were all the same size. That in itself made the new arrivals feel very accepted and pleased to be here. The look on their faces confirmed that. I think all of them must have had some of the same bad experiences that I'd had. But here we were all on the same level, eye to eye.

Elves arrive by train on their journey to the North Hills.

"Many traveled for weeks to get here. Most all of the elves had to take trains and ships for part of the journey. Many others hiked from great distances. But they had one thing in common: They were all enthusiastic about being part of Santa's vision. They wanted to join him in being a blessing to children all over the world.

"The following year, at least a hundred more little people arrived. Most all of them had a trade or talent, or just enjoyed helping in any way that was needed. With a broad range of skills to work with, we started designing the layout of the village and the production floor. Santa wanted us for our goodness and our skills. Our height wasn't an issue. And nobody called us little anymore.

"As our numbers grew, it was getting harder and harder to re-member everybody's name. Also, some of the names belonged to different nationalities and were long and difficult to say. Santa asked everyone to think of a nickname for themselves. We all liked the idea and it worked out great. That's why everyone here is known by a single name.

"At first, we didn't understand each other since we arrived from many different parts of the world. It took a little while to work it all out. Mrs. Claus and Santa had fun interpreting for everyone, but they couldn't be everywhere at once. So, we all started learning other languages. In about a year or so, our conversations were getting much easier. The main language here is still English; everyone learned it over time. Still, most of the elves speak many languages now.

"I mentioned we had designers. But that wasn't all. We were also blessed with lumberjacks, carpenters, painters, teachers, seamstresses, cooks, doctors, nurses, mechanical engineers, gardeners, civil engineers, handymen, and many other walks of life. We all shared the same goal: to make Santa's dream come true.

"As soon as the lumberjacks went to work cutting trees for lumber, we began to build homes for our families. Santa taught the senior raindeer how to drag the fallen trees out of the forest. They would bring the wood into the village, and then into the stables. At that time, the stables served as our woodcutting headquarters. For the meanwhile, the raindeer bedded down in a fenced-in area. It took only a few weeks to accumulate enough lumber to start building. A team of elves would transport the lumber over to the carpenter elves, who worked together like a well-oiled machine. The homes would now come together quickly.

"All the while, the ladies worked in the garden. Mrs. Claus helped with the design and layout of the garden. It had to be quite large to feed all the elves, you know. Many of the elves had brought seeds and seedlings or little fruit trees with them. This gave us a good start. Little did we know how good our garden would grow. For, lo and behold, as soon as we planted the seeds and trees in the rich soil, our harvest grew rapidly. We were amazed and grateful for our good fortune. Many of the elves had great ideas for the garden, and it flourished beyond our wildest dreams.

"Santa was so impressed with the elves' ideas and expertise. He thought, why not start a team to work on these ideas? Thus was born the Invention and Design Team—later called the Design Department, headed up by Bubbles. Some of their ideas seemed too far out at first, but they usually worked. The team made many of our jobs a lot easier. Their new concepts also speeded up production. Our toy makers were able to double their output so that a lot more gifts reached many more children. That was the year we really started to grow."

I asked Slim if he was sorry to leave any friends back in Kaskinen. He said, "Yes, we all did, and for that reason alone, it was a little tough on Happy and me. However, there are times when we, as children, have to step up to the plate and accept change. We have to trust our parents, that they are making the right decision for the entire family, as did my Mom and Dad when we moved here. When we came here, Happy and I not only had each other to play with, we had the parrots too, Goober and Sammie. Wow! They were, and still are, barrels of fun! Lon, they'd make anyone laugh! We also had the raindeer. During that time, Santa and Mrs. Claus, and Mom and Dad spent as much time with us as they could, and they trained us to help out too. Happy and I trusted, and everything turned out better than we imagined. We have more friends now than we ever dreamed we could.

"We never have a desire to leave, Lon. We're truly one big happy family. And another thing…we're all needed here. That's a great feeling no one can take away. It's more than wonderful to feel needed. We all have a job, we take great pride in our quality of workmanship, and we have a lot of fun doing it. Santa had a plan, and all of us worked to bring it about. We're so glad we did; we've never regretted it.

"I'll tell ya, Lon, everyone here has their own unique story. Every elf you talk to will take you on a different journey. Just listen, and you will learn how all this came together. Every story adds a piece to the puzzle of how everything has worked out for everyone's good here at the North Pole.

"Take the raindeer, for instance. When we came here, we only had six raindeer. I remember when Dancer had her twins. You probably know that three years in a row, she gave birth to twin raindeer: Comet and Cupid, Bonner and Donner, and Blitzen and Blitzer. Everyone was so excited about the new additions. But my favorite raindeer will always be Veben and Vixen. They were born in Finland. Other people had dogs and cats for pets, but we had raindeer. So you know we stood out like a sore thumb. But the raindeer loved us, and we loved them. People would always come by to see our pet raindeer.

It was amazing how well they behaved when visitors were around. They fit in easily with the family.

"I never did tell Mom and Dad till later in life, but Veben and Vixen would let Happy and me ride on their backs. We would hold onto their antlers and ride and ride. Only on our property, of course. The raindeer were so relaxed. They didn't seem to mind at all, so we were never scared. Thank God, we never got hurt, or that would have been the end of that.

"Lon, I tell you, all of us elves here at the North Pole were meant to be here." We walked over to the J'Yakaboo River and found Happy sitting on a smooth bench under a tree. He was watching three elves who were having a ball fishing. We joined him. Happy said, "Over there is Scars. He always has a hook in his finger or elbow. One thing he surely isn't, is a fisherman. But, he likes to grab his pole and be with his friends by the water. His other two buddies are Bear and Sparkle. Now, Bear is the great outdoorsman of the bunch. He always sets up his other two buddies before he starts fishing. Sparkle, he usually catches the least amount of fish, but his eyes get as big as plums when he hooks one."

Just then Sparkle shouted with joy, "I've got one, Bear! Look, Scars!" His eyes lit up and got all sparkly. Sparkle handed his pole over to Scars. "You pull this one in, Scars." Then Bear yelled out, "Don't lose it! Keep it tight!" These elves were the best of pals. Scars said, "Boy, that's about a two pounder!" Sparkle disagreed. "No, I bet it would go four or five pounds." Sparkle's fish seemed to grow after it was out of the water. Slim, Happy, and I got the biggest charge out of watching them. The fish probably weighed a pound at most, and Bear surely knew it. I decided elf watching was more fun than fishing.

Slim said, "Lon, here comes Boots. Let me introduce you. 'Boots, meet Lon.'" Boots sat down right beside me. Slim had to go take care of some business, so he said, "Boots, why don't you tell Lon your story of how you came here?" I thanked Slim for the time he had spent with me, and he went on his way.

I found out that Boots came from Zimbabwe. Bear was his son. They had fished together for their survival in Africa. Here at the North Pole, fishing was mostly just fun. Boots said, "My wife is Pearl. She works in the laundry. I'm the one in charge of packing Santa's bags, the gifts he delivers on December 24th. He always compliments me on how well I do my job, and that makes me feel good. Every year, Santa visits more and more children, so I've had to get more and more efficient. I've learned to pack according to country and city, and the bags are full and tight. This makes Santa's job easier.

"In Africa, my family and I always lived in danger. Our home was a small mud hut. My son fished for food, for survival. When we had extra, we would sell it to the rich people. One day a rich man purchased some fish from me. He took the newspaper from under his arm and tossed it to me to wrap up his fish. I said, 'Thank you, sir,' and started to place the fish on the page when I saw something out of the ordinary. Right there before my eyes was the ad from Kris Kringle. I tore it out and slipped it into my shirt.

"When I got home that night, I showed it to my wife and son. Pearl said, 'Let's pack up and go.' Bear said, 'I'm with you, Mom and Dad.' I said, 'Calm down. Let's think about this.' We all knew it would be a very long trip. Pearl was determined. She said, 'We can do it! We will be around our own kind of people. We will have a home and food. We don't know what will be expected of us when we get there, but we can do this!' So, we started planning, and just one week later we were off to the North Hills. All of us had backpacks and fishing gear. Lon, there were times we didn't think we would make it. We wore out our shoes getting to the North Hills. In Africa, we never even wore shoes. As we went farther north, it got much colder than we ever would have dreamed it could be. We had coats, gloves, and boots. People would look at us funny, but our minds were made up! 'We're going to Jemdaza, North Hills,' we told everyone.

"We took every ride we could. We rode horses, oxen, camels, small boats, and big boats. People were kind to us, but they still thought we were crazy. We stopped many times to work. We would pick fruit and vegetables; we even worked in copper mines. My wife ironed and cleaned clothes for people. We all did what we could do. When we had enough money, we would move on again. This process took many, many months. However, my family and I had a deep longing to do better, so we didn't care how long it took to get there. What we did know was each day we were one more day closer to being there, and that gave us enough hope to know we would make it.

"Before I saw the ad in the newspaper, we didn't know of Kris Kringle. We didn't know this trip was way out of our league; we were ill-equipped for it. But, desire took over and we coped. We worked for our passage on a ship headed for Greenland. From there, we traveled to Cape Morris Jesup. Then, we caught a ride on a train to Jemdaza. We had thought it all out; we had a plan. My wife and son never wavered. They encouraged me, I encouraged them, and we never looked back.

"The closer we got to Jemdaza, the more our excitement grew. It was funny. We had never before been out of Zimbabwe, but we felt like we were going home at last. I want you to know, Lon, a long time ago a lot of us little people got separated and were scattered all over the world as many of the elves were adopted. But now, we would be reunited. We were wanted by this Kris Kringle, and we had a desire to meet him, and be with him and his dream. Of course, at times it was hard on our family, and I had doubts, but I never told Pearl or Bear. Once we made it to the train that would take us to Jemdaza, I became confident. I remember looking at them and saying, 'We're going to make it!'

"Do you know the train to Jemdaza? If you look to the left, there are small towns, fields, and beautiful wilderness. But on the right there is nothing but snow and hills—all white. The trainmaster told us, 'You won't make it. There's nothing out there but a hundred miles of ice and snow.' With a tear in my eye, I said, 'Are you sure about this? We have traveled for nine months to get here.' The trainmaster said, 'The only thing I can tell you is I've seen many, many small people stand where you are now. They all left for the North Hills, and I've never seen any of them come back. Good luck!' Well, this trainmaster didn't know what he just said! His words were meant to discourage, but they gave us hope again, and I became very bold. I told my wife and son we were going shopping, then on to the North Hills!

"In Jemdaza we spent the remainder of our money. The ad said bring tools of your trade, so I purchased fishing line, hooks, artificial bait, and a lobster cage. My wife bought a washboard and brushes to scrub clothes. We stuffed what we could into our backpacks, grabbed the rest, and we were off again. Only one hundred miles more and we would be there! We were just exhausted, but now we knew we would make it. We had learned many new skills by trial and error on the trip. Necessity was a great teacher. We kept our conversation positive and talked about how this was the adventure of our lives. But I felt responsible for bringing my family along on my dream and I couldn't keep doubts from creeping in sometimes. What did I get them into? Still, we had come too far to turn back.

"After we'd walked about eight miles, we could go no farther and we sat down to rest. I was afraid the cold temperatures would be the end of us. But just then the North Wind told Ivy, 'There is a family of three coming from Jemdaza. They're very tired and cold. They have stopped, and I don't think they're going to make it to the North Pole. I think they're at the end of their journey.' Ivy immediately said to the North Wind, 'Blow on me so I can make a loud enough noise that will alert someone to come find me.' So the North Wind blew on Ivy, and Ivy tilted his branches to send a whistling noise strong and hard toward Santa's Village.

"Santa heard Ivy's whistling sound and he asked the elves, 'What do you think that is? I'm going to the woods to find out.' As Santa got closer, he realized it was Ivy. Ivy then said to Santa, 'You have three very tired, very cold elves traveling from Jemdaza to the North Pole. They have sat down in the snow because they are exhausted. I don't know how long they have been there, Santa, but I do know they may not make it. If you hurry, you can save them before it's too late.'

"Santa hastily thanked Ivy then rushed as fast as he could to the stables. 'Tank, get my sleigh and all twelve raindeer hooked up! Right now! Please! There is a family about ten miles out of Jemdaza. We've got to move fast!' Tank said, 'Come on, Dasher, Dancer, Prancer, Vixen, Comet, Cupid, Donner, Blitzen, Flasher, Veben, Bonner, and Blitzer! This is an emergency!' Mrs. Claus came outside, 'What's wrong?' she said. 'Susie, I need blankets, right now! There's a family traveling from Jemdaza, and they need our help just as soon as I can get there!' Susie felt the urgency in Santa's voice and quickly gathered up the blankets. While the raindeer were being hooked up to their reins, Santa told them why they had to rush to get to these people. With the raindeer harnessed, Santa said, 'Let's go! Hurry as fast as you can!'

"At Santa's command, all the raindeer immediately started to run. 'Go—Dasher! Go—Dancer! Go—Prancer! Go—Vixen! Go—Comet! Go—Cupid! Go—Donner! Go—Blitzen! Go—Flasher! Go—Veben! Go—Bonner! Go—Blitzer! Go! Go! Go! I know you cannot fly, because it's not nighttime, but we have to travel as fast as your legs will take you—for this is a very serious circumstance!' Santa held tightly to the reins. The raindeer ran like a flash into the distance, as if challenged to a race, and with the bottoms of their feet barely brushing the new-fallen snow. They understood exactly what Santa wanted them to do."

Boots sure had an exciting story to tell! He continued. "The North Wind, Ivy, Santa, Mrs. Claus, the elves, and the raindeer were all working together as a team to try to save me and my family. The North Wind spoke to the South Wind 'Try to keep heat on that family!' Hours went by, then Santa spotted us. We heard the bells coming toward us. Bear, Pearl, and I stood up. Our first thought was, 'We're going to be eaten up!' We had never seen raindeer before, and they were huge! Their antlers were enormous! The raindeer and sleigh circled around us as we huddled in the snow, then they pulled up beside us. Santa noticed we looked African, so he spoke to us in our native language. Roughly, the English translation is, 'I'm Kris Kringle, but everyone calls me Santa.' We all cried as we exchanged a few words with Santa, thanking him for rescuing us. Santa lost little time in helping us into the sleigh. He quickly placed blankets all over us to keep us as snug and warm as possible. He tossed our backpacks and equipment into the back of the sleigh and told the raindeer to take it easy going back, since everyone was now okay.

"Pearl discovered some sandwiches and fruit packed in among the blankets. Susie—Mrs. Claus—had thought to include them as a nice surprise. As we got close to the North Hills, we saw a huge mountain surrounded by woods. Then we were there, safe and sound. When we got out of the sleigh, so many elves came up to greet us with the friendliest and warmest welcome. Strength was returning to our bodies now. We looked at each other with tears flowing from our eyes and said, 'Thanks to Santa, we made it! We made it!' I hugged my family in joy and relief.

"We watched as Tank put the raindeer away, brushed them all down, fed them, and watered them. As far as we were concerned, they were the heroes of the day—along with the North and South winds, and Ivy. We realized right away that everyone here does their part to make things happen at the North Pole.

"Lon, over the years, we were taught English by Santa, because that was the universal language. Santa still speaks African to us, and I teach it at the school. Everyone studies language skills of all kinds here. But I'm getting a little off the track here—so back to the story.

"Santa told everyone who came to the North Pole that if any of us ever wanted to leave, he would finance our trip back to where we came from. But no one has left yet. Why would we leave? We're home.

"From that day on, all the elves made it a point to visit the raindeer at the stables often. We take treats along, and most of the time an apple or a carrot, which are their favorites. Tank always takes the best care of Santa's raindeer. His assistant Cheeks looks after the smaller raindeer. Cheeks is known for his bright apple-red cheeks."

Boots said, "Lon, it's been wonderful talking with you. My family and I are so thrilled you're safe here with us." His story had been so touching. I thanked him and we said our goodbyes, just for now. As we shook hands, he pulled me in for a hug. Then I was off on my next adventure.

Chapter Ten
The Bubble Dome

Bubbles and his staff manufacture glass inside the mountain.

I totally enjoyed my conversations with the elves. It was as though they wanted to talk to me as much as I wanted to talk to them. I supposed it was because they didn't often get to speak with anyone from the outside world.

I met up with Bubbles on my way over to the Design Department. He asked me to join him at the Whispering Pines Club, and I said yes since I was always happy to see him. We discussed many things over a mug of hot spiced cider. He shared with me how the Bubble Dome had come about. I listened very intently so I wouldn't miss any details. I told him he was an awesome design engineer. He laughed and said, "All I do is look at a situation and try my best to make it better." I was so impressed, I told him, "Your creativity on this project is one of the greatest design concepts I have ever seen in my entire life." Indeed, Bubbles' Bubble Dome left me wondering how soon I would be able to tell everyone back home about it.

Bubbles explained, "When I arrived at the North Pole, I observed the few buildings that were here at the time: the raindeer stables, Santa and Mrs. Claus's log house, and Wrinkles and Joy's little home. I also noticed their struggling gardens.

"Obviously, the biggest problem was the weather, since winter lasted the year-round. Because of the cold, all the plants had to be grown indoors. Everyone had every plant imaginable, all over the inside of their homes. It was really funny. Everywhere you looked there were all kinds of herbs and flowers, many of which I had never heard of or seen before. The inside of Santa's log home was like a tropical paradise. What an overwhelming pleasure! There were plants with huge leaves and plants with very tiny leaves. Some had budding flowers of vibrant hues that produced healing potions, while others were used for colorful décor. And, of course, there were fruits and vegetables of every imaginable kind. I learned that the rich soil and special river water made all the plants grow quickly. Also, one big advantage from all of these plants was their wonderful fragrance.

"When the elves came home from work, this aroma soothed them to sleep. When they awoke a few hours later, the scent actually made them feel fully revived for the day. These indoor plants made the homes look more like greenhouses, but they didn't mind, because it only made their living quarters more homey. Santa and Mrs. Claus and the elves sang to their plants every day, making them flourish well and fast.

"We were not protected like these indoor plants, however. So, I went to work on an idea to take care of Santa, Mrs. Claus, Buddy, and the elves and their children. I knew I had to keep testing until it worked.

"I began my research on a type of ore found in our mountains here. Luckily, I had a very dedicated team to assist me—small in numbers but great in skill and heart. This special ore I named 'vita ore stone.' My team set up my experiments inside the cave so as to shield us from the bitter cold outside.

"We heated up the stone to three thousand degrees. This process took many long hours, but it was necessary to reach the total melt-down point. How lucky we were that the heat kept us very warm in the cave! Since we had several production rooms inside, the heat circulated through the pockets of air, the large room openings, and all through the surrounding rooms. It was as if we had natural tunnel vents throughout. What a great advantage this was, in the midst of the bitter cold outside!

"After the ore melted, we used a large ladle and carefully poured the liquid into flat molds. This process had to be done very rapidly to produce panes of glass. While the ore was cooling, we dumped large mounds of snow onto the glass, which created a frosted effect. Then after a short while, we lifted the slab out of the mold. We now had a sheet of glass between six and eight inches thick, and the result was amazing. Looking from one side you couldn't see through it at all, because of the frosted effect. But from the other side, it was as though you were looking through clear glass. We realized these would make perfect windows for our log homes, so we began making many panes. At this point, Santa hadn't seen what we were up to, but we wanted to be sure of our results before we brought them to him. Just by chance, two of my elf workers stood two pieces of glass right next to each other, and we couldn't get them apart no matter how hard we tried. We finally realized the glass was magnetic. That's when it occurred to me to create a dome to protect us.

"Wrinkles thought it was 'too cool!' when I explained the process and demonstrated how it was done. The experiment was now a success, and it was time to show Santa. Wrinkles went into the woods to find Santa and returned with word that Santa would do his best to get back as soon as possible.

"While we waited, Wrinkles gently reminded me, 'Whatever you do, try very hard not to smack your gum around Santa.' Wrinkles knew how enthusiastic I am about gum. I laughed and agreed that I would try my best not to smack. Wrinkles added, 'Santa won't say anything to you about it, but you don't want it to annoy him.' You see, it seems as though I always have gum in my mouth. I just love gum. Any flavor, anytime. One of my friends, Chuckles, actually invented some gum. He made it in delicious flavors, and you could make huge bubbles with it. I was known to blow the biggest bubbles at any given moment and without warning.

"Santa arrived and brushed off his snow-covered clothes as he entered the cave of the mountain. He pulled off his hat and gloves and exclaimed, 'It's hot in here! What are all of you up to?' I was nervous, but Santa quickly calmed me down. He said, 'Thank you, Bubbles, for wanting to share all your ideas with me.' Santa had a way of making everyone feel special, and I began to get very brave. I had collected all of my drawings and spread them out for Santa to see. He looked at them and showed interest in every aspect of my ideas. I said, 'Santa, I call this stone "vita ore stone." I took it from inside the mountain and we melted it at a very high temperature.' As I showed Santa the process, he was shocked to see how the snow caused an instant frosted effect on the glass. I then explained to him how this would work perfectly for windows in all the homes. Since the glass was six to eight inches thick, it would act as a barrier between the cold outside and the warmth inside. Another great feature was that the light coming through the windows would be just enough to keep all the plants nurtured in their growing stages. Then I showed Santa my big idea, the dome.

"I fingered through some of my drawings and found the sketch of the entire area with the proposed dome. I explained, 'We have glass beams that can be made to support the ceiling. And we know through many tests that this type of ore is rock-solid. So, we can pour the hot liquid through a twin-roller assembly, and it would be plenty safe enough to make much larger sheets of glass. What's really unique is this glass is magnetic. When two sheets are put together side by side, you cannot pull them apart. This means we could use it to cover the whole village, the garden, all the way over to the side of the mountain. We could do the garden first, then keep expanding the dome until it's completely over us. This dome would definitely keep the heat inside with no problem.'

"After I showed Santa all my drawings, in as professional a manner as possible, he said, 'Let's do it, Bubbles! We'll do the windows first.' I replied, 'Mission accomplished, Santa!'

"We built the first homes with our vita ore stone windows, and some of the other elves gathered around to admire them. They were so excited about this new invention, and word started to spread. I watched Santa as he did a little experiment of his own. First, he stood outside one of the houses, looked through a window, and reported that he couldn't see anything. Then Santa bent down, entered the house, and knelt down in front of the window. He peered through the glass from the inside and waved to the elves outside. Everything was clear for Santa, just as if there were no glass there at all, but because of the frosted outer surface, no one could see him. Santa smiled and let out a 'Ho-ho!'

"There was no doubt the experiment was a huge success. I was so happy that Santa was thrilled about my invention that I forgot to be careful with my gum! I blew a Bubble so big and so hard, when it popped it covered my whole face. Santa thought it was hilarious and he laughed for quite a spell. After he regained his composure, he congratulated me and told me how proud I made him.

"Santa then asked me if I was certain the dome idea would really work. I said, 'Without a doubt! Yes! In fact, I shared this invention with you, Santa, only after our tests were successful. When we found out this glass was as strong as mountain ore, that's when we were convinced it would work!' Santa was elated. He said, 'First, we will finish all the windows in all the homes and then we will start on the dome. As more elves arrive here at the North Pole, and as more homes are built, we will add more windows, but we will continue working on the dome since we need to get this done.'

"The next day, we were in full production, working around the clock to move the vita ore stone. We split up into teams—some would melt the stone, some would pour the molten liquid, some would roll out the glass, and so on. We had a real production assembly line to speed up the process. Precautions were taken so that the glass pieces would not touch each other until we placed them together to form the dome.

"We built a fire in a deep pit to melt the large pots of stone, and it burned nonstop. It wasn't long before we saw the dome take shape. Later in the year, of course, we switched to making toys for the children. When the season was over, we resumed building our homes and the dome.

"We often reflect on our progress since we came here, and we marvel at all we have accomplished in such a short span of time. Although at times that year was somewhat tough and tiring, on the other hand, it was a very eventful and prosperous year. We had all just moved here, and while getting settled, we still had time to build not only the homes, but surprisingly the dome as well.

"Oh, I certainly don't want to neglect mentioning how invaluable the ladies were throughout the busy time. They helped gather stone from the mountain. They transported lumber to the carpenters. They prepared food. They worked in the garden, and they did many other things in between. They worked right by our side and were a big asset indeed.

"Those first few years, when we weren't making toys, all we did was build. It took more than three years to complete all the homes inside the dome. But it was most important that we do all this for our protection from the weather and for our survival. All this was necessary to make Santa's dream grow.

"What you see, Lon, is not at all how it was when we arrived. We really loved the whole process of making all this happen. You can't imagine the thankfulness in our hearts for how it came together so fast, right before our very eyes. The day it was completed, there was rejoicing in the streets. We created heat under the very coldest conditions! If only you could have been here for that awesome celebration.

"After the village was completely enclosed, I would watch Santa just standing there contemplating the snow melting off the dome. He was really intrigued with this whole idea. It truly was amazing how the sun's rays would heat up the inside of the dome. The upper part of the dome remained at seventy-four to eighty degrees, while the lower part stayed a comfortable sixty-eight degrees, a perfect temperature for us. The joints were sealed tight, so we never had to worry about snow melting and leaking inside the dome.

"Another great thing was how the sun shining through the glass caused our garden to grow hardy and rapidly. In fact, we could grow anything all year long in different areas of the dome. Often, we would reflect on how very fortunate we were.

"After we accomplished this invention together, I was fired up to get going on other improvements—I was on a roll. As I thought of new ideas, I would brief Santa on them, and then put them into production. Santa always backed me on my ideas, and I thrived on making them come to life. I also created easier ways to accomplish not only my work, but the work of others when needed. I liked creating short-cuts for the elves so they wouldn't be overworked. But no matter what the invention, first and foremost the elves, including me, have always concentrated on making toys for the children of the world our top priority. That rule never changes.

"Well, Lon, as the years passed by, this village became more like home. It took about ten years to finish our main projects: the homes, the dome, the garden, the production floor, the lumber room, the kitchen, the dining room, the streets, the stables for the raindeer, and all the rest. Of course, I was honored when the dome was completed. One of the first things Santa said to me at the ceremony was, 'From now on, you can chew gum and blow bubbles anytime you want to. Ho-ho!' It never really bothered Santa to begin with. He liked to tease me about it from time to time is all.

"Santa and Mrs. Claus presented me with an award. Santa said, 'Bubbles, in honor of you, from this point on we will call the dome the 'Bubble Dome.' All the elves were there and they showed their appreciation to me. Every year after that, on the first of April, and during Carnivale, Santa makes a toast to me in remembrance of my first and biggest invention here at the North Pole, the great idea that changed all of our lives.

"When the Bubble Dome was first finished, Goober would sing to Sammie, 'I'm flyin' to the moon, la-la-la…catch me if you can, my Sammie-Ma'am.' And as the years went by, Goober and Sammie entertained each other, playing hide-and-seek in this vast and spacious Bubble Dome. They loved how they could be higher than everyone else, and you could tell they were happy and content. We all delighted in their singing. They acted like they didn't have a care in the world. Even these parrots' lives had changed dramatically for the better.

"With the completion of the Bubble Dome, we started working on many new projects. The biggest was the Twin Prop Electric Wind Tunnels. Shadow came up with a way to produce electricity for the village and drew the designs on how it would work. This became another of our greatest undertakings."

Wrinkles walked up to join us and said, "Lon, you have seen the whole Christmas Village Complex now, so what do you think?" I replied, "Wrinkles, in all my life I have never seen anything like this. It is certainly going to be very difficult for me to leave. All the elves I've met have been more than kind to me. Bubbles just told me the story of the Bubble Dome. And that's just one of the amazing stories I've heard since I've been here. Wrinkles, this really is one great place. I'm overwhelmed by everyone and everything. Many thanks to you for allowing me the opportunity to experience your special world." Wrinkles and Bubbles smiled at me, and I smiled back at them. We basked in the moment. Certainly, we all felt honored to be with each other.

Chapter Eleven
The Twin Prop Electric Wind Tunnels

The Twin Prop Electric Wind Tunnels in operation.

Bubbles took me over to the Design Department and introduced me to Shadow. He got this nickname because he followed Bubbles everywhere. Shadow was a pleasant fellow. We shook hands and he welcomed me with the traditional hug. Shadow didn't need much encouragement to talk about his electric wind tunnel invention, but Bubbles urged him anyway. Shadow elaborated about how the dome was built to protect the North Pole, but then they needed to find a way to produce electricity.

"When I first shared my ideas," said Shadow, "everyone thought I was nuts. Nevertheless, I wasn't discouraged because I truly had faith that my design would work, so I got busy. I put my complete designs down on paper. This was before we had computers. I showed my designs to Bubbles, and he suggested I build a model of the twin props. I started putting a scale model together in my living room, working and reworking the parts. I accomplished a lot in a short period of time, but my home was starting to look like a mechanic's garage. Still I pressed on, because I was determined to lick the problem. The result was with a three-foot tower with blades I could crank. This was working out, and it was really fun!

"Now, to test the props…they turned with little effort. I let out a big sigh. If we could do this on a large scale outside, I had this gut feeling that the wind would surely turn the props. In my mind I could see the props turning, electricity being produced, and the power traveling through the wires to the transformers and charging the batteries. The batteries would store up extra power we could draw upon as needed. I saw the image of a light fixture on a wire. When I flipped the switch, the wire would touch the rods, and the fixture would light up instantly. As long as I kept spinning the props, we would have light.

"I designed another prop halfway down the pole. Now we would have twin props making double the electricity at the same time. Well it worked, but this was still only a model. This entire process took me a couple months to complete, and I didn't get much sleep during that time. I was lucky that my adrenaline kept me charged up. The important thing, Lon, was that the concept worked, and I finally had a working model to show Bubbles. I began to think, maybe this is what I was born to do. In so many ways it has been very rewarding and so much fun to be a part of. And that is the best combination.

"Well, I invited Bubbles over to my house. I showed him the model and explained the entire process. He was flabbergasted. Right away he went to get Wrinkles. Happy answered the door, and Bubbles saw that Wrinkles was having dinner with his family. Normally, Bubbles would never intrude, but this was earthshaking. He burst into Wrinkles' dining room and said, 'You've got to see this! Come with me right now to Shadow's home to see his invention. It's a genius idea!' Wrinkles took Bubbles' word for it and said, 'Okay, Bubbles, let's go take a look'

"Bubbles hurried Wrinkles to my house to see my wind tunnel invention. I explained the entire concept to Wrinkles, the theory and how all the mechanical parts worked. I asked them to bear with me; I had to make the room completely dark in order to reveal the process. Bubbles blew out the candles for me and with great anticipation I started to spin the props. To their surprise, when I flipped the switch, voilà! a light glowed above us and we could all see each other. It was wondrous. Wrinkles shook his head and in a loud voice said, 'This is totally unreal! We need to get Santa immediately!' Goodness, he was gone in a flash; he left so quickly it was as though he had disappeared.

"Now it was Wrinkles' turn to interrupt Santa's dinner. But Santa could tell that Wrinkles had something of the utmost importance on his mind. 'What's up, Wrinkles?' Wrinkles replied, 'Oh Santa, you have to come see this! Please, come quickly!' Mrs. Claus overheard them and told Santa she would be glad to keep his dinner warm until he got back. Wrinkles brought Santa to my house in no time flat. Santa entered like the North Wind, sat on a stool close to my machine, and examined it. Bursting with curiosity, he said, 'Well, Shadow, you have my undivided attention. What in the world is going on here? By the looks of this room, ho-ho, you have been very busy with important machinery parts of some sort, so fill me in.'

"All eyes were on me, and I began to explain the entire invention once again. Santa grinned from ear to ear. His eyes grew bigger and he said, 'Wow!'" After he caught his breath, he asked, 'Shadow, how big do these have to be? Is it possible these wind tunnels could light up the entire Christmas Village?' I hesitated. They all watched for my reply. Then I mustered up the confidence to speak, 'I know this will work!' Santa wanted to know how long it would take to build. 'Well,' I said, 'I've thought about that too. It should be ready in approximately six to nine months. If the woodworkers, metalsmiths, and elf helpers join with us together as a team, we'd have a very smooth operation and it could be done maybe even sooner.' Santa asked, 'How many of these units will we need?' I replied, "If we assemble three units, we will have all the electricity we need.' Santa said, 'Great! Let's get started first thing tomorrow.'

"We met early the next morning. Bubbles said they had found a vein of iron ore in the mountain that could be melted down to make metal blades for the props and the tower. He started organizing the layout for the mechanical twin props, and everyone went to work on the design. Lon, it was an amazing thing to see the towers coming together.

"As is usual with any kind of construction, it took us longer than planned to complete the whole operation. Still, just under fourteen months wasn't bad for a project of this magnitude that had never been tried before. Some sections took longer to build and assemble because many of the parts had to be ordered and brought in on the train. The metalsmiths worked diligently, hammering out metal, shaping and assembling all the pieces. We had wire and metal flying in every direction. The batteries were all put in place to store up power. After ten months, the wind tunnels started to take shape. The three towers were twice as tall as the highest trees in the forest. The props were forty feet across. Much scaffolding was used to erect these huge twin prop electric wind tunnels. When we were finished, the crew disassembled the scaffolding, and all the wood was put back into the lumber room to be reused in making toys. Santa doesn't like to waste anything that is still perfectly useful.

"One of the last steps was to have the electricians place lights throughout the entire village. Then, all the elves gathered together to see if my invention worked. They had put so much time and effort into the project, we all held our breath as the props were turned on. Santa and Mrs. Claus craned their necks looking up at the towers. The props were turning smoothly and ever so quietly. The battery sources were being charged up at the same time they were being used. It was a new type of battery power recycling. While everyone stood with anticipation in the middle of the village, Santa made an announcement. 'Shadow now will turn on the main switch to light our village.' To my great relief, all the lights came on. What a sight to behold! Everyone was speechless and bedazzled, as if frozen in ice. There was an overall feeling of wonder, pleasure, amazement, and delight as the night instantly lit up like daylight.

"Santa smiled, shook his head in awe, and asked me to say a word to everyone. As the crowd grew silent, I spoke softly. 'The design staff has been working on motors to run our power saws and sanders, which take the place of elves peddling to make the belts turn the cutting blades. This can now all be done by electricity. This new system will free up so much more of their time to do other things. We plan to have all the power tools hooked up and running by the end of the year. I want to say thank you to everyone who has worked on this project.' Everyone applauded, and Santa said, 'I have one more announcement. I have given this much consideration and thought. When a person accomplishes an achievement of this magnitude and benefits Santa's Christmas Village and all the elves, I want to use the option to honor that person. Therefore, I proclaim December 28th of every year as Shadow Day, in honor of Shadow and his extraordinary twin prop electric wind tunnels. Congratulations, Shadow!' All the elves were cheering and shouting, "Congratulations, Shadow!' Everyone made me feel so appreciated. What a day to remember. And we had electricity!

"Well, Lon, that's my story." "It was wonderful, Shadow. Your invention is so valuable to the whole village. Thanks so much for telling me all about it." Shadow said, "Oh, you're most welcome, Lon. Now, how would you like to find out everything about our garden right from the horse's mouth, so to speak? Our garden is essential to our well-being and ultimately to our common goal of bringing joy to children. Skooter is our master gardener. Would you like to meet him?" There was not a speck of hesitation on my part when I told Shadow, "Absolutely! Count me in!"

Chapter Twelve
The Garden

The waterwheel in the J'Yakaboo River by the apple trees.

When we found Skooter, he was tending the garden. Being master gardener didn't mean he was above getting his hands down in the dirt. Shadow introduced me to him and left me in his capable hands, green thumbs and all. Skooter knew his horticulture inside out. He could name any plant and tell you how to care for it. He also understood bees. Skooter and his assistant, Patches, were both bee experts.

Skooter explained how the queen bee ran her colony, with worker bees gathering pollen to produce honey. The honeybee hives were necessary for the pollination of the plants. They also produced honey for use at the table and in cooking.

Skooter told me the bees never stung anyone, since they understood that humans and bees needed to work together. As if to prove the point, a bee landed on my hand. I didn't move. Just as Skooter had said, it didn't sting me. The bee stayed a minute then flew off when it was ready. It was just taking care of business, collecting pollen to make honey, and I was a rest stop. The same flowers that decorated the elves' homes and made them fresh and sweet smelling were sources of pollen for the bees.

Skooter told me, "Lon, when the Bubble Dome was completed, the temperature started to rise. When it hit sixty-eight degrees, it held right there and the snow began to melt in the area covered by the dome. By that time we had a clear understanding of conditions at the North Pole. We watched as the J'Yakaboo River thawed under the dome. It ran through the village and the garden area and has been a real treasure to us for many, many years. It continues to help us produce exceptional fruit, vegetables, medicinals, and flowers.

"Mrs. Claus worked on the layout of the garden with the other ladies. They did a superior job. When Santa appointed me to be in charge of the garden I put my talent to good use, along with Patches, to develop the garden to its present state." I said, " Skooter, it is a beautiful garden." Skooter showed me around, listing all the wonderful varieties as we went. "Lon, here are six kinds of apple trees. We have Red Delicious, Yellow Delicious, Jonathan, red Rome, Mutsu, and Granny Smith. Some types of apples are better for eating, and some are better for baking. There are five beautiful rows of trees in our apple grove.

"Then we have our red plum and purple plum trees. Over there are the peach trees in three wonderful varieties. Close to them are our many apricot, pear, coconut, and banana trees. We also have a few walnut trees. We raise peanuts and almonds. Quite some time ago, some of Santa's friends gave him three trees: an orange tree, a grapefruit tree, and a lime tree. Santa and Mrs. Claus gave them all to the garden, and now we have dozens of each variety. We try to keep the trees at the outer edge of the garden, because we don't want the plants to be in the shade all the time. We have also relocated some of these trees to the village and throughout the compound.

"Now, let me show you the remainder of the garden. The J'Yakaboo River runs through the garden here and under the dome to the outside, then under the polar ice caps." A simple wooden bridge spanned the river, and we crossed it to the other side. "Look at our acid-free tomatoes, Lon. We also grow the big purplish beefsteak tomatoes, Italian plum tomatoes, and sweet mini cherry tomatoes, plus all varieties of squash, huge pumpkins, seedless cucumbers, and sweet corn.

"Here we have red and purple raspberries. Strawberries are plentiful too." Skooter urged me to try the berries. He must have seen me salivating. I bent down and picked a handful—I just couldn't resist. They were plump, juicy, and extra sweet. Several varieties of berries were climbing up along the mesh against the Bubble Dome wall. Nearby were both tart and sweet cherry trees.

Skooter said, "Over here we have many kinds of pepper for seasoning. Most of them will go to the drying room, along with a lot of the fruits and vegetables. That is how we obtain new seeds to plant." The garden contained so many different vegetables, I can't remember them all.

"All of our fruits and vegetables become very hardy and full of flavor mainly due to the Bubble Dome," continued Skooter. "They grow fast too. A unique feature about our garden is that it never has weeds." I had never seen soil this rich before, and so very fertile. Skooter told me, if you picked an apple, in a few days blossoms would appear on the tree, and in just weeks little apples would start to grow. The fruit and vegetables never rotted. Some took longer to grow— like the pineapples. It took years to grow those. But Skooter said there was always a huge variety and plenty to eat.

I was curious about two rooms over to the side. "Follow me, Lon, and I'll show you." Skooter opened the door. "Here are our gentle plants," he said. All the plants were off the ground so they could be tended with extra care. There were carrots, leaf lettuce, radishes, and every kind of herb, used for flavor in cooking and baking.

The garden took up only five acres or so, yet it yielded enough food to sustain the entire village. The Bubble Dome, the special soil, and the life-giving water from the J'Yakaboo River all made it possible. It was magical!

"The rule is anyone can enter the garden at any time and pick whatever they want to eat," said Skooter. "Santa only asks that you eat whatever you pick. In other words, don't pick an apple, take one bite, then throw it away. Santa says, 'If you take an apple and you don't want it all, split it in half and share it with someone else.' Santa hates waste. And it makes perfect sense. Everyone here honors the garden. In our homes, we often start new seedlings so we always have new trees growing.

"We also have grapevines running through many winding sections of the village. There's what's called the 'elf walkway' in this area. The elves use it on their time off, to relax. They take long deep breaths, just to inhale the intoxicating scent that lingers in the air. It's a very soothing and satisfying, rich aroma…and ohhh so pleasant and soothing to the senses. Every day, at different times of the day and evening you will see many people on the benches, sitting with a friend, daydreaming, or listening to the river. Before they leave, they often cut some flowers to bring home. Throughout the garden there is latticework with climbing roses and blooms of all kinds. All of our homes always smell of fresh, fragrant flowers. And Mrs. Claus makes herself available to help with flower arranging.

"You'll be interested to know, Lon, that we also have a team of elves who are in charge of canning and freezing. We have two underground rooms that serve as walk-in freezers. The frozen ground keeps them cold, and it works great. And here's the storage room where the canned food is kept." Skooter said Bubbles found a way to make thin glass jars out of vita ore stone for canning. There were rows and rows of fresh canned fruit and vegetables in the storage room. I also saw sacks of potatoes and nuts piled high.

Skooter said, "There's Patches over by the hives collecting honey. Since we've been sleeping for three months, we're way behind, and Patches is very busy."

"You've heard how everyone here at the North Pole ages very slowly? The only major thing that changes is our hair. It gradually turns white over time. Fingers, our hairstylist, is excited about a new dye that will last for five years. As the hair grows, the color works its way down toward the roots. The design staff and Lavender, our herbologist, have been working on this formula for some time. They call it 'organic hair color.' They have developed four colors: reddish, black, blonde, and ash tones. Fingers is testing it out this week. She has investigated various reasons as to why this coloring works the way it does. As best she can figure, it has something to do with our water source. We should find out soon." I thought, many a lady I know back home would love to have a sample of this dye.

Skooter asked, "Have you had a chance to eat the goodies from the Baker's Dozen, Lon?" I could happily tell him I had. "The lady elves make bread from the wheat. The aroma of wheat muffins with blueberries permeates the morning air, and people passing by the bakery on their way to work invariably stop to get a treat. We have specially blended flavors of grains for our breads that really take it up a notch from the usual, since our ladies love to experiment at the Baker's Dozen."

While Skooter was showing me around the garden, Bear came to check his lobster and shrimp traps. Whenever he pulled the traps up out of the river, there would always be lobsters and shrimp inside. He always caught something. It was uncanny. Many elves enjoyed fishing the river in the garden area for fun and sport. They found it relaxing. The Bubble Dome kept the water about twenty degrees warmer than outside, so the fish liked to gather there. This was obviously to the elves' advantage. They always went home with a sizable catch.

Skooter told me about a favorite sport of the little elves. They would string popcorn so the parrots could have a snack. Then they would wrap the string around the baby trees, since they were much easier to reach. As the parrots flew around getting their snacks from the trees, they'd sometimes get dizzy, and this made the little elves laugh. It was all harmless fun. The parrots got their snacks, and they kept the little elves in stitches.

Skooter said, "One day when I was watering the plants, I really worked up a sweat. Bubbles happened to come into the garden to get an apple to snack on and he stopped to speak to me. During our whole conversation, massive sweat dripped from my forehead and soaked my shirt through and through. Bubbles didn't say a word, but when he returned to the Design Department, he and the elves went to work on a new invention. It didn't take long. After only a few weeks, they built a waterwheel in the garden. The wheel would pick up water from the J'Yakaboo and dump it into troughs that, in turn, watered the trees, fruits, and vegetables. It worked wonderfully.

"Santa, Mrs. Claus, Buddy, and many of the elves came to see the new invention. Everyone thought it was a great idea—less stress and a cooler Skooter. Santa said, 'Another job well done!' But he wondered what would happen if too much water got on the garden. Bubbles said, 'All you have to do is take this rope and pull it until it moves the water trough, and then the wheel dumps the water back into the river.' Santa said, 'What keeps the wheel turning?' Bubbles answered, 'The river runs continuously, and the current turns the wheel.' 'Brilliant success!' Santa said, as he looked on in amazement. I will never forget what Bubbles and the design elves did for me, Lon. They sure made my job much easier."

I told Skooter I'd never seen a garden with so much color and lush growth. I hadn't noticed any bugs, except for the bees, and I asked him about that. Skooter said, "You're right. They just don't come around. You know, Lon, I think I have one of the best jobs here." I said, "I'll bet you're right, Skooter. Thank you so much for this chance of a lifetime. It's been an awesome tour. I told Santa I would join him over at the yearly business meeting, so I need to leave you now. Thanks again, Skooter." Skooter shook my hand and said, "I've enjoyed talking to you, Lon, and I hope we can do it again soon. Right now though, I'd better get over there too!"

Skooter and I had to hurry to make it to the meeting on time and the brisk Christmas music helped us quicken our pace. The supervisors of all the departments were there. Santa read the roll call and each supervisor replied with "Here." The departments were as follows:

- Alterations and Sewing Department
- Canning and Freezing Department
- Carpenter Department
- Computer Department
- Dairy Department
- Day Care Department
- Design and Engineering Department
- Doctor
- Garden Department
- Kitchen and Dining Department
- Lumber Department
- Mail Room Department
- Wrapping Department
- Paint Department
- Picking Department
- Recreation Department
- School Department
- Shrinking Department
- Stable Department
- Toy Storage Department

Santa said, "Thank you all for attending. I know this may be boring to some, but we must cover business here at the Christmas Village. We have much to accomplish this year. Now, I know many of you have already started work, but I have some important last-minute information I want to tell all of you.

"All the requests you asked for have been shipped in. Buddy has been picking up supplies all during January through March. All of you need to check your departments. Also check storage to make sure you received everything you asked for. There is extra stock in the storage facility. Try to make as much as possible fit in your department. We want to clear out the storage room. Some of the items that came in were several new tools: levelers, rulers, belts, new files to sharpen the saw blades, spray paint equipment, paint and brushes, and hundreds of new shades of color.

"The Sewing Department made all new aprons for this year. Every department, please let the Sewing Department know how many you need.

"Day care, you have new toys to try out—they're coming your way. Please get back with me on how they work. We also have new laptop computers for all our students. Loads of new books from the precious Niemerg family came in. Mail Room—good luck! It's a thrilling time now, since things are really picking up. You'll have some beautiful new rolls of wrapping paper to work with this year. The Garden Department received new squash and okra seeds, along with rhubarb roots and sweet potato plants.

"The vaccines have arrived; they are all in the freezer. Let's try to get everyone vaccinated this week.

"Everything the departments have asked for has come in. If you have any questions, please see me. This is going to be another great year! I just know it! We all have enough to keep us very busy—and have fun doing it, of course—since we have many, many children's requests to fill. Children so look forward to Christmas. We want this to be the best year ever! This concludes our annual business meeting. After today, it's fun time! I tell you, it's fun doing what we love to do—making toys!

"Oh, one last thing. We have three new departments. You will all have a chance to tour them. First, we have the Shrinking Department. After packages are wrapped and tagged, they will go through the shrinking machine. This is a new machine that was designed about three years ago. The design team has ironed out all of the kinks, and the machine is now ready to roll. We will be using this new equipment in the new Shrinking Department.

"The second new department is the Design and Engineering Department. This is a new expanded version of the Design Department already in operation and headed up by Bubbles.

"The third department is the new Recreation Department. The kids can use it whenever their schoolwork and chores are done.

"Once again, thank you for coming. Let's have a great year. Remember to clean out the storage room. Thank you, everyone! And if there is anything else you need, let me know right away. Now, let's go grab a snack at the cafeteria and enjoy the remainder of the evening together."

Food and conversation sounded like the perfect idea. Diamond, Crunch, Ruby, Munch, and Ice had cooked up a storm, and the kitchen crew had placed all the delicious food on the table. Buttons filled baskets with a variety of breads then joined us. This snack seemed more like a meal—it was yummy and filling. Thank goodness they didn't forget to roll out the dessert cart.

Chapter Thirteen
The Paint Room and Day Care

Elf Giggles enjoys his new paint gun.

I had been looking forward to this day every since I arrived at the North Pole—a few days ago. My world had been turned so topsy-turvy, it seemed like a lot longer. I was about to see Santa's toy making operation in full swing. When I entered the production floor, the elves were cutting wood and making toys, and the conveyer belts were moving the toys down the assembly line. Apparently making toys was as easy as riding a bike: Even though they'd been sleeping for three months, the elves picked up right where they'd left off.

I spotted Giggles in the paint room. He was the head painter and he was getting ready to use this year's new paint equipment. I also recognized Sky, his assistant. Blitz, Blaze, Swang, and Dance—the only girl painter—were there too. Dance and Swang did all the detail painting. Everyone was getting the new equipment in order. Blitz was filling up one of the five paint holding tanks. Each one had it's own trigger. Blaze was putting the lids on the tanks. Swang was untangling the hoses. Dance was lining up toys on the conveyer belt. Sky was placing the packing trash outside the room. I made sure to stay out of their way, and in no time they had the new equipment ready to go.

Giggles got off to a great start with the new spray gun. The painting seemed to be going very smoothly. Blitz was pouring more paint into the holding tanks, when all of a sudden everything went haywire. The spray gun clogged and Giggles realized the wrong paint was coming out of the nozzle. Fire trucks became yellow, and the others toys were spotted with a rainbow of color. Giggles continued to pull the trigger on the paint gun in hopes of unclogging it. Then there was some kind of chain reaction, and the tops of the holding tanks blew off. All of the elves were covered in paint. An "Oh, my goodness!" popped out of my mouth. Everyone else gave each other a "What just happened?" look. They were all pointing at each other; no one wanted to accept the blame for this one. Swang said, "What did you do, Blaze?" Blaze answered, "Me? What did you do?" It got to be quite hilarious as they all blamed each other, round and round in a circle, not knowing what to do.

I was laughing long and hard as this conversation of blame went on. Finally Giggles said, "Hurry, we need to get all of this cleaned up really fast, before someone sees this mess. Sky, you start on the equipment. Blitz, you and Lon go get two buckets of water." Giggles was including me in the crew. I had arrived! He continued. "Dance, you and Blaze start on the floor. Swang, you can clean the tubing. Let's get all of these paint lines straightened out—hurry!

It sure took a while, but with team effort, we finally got all the paint cleaned up. All the equipment looked new again. The correct paint was in the holding tanks. The paint lines and spray guns all matched up. Wow, what a job! The lids to the holding tanks were in the locked position, fastened down real tight this time. Although the mess was gone, there were dried paint blotches all over everybody's clothes, aprons, and beards. The elves looked at each other and had another big laugh. That's when Giggles said, "Maybe we should look at the directions. Dance, start reading." She read the following out loud:

Number 1: Make sure the correct paint is in the proper holding tanks.

Number 2: Make sure the five clear lines go to the correct holding tanks.

Number 3: Make sure that when the trigger is pulled, the paint coming through the clear paint line matches the color on the paint gun.

Number 4: Before you use another color, move the trigger switch to the proper color, otherwise it will clog the paint gun.

Number 5: Never spray when you're adding paint to the holding tanks.

Number 6: Never unlock the lids on the holding tanks when in use, or paint will spray everywhere.

Number 7: Always use goggles when handling paint to protect your eyes.

Number 8: Use water-based paint only.

As the directions were being read, we all realized everyone had made at least one mistake. But now they had corrected them. That's what really mattered. Soon after we got back to work, Santa stopped by and asked, "So, how is the new equipment working out?" Everyone spoke at the same time, "Great!" "Wonderful!" "Super, Santa!" Blaze added, "It's going to make our job so much easier." Santa stayed long enough to see how it all operated and spoke to everyone down the line. He said, "This equipment is so much better than painting by hand—it really speeds up the process. Hey Sky, what do you think?"

Sky said, "I like it. It's like having five paintbrushes in your hand at the same time, all with different paint." Santa asked Blitz, "How do you like the colors?" "They're very beautiful, very wonderful colors, Santa. One spray over the toy, and it's coated smoothly and evenly. This new machine is exceptional! I don't know how we worked without it until now. We're all very pleased with it."

Santa continued to check everybody out. "Blaze, how is Giggles doing with the new trigger systems?" Blaze said, "As you can see, Santa, he's doing a great job." Santa said, "Dance, does the new paint flow okay when you do the detail work? Do you like the new system?" Dance replied, "Oh, I really like the paint's glossy finish very much. It shines like you're looking into a mirror." Santa turned to me. "And Lon, what do you think?" "Well," I said, barely holding back a giggle, "just from what I can see, it seems like this new equipment is going to speed up the entire process tremendously, and I think it's pretty fantastic!" Santa said, "Giggles, you and your staff, keep up the good work." On his way out the door, Santa gave me a sly look from under his bushy eyebrows and said, "Hmmm, it looks to me like the elves have more paint on them than the toys." Then he winked. Santa was having a private laugh with me, and I would have another fun story to share later.

As soon as Santa left, I went back inside, and we all burst out laughing again. Giggles said, "What a lesson. Next time we read the directions first!" It took hours before the Paint Department got caught up. There was a lot of repainting to do, and the toys were backed up clear into the Lumber Department. Swang and Dance took care of all the touch-up and detail work. Soon, the fire trucks were red again, the wheels were black, the bell was gold, a clean rope was added to the bell, and there was a tiny new water hose on every truck. All the toys were spiffed up. The dump trucks were yellow, black, and white, and you could haul and dump rocks or dirt with them. I spotted Whistles bringing in new aprons from the Sewing Department. That was right on time. The whole department was running smoothly, and these elves had a right to be proud of themselves. Things were back in order again. Santa would soon be reading to the little elves at the day care, and I wanted to be there, so I wished the painters a great rest of the day and took off

Santa was just taking a book out of his back pocket when I arrived. All the little elves were gathered around, sitting on the rug in front of Santa's chair. Peace cared for the children while their parents were at work. She stood next to me by the door, but no one was looking at us. All eyes were on Santa. For the first time this year, Santa was going to read them a story. Peace leaned in and whispered to me, "It's always a joy to see Santa spend time with the little ones. Sometimes Mrs. Claus, or some of the elves will take a turn. The children love visitors. Santa greets every child by name. He's very special and he makes all the children feel special too." The little ones were ready to listen and learn. Then Santa started.

"The name of my story is 'The Missing Gold Watch.' Once upon a time, there was an elf called Flash. He was a developer of electronic games. Flash was a very snappy elf. He never dressed down for work. He was always clean, his hair was neatly combed, his boots were polished, and his shirts were crisply ironed. He always looked like he was going somewhere special. Everyone thought he was mighty snappy. Flash also had a very special pocket watch. It was 24 karat gold, Swiss made, and very expensive, with a gold chain attached. It was as sharp as he was.

"One day, when he arrived home from work, Flash was preparing to take a shower. He took his watch off and placed it by the open window and hung up his clothes. When he turned, he noticed his watch was gone. Just then, Pockets, a young elf, was walking by the window on his way home. Flash yelled out, 'Stop! You took my watch. Give it back!' Pockets said, 'I didn't take your watch.'

"Flash put on his robe and ran outside to confront Pockets. Other elves started gathering around to hear what the fuss was about. Pockets was totally embarrassed, so he turned all his pockets inside out and said, "See—I don't have your watch, Flash! I didn't take it!" He took off his thin coat to prove it to the crowd. He didn't have any watch of any kind on him. Flash didn't say anything more, but he was still convinced Pockets stole his watch. He thought he must have quickly stashed it someplace. Everyone standing around thought poorly of Pockets. They were whispering and pointing. Poor Pockets. He felt so bad.

"A week went by, then Flash had an idea. He owned another pocket watch. It was older than his good watch and served as a back-up. Flash pulled a box out from under the bed, opened it, and took out the old watch. He placed the watch by the window where he had last laid his 24 karat gold, Swiss made, very expensive watch, and he waited for Pockets to come by. "Now we'll see if he takes this one," he said.

"Flash hid in the closet and watched. He wanted to catch the thief red-handed. But nothing happened. Every day, Flash would come home from work and set his trap, but no one ever took the watch. Then one day, Flash heard a noise. He looked toward the window just in time to see Goober—Santa's parrot had picked up the watch in his beak and was flying away! Goober hurried straight home to his tree house at Santa's castle, with Flash close behind. Flash observed Goober stowing the watch inside the tree.

"When Flash told Santa the entire story, Santa went straight to Goober's tree house, and that's when he found two pocket watches. Also a ring that belonged to Joy, Wrinkles' wife. Two scarves that belonged to Mrs. Claus. Plus a handful of other assorted items. Well, Santa had a long talk with Goober that day, and Goober said, ' I'm sorry, and I will never do that again.' Santa said, 'It's Flash you need to apologize to, Goober.' So he did. He told Flash he was sorry, that he had learned a very important lesson, and he promised he would never do it again. Flash was now totally embarrassed, because he had suspected Pockets. Pockets must have felt like two cents standing there in the street, being accused of a crime he didn't commit. Flash said, 'Santa, what am I going to do?' Santa suggested he tell Pockets how sorry he was. 'I'm sure Pockets will understand, Flash, and I think he will accept your apology.'

"Flash decided he would apologize at lunch the very next day. The time came, and the two whistles blew, signaling lunchtime. Everyone headed for the cafeteria. While they were all eating, Flash stood up and rang the bell. He said, 'May I have your attention, everyone?' There was total silence as Flash shared his story about the pocket watch. When he was done, he turned, looked at Pockets with tears in his eyes, and said, 'I'm so sorry, Pockets.' Flash felt so bad. Pockets stood up and said, 'That's okay. I understand, Flash, and I accept your apology. Let's be friends.' Flash said, 'Pockets, from the bottom of my heart, I beg you to take a gift from me, my best 24 karat gold, Swiss made, very expensive watch. I want you to have it.' Pockets shook his head and said, 'No, that's okay.' Flash insisted, 'Please.' Santa nodded to Pockets to take the watch, and Flash and Pockets gave each other a big hug. To this day, Flash and Pockets are the best of friends. This is a true story. The End."

Santa said, "I want to say a couple of things about this story that all of us should never forget. First, never accuse anyone of stealing. Second, never embarrass anyone, ever. Third, remember everyone has feelings. Fourth, when you're wrong, always say you're sorry. And last, always be a true friend.

"I must go now, so have a great day, everyone. I have to run along and feed the raindeer." Santa waved goodbye. All the elves were clapping for Santa and rushing in around him for a hug. They were so happy he had spent quality time with them.

Peace distributed some of the new toys for the season. One of the children's mothers gave her a hand. Peace took care of twelve little children, and she was always quick to say how well behaved her little elves were. But after all, they were a lot of responsibility, so all the elf mothers chipped in. As normal toddlers, the children were pretty hard on all the toys. That made them a great testing ground for new, untried toys. Santa and the Design and Engineering Department counted on them to do their best to destroy them. Only the toys that were loved, and that survived, were put into production for Christmas.

Peace said to me, "Santa always enjoys talking to the little elves and holding them. He stops in at the day care as often as he can. The thing I love most about Santa is he stays in touch with everyone. He's always so closely connected, always so concerned about the progress of every elf—from their childhood and throughout their lives. Santa teaches us great lessons. He always says, 'Keep growing in knowledge. Keep learning, and be an asset to your community.' One thing I know for certain: We love Santa and Mrs. Claus, and we know they love us."

Chapter Fourteen
The Clubs

Dallas and Turf play a game of pool.

What a sweet and uplifting time I had spent at the day care with Santa, Peace, and the children. Santa's story was a charmer, and the children learned a lot from it. They had a great bond, Santa and the children.

Santa had also introduced me to too young elves this day, Dallas and Turf. They were going to spend part of the day with me. Santa said, "Lon, these two young men have a school assignment. They're doing a report on being polite and social. If you don't mind, they would like to write about your day with them. Is that okay with you?" I replied, "That's fine. I'm happy to help," and Santa went about his business.

I shook hands with Dallas and Turf and said, "I'm all yours! What are we going to do today?" Dallas replied, "Today we are going to take you on a field trip to our village clubs." Turf added, "We want to introduce you to some elves and show you how we spend our time at the clubs." I said, "I'm ready, guys. Let's go!"

Dallas said, "The first club we're going to is called the Whispering Pines. This is a recreational and social hangout for the younger elves, but anyone can visit any of the clubs. Ice and Tapper run this club." We entered a wonderful world of games. There were pool tables, a ping-pong table, chessboards, dartboards, pinball machines, a juke-box, and a dance floor where they gave dance lessons. A snappy tune was playing on the jukebox, drowning out the outdoor music. Dallas said Tapper was a great dancer. She enjoyed teaching all kinds of dances to the elves. Ice and Tapper loved to dance together when they had free time. After work, Dallas and Turf hung out here. Everyone liked to socialize at the bar, which sat in the middle of the room, like an island. All the games lined the outer walls. Dallas said, "There's an area over there were the adults can play card games and checkers, but usually they get together at each other's homes. They like to give us younger elves our space."

Ice worked the bar. He made every kind of drink you could imagine, from exotic punches and luscious fruit drinks—like blueberry freeze, plum twist, strawberry splash, peach freeze, and green river—to an infinite variety of teas and coffees, hot or cold. If you ordered one drink a day, it would take you a full year to get through the whole menu. Turf said all the pubs and clubs served soft drinks only. Dallas said, "We all like coming here because it is so much fun." Ice was welcoming and open with all the young elves. Tapper helped out at the bar. This popular club had so many customers, the front door was always opening and closing. The Whispering Pines was known to have the best drinks and the jolliest atmosphere.

Turf said, "Order whatever you want, Lon. All the snacks and drinks are free at the clubs. They always keep fresh fruit on the bar and the tables." Dance was sitting at the bar with some friends. She said, "Hi, Lon! I hope you enjoyed our paint room fiasco today. I'm glad we finally got it all cleared up and running again. Help yourself to some refreshments. There's plenty. Santa always sees to that. Have a good time with the guys now!"

Dallas and Turf started a game of pool while we were talking. The pool table was cleverly engineered. With just the push of a lever, it would raise or lower. Based on the size of the players, the table could adjust to accommodate any height. Planning and consideration went into everything these folks did. There was a beautiful fireplace in the corner, which helped give the Whispering Pines Club the feel of a winter lodge. I could see why this could be a cool hangout. We finished our drinks, and Turf said, "Next stop, the River's Edge Club!" Dallas and Turf both seemed to be enjoying a day away from the classroom.

"River's Edge is an ice cream shop run by Blue Eyes," said Turf. "She has the bluest eyes." Dallas and Turf introduced me. "Hello, Blue Eyes, this is Lon." She was making waffle cones. She said, "I know it will be busy later this evening, and I'm going to need these. So, Dallas, Turf, why aren't you in school today?" Dallas answered. "Today is the day we're showing Lon around our clubs, then we're going to do a report." "Cool," said Blue Eyes. "I know it's early, but would you guys like an ice cream?" Turf replied, "Give us three of your specialties." She pulled out three homemade waffle bowls and layered the bottom with bananas, then added four scoops of ice cream: vanilla bean, wild strawberry, German chocolate, and crushed pineapple. Then came four small scoops of fresh toppings: strawberry, pineapple, chocolate bits, and shaved coconut. Blue Eyes then globbed real whipped cream all over the top, spooned on some fresh cherries, and sprinkled it all with pecan pieces. Dallas's and Turf's portions were the size of a child's cup. The elves didn't require much. She made mine three times as big, and I wasn't complaining. We ate out on the deck overlooking the J'Yakaboo River. This was the life.

It was a very calm place, and it made our conversation easy. I asked Dallas and Turf if they liked it here. They told me they were both born at the North Pole. "We have so many friends, Lon," said Turf. "Our parents told us we're protected here, and no one can pick on us or tease us. Of course, Santa watches over us too. And there is so much to do here. In answer to your question—we really love it here." Dallas seconded the motion.

"So, how do you like it here by the river, Lon?" asked Dallas. I replied, "It's wonderful." Turf said, "The ice cream isn't bad either, is it? Blue Eyes also makes fruit blitzes, shakes, freezes, and just about anything you can dream up, even ice cream cakes. There are always intriguing new desserts here at the River's Edge." We thanked Blue Eyes for the scrumptious sundaes then headed for our next stop.

Turf said, "Now we're off to the candy store. It's called the Knotty Pine Club." As the name implied, the club was built out of beautiful knotty pine boards. I couldn't wait to go in. Chuckles was the confectioner at the Knotty Pine Club. He gave us a big hello and said, "Hey, no school today?" Turf said, "No, we're on a field trip. We're working on a special report. We're showing Lon all of our clubs today." Everybody seemed to know the boys should be in school. I think they were making sure the guys weren't playing hooky. I liked how the elf community showed their concern for each other. This club was really a candy store. There were oodles of special lollipops on the counter. Rainbow pops, chocolate pops, chocolate covered fruit pops, to name a few. Chuckles said, "The strawberry lollipop dipped in chocolate is our number one favorite. We have chocolate bars of all kinds too." There were rows and rows of candy. You name it—the Knotty Pine Club had it!

I said to Chuckles, "Didn't you create a special Bubble gum? Bubbles told me how much he loves it." "Yes, that's right!" said Chuckles. "I'm always working on new flavors of candy and gum I make sweet candy and sour candy, creamy bonbons and crunchy logs, big chunks you have to bite into and little pieces you can pop into your mouth. I like variety." Dallas said, "Lon, do you like candy?" I didn't have to think about this one. "I love candy, Dallas. And I'm amazed to see so many new and fascinating flavors and textures here." "Let's choose a piece and sit at one of the tables," said Dallas. When we were settled, Turf said, "We all enjoy coming here to talk and to plan. Sometimes we pick up a piece of candy, like a special blend lollipop, to eat while we're walking along the river and through the village. This candy store is always stocked. Chuckles never disappoints."

Chuckles was busy making peanut brittle and Santa's favorite, candy-coated baked almonds. This master candymaker liked to use a wide variety of nuts in and on his velvety smooth chocolates. He strived for perfection and made it look effortless. While we were talking and eating, elves kept coming and going. They would grab a napkin, take a piece of candy using the tongs, and off they went. It was time for us to go too, so we thanked Chuckles and headed out to get some lunch.

We decided on the Cozy Creek Club. All the young crowd enjoyed coming here for pizza. Luckily we arrived at the beginning of the lunch hour, or the place would have been packed with elves. My guides introduced me to Ola and Phillipi. They were Italian culinary geniuses. Their menu offered vegetable pizza, seafood pizza, and endless types of cheeses, thanks to Britches, the dairy farmer. They also had dessert pizza. There was a sign on the door that read, BYOM, which meant "bring your own mug." Dallas and Turf had mugs clipped to their beltloops. Ola and Phillipi were kind enough to present me with my very own wooden mug with "Lon" carved into it. I thought that was awfully special, and thanked them profusely. I chose a slice of cheese pizza and took my new mug over to the drink machine.

"Let me tell you a little about the drink machine, Lon," said Dallas. "Lazer is the syrup specialist. He takes the syrup from real maple trees, boils it down, and mixes it with concentrated tropical fruit juice blends. Then he places the syrup in the drink machine. Put a few squirts in a mug of water, and you've got a nice refreshing 'flavored water.'" The pizza was ambrosia and the flavored water was like nectar. "Thanks for picking this place, guys," I said. "There is usually a long line to get in here in the evening hours," said Turf, "but we're here at a good time. We can stay a while longer and talk." We chilled out for a bit, enjoying our meal and leisurely conversation. But alas, we had to move on. I thanked Ola and Phillipi for the wonderful food and the thoughtful mug, clipped the mug to my belt, and reluctantly left.

"Where to next, guys?" I asked. Turf said, "We're off to Echo Valley Club. I think you'll like it, Lon." The Echo Valley Club was decorated with a Mexican flair. The walls, ceiling, carpet, furniture, and accessories were all ethnic and bright. Endless strands of tiny lights were strung around the room. The place reminded me of a hacienda. Cisco said, "Hello, guys…come on in." Turf said, "Meet Lon." Cisco had a broad smile and a warm handshake. Dallas said, "This place is also jumpin' at night. Usually it's standing room only. They specialize in hard and soft tacos, burritos, and nachos with cheese." Cisco said, "What can I get for you?" "Nothing today, Cisco." said Turf. "We've been taking Lon on a tour of the clubs and sampling everything along the way. I'm afraid we're stuffed. But we wanted to make sure Lon got to see the Echo Valley Club." I said, "Slow down, guys. Thank you, Cisco. I will have a burrito and two soft tacos, please. Remember, Dallas and Turf, I'm four times your size." We all laughed as they sat down and watched me eat.

I asked Dallas, "Why doesn't everyone eat at the dining hall?" "Oh, the chefs prepare a light breakfast and lunch, but Santa gives them the evenings off. So, we visit the clubs for dinner." "Well, now I understand one reason why the clubs are so popular!" I said. As I was finishing up, Santa walked in. "Hello, Cisco. Hello, Lon. How are these two treating you?" "Great, Santa. Dallas and Turf have been great!" Santa turned to Cisco, "May I please have two burritos and four hard tacos?" Dallas's and Turf's eyes got so big when they heard Santa's order. I looked at the two of them and said, "Told you so. We need more food than you!" We all laughed.

Santa was wearing a shirt with colorful Christmas packages scattered in a bright pattern. I saw Mrs. Claus walk by on the street. Her apron matched Santa's shirt, of course. The boys needed to move on, so we said goodbye to Santa and Cisco and headed out the door. The whole parrot family flew by on their way for a snack of their own.

We went over to the Blue Water Club. Dallas said, "This is known as the grease pit. Smiles runs it. It may sound bad, but it's one of the healthiest clubs we have. Smiles enjoys serving up vegetable burgers. They look just like hamburgers, but the ingredients are all vegetables. The fishburger is also terrific tasting." Smiles showed me around. He said, "I hope you like vegetarian, Lon. After you get your sandwich, come over here for the condiments. We have tomatoes, lettuce, pickles, onions, cheese, and hot, mild, and barbeque sauce. You might like some ketchup on your crispy French fries. It's over here."

The inside of the Blue Water Club was decorated like an ocean. I asked Smiles who did all his detail painting. There were three painters: Dance, Swang, and JoJo. JoJo was the elf in charge of design and layout. The detail here was accurate and realistic. I felt like I was swimming with dolphins, whales, tropical fish, any kind of sea life you want to name. And all of their vividly painted eyes followed me around the room. I began to feel like I was really underwater. Turf snapped me out of my hypnotic state. "This is known as the 'fun place,'" he said. "Smiles always creates a good time for everyone." We didn't stay to eat. Time was running out, and we had other places to be. We thanked Smiles and drifted out into the street.

We headed over to the Eagle Ridge. S. T. met us at the door and shook hands with me. "Santa said you guys might stop over. Welcome!" This was the club all the adult elves liked to go to. It offered card games, darts, and of course shuffleboard. The old jukebox played 45s. Everything in this club was old-time—cool stuff. Younger elves never, and I mean never, came in here. This gave the more mature elves their own place to hang out and chill. Dallas said, "Some business decisions are made here, in a more relaxed setting, but it's mostly used for just plain fun." It sounded like just my speed.

S. T. said, "Can I get you anything?" Dallas and Turf spoke up a little too fast, "Can't stay long. We have many more clubs to visit. Thanks anyway, S. T." I smiled and shook my head. I could see this place wasn't for the young ones. When we got outside I said, "Thanks for the bum's rush, guys." We shared a knowing chuckle and moved along.

We stopped briefly at the Baker's Dozen, run by Buttons. The aroma made me swoon, as usual. Buttons had all kinds of fruit breads, wheat breads, white breads, twisted cinnamon breads, and more. Some with frostings, some with special glazes, some with sprinkles or flavored sugars, and so on. You name it, he had it. Elves would stop to take home fresh bread every evening. It was the perfect food to eat with a good cup of hot chocolate, tea, or a specialty coffee.

Buttons was busy taking bread out of the oven, so we didn't bother him. Dallas said, "Lon, try a slice of zucchini bread." It was great!

"Buttons invented this recipe last week, and now it's one of his favorites—ours also."

We had just about come to the end of my guided tour. Turf said, "Well Lon, that's all of our clubs and hangouts. We always have big parties over at the bowling alley, but it's closed for now, until our big annual Texas Cowboy Bowling Party. Sorry about that."

"We have one more stop, don't we, Turf?" said Dallas. "The last thing we want to show you, Lon, is our big screen theater. There's always a movie on Friday and Saturday nights. We bring popcorn, our favorite snack, and our BYOM." I looked at Dallas and Turf and said, "I think the elves play as hard as they work and study." Dallas said, " You're right, Lon. Our teacher, Miss Needles, always pushes us to do better. After we put in a long day at school or work, we balance and refuel with friends and family. Santa encourages games to keep our minds nimble and activities to strengthen our bodies. We're nothing if not well rounded. And we can thank Santa for that. The interesting thing is, it all helps us fulfill Santa's main goal, delivering toys to more and more children around the world. And we have a good time doing it too. It's funny how that works, isn't it?" I had to agree. I thought, all the elves at Santa's Christmas Village should feel very blessed.

I thanked Dallas and Turf for a great time. I now had two more friends. We managed a quick hug and then they were off to do their report on our day. I hope it was as much fun for them as it was for me, because I will treasure it and talk about it for the rest of my life!

Chapter Fifteen
The Wrapping Department

Dutch and Spin had given me precise directions to the Wrapping Department earlier that day. So, why wasn't it right in front of me now? I thought I was exactly on the spot where the doors should be, but there were two huge Christmas presents and nothing else. Each box appeared to be about eight feet tall and three feet wide. How could I go so wrong? At least, some lucky someones were going to be ecstatic when they received these enormous gifts. They must have been very, very good this year.

I walked up to the presents and touched one. This wasn't wrapping paper at all. The "presents" were two gigantic doors painted to fool the eye. And what I thought was a huge white bow with an elegant satin loveliness to it, was also just a painting. One door had a huge gold bell in the center that shined like the sun. The other looked exactly the same, except the bell was silver. Only true artists could have created such a convincing illusion.

To the right of the doors, the fun continued. There was a specially made paintbrush with a mahogany wood handle attached to the wall. Or was there? This too was only paint. Along the handle, it read "Meschbach." The name rang a bell. Buddy had told me Herr Meschbach had done most of the paintings in the castle. Underneath the signature was written, "Press here to make the doorbell ring." I pressed the handle of the paintbrush, and almost immediately a couple of elves opened the doors and let me in. I said, "The Wrapping Department, I presume?" "Yes, indeed," said the elves in unison.

It was Ben and Ken. They informed me that not only did Meschbach paint the doors, he designed all his own brushes to achieve the very highest quality for his work. Ben said, "He painted walls and ceilings in the castle too. One ceiling that stands out to me is the daytime ceiling, with angels flying all around. It looks like heaven in an endless sky. Truly breathtaking. He also painted a midnight sky ceiling, and in another room he painted a wall to look like the green mineral malachite, with striations and all." Ken said, "We love to roam through the castle and look at these paintings from time to time. They're very relaxing. They lend a homey air to the castle." I said, "He certainly is a great painter, one of the best of his generation, I'd say."

"Well, I guess we'd better move along now, Lon," said Ben, "if we want to view the wrapping room before they close down for the day. We walked through the small foyer and into the main work area, and I chuckled at what I saw. The walls were papered with a hodgepodge of wrapping paper. Prints big and small, stripes narrow and wide, flowers brilliant and muted, were all plastered next to each other. There were shiny borders and shimmering textures. It was a striking example of the whole being bigger than the sum of its parts.

Hanging from the ceiling beams, all over the room, were streamers and ribbons of all different lengths and colors. It looked as though someone was getting ready to throw a party, but serious work was done here. Without a doubt, this was an absolutely exciting room to be in.

The flooring was a beautiful natural pine with little variegated red presents and gold bows painted on the boards. The whole room was a tribute to the joy one feels when looking at a beautifully wrapped gift. Someone had put a lot of thought into designing this room. Ben told me that JoJo had a lot to do with it, along with Violet, Tango, Yoko, and Peppie. No wonder all the elves loved their jobs! They made their environment fun, which had a way of making the work fun. In the Wrapping Department, the medium was definitely the message.

Music filled the room in a continuous loop of upbeat fun songs that made you want to dance all day long. And the volume was the same anywhere you stood. The elves danced around from station to station to get their work done. They said it was good fun and great exercise too. It always put them in a cheerful mood. I thought, what a wonderful place to work. It actually looked more like play. They had me dancing too.

I got to see the toys coming off the conveyer belt from the Picking Department into the wrapping room. Violet was head of the Wrapping Department, and Peppie, Yoko, and Tango were her assistants. They also had many helpers. The elves would pick up the item, remove the name and address tag, box the item, then properly tape up the box and wrap it. They had rolls and rolls of paper decorated with ornaments, Christmas trees, Christmas lights, Santas, and raindeer, and all were very colorful.

Violet and Peppie enjoyed deciding on ribbon and wrapping paper together. Yoko and Tango worked as a team also. It seemed to me the elves always preferred to do things together.

Many helpers were also wrapping and decorating packages. They had to make sure the packages were properly tagged before putting them on the conveyer belt that took them to the Shrinking Department. All the elves here did beautiful work. But that was typical. All the elves everywhere in Santa's Christmas Village did beautiful work.

Right here I need to tell you about Violet. She was as vibrant as her name sounds, so much fun to be around. She had such a sweet disposition and a great attitude. Anyone who chummed with her, felt better when they left. Santa and Mrs. Claus sensed her genuine warmth when they first met her some years back, and they thought she would be a real blessing as the head of the Wrapping Department. They were absolutely right. She was always so excited to come to work every morning. In fact, she was the first one there. Making sure all the packages were perfectly wrapped and with just the right bow to match, was of extreme importance to her. Her top assistants, Yoko, Peppie, and Tango, were just as committed. Each and every gift was wrapped with love and pride, as if it were their own to unwrap. All the workers in this department shared in the fun. It was of utmost importance to make each child happy on Christmas. They would imagine the glimmer in the children's eyes when first spying their wrapped gifts under the tree. That alone was worth its weight in gold.

Violet loved her job so much, that before going to sleep, she would let her mind wander into a dreamland of what could make her department even more fun. When the right time came to share her thoughts, she would call a "fun meeting" with her top assistants. Every year they would pool their ideas and dreams and come up with a new improvement for the department. They were all excited about one special idea in particular that had been in the works for a few years now, but no one knew it except the Design Department—newly named the Design and Engineering Department, Violet, Yoko, Tango, and Peppie. This was a top secret project.

Violet, Yoko, Tango, and Peppie collectively decided to come up with a special machine that would wrap each Christmas package. Violet envisioned it speeding up the wrapping process. Yoko thought there should be several machines and they should have personality, maybe like a robot. Tango wanted each robot to have eight arms. Two arms would measure, wrap, and cut the paper, while another two arms turned the package. Two more arms would handle the ribbon and taping, and the remaining two arms would pick the package up, add any optional trinkets on top, and then place it on the conveyer belt that would shuttle it over to the Shrinking Department. Peppie was interested in the facial part of the robot. She wanted to help design the head and features, and give them a sweet look. They all agreed each robot must be colorful and have pizzazz.

Right from the beginning, Violet kept in touch with the Design Department and sent all of her team's ideas over to them for development. Bubbles and his staff were too busy to take on another assignment, but Dutch and Spin were thrilled to get a big project as their own. Besides, it was a kick to work with Violet and her assistants. Ideas got to spinning around in their heads. They had to work fast to get the robots into full operation the following year. This was a chance for Dutch and Spin and their crew to make a big splash.

The months flew by, but there was nothing to worry about. The robot team was way ahead of completion time because they enjoyed the work so much. Dutch and Spin had fun adding a mischievous touch to the robots. Every time the robots finish wrapping a gift, they turned and winked. This was a real elf crowd-pleaser.

Winkie gets ready to wrap another package.

Violet had been watching me watch the robots. She said, "Aren't they great? Dutch and Spin really pulled it off, Lon. We got our Ultra-violet Wrapping Robots in time for the busy season. Would you like me to explain how they work?" With great enthusiasm, I said, "I would be very interested, if you have the time." She said, " I am honored," and launched into a description of the entire process.

"The Picking Department sends the packages here, then we sort them by size. We set a toy onto the tray in front of each robot and enter instructions into the computer as to which paper and ribbon to use. With the push of the start button, the robots take over. The package is wrapped and tied with a bow in a total time of twenty seconds, and when the robot is finished, it winks. When we're done laughing, we start again. The little elves have nicknamed the robots Winkie, Dinkie, and Pinkie. Everyone loves to come to the Wrapping Department and visit them.

"A really fun part is our keyboard. It gives us endless choices for paper and ribbons—color, size, pattern, you name it. We just program our preferences into the control panel. After the wrapping and ribbon are done we press another button to display all kinds of trinkets on the screen. If we think the package needs a little something extra we choose a trinket, and the robot adds it as the last step. The results are always a knockout. We're like kids on Christmas morning!

"Dutch and Spin have even more developments in mind. They are now working on a highly advanced computer program that will enable us to talk with the robots. That way, we can tell them which paper and ribbon to use, instead of entering it into the computer. This will speed up the process immensely."

I was so engrossed in Violet's explanation of how the robots worked, I accidentally got too close to one of them as it was wrapping. All three robots instantly stopped and looked at me. Their eyebrows scrunched up and their eyes closed. I backed up immediately. They were becoming so human to me, I thought maybe I had offended them. Then their eyes opened and they started wrapping again. "What did I do?" I asked Violet. Well, it turns out I had broken the laser beam around the robot, and that made all the robots stop. Violet chuckled, "Don't take it personally, Lon. Dutch and Spin added this safety feature to protect anyone from the robots when they are in motion.

"I will never forget the day we unveiled all three robots. It was a sight to behold! Hundreds of elves were filing in and out just to catch a glimpse of them in action. Mrs. Claus had everyone come over to the dining facility, where they made a toast to honor us—Yoko, Tango, Peppie, Dutch, Spin, and me. Mrs. Claus thanked everyone for all their fine work and said, 'We will name the robots "The Ultraviolet Wrapping Robots" after Violet, because she had the creative vision to think of this innovative project in the first place.' I felt so honored, and I'm sure I must have blushed. I thanked Mrs. Claus, and everyone held up their glasses as they toasted our project team.

"Then Santa said, 'These Ultraviolet Wrapping Robots are just wonderful, because, they not only make the job much quicker, they also allow the workers to spend more quality time with their families and friends.' Santa always says that time spent with family and friends means even more than a present. Of course, little children need their presents more than anybody else. It's only as children get older that they understand just how important family and friends truly are. When they're little, presents are huge as a sign of love. Still, I'll have you know, Lon, that I never turn down a present! Presents are always great to receive. Yet, Santa has another favorite saying: It is more blessed to give than to receive. Wow, how meaningful and true." I had to leave Violet and her crew, but did so with a smile. After all, a robot had winked at me today.

Chapter Sixteen
The Shrinking Department

The package shrinking machine makes light work for Santa.

My next stop was the Shrinking Department. I was very curious to see Ish's invention, the mysterious package shrinking machine. It had taken several years for the serious-minded design team to take the idea from paper to reality, during which a few experimental versions had been in use. But now it was perfected and given its very own department. The machine would be a great boon to Santa's main work, delivering toys to children.

Ish met me with a hug and he was a bundle of excited energy. He was so happy to be sharing his story with me. "Me too!" I said. Ish told me that one day, like a bolt of lightning, the thought just popped into his brain: What if the big Christmas packages could be shrunk down to the size of a coin? It would certainly make work easier and faster for Santa and the raindeer. Santa would be able to reach more children while making fewer trips. The raindeer wouldn't have to pull so hard or so long, they could get around faster on their Christmas Eve flight, and they would recover their strength more quickly. More gifts packed into less space, plus less weight, less stress, fewer trips, quicker recovery, and more happy children—shrinking would make the whole system that much more efficient, he thought. This was a no-brainer.

Bubbles and Shadow gave Ish permission to develop the design as long as it didn't interfere with the many other projects the department was already working on. Shooter and Snickers were so excited to help that they put in overtime. Every night, Ish, Shooter, and Snickers went to work. If they couldn't do it, nobody could. Then Shooter had a breakthrough moment. He said, "Ish, I think if we use laser technology, we can lick this thing." This was a real technical challenge.

Santa marveled at all the things that came out of the Design Department. Ish said, "Lon, we worked on so many prototypes. Santa tried out some of the results. We had to scrap a lot of ideas, but Shooter and Snickers always pushed me to complete the job. I don't think anybody ever accomplishes great things all by themselves. We finally developed the laser technology. We enclosed the entire laser inside a machine that took up about a six-by-eight-foot space and the conveyer belt ran through it. We were getting real close.

"I remember when Bubbles and Shadow first watched the big packages going through the machine and coming out the size of a coin. Bubbles picked up a tiny package and was amazed to see that he could read who and where it was to be delivered to. Bubbles said to me, 'Now you've shrunk the package, how do you bring it back to its proper size?' I said, 'Well, that's our next challenge.' So Shooter, Snickers, and I went back to the drawing board. Lon, we tried cooking the package, freezing the package, heating the package. We tried sending it back through the machine, front and back, but to no avail. Nothing worked. We tried throwing it, blowing it, spraying it with water, but we still had a package the size of a coin.

"The whole design team was sitting in the design and experiment room, when Hood came in. He was the smallest elf and he enjoyed running our errands. He would get us our food, drinks, tools, anything we needed. He always wore a hood because he thought it made him look taller. That's how he got his name. It led to some slapstick fun. Many times he would have his arms full of stuff and his hood would fall down into his eyes, and he'd stumble so that everything flew out of his hands and all over the place. Well, this day we showed him the coin-size package. He liked it so much we let him keep it awhile, and we sent him out to get coffee.

"Hood was taking longer than usual, and we were wondering what trouble he'd gotten into. It turned out he had tripped and fallen on his way back from the village. Coffee mugs flew everywhere. Buddy happened to be nearby, so he helped Hood up and they went to wash the mugs and get refills. On the way back, Hood looked for the tiny package. He spotted it over by the pine tree but now it was full-size! Hood was kind of surprised but he did what he had to do. He placed the package on the tray and returned to the Design Department. As soon as Hood walked in, we rose to our feet in astonishment. I said, 'Hood, what did you do?' Hood started to apologize, 'I fell. I'm sorry it took me so long to get back. Buddy helped me wash the coffee mugs and—' I cut him off. 'Never mind about that. We've got to know how you enlarged the package.' Hood wasn't sure how that had happened, so we started experimenting. We tossed the package down; nothing happened. We poured coffee on it; nothing happened. We put the package next to the mugs on the tray; nothing happened."

Ish continued his story of discovery. "Bubbles turned to Hood and said, 'We need you to do everything exactly as you did before.' Hood said, 'I will gladly do this as many times as you want, so long as I don't have to clean up the coffee.' Bubbles laughed. 'Okay, we will clean up the mess.' We started from the very beginning. First, we sent the package back through the shrinking machine, but this time we shrank a second package for the sake of our experiment. We put one coin-size package on the tray with the mugs, and the other I slipped into my pants pocket.

"Hood took the tray with the five mugs and the small package and walked toward the village for more coffee. All the design staff walked behind him, and we volunteered Buddy to reenact his part. Hood filled the mugs, headed back to the Design Department, and dropped the tray in the same spot. I cleaned up the mess. The package was still small. Bubbles said, 'Where were you standing, Buddy?' Buddy took his place then walked over to Hood very fast, helped him up, and asked if he was all right. We all paraded to wash and refill the mugs then followed Hood back to the spot where he'd fallen. The package was in its spot by the pine tree—and it was large again!

"Now came time for my experiment. I pulled the second package from my pocket and placed it under the same evergreen tree. Poof-pop! It grew to its regular size! The key turned out to be the evergreen tree. We tried it again and again. Every time, the coin-size packages grew when we put them under an evergreen tree, different evergreen trees. That meant the tiny packages would change to full size as soon as Santa placed them under a child's Christmas tree. This was revolutionary!

"Bubbles had a good point. 'What if the home has an artificial tree? What happens then?' We finally did get it figured out. Santa brought an evergreen tree branch along with him for emergencies. When he encountered an artificial tree, all he had to do was place the packages then wave the branch over them. It was a thing of beauty. It was now time to show the package shrinking machine to Wrinkles and Santa. At the far end of the room, the ladies had set up a real Christmas tree all decorated and lit up—and an artificial tree all decorated and lit up. Wrinkles and Santa arrived for the demonstration and Santa said, 'Ish, Shooter and Snickers, I've heard a little about your idea. You all have my complete attention.' I said, 'I will go first, Santa. Here's how it works. The packages leave the Wrapping Department and travel along the conveyer belt through our shrinking machine, where they are reduced to the size of a coin.' Right on cue, tiny packages rolled out the far end of the machine, and I opened up the machine to show Santa how the laser technology worked. Santa and Wrinkles were speechless. Snickers picked up two little packages and demonstrated, 'Santa, when you place a package under the evergreen tree like this, it enlarges to its proper size.' Poof-pop! The package zoomed up to its original size. Snickers then said, 'If you place a package under an artificial tree, you then wave a small evergreen branch over the package like so, and it will enlarge also.' Poof-pop! The second package grew big.

"It was Shooter's turn to get in on the act. He launched into all the reasons for using the machine, how it would increase efficiency and help Santa and the raindeer deliver more toys. Bubbles said, 'Well, that's our presentation. I want to thank all of the design staff. Santa, if it weren't for Hood, we never would have figured out how to enlarge the packages. Hood gets the credit for that.'

"Santa was obviously touched by all the work that went into this project and the impact it would have on his Christmas Eve deliveries. He said, 'I have much to say. I am having a get-together at my home tonight. I want all of you to be there. Hood, you also. All six of you, tonight at 7:00 P.M.' Then he left. Wrinkles said, 'All of you have done a great thing. This is a tremendous project, and I thank you also.' That day, Mrs. Claus, Buddy, and everybody came by to see our new invention, the amazing package shrinking machine.

"Dinner at Santa's was excellent. The whole design team was so excited. Bubbles tried really hard not to blow Bubbles. Santa said to Bubbles, Shadow, Snickers, Shooter, Hood, and me, 'From the bottom of my heart, a big, big thank-you!'

"Santa gave all of us a special gift that night. It was a music box with an evergreen tree on top, to remind us of the package that fell under the pine tree. By now, Santa had heard the whole story of Hood's breakthrough discovery on the way to pick up coffee for us. Santa said he was still laughing about that one. He spoke to Hood. 'This year, Hood, you will ride with me to deliver packages to all the children who sent a request to Santa. But no hot coffee in the sleigh, ho-ho!' So Hood rode with Santa that year. What an honor for the littlest elf. That day, Hood felt six feet tall."

Chapter Seventeen
The Mail Room

*The doors to the Mail Room, where children's letters
to Santa are handled with care.*

I remember when I first saw the Mail Room. It had two massive doors. They were tall, thick, very secure, and extremely beautiful. The doors were made of cherrywood intricately carved by expert crafts-men. A large wreath decorated with sparkling bright lights hung on each. Above them, "Mail Room" was hand-carved into the wood.

When I opened the door I was bowled over by the huge hub of activity. The first thing that struck me was the four elves on ladders sliding back and forth along the wall and filing letters. Persona and Mooksie came up to me and distributed hugs. They were in charge of the Mail Room. Persona said, "We knew you were going to visit to-day, Lon, so we all wore name tags. We heard you enjoy talking to the elves, and so we thought it would make it easier to get acquainted. Let me introduce you. Here is Glisten, Sienna, Blush, Charm, Mist, Oberon, Sporty, Jasper, Timber, Hot Rod, Chaps, Zoie, and Roxy. There are a total of fifteen of us here in the Mail Room." Everyone said, "Hi, Lon," at the same time.

I'll tell ya, this room was super organized and very, very clean. Persona told me the number one rule was, "Don't lose a letter—not one, not ever." Ten elves worked at desks in the center of the room. Oberon was putting handfuls of mail into a machine that counted the letters, then dropped them onto the table in the center of the room designed to hold thousands of letters. It seemed like that would keep Oberon very busy since there were bags and bags of mail next to the counting machine and the table was already filled. I looked closely at the mail and saw letters from all over the world: the United States, Australia, Canada, Russia, Germany, Chile, and Togo, to name a few. The elves were picking up letters from the table, one by one. They'd open a letter and read it. These were children's letters to Santa.

After reading a request letter, an elf would put the name and ad-dress and what the child wanted into the Wiz computer. The Wiz computer was really neat. After they logged on, all they did was speak to it. It was voice-activated. The Wiz would take it from there, record-ing each child's information from beginning to end, until the Christmas requests were filled.

Glisten picked up one of the letters from the table and opened it up. It was a thank-you to Santa. Glisten said, "We don't get thank-yous from every child out there, but the many we do receive are posted on the wall." With that, Glisten stuck the letter up on the wall. I didn't see any pushpins or tacks. "What's holding up the letter?" I asked. Glisten smiled as he told me it was a special paint with a sticky fin-ish. It was called "snowflake white," and it was all thanks to Jasper.

Mooksie told me how it all came about. "Many years earlier, Jas-per was in charge of hanging up the thank-you cards on the Mail

Room walls. The pushpins were always sticking him more than they did the wall. One day he'd finally had enough, so he asked the Paint Department and the Design Department for help. It only took a few weeks for them to come up with a new kind of rubbery stick-like-glue paint that Jasper called snowflake white. The Paint Department painted it on all the walls in the Mail Room, and it worked wonderfully. It also sped up the process of putting a letter on the wall. Just slap and stick. The new paint turned out to have an even greater benefit. Now there were thousands of letters on the wall, and all the elves loved to come in and read them. Thank-yous always boosted their confidence and made them feel appreciated. Santa was extremely pleased."

Hot Rod, Sporty, Jasper, and Chaps were in charge of filing the many letters into their proper locations. Their ladders slid back and forth along the twelve-foot-high walls like greased lightning. Chaps explained, "We keep all the original letters, just in case there's ever

Elf Chaps on a ladder, filing children's letters written to Santa.

a problem with the Wiz computer. However, Wiz never makes a mistake, and the reason is because we have the master computer, which is run by Mooksie. Our master computer checks all the other computers. So, here we have computers checking computers."

Hot Rod said, "Lon, over here is the picture gallery. The children who send thank-yous sometimes send pictures too. When they do, we post them all over here." I stepped over to look at the photographs and said, "I've never seen such joy on children's faces. There must be thousands of them, all of the children opening up their gifts from Santa." I was looking to see if I recognized anyone I knew.

Sporty said, "Lon, over here are the pictures children color in their coloring books and send to Santa. We post them so all can see. Whenever the walls get filled, and everyone has had a chance to see them, then Roxy and Zoie take down the pictures, drawings, and the thank-yous and place them into albums, so Santa and Mrs. Claus can look at them whenever they want. Santa has a special section for albums in his library. Poring over them is one of their favorite pastimes." The wall was almost completely full, so it must have been almost time for a new album. If you stood in the center of the Mail Room and panned the room, it looked like a museum. On their breaks, everyone enjoyed visiting to read the thank-you letters and see the children's happy photos and adorable pictures.

Sienna had a special job in the Mail Room, and she was happy to fill me in. She said, "Lon, if we get a letter written in a language we can't understand, my job is to scan the letter into the computer. The Wiz translates it into our universal language, English, so we can start to fulfill the child's request." Sienna showed me a bunch of letters from different countries and how she processed them. This was yet another demonstration of elf efficiency. In fact, I was starting to think, I might want a Wiz computer of my own. I asked Mist, "Where do these computers come from? I've never seen anything like them." Mist said, "We have a friend who is a huge contributor to the Kris Kringle Foundation, and he owns a computer company. We get all their newest technology to test, and they always check with Santa to make sure the new Wizes are working as they should." Charm's job was to double-check the names and addresses with her master computer for accuracy. However, she never found a single error, because the new Wiz just never made a mistake.

Blush said, "Lon, there was a time we had major problems with computer hackers. They would go into our computers and place viruses, and totally destroy our memory chips. This was a huge problem. We would have to go back to the letters that were filed away and enter everything by hand. This took much time. However, with the new Wiz monitors, if anyone is trying to hack in, Wiz picks up on it immediately. The Wiz is so powerful, it sends the virus back to the user who is trying to wreck our computer and shuts them down on a dime. We never hear anything about hackers and viruses anymore. Our master Wiz wipes them out before they have a chance to get in." I said, "Persona, where in the world can I get one of these?" "Sorry, Lon," she said. "This computer is still experimental and not generally available."

Anyway, the Wiz was way cool. It sent requests over to the Picking Department, where the item would be taken out of inventory. There the item would be tagged on the Wiz printing machine and placed on the conveyer belt, which carried it over to the Wrapping Department. Next came the shrinking machine, then on to storage, to be delivered on December 24th. The carpenter elves used the Wiz too, to keep track of inventory. Wiz seemed to keep everyone organized.

The mail was the lifeblood of Santa's whole system. Without request letters from children, Santa would have a hard time figuring out what every child wanted. Asking for what you wanted made everybody's job that much easier. Buddy picked up the mail brought in by the train to Jemdaza and took it to the Mail Room, where everybody treated it like gold. The closer it got to Christmas, the more trips he made. Once a month in January through May turned into twice a month in June through September. By the time October rolled around, and clear till Christmas, Buddy was going to the post office in Jemdaza every week. The mail was as big as a mountain. Santa monitored the daily updates from the Mail Room with keen interest and an eagle eye. He always wanted to know what each and every child had asked for, and on December 24th none of them would be disappointed.

Chapter Eighteen
Lumberjacks and Carpenters

Elf Luigi and Elf Stefano cut down a tree.

I have tried my best to explain and document everything I encountered at the North Pole. Santa's Christmas Village was extraordinary and ordinary at the same time. The fact that I was being saved and entertained by Santa Claus and his elves was out of this world. And yet I found them to be like people I knew back home, people who cared about each other and who shared strong community goals. Business meetings and canning will probably always be boring to me, no matter where they take place. But I do understand that even Santa has to plan out his life, or where will he end up? So I looked at the bright side, opened up my mind and heart, and experienced as much as I could—the fun and the not so much fun—in the short time I was there. By far, there was a lot more fun!

I had a hankering for a cup of coffee at the Eagle Ridge. Luigi and Stefano were already lounging in the club when I got there. They were both senior lumberjacks from Italy, and they asked me to join them for a he-man cup of coffee—black, no sugar, no cream, just dark, rich coffee. I took a sip, gagged, and said, "A little strong, isn't it?" They both laughed. Stefano said, "That'll wake you up and snap your mind to attention!" I smiled and said, "You're right on, Stefano. Tell me, how did you get your name?" He said, "My real name is Alfonso Ulrich Hawthorne." I used seven letters in my name to spell Stefano. Everyone calls me Stefano." I smiled. "Alfonso Ulrich Hawthorne. Oh, that's a short name," and we all laughed. I said, "I am so pleased to meet you," and we did the elf hug.

I said to Luigi, "So, what is your real name, Luigi?" "Dexter Culbertson Christensen. When I needed a nickname for Santa's Village, I already had one. Luigi is what my uncle always called me. I don't know why; I guess he just liked it better than Dexter. Anyway, it felt like home, so I stuck with it." We shook hands and had a quick hug, and I said, "Pleased to meet you, Luigi."

Stefano and Luigi told me how much they enjoyed their jobs and explained the rules of lumberjacking to me. I took notes:

Rule 1. If a tree is damaged at the base, or lying down in the forest, we can use it.

Rule 2. The entire tree is to be used, even the branches.

Rule 3. All the scrap wood is also to be used, for example, in our woodburning stoves.

Rule 4. Only trees extremely close together can be taken, and the trees with space around them are left to continue to grow.

Rule 5. The worker elves will assist the lumberjacks by planting two trees in the area where one tree is cut down.

Rule 6. If only the branches are damaged because of ice and snow, take only the damaged branches and leave the rest of the tree alone.

Rule 7. A tree cannot be cut down if the process would damage other trees.

Rule 8. Never do clear-cutting of trees, where whole acres of trees are removed at once.

Luigi said, "These are the rules we live by. They are never to be broken. If ever we have a question about the rules, we always talk to Santa." I asked Stefano, "Who works with you and Luigi cutting trees?" Stefano said, "Well, we have Rawhide and Tacoma. Those two climb the trees to cut branches off. Then Wisp and Jesse gather them up for use. They separate the good wood from the bad, and the bad wood gets used in the woodstoves. Santa and Buddy haul the wood out of the forest and take it to the lumber cutting room, with the help of the raindeer who pull the sleigh. With our 'cut one, plant two' policy, we will never run out of trees. Our forest keeps growing, and it helps the environment too. Santa is thrilled about that.

"Let's see…what else? Luigi and I cut down the trees. Then Fern and Nimbus are in charge of planting new trees, and also stacking lumber up in the lumber room. They take the planting very seriously, and we're all grateful for that." "Don't forget the carpenters." said Luigi. "They take the lumber from the lumber room every day. The forest is put to good use. We don't waste a toothpick. We protect our woods, and the forest protects our Christmas Village. We make sure our forest stays healthy and growing." I was beginning to appreciate the balance of nature at the North Pole. After this day, I became a wiser man about trees and how they fit into the whole of life on Earth. I realized no one is ever too old to learn. I thought, how smart and practical Santa and the elves are to care so much about their woods.

Stefano said, "Santa really enjoys walks in the woods. He often uses it as his private time. One day, we heard Santa talking to the North Wind. The North Wind didn't talk back, but Santa felt the North Wind could hear and understand him. He was telling the North Wind all about his plans to help children. Come to find out, the senior tree, Ivy, was listening. The tree opened his eyes and said, 'Hello, Santa.' Santa froze in his tracks. Ivy continued. 'Yes, I can talk. The trees produce a toxin, to keep poison ivy from growing all over them. To protect myself, I've allowed poison ivy to grow at my feet and all around my trunk. Since the elves hate poison ivy, they avoid me totally. This is why I am called Ivy. Smart, huh?' Santa smiled and said, 'Ivy, you are a clever tree!'

A heavy growth of poison ivy protects the tree Ivy.

"Ivy said, 'For so many years I have listened as you have shared your vision and dreams with me about children all over the world. I have always been so fascinated with your ideas. I've heard Stefano and Luigi's many conversations about their eight rules for taking a tree. I've seen the replanting that Fern and Nimbus do. I spoke to the North Wind many years ago, when you first arrived, Santa. I told Blow of your dream and vision. Blow is another name for the North Wind. Then later on, I told Blow about the elves coming to the North Pole. I also told him about the eight rules for the tree cutting. Blow and I talk all the time. I ask Blow to calm down at times, so the lumberjacks can do their jobs. I realized early on, the elves only took what they needed. So now, when Blow spots Stefano and Luigi, he chills out.'"

Luigi picked up the story, which had me spellbound. He said, "Ivy and Blow converse all the time. If it is in their power to protect the village and keep it safe, they will do it. Ivy said, 'Santa, do you know why you don't get unwanted visitors snooping around? It's because the North Wind blows snow and creates a cold beyond cold, so that anyone getting close to Santa's Christmas Village is compelled to turn around and go back where they came from.' Indeed, unlike the old days, since Santa established his village, only a few people have made it to the North Pole, Lon. You're one of them!

"Ivy revealed more secrets to Santa. 'Blow usually allows only small people through, whom we now call elves. Of course, Blow knows Buddy very well, so even though he is a tall person, he is allowed through without incident when he goes to pick up supplies and mail for you. Buddy is able to travel unharmed when he meets your benefactor guests, January through March. Blow realizes that those tall people are friendly too and leaves them alone, as with Buddy.

"'Blow also teams up with Heat. Heat is the South Wind and is much warmer than Blow. Blow and Heat understand each other, and they work together to protect your Christmas Village from unwanted visitors.' Santa was just amazed, and said, "Now I understand why no uninvited visitors come to Santa's Christmas Village at the North Pole!'

"'The reason Blow allowed you to enter the North Pole, Santa,' Ivy continued, 'was that he felt you were special. There was an aura about you. Your love for children and wanting to make them happy, it all shined through. Blow, Heat, and I are so excited to have you here. And to think all three of us have a small part in helping children around the world. It makes us feel worthwhile. We're so thrilled to have you here at the North Hills. We like your new name for it too—the North Pole.'

"Many years ago, a few men did get into the North Hills," said Stefano. "Ivy told Santa about it. 'Before you settled here, Santa, tall men traveled into the North Hills, either by design or by accident. But that's all changed now. When Blow starts to rest, Heat stays alert. I'm also the timekeeper. I make sure only one of us—Blow, Heat, or myself—rests at any given time.' Santa tells Ivy, Blow, and Heat all the time how very important and special they are, Lon and they feel the same way about him, the village, and what he stands for.

"Ivy and Santa have been friends for many years now. Santa goes into the woods to talk to Ivy as much as he can. When Santa told us this story, we were just as amazed as you are, Lon. Apparently, Santa asked Ivy if he could tell his wife Susie about the others. Ivy said yes, and over the years, Santa and Mrs. Claus have been great friends to Ivy, Blow, and Heat. Ivy said, 'Santa, you can tell anyone you want about us. However, if I choose not to open my eyes and talk, then you're going to look like you're off your rocker.' We all laughed at that. Never in a million years did we think Santa was crazy, although it took some years before Ivy spoke to us. Blow, Heat, and Ivy always know what's going on at Santa's Christmas Village, and Ivy only speaks to people who support Santa's work. Finally, Ivy said to us, 'The roaring East Wind didn't mean to, but one day his white lightning accidentally struck me, bringing me to life. It then shot off and created the North Wind and the South Wind, and we are eternally grateful for that.'" All I could say was "Wow! What a yarn, guys!"

Luigi and Stefano invited me over to the cutting area. The head carpenter's name was In. In wanted to be included in everybody's conversations. His ears could pick up voices a block away. He made me feel very comfortable around him. He had me put on protective eyewear so that I could observe how they stripped the bark from the trees and cut the wood into lumber. Then I helped stack up lumber in the lumber room. Boy, this was a full-time job for the elves, but somehow there was always enough lumber in the lumber room, stacked up and ready for the carpenter elves to do their job. I thanked Luigi and Stefano for sharing their time and their fascinating stories with me.

Then there was Hype, the most energetic of the carpenters, and very good at what he did. Hype seemed to be in perpetual motion. He just went on and on. He'd quick cut out a pattern, then start another one right away. Fast was his middle name. He really enjoyed working on wood.

Hype introduced me to Red. He had red hair, a red beard, and a red mustache. He was Mr. Perfect. Everything, and I mean everything, had to be exact! Cutting out patterns, putting them together—it all had to be right on the money. Red had a deep desire to make all the toys superb. He thought every child deserved that. He enjoyed his job and it showed. The rest of the carpenters found him inspiring and all the toys came together so very nicely.

Speed could cut out toys almost without a pattern. His name alone probably tells you that he could stack and cut toy patterns faster than anyone else. He knew his job like the back of his hand. Speed was a modest fellow and if you complimented him, he would say, "Aw, it's just that I've done this for so many years, I just know what to do." He was as modest as he was quick.

When two pieces of wood come together, it creates a seam, and the wood has to match up perfectly. Seams was the best at cutting out angles to get a flawless joint. The carpentry shop was lucky to have him, and Santa knew it.

"That covers our team of carpenters," said Luigi. "These five men can stack up wood patterns and assemble everything from trucks to dolls impeccably and in no time flat. They really are a great team. They work together very well to move the toys from the cutting room to the Paint Room in good time, and they make it look easy.

The Carpenter Department was known as information central. These guys knew everything about everyone: who was in love, who was getting married, who would soon have little elves. You couldn't keep a secret from them. They knew about every new invention as soon as the idea popped out of somebody's mouth. These men were always in the middle of everything. While the music played, they built toys all day and talked as much as they built. That was their workday.

The day I was visiting, patterns were already cut out and stacked up. Everybody was assembling the toys. They all said hi to me and welcomed me to their department. In said, "Hey, guys, let's tell Lon the story about the chefs."

Red grinned and said, "That is a great story. It's about Munch, Crunch, Diamond, and Ruby, four of our chefs, and five meddlesome carpenters. One day, Speed said he thought Munch and Diamond, and Crunch and Ruby might be in love with each other. In said, 'Well, they are appealing, cheery, and single.' Hype said, 'Maybe we can hook them up.' I said, 'I think they would make ideal couples. What can we do to get them together?' Speed said, 'Well, they all cook together, so this ought to be easy.'

"We thought a bit, then In said 'I have an idea. Let's send a note over from Diamond and Ruby to Munch and Crunch. Speed's the best writer, so he can write it.' Speed said, 'All right. Let's see...' And here's the note we wrote:

To Munch and Crunch:

How about joining us for a game of pool at the Whispering Pines tonight at 9:00 P.M.?

If the answer is yes, please check here ___.

If the answer is no, please check here ___.

> *Your friends,*
> *Diamond and Ruby*

"In said, 'That's great! Hood, would you mind taking this over to Munch and Crunch?' So, Hood took the note to the kitchen, handed it to Crunch, and said, 'Please read this and give it back to me.' Crunch and Munch read the note. Crunch elbowed Munch and said, 'Check yes.' Munch didn't have a pen, but Hood did and he pulled it out.

Crunch checked yes, then he folded up the note and gave it to Hood. Hood walked right past Diamond and Ruby without a glance. He took the note back to the carpentry room. Hood told us everything that had happened, and we couldn't keep from laughing at our little deception. Crunch and Munch wore big smiles all day.

"Later that day, Diamond and Ruby asked us if we knew why Crunch and Munch were smiling at them. 'No, I don't,' said In. 'Well, it's very odd.' said Ruby. 'Should we smile back?' 'Well, yes,' said Diamond. So Diamond and Ruby smiled back at the twin brothers throughout the day. Munch said to Crunch, 'I didn't see Hood give the note to Diamond or Ruby, but they're smiling at us. That's a good sign.' Nothing more was said.

"Back at the carpentry room, In said, 'Now, how are we going to get the girls over to the pool room?' Hype said, 'I know! Let's send the same note to the girls from Munch and Crunch.' Now the note read:

To Diamond and Ruby:

Do you care to join us over for a game of pool tonight at 9:00 P.M.?

If the answer is yes, please check here ___.

If the answer is no, please check here ___.

> *Your Friends,*
> *Munch and Crunch*

"In went to get Hood, and Hood took the note over to Diamond and Ruby. Ruby showed Diamond the letter. Diamond said, 'Check yes.' Ruby said, 'So this is what Crunch and Munch were smiling about all day!' Hood brought the note back to us. We were having a grand old time.

"The Whispering Pines was always a happening place. Hype said, 'How are we going to clear out the Whispering Pines Club?' I said, 'How about a movie for the kids, at Santa's?' We all consulted Santa, and he said, 'I will get Buddy and open up the pool at the castle. Then everybody will leave the Whispering Pines Club to go swimming. For we know that the elves just love having fun in the water.' Leave it to Santa to have an even better idea.

"Munch, Crunch, Diamond, and Ruby were so giddy all day, they couldn't think straight, and they were messing up all the food. They were all falling in love. Thank goodness they somehow got through the day.

"When they met at the Whispering Pines, the drinks and snacks were already set up. Crunch and Munch thought the lady elves brought the snacks, and Diamond and Ruby thought the guys brought the snacks. We were keeping a low profile in the back room, playing cards and eavesdropping." In said, "We were really watching how the pool game was going. Crunch and Ruby played ping-pong. Munch and Diamond played pool. Not for just an hour, but this went on all evening. We finally gave up and went home.

"We found out later what happened after we left. Ruby finally said, 'Hey guys, thanks for inviting us out tonight. We were so thrilled you sent us the note. We immediately signed yes.' In unison, the guys said, 'What?' Munch said, 'You two are the ones that sent us the note, and we checked yes.' They all broke up laughing. Ruby said, 'Why don't we find Hood and figure out what's going on?'

"The next morning, they cornered Hood, and he explained the whole conspiracy. Crunch, Munch, Ruby, and Diamond appeared in the door to the carpentry room, and all of our machines froze. Everyone was looking at each other and pointing. Shoulders were up in the air as if to say, 'I don't know anything.' Faces were turning red. Seams wore an 'I told you so' look. The chefs just stood and watched for several minutes, enjoying our embarrassment. Then they simply said, 'Thank you' and everyone laughed with relief.

"The chefs went back to the kitchen, and today they paired off differently. Crunch and Ruby were working together, and Munch and Diamond were working together—for a change. These four had finally admitted they were in love. The carpentry cupids had saved the day.

"Meanwhile, back at the carpentry room, we were all talking about what had just happened. We were intoxicated with power, and we wondered what trouble we could stir up next. Hype, Speed, Red, Seams, and I thought the whole thing was such a riot."

We all were laughing at the carpenter's matchmaking tale, and I said, "What a story!" Red said, "Those were some of the first couples to get married here at the North Pole." I said to Red, "Are you guys always trying to stir things up?" In replied, "You bet. We're always in the middle of something!" Seams said, "Come on, you guys. We have a lot to get done today." So, back to work they went, and I was off to visit the happy chefs in their kitchen.

Chapter Nineteen
Chefs From Around the World

Chef Crunch and Chef Ruby assist Mrs. Claus in the kitchen.

The chefs invited me over to the kitchen and dining facility. The kitchen was huge. The pantry had plenty of storage space for canned fruits and vegetables. Garlands of onions, garlic, and peppers of all kinds were draped high on the cabinets. Baskets of fruits and vegetables hung from the ceiling. The refrigerator and freezers were packed with fish, lobster, and shrimp. The chefs had everything they needed right at their fingertips.

When I arrived, Smitten was there to greet me. He said, "Hi, Lon, I'm Chef Smitten, originally from France. I am one of the chefs here at the North Pole. We're all so thrilled to have you here in our kitchen. Let me introduce you to the other chefs. I know some of you have met, but I will introduce you again." Chef Munch and Chef Crunch shook hands with me. Together they told me, "We're the twins from Germany." With a big grin, Crunch said, "We love to sample all the cooking here because we want to make sure everything is sublime." Smitten said, "Here are the twins' wives, Diamond and Ruby. They are from the United States." I was meeting the famous couples brought together by the matchmaking carpenters, and they were charming.

As we shook hands, Ruby said, "Lon, we hear you make a great broccoli cauliflower salad and a yummy carrot cake." Lon replied, "Oh, so I've been told. If you want, I'll gladly show you how I do it. Do you have time right now?" Ruby said, "That would be great!" I said, "It's my pleasure, Ruby. Ready to get started?" "Don't forget me," Quicken said. He and Ice were just coming in the door. Quicken was from Holland, and Ice was from Australia. I was thrilled that all seven chefs were now present in the kitchen at the same time, because I would need a lot of help to make enough salad and cake for two hundred and fifty people. I had never cooked for that many before. Smitten eased my mind by reminding me there was plenty of kitchen help to get it done. I began by listing the ingredients for the carrot cake. Here is the recipe:

Golden Carrot Cake

2 cups granulated sugar
1 cup vegetable oil
4 eggs
2 cups finely grated carrots
2 cups flour

1½ tsp. baking soda
1½ tsp. baking powder
1 tbsp. ground allspice
1 tbsp. ground cinnamon

Preheat oven to 375 degrees. Grease and lightly flour two bundt cake pans.

In a large mixing bowl, blend sugar, oil, eggs, and carrots. Set aside. In a medium mixing bowl, combine flour, baking soda, baking powder, allspice, and cinnamon. Gradually add dry ingredients to carrot mixture and stir until blended well. Pour into a bundt cake pan. Bake 1 hour or until toothpick inserted in center comes out clean. Cool completely and pop out of pan.

Quicken said, "Lon, how many will this serve?" I guessed approximately twenty-five people. "So, let's make ten batches," he said. Everyone started working as a team, shredding carrots, measuring flour, pouring sugar. Smitten went to get the olive oil.

Elf Lavender with her herbs and spices.

Lavender brought us more cinnamon. She was wearing a hat with dried herbs all over it. It was a hoot! I loved how these elves expressed themselves. The effect was eccentric and endearing at the same time. She said, "Here's the cinnamon, Lon. You know, when we moved here to the North Pole, I brought endless amounts of all kinds of seeds, plants, and herbs. We now have spices of all kinds, whenever we want them." Diamond and Ruby were coating the pans with shortening and a light dusting of flour, to prepare them for the batter. Ice and Diamond were already cutting up broccoli and cauliflower for the salad. Quicken said, "What goes into the salad?" Here's the recipe I gave them:

Broccoli and Cauliflower Salad

2 heads cauliflower

2 heads broccoli

1 large sweet onion

1 cup mayonnaise

1 cup Miracle Whip

½ cup sugar

½ cup vinegar

1 cup chopped pecans

½ cup cranraisins

Cut broccoli and cauliflower into small florets. Set aside. Cut onion into small pieces. Set aside. In a bowl, blend mayonnaise, Miracle Whip, sugar, and vinegar. Stir in pecans, cranraisins, and onions to mix. Add broccoli and cauliflower to mixture. Chill 2 hours and serve.

I said, "I've never been in a kitchen where everyone was working so well as a team." Crunch thanked me as he read the icing ingredients. He was really into his work.

Crème de la Cream Cheese Frosting

1-8 oz. package cream cheese

¾ stick butter

1 tbsp. vanilla

2 cups confectioners' sugar

1 cup chopped pecans or walnuts

Mix ingredients and beat until smooth. Lather frosting onto the cake after it has cooled.

"That's it, times ten, for our ten cakes," I said. In about an hour, our cakes were done, and the chefs were grabbing the oven mitts and sliding the cakes out of the ovens. The salad was chilling in the refrigerator. All the elves were excited to have a taste, but they restrained themselves. Lunch would be served from noon to 1:00 P.M., and we still had a few hours to go. The chefs needed this time to prepare many more lunch dishes. Munch said, "Hey, guys, we still need a potato dish." I spoke up quickly, "I've got one." Ice said, "Let's hear it."

I told them about my sweet potato casserole. "First, you layer the bottom of a deep-dish bake pan with one large can of sweet potato slices or chunks, then you sprinkle brown sugar lightly all over it. Scatter small chunks of pineapple on top of that, and add chopped pecan pieces. Bake it for half an hour at 300 degrees." "Sounds great," said Smitten. So, Munch and Crunch handled the sweet potatoes while Diamond, Ruby, and Quicken prepared the pineapple. Smitten went to get more brown sugar.

Santa poked his head into the kitchen and said, "How are things going today?" He was wearing a shirt with Christmas bells all over it. He took a whiff of the heavenly kitchen smells and smiled. "Smells wonderful! Lon, I've heard you would be in the kitchen today. Any specialties?" I said, "Yes, of course. A sweet potato dish, and a broccoli-cauliflower salad, and a carrot cake with creamy frosting." Santa said, "Wow! That's making me very hungry, and the aromas in this kitchen are so appetizing! I can hardly wait for lunch today." I said, "Wait till you try Crunch and Munch's lunch meat recipe. They add secret spices, and it's wonderful. You would never guess you're eating catfish. They brought the recipe with them from Germany. Trust me— it's really good."

Diamond, Ruby, and Quicken were busy cooking, and I was talking with Ice. Out of the corner of my eye, I saw Santa sneak some bites as he left with a "Ho-ho!" Ice said, "Lon, so many of the elves have talent. We're very fortunate that Santa allows us to do whatever jobs we know and like best. Santa always enjoys the kitchen. He thinks its great that the elves eat together. It saves so much time, instead of having everybody go to their separate homes for lunch. He feels they work so hard, they deserve a relaxing meal with their friends. Santa's always thinking of ways to save the elves time and work. When they eat in the dining room here, it saves time, energy, and it's so convenient."

Ice continued. "We make a huge variety of dishes and serve them buffet style so everyone can choose the foods they like. Wow, look at this. We're going to have a big turnout for lunch. Word has spread fast. All the clubs must have closed so everybody could try your new dishes, Lon. Let's go join them."

Everyone wanted a piece of carrot cake. They had never seen a cake with small bits of carrots in it. Zucchini bread yes, carrot cake no. They were all talking about how tasty it was, especially with that smooth, rich icing. The chefs surrounded me, chatting and enjoying the excitement. I had contributed something special that day. All the helpers in the kitchen were asking me questions about my recipes. Ice and I waited till everyone else had been served then we sat down with the other chefs. I intentionally tried to listen more than I talked. I wanted to focus on what they had to say.

Crunch and Munch started first, telling me how they had brought all the tools of their trade when they arrived at the North Pole. Crunch said, "Lon, we had pots, pans, spoons, spatulas, tools, and appliances of all kinds for the kitchen. Later, Bubbles made us some new utensils for stirring." Munch said, " I remember all the spices we brought. I tell you, Lon, we stank up the whole train, all the way to Jemdaza. The conflicting smells were too much for an enclosed space, and everyone wanted us off the train! It was too funny. Well, we finally made it here, and we're so glad to have done what we did." He turned to Crunch, "Do you remember the lady on the train who kept sneezing? It must have been the spices. She was sure glad to see us leave. I'll have to admit, the smell was a little overwhelming, even for me. But we weren't allergic, so we could just laugh it off. And do you remember how our pots and pans clanged together, nonstop? They made such a racket, nobody could sleep." "I think everyone was glad when that trip was over," Smitten said. "Our bags had 'North Hills or Bust!' written on them," said Munch. "No one had to ask where we were going! We looked like a traveling flea market! The bottom line was that our minds and hearts were made up. We were headed to the North Hills and a better life!"

When all the chefs met for the first time, they really hit if off. They shared special recipes from their different countries. They appreciated the nuances of cooking and baking, how a certain technique or a single ingredient could make a dish exceptional. They had a common passion, and it was food.

Crunch continued the story. "For many months, we tried all types of dishes from around the world. Some were unusual and took some getting used to, but others were without a doubt sensational. You never want to miss dessert, Lon. We keep coming up with new ones all the time. We hung a sign up in the kitchen that says, 'There's Always Room for Dessert!'"

Ruby said, "Do you remember when the children in Mexico sent in their toy requests? They included their favorite recipes for us to try. We ate Mexican food for weeks. It was very good food, a little hotter than I was used to, and I mean spicy hot. Ice made colder-than-usual drinks that month to keep our mouths cooled down. We got used to it though, and now we often crave them, so they're always on the menu." Quicken said, "We always love it when children send us their most favorite recipes. I think it makes them feel more attached to us too, and that's cool."

Smitten said, "It's kind of obvious how Chef Ice got his name. He loves to make everything cold: cold desserts, cold soups, cold drinks, ice-cold jello, to name a few. Everyone enjoys his banana supreme splits. I make all of the sauces for his desserts: pineapple sauce, strawberry sauce, chocolate sauce, and so on. He uses layers of bananas, ice cream, sauces, all sorts of flavors of whipped cream, assorted nuts, and cherries—whatever you want. His waffle cones look like boats. The small elves just love Chef Ice's desserts."

"Ice is also the very best drink maker I have ever met," said Ruby. "We call him the 'master drink mixer.' He'll make you apricot iced tea, blueberry cream iced tea, strawberry lime iced tea, and many other kinds of iced teas. If you don't see your favorite on the menu, he can still make it for you. For his most recent creation he adds drops of his secret fruit syrups to certain beverages to get a flavored drink that really quenches your thirst. He experiments every day, and I guess that's why he has so much fun. He really is a master at it—and the drinks prove it." Smitten said, "I always enjoy his slushy drinks. He uses a very fine pebble ice to start and adds flavored fruit. He has an awesome variety of candies, sauces, and syrups you can choose from, or he will make a recommendation. They are a must-try! Ice's talents never end. He specializes in ice cream drinks too. One of my favorites is a velvety smooth white chocolate-coconut mocha shake. It will make your tongue slap your backbone. I'm serious, Lon!"

Then there was Chef Quicken. She had to be the fastest chef I'd ever seen. She could cook up a storm and when the dust settled, the food was on the table. She worked from hundreds of recipes, and you didn't want to get in her way. She moved to the right while she was working, so you always wanted to stand on her left. She was art in motion. The helpers in the kitchen were also apprentices to the chefs, and Quicken loved to teach them everything from old techniques to new tricks.

Smitten brought a smile to everyone's lips. He was in love and it was infectious. He just didn't know who he loved yet. After a time, he realized it was Yawn, but I'm not sure if she knew. Smitten's specialties were making people feel comfortable and stirring up great sauces. He was the "sauce king" in the kitchen. One time, he made me a French pastry with a sweet pomegranate mint sauce and placed chocolate shavings on top. The mint came from the garden, of course. It was delectable.

Chef Diamond and Chef Ruby were true culinary geniuses, and everyone called them "the artists." It was not uncommon for the rest of the elves to gaze at their plates for a long time before taking a bite. They would "oooh" and "ahhh" over the shapes, colors, textures, aromas, and ornamentation, and smack their lips in anticipation. When they finally took a bite, there were always thumbs-up reviews. Diamond and Ruby enjoyed their faithful following in the dining room. These creative chefs had a passion for presenting works of art that could be eaten, and their audience showed their appreciation. The consensus was "Yummy!"

Diamond and Ruby took special pleasure in making beautiful cakes. The icing would cascade over the top and down the sides of their original creations. Using small paring knives, they would carve rosettes and leaves from colorful pieces of fruit and adorn the cakes with them, creating lovely arrangements. Chef Diamond and Chef Munch were married, as were Chef Ruby and Chef Crunch. From what I observed throughout the day, the Munch and Crunch brothers commanded respect in the kitchen. They were really top-notch.

The kitchen staff wore their tall white hats with dignity. All looked like first-class chefs. They honored me with my own hat, and had added a special touch. On the front was embroidered, "Special Guest—Chef Lon." The dinner conversation was interesting, as usual. We were just finishing up when Santa held up a plate with a slice of carrot cake and said, "Last piece—does anybody want it? Ho-ho!" Well, it was just a tease since Santa had already decided to eat it himself. Mrs. Claus scolded him mildly with, "Santa!" and he replied, "It's too good, Susie," then finished it off. Santa licked the last of the frosting off his lips and told me how much he enjoyed it. It was obvious to everybody, and we all laughed.

After lunch I helped clean up the kitchen, and we got everything spiffed up and put back together. I asked Whippersnapper, one of the helpers, about the pink marble countertops. He told me, when they were digging out the vita ore stone to make the glass, they found a vein of pink marble. It was so pretty, they decided to use it on the kitchen counters and as an accent in other parts of the castle. "You're right, Lon," said Whippersnapper. "It is beautiful, and it keeps our spirits light and happy in the kitchen."

Thanks to Johnathan Andrew Witherspoon, the kitchen was equipped with modern appliances. Whippersnapper said, "We're always upgrading here." Everything looked new. The kitchen cabinets were made of maple, with a light pinkish wash that highlighted the grain of the wood. "The painter Meschbach had something to do with this champagne maple look," said Whippersnapper. "Visitors to the castle often wish they could take Meschbach home with them, to have him redo their kitchens. Too bad he's so busy flying around the globe with a nonstop schedule. We're definitely blessed to have his art in our everyday lives.

"The stained glass inserts in all the cabinet doors were done by Lady Whisper. She is an older elf and speaks in a soft voice. Her work is just marvelous. She had Bubbles make her some really thin glass for this purpose, then she colored it as you see here. Many of the elves also are lucky enough to have some of her work in their homes. Besides door inserts, she makes lamps, shades, chandeliers, and other pieces of art. Mrs. Claus has some of her creations in her home too. Lady Whisper teaches the little elves the art of stained glass once a week. She is quite an artist, and everyone shows her great respect."

All the chefs had some special musical talent and they entertained while the elves ate. Diamond and Ruby played the violin. Smitten was on the bass guitar. Quicken tooted the flute. Crunch and Munch blew saxophone. Ice sang. All the kitchen assistants served up the food, while the main chefs played to beat the band. Everyone, and I mean everyone, really enjoyed the dinner music. Santa always lit up around Christmas music. He said, "I am so fortunate to be among such great people in my life."

The dining hall made a wonderful setting for music. It had forty stained glass chandeliers. Oak tables lined the walls, and some were placed in the center of the room. The dishes and silverware also had a stained glass finish, thanks to Lady Whisper. And everything was always crystal clean.

Diamond had a new story for me. I was delighted to listen. She said, "Lon, you should hear the one about last year's Annual Decoration and Cook-Off Contest. It was the lady elves against the men. The lady elves had won every year since we started. There may have been a tie one year—but that was the exception. However, last year the men decided it was their turn to win, and they took it up a few notches.

"Slowpoke, come over and join us." Slowpoke sat down and shook hands with me. Diamond said, "Slowpoke, tell Lon about last year's Annual Decoration and Cook-Off Contest." Slowpoke smiled and said, "I'd love to, Diamond. Santa asked me to come to his office, Lon, to have a private talk. I felt very honored. As I sat down in a comfy chair, he said to me, 'Slowpoke, I know there are times you get teased because your pace is slower than some of the other elves, but you have always had their respect, and that's one of the reasons I need to ask a favor of you.' Of course, I was honored that Santa was seeking my help and more than willing to lend a hand. I said, 'What can I do for you, Santa?' Santa said, 'I'm appointing you to be the one in charge of the Annual Decoration and Cook-Off Contest. The men have lost every year, and this year I want us to win. No one knows I'm going to appoint you. Now I know this is a huge responsibility. Are you ready for the challenge?'

"My knees were shaking; I felt quite taken aback by Santa's request. Yet I was also thrilled to say yes. 'Okay, good! You have six weeks to get this done. Last year, the men's challenge was on September 2nd We won the coin toss this year, so we can have the advantage of going second. The ladies go first, on September 1st. All of us are counting on you, Slowpoke. You're very smart, so whatever you want all of us to do, we will do it.' I shook hands with Santa and put my finger to my lips as I left. 'Top secret!' I said. Then I immediately started planning. Everyone was kind of curious about my meeting with Santa, but I kept mum till Santa could make his official announcement.

"Three days later, I called a meeting of all the men elves. Santa spoke first, 'The elf in charge of this year's Annual Decoration and Cook-Off Contest is Slowpoke.' Everyone politely clapped, but I could tell by some of their faces that they had their doubts. I remember stepping up front to talk. I started my speech with 'This year we will win!' Everyone cheered. Now everybody would find out what Slowpoke was made of."

Slowpoke continued. "I picked a name for our festive night. It was 'The Christmas Bash.' I told the guys, 'Over the next six weeks we'll need to put a lot of time and energy into this, collectively. So, let's get crackin'! Bubbles, we need new plates, and I'd like the design on them to be a Christmas tree with painted lights. We need gold glasses with candy cane stems, all red and white. We need red napkins with little wreaths all over them, and the forks, knives, and spoons should match. The dessert dishes will have the same pattern as the dinner plates, but be one-fourth the size.'

"The chandeliers were all covered with big green bows and had streamers hanging down from them, Lon. It was a real nice touch, and the light reflecting on them made the ribbons look quite dazzling.

"The tables were decorated with candlestick holders in a poinsettia design. In the center of each flower was a candlestick. The tablecloths were a soft gold fabric trimmed with gold tassels at the bottom edge. The gold wasn't gaudy; it gave just enough shimmer to make a stunning impression. We scattered small silver box ornaments here and there on the tables. They had little white after-dinner mints in them. The chairs were draped with big green bows and steamers, to match the chandeliers. Can you visualize how festive and colorful the room looked, Lon?" I said, "Most certainly! Tell me more, Slowpoke."

"Upon entering the dining hall that special night, everyone was struck with excitement and awe. You could hear gasps of surprise, as though they could hardly imagine this to be real, especially coming from the guys. That's not all. The carpenters had arranged live poinsettias in the shape of Christmas trees. They very cleverly devised a stick-type tree with shelves to hold the plants. The center post was six inches square and eight feet tall. Around it, circular wooden shelves started out big at the bottom and got small at the top. They slipped over the post and were attached at about every twelve inches. We crowded the poinsettias on the shelves so that all you could see was this big red poinsettia Christmas tree. The poinsettia pots were covered with shiny green foil that glistened as if the tree had lights on it. We used so many pots that we lost count. It was absolutely stunning!

"We had a total of twenty trees, all the same size, lining the dining hall. It had all been carefully planned from our first meeting. I had pointed out that we'd need to hurry and get these numerous poinsettias in the planting stages immediately. It worked perfectly. We wound up using the older, larger poinsettias on the lower shelves and the younger plants on the smaller shelves toward the top.

"We cut out snowflakes of all sizes and hung them from the ceiling on clear fishing line, so it looked like it was snowing. We covered the walls with them too. The poinsettia trees looked breathtaking against the background of white walls.

"All the elf men wore black pants and royal blue shirts with white icicles all over them. Our suspenders were black to match our pants, and there were icicles scattered on them here and there too.

"Our dinner was elegant and everyone raved about the food. We had the following:

- Two Christmas cookies shaped like bells placed on either side of the plate
- Apple butter slices formed into wreaths, on a small dish beside the dinner plate

- Fresh, mixed green salad with a creamy apricot drizzle sauce on top
- A small cup of cucumber bisque soup
- Fresh citrus Waldorf salad
- Lightly sautéed zucchini slices
- Buttered baby carrots with an orange honey glaze
- Double-baked potatoes stuffed with a sour cream mixture
- Marinated lobster
- Our chef's special seven-layer white chocolate cake with a French butter cream frosting
- Spiced cranraspberry sherbet or peppermint ice cream
- Christmas Holendoz as our drink

"The chefs had outdone themselves. Everything was transcendent." I said, "That meal sounds terrific." Slowpoke licked his lips and said, "You have no idea. Now, I'll tell you how our special dessert was served. Just after the main meal was over, music played as the chef helpers came out of the kitchen single file with serving trays of flaming cherries jubilee balanced on top of their heads. Now, that was quite a show to see! They circled the tables then took their places at measured distances around the room. The entire room came alive with clapping and whistling and cheering. The chef helpers served everyone at the same time. After that meal, we all felt like we wouldn't eat again for a week. For the rest of the evening, Munch and Crunch played their saxophones and Ice sang. Hopes were high. Surely, this was the year the guys would win the contest. It had turned out to be a beautifully choreographed feast."

Diamond said, "Now, let me tell you what we did. Mrs. Claus appointed Ellie to organize the ladies' portion of the Annual Decoration and Cook-Off Contest. Ellie is so elegant. She plays the harp and works in the Sewing Department. At our planning meeting, Ellie said, 'This year our theme is "A Victorian Party." I will call off the things that need to get done:

1. Flowers for the tables
2. Presentation of tableware
3. Candles
4. Food
5. Servers
6. Decorations
7. Two trees at the entrance decorated with Victorian lights and ornaments
8. All the ladies dressed in Victorian costume
9. Music by the Lady Hornets

"'Diamond, Ruby, and Quicken will be in charge of the food. And the rest of us all know what we have to do for the next weeks. So let's beat those guys again this year!' All the lady elves signed up for jobs and wrote lists of things to do to make it all happen. Ellie said, 'Everyone, keep a secret now!' And the competition was on."

Slowpoke picked up the story again. "September 1st was the ladies' Victorian Night. We knew it was going to be an extravagant evening, so all the men wore tuxes, and the ladies dressed up Victorian-style. The event kicked off at 7:00 P.M. The Lady Hornets were playing their harps, flutes, and violins. The tables were decorated with pink roses, all in soft colors. There were two trees at the entry doors richly decorated with precious Victorian ornaments. The tablecloths and centerpieces had a Victorian touch of class. Ruby, Quicken, and Diamond, along with their helpers, served shrimp linguini, vegetables, baked potatoes, bread and butter, and strawberry soup. Fresh fruit was cut in the shape of flowers, and the ice cream cake was trimmed with rosettes made from frosting. We danced throughout the evening and had a splendid time. "The next night would be the men's night to pull out all the stops. We were determined to make September 2nd a true Christmas Bash."

Ruby said, "Let me tell Lon about the Christmas Bash. Well, that day we all brought our lunch in a paper bag. No one, certainly none of the ladies, could get near the kitchen or the dining hall. Preparations were underway for the men's big surprise. Exactly at 7:00 P.M., the band struck up and Ice sang. All the lady elves were dressed in their best Christmas finery. When we entered the dining hall, we were literally speechless. Many of the ladies had tears in their eyes. The poinsettia trees, the snowflakes, the table settings—every detail was dazzling. We told Slowpoke we were sure the guys had won. It was breathtaking and we knew the food would be just as good."

Slowpoke said, "To tell you the truth, I think the men were shocked to win. The ladies always did a fantastic job. Us win? As much fine work as everybody did, we still thought it would be too good to be true. We talked about it for weeks afterward, how we beat the lady elves that year. Santa and everybody loved the decorations so much, we left them up till Christmas."

Slowpoke smiled. "The best part was no one picked on me after that night. And, of course, we still filled Christmas orders for all the children of the world that year, as usual. Dreamer painted me a keepsake of that night—a picture of the dining hall fully decorated for the Christmas Bash. Wait till this year's contest, Lon!" I had to say, "I just wish I could be here to see it, Slowpoke."

Chapter Twenty
The Guest List

Santa gets ready to speak with his guests during their visit to the North Pole.

I was enjoying lunch at the Cozy Creek Club with Mrs. Claus. Ola and Phillipi had served us the most delicious pizza and root beer. Mrs. Claus was telling me about the guests who visit January through March. She said, "Lon, it all started when Johnathan Andrew Witherspoon gave Kris a map to the North Hills. Johnathan also gave us money so Kris could make even more gifts for children. He felt he was doing something worthwhile by helping Kris build his dream. Prior to Johnathan's passing, Kris kept him up-to-date with how he was using his donation money. It gave Johnathan so much pleasure to be a part of our efforts for children. He transformed himself from a 'scrooge,' as he called himself, into a charitable benefactor. Johnathan passed away happy and at peace, and he left all of his wealth to Kris and myself, for Kris's work.

"But earlier, as Johnathan was becoming too ill to travel, he did another wonderful thing. He wrote all of the wealthy associates he had done business with for so many years and told them about Kris's dreams for children. Kris and Johnathan decided to invite these business people to the North Pole, so they could see our dream in action. There were so many of them, we had to rotate the list. The first group came in January, the second in February, and still others in March. Johnathan had spent six solitary years at the North Hills, but was never able to see the community we had established here, called the North Pole. He regretted that very much, as did we. Still he continued to be our greatest supporter and cheerleader.

"As the many guests would come and go, they fell in love with everything and everyone here at the Christmas Village. They all, and I mean all, were mesmerized by the huge mountains that surround us, and all the work that was being done here for such a great cause.

"The first group of visitors were very wealthy businesspersons who gave to many causes. There were about twenty of them altogether, many with spouses, and when they returned home they all talked about everything they'd seen. Then they had meetings to form what is known today as the Kris Kringle Foundation. They wanted to be a blessing in some way to children all over the world, to be a part of helping Santa's dream come true. Word spread abroad, and before you knew it, the facility here at the North Pole really began to grow.

"We were here about fifteen years when Johnathan passed away. But with his twenty business friends all helping in many ways, the guest list grew. More and more organizations, couples, companies, and individuals started giving large sums of money. When the list grew to more than two hundred, those guests also wanted to come and see what this North Pole was all about. Today, the foundation keeps getting bigger, and donations just keep pouring in. And that's where I come in. I now run the Kris Kringle Foundation. Santa and I always put the visitors list together each year so some of the participants who haven't been here can have a chance to visit. Here is the original list of twenty benefactors, those who have been so loyal to us from the very beginning:

1. Mr. and Mrs. Brinkley
2. Mr. and Mrs. Buckner
3. Mr. and Mrs. Sebestyen
4. Mr. and Mrs. Fultz
5. Mr. Isenbarger
6. Mr. and Mrs. Harris
7. Mr. and Mrs. Scott
8. Mr. and Mrs. Swaney
9. Mr. and Mrs. Franzen
10. Mr. and Mrs. Niemerg
11. Mr. and Mrs. Thomas
12. Mr. Dimmerling
13. Mr. and Mrs. Mattox
14. Miss France
15. Mr. and Mrs. James
16. Mr. and Mrs. Hoober
17. Mr. and Mrs. Shepler
18. Mr. and Mrs. McCarley
19. Mr. and Mrs. Hamilton
20. Mr. and Mrs. Snell

"I'm telling you about these twenty, because they should be remembered and honored. They never stop giving. They are fortunate to be very wealthy, but that doesn't mean they are obligated to donate to Santa's Christmas Village. Still, the more money they make, the more they give, year after year. We've met many more of our benefactors over the years as their numbers increased. What a thrill it is to welcome them here.

"We have another top twenty list. That list contains the names of individuals and couples who do special things for people throughout the year, but don't have the means to contribute money. It's quite a process to try to juggle who comes here next. We meet all different nationalities, all of them wonderful people. They all say how grateful they are for the chance of a lifetime, to be here at the North Pole with Santa and me. Only a few families have visited more than once. But no matter how rich or poor you are, you can still get on one of the lists, according to what you give or do. Whoever is chosen receives special instructions on how to get here. Buddy is always happy to pick up our guests at the train station in Jemdaza and bring them here to the Christmas Village.

"While our guests are here, the elves sleep, of course, and the production facility is shut down. But Goober and Sammie, and Sir

King and Lady Queen keep everyone in stitches. We have so much fun with their offspring too, watching them grow and listening to the parrots as they learn to speak. The parrots and dogs are always running and playing; they're great company while the elves are asleep. They're definitely a lively and comical bunch, and they keep us young. Santa and I don't know what we would do without them. They fit right in, just like family.

"As for me, I really like being in my kitchen cooking and baking during this time, and entertaining our guests here at the castle. We do have a maid and butler who arrive on January 2nd of every year. They stay until March 28th You just missed meeting them, Lon. The elves aren't reawakened till March 31st, of course, and they go to sleep every January 1st, so they've never met the maid and butler either. But those two are a tremendous help while they're here.

"I tell you, Lon, we are endlessly grateful to all of our contributors to the Kris Kringle Foundation, and we stay in touch with each and every one of them during the year. We enjoy talking to our many friends throughout the world via our satellite phones. No matter how many people give money, time, or whatever to our foundation, Santa and I make calls to all of them. We email them or we mail thank-you cards. We also send out a newsletter to our charitable friends two times a year. We keep everyone updated about Santa, the raindeer, Buddy, the elves, and all the things that are going on here at the North Pole. Lon, it takes everyone to bring Christmas into all the homes on Earth at Christmastime, and they deserve to know how things are going and share in our joy.

"Our tours and help lists give our guests many options to explore during their stay here. They can feed the raindeer at the stables, or they can assist in the kitchen or the garden. Our guests can visit the production facility, and they can look through the window of the room that holds the Shimatta feather. The Sleeping Chamber is off-limits though. Not Buddy, not myself, not even Santa is allowed to disturb the elves' sleep. This is their time of no interruption. You'd think our guests might be hard to keep up with, since they visit when all of the elves are asleep. But it's just the opposite. Far from being waited on hand and foot, you'd be surprised at how many people come here just to help out. It is truly amazing how much work our guests save us when they are here.

"During our three-month shutdown, Lon, going outside of the castle by yourself and going into the production facility are totally off-limits to all of our guests. The only way it is allowed is if you are escorted by Santa, Buddy, or myself. Nothing, and I mean nothing, can be touched, unless one of us is with you. No exceptions. When you enter the castle from the production facility, the door is sealed shut. This rule may seem a little harsh at first, but trust me, it is enforced so everyone can stay safe. We have a lot of power equipment on the production floor, and we don't want anyone to get hurt. It is also very important that we don't disturb the elves' work in progress.

"Once entering the castle, everyone has free rein. All except the pool area, that is. We lock the pool door and don't let anybody swim unless Buddy is there to lifeguard. Once again, this is a safety measure. However, the pool has very flexible hours when the guests are here. They enjoy it so much and always tell us they hate to get out of the water.

"There are so many activities to keep our guests occupied. The game room offers lots of diversions. The theater always has a movie running. The spa is new and a must to experience before leaving. Last year the hot tubs were added, so everyone can get totally relaxed before going home. It's quiet and soothing, like a resort haven.

"Our guests stay four to eight days at a time. We leave the Christmas decorations up for them—red and green, blue and white, gold and silver, with bells, bows, and wreaths. They are in such awe when they first step inside the castle. Their eyes and mouths open wide. The staircase is decorated with garlands and twinkly lights, and it goes up ten stories. Some people can't take heights; they get dizzy, so we warn them not to look down. The elevator goes up fifty stories to the very top.

"Our castle was built into the side of the mountain, which protects us. The mountain is approximately two thousand two hundred feet high and is surrounded by more mountains and the woods. Bubbles has told you about our Bubble Dome, so you know that you can't see our facility from the outside. You can see the twin prop wind tunnels though, all three of them. You can see part of the raindeer stables from the higher stories in the castle. Everyone enjoys looking through the windows or stepping onto the balcony to look out over the North Pole. No doubt about it, it is a magnificent sight. The twin prop wind tunnels and stables are white and blend into the snowy scenery. When our guests go to their rooms to unpack, they are overwhelmed by the view through their windows.

"Once our guests are all settled in, Santa and I meet with each individual or couple privately. We want to get to know them and demonstrate how special they are to us. All the time, they tell us how thankful they are to be invited here and how beautiful it is. And we're genuinely happy to have them here. I can tell you something about our oldest loyal contributors, Lon. Let's see...I'd better consult my list so I don't leave anybody out.

"Let's start with the Brinkleys from Amsterdam, Netherlands. They own a major steam room and sauna company. They shipped us a new steam and dry heat sauna system for our new spa. Oh, Lon, these are great for cleaning out the pores of the body, and help in losing weight. We all smiled when Mr. Brinkley told us that. I remember Santa asking them, 'Will it really work?' Santa and I could hardly wait. They brought their master sauna installer, Gulford, with them to set everything up. It took him only four days to complete the job, beginning to end. We thanked Gulford for doing such a great job and stepped inside to christen the equipment. It was divine! Now our guests can also have a great time using these health rooms. Mr. and Mrs. Brinkley said their two daughters back home often have sauna parties at their house. Their friends join them. They play music, use the pool, grill outside, and just chill. Mrs. Brinkley said, 'We have taught our children to always share what they have.' A wonderful motto, don't you think, Lon? We couldn't thank the Brinkleys enough.

"Then, we've spent happy hours with the Buckners from Sarbrutten, Germany. They brought us a marvelous clock as a gift. They asked Santa if it could be mounted in the production facility, and Santa thought it was a great idea. It's huge! It can be seen from anywhere on the main floor. This clock was built by the Buckner Clock

Company. It doesn't show the time; rather, the hands point to the months, January through December. Then in the middle of the clock it reads 'North Pole.'" I remembered seeing that clock on my tour of the production floor and said, "Oh yes, Mrs. Claus, it is so big, no one can miss it!" Mrs. Claus said, "Near the top of the clock, it reads "December 24th," our goal date. Santa also has a smaller one like it in his office. We thanked the Buckners for designing these amazing clocks especially for us. We are so grateful for all the donations and support they have given us throughout the years.

"I have to tell you about the history of their clock company, Lon, because it is so interesting. Mr. Buckner told Santa and me his grandfather owned and operated a watch repair shop for many years. That's how he supported his family. Ever since he was two years old, Mr. Buckner spent hours in his grandfather's shop, and his grandfather noticed how intrigued the little tot was with the watch mechanisms. 'Of course, Grandfather thought that you're never too young to learn,' Mr. Buckner told me, 'so he started teaching me. Little by little, I grasped all kinds of watchwork knowledge. I never got tired of opening watches to see how they ticked. I learned to repair every kind of watch there was.' His fascination with watches developed into his clock business. Today, their company sells clocks all over the world, and they are known for their unparalleled perfection.

"As if Mr. Buckner didn't have his hands full with his clock company, he also took up designing buildings. He's quite innovative and talented. Each year, he takes time off to bring his crew up here to build for us. He not only builds homes, but businesses too. He loves to create custom cabinets in kitchens. We've seen his portfolio, and he has built some amazing buildings. 'Whatever you want,' he told us, 'my crew and I can build it. One of my favorite sayings is, "What you want is what you get, and then some more—because we aim to please!"'

"The reason for telling you all that, Lon, is because Mr. Buckner was a very important key in the beginning stages of planning the castle. He was the first one who showed us blueprints for the proposed building. His concepts were far beyond anything Santa and I ever thought of. Good heavens! We could hardly sleep at night, thinking of the fantastic building that would be ours.

"Before Mr. Buckner and his crew started to build the castle, he said, 'Santa and Mrs. Claus, when I design and build something, it's not work to me. I know my job well and I'm good at what I do. But it's a pleasure too. I relish this sort of thing….It's just me having fun. When I was chosen to be in charge of designing and building the castle, it made me feel like a kid in a candy store. To have this opportunity…you have no idea. It is with honor that I take on building your North Pole castle. For me, it's a great blessing and the opportunity of a lifetime. I thank you both so much.'

"Well Lon, if you could have seen him and his assistants working here on the castle, you would have been proud of them. They worked so well together, never an argument, and they had such fun. Mr. Buckner was always making remarks that just cracked us up. He is a natural jokester. I guess some people are just born with that gift. He told us he got it from his grandmother. I will have to share some of her stories with you on another occasion, because she was quite a corker too. But for now, I am happy to say that the Buckners stay in close contact with us, and they are a super-fun family to know!

"Another family is the Sebestyen family. They're from Ottawa, Canada. Mr. Sebestyen is also in the clock business. He's the fourth generation in his family to own a successful specialty clock company. He specializes in one-of-a-kind clocks with unique carvings. The whole family gives a hand in keeping the business going. They also get a lot of repeat business over the years, because they provide such excellent customer service. Mr. and Mrs. Sebestyen surprised us with a very beautiful grandfather clock made of cherrywood for the castle. My, oh my, it took four men to deliver it and set it in place. It plays delightful Christmas songs and on the hour it chimes soothing tones. It is very pleasing to the ear. Santa loves it. They also brought a small mantel clock for each of the elves' homes and delivered them personally. The Sebestyens are tenderhearted people. It was hard for them to leave, because they felt so attached to all of us here, like family. But we keep in touch by phone until we can see them again. They remain good friends, and every year faithfully they contribute to the foundation.

"Another very giving family is the Fultz family. They're from Juneau, Alaska. They own a huge golf cart manufacturing company. They brought us the two golf carts. Both are white trimmed with red. One reads 'Santa' and the other reads 'Mrs. Claus.' The carts are powered by cutting-edge technology—spinning magnets. They have some lovely features: a really neat foghorn, a back-up charging system, a clipboard for notes, a fold-down mirror, and a drink holder with a cooling system, to name just a few. There is a very special feature I want to tell you about. They have a thumbprint starting system. When Santa starts up the cart, all he has to do is place his thumb on the scanner by the steering wheel, and the vehicle starts. My cart uses my thumbprint. Santa and I really appreciate this safety feature. It means no one can get hurt by accidentally turning them on. Both carts have a four-seat wagon so a whole bunch of elves can ride with us. They also have a bright red and green flag on each. Sometimes the elves need us in a hurry, and these flags let everybody know where we are when we're scooting around.

"The Fultzes also brought three bright orange carts for the workers on the production floor. They're a little different from ours. They're equipped with a square wagon on the back so they can haul supplies to all the different departments. You saw some of these carts pulling floats in the Carnivale parade. Lon, the chefs really enjoy these carts because they can bring fresh fruits and vegetables from the garden to the kitchen in one trip. We thank the Fultzes every time we use our carts because they save us so much time, and time here at the North Pole is very important.

"Next is Mr. Isenbarger from Michigan, in the United States. He owns and operates a very quaint, small, but very nice customized china and glass manufacturing company. He's been a very wonderful and faithful friend to us for many years. He has an extraordinary personality that attracts people to him. He is a very likable gentleman, so polite to everyone he meets—almost to a fault. He comes across like the CEO of a big company, but he considers himself a simple man living in a small town.

"Mr. Isenbarger was so thrilled to meet us that he stuttered and sputtered. We told him we're just two normal people, Santa and me. Once he calmed down, he helped unload a complete set of chinaware for four hundred people, to be used in the dining facility. The dishes and cups have 'The North Pole' printed across the middle. Mr. Isenbarger said, 'If you break any, you can have free replacements forever, since they are guaranteed never to break!' He gave us gold silverware and glass stemware to match. The drinking glasses are all trimmed in gold and etched with 'The North Pole.' Then he brought in a very beautiful custom-made set that he designed himself, for Santa and myself.

"Mr. Isenbarger was so anxious to give us a personal demonstration of this unbreakable tableware, we just couldn't refuse him. So, he proceeded to drop a plate and drinking glass onto the marble floor. Santa and I jumped back to avoid the broken pieces, but there were none. They didn't even crack. Mr. Isenbarger got a huge laugh out of our expressions. He then took a large soup bowl and tossed it on the floor, really hard. Then he threw a few cups down. Now we were enjoying watching him. He said, 'Santa and Mrs. Claus, I have proved for many years that there is nothing you can do to this glassware to break it. So, have fun trying.' We thanked him for his very generous gifts. He was actually one of the very first supporters of the Kris Kringle Foundation. We would like to see him more often, but he stays so busy.

"The next couple who graciously support us are Mr. and Mrs. Harris. The Harrises are from Madrid, Spain. They have done a lot of investing with stocks, bonds, and properties. Mrs. Harris presented us with a very elegant tablecloth she crocheted herself. It is made of delicate satin crocheted lace, and I treasure it. She spent many months on it, and the craftsmanship is impeccable. She told me, 'As soon as we were notified we would be guests here at the North Pole, I went to work on it.' The tablecloth has a picture of a beautiful mountain scene with woods surrounding the mountain. In the middle of the picture, it reads 'The North Pole.' Santa and I were so impressed with her thoughtfulness. It adorns our dinner table often. Mrs. Harris mentioned that her husband always took very good care of her and has given her so many marvelous things to make her happy. Therefore, she wanted to do something for other people, to keep the giving spirit alive. Since they left here, she has made eight more tablecloths as gifts, and is still making more. We also thanked them for their financial support. We keep in touch and always love hearing from them.

"I remember the Scott family. They were from Na'gpur, India. The Scotts own a major rug company. Mrs. Scott loves to talk, and she knows a lot about a lot of things. We loved to listen to her. She told Santa and me how their company got started and in general kept us spellbound with her knowledge. Mr. and Mrs. Scott are giving people. No doubt, that's why they are so blessed. They gave us two snowy white Persian rugs with 'The North Pole' woven right in the middle. We put the larger one in Santa's office. The smaller rug is in my office. They also included rugs for the dogs, Sir King and Lady Queen and their pups. On top of that, the Scotts donated colorful Persian rugs for every home, so all the elves' can enjoy their beauty. They are great givers to the foundation. Santa feels that if more people were like the Scotts, this world would be even more awesome than it already is.

"Moving along, we come to the Swaneys from Nass, Ireland. They gave us gold doorknobs for the front doors of the castle. Of course, they are inscribed with 'The North Pole.' They also installed similar doorknobs on all the homes in the village. The Swaneys own their own door fixture company and made these especially for us. We felt very honored to have them as our guests and they felt honored to be here. We got into many conversations about door locks. They were very knowledgeable and charming. This couple is always so giving, not just with financial contributions for our Kris Kringle Foundation, but of themselves. Santa and I admire such individuals as these.

"The Franzen family from Mexico City, Mexico, owns a company that produces doorknockers and windows. They presented us with doorknockers for the castle and all the elves' homes. The castle knocker is unique. You don't hear anything outside when you knock, but it buzzes inside the castle. It sure puzzled our Design Department. They think it's a brilliant idea but they can't figure out how it works. It makes quite a first impression with the other guests. We thanked the Franzens—for their generous financial help to the foundation too.

"Now let's talk about Mr. and Mrs. Niemerg. The Niemergs told us all about the publishing company they own. It sounds like quite a business. Mrs. Niemerg is about our height, but Mr. Niemerg is the tallest man we have ever talked to. They are from Stockholm, Sweden. Imagine this: They presented us with a complete library. Mr. Niemerg said, 'You will notice there are two copies of each book—one for your home library, Santa, and one for the Quiet Hollows Library. That way all the elves have a library to enjoy.' We appointed Trinket Head Librarian. What a learning gift for all of us. But poor Buddy. He was picking up shipments for weeks and weeks. He never complained though, not even once, about the endless trips he made. I guess it's because he knows it's all part of the dream. I know all of us benefit from reading the books the Niemergs have given us.

"Santa is really happy that we have a lot of books for the little elves too. He has already taken quite a few to his office to preview. I saw one titled *How to Win a Friend* I thumbed through it, and it is all about pampering techniques. The book lists one hundred ways to pamper someone, to win them over as a friend. I really like that one.

"Mrs. Niemerg said they never have problems with their children getting to bed each night, because either she or Mr. Niemerg always reads them a story, which the children have picked out. I thought to myself, what a nice family time together. Even though children don't realize it when they're really young, when they get older, these moments at bedtime will certainly be a keepsake memory. Money can't buy that! I wish we had been able to spend more time with Mr. and Mrs. Niemerg. They are a great treasure. They shared many stories with us and all of them were so interesting. We hated to see them leave but we do keep close contact with them, and they with us. Once again, the Niemergs are also very generous donors to our Kris Kringle Foundation.

"To this day, books arrive here from all over the world, thanks to the Niemergs. The Quiet Hollows Library is a great place to visit, read a book, and have a cup of tea or coffee. It's busy all the time. We're so glad of that, because Santa and I know the more you read, the more you want to read, and the smarter you become. Santa tells the children in the day care who don't want to learn to read, 'Just think of something that puts you in a good mood. Then, whatever that something is, find a book that talks about it. Chances are, you will begin to love reading without even realizing it. Then you will want to share what you read with others, like your friends, sisters, brothers, Mom, and Dad.' Santa is very smart. One reason is he loves to read. Santa also tells the little elves to choose good things to read that will help them and others in their lives. That's how reading can make this world a better place to live in. Santa always has something helpful to say to the little elves to raise their level of thought.

"Next we have…let's see…oh, yes, Mr. and Mrs. Thomas. They are from Kiev, Ukraine. Santa greeted them in their native language. They felt very special to be visiting with us. They gave us a magnificent gift: a DVD library. We have educational DVDs, how-to DVDs, and movie DVDs. It's a massive collection. We store the entertainment DVDs in the movie room; all the rest are in the Quiet Hollows Library. This is brand-new technology for the elves. They're still overwhelmed by having all this drama, comedy, and instruction at their fingertips. All ages benefit from it. That includes Santa and me too. We are all very blessed.

"I remember when Mr. Dimmerling came here from Madrid, Spain. He owns his own electric company, and he gave us a gift of twenty transmitters for Santa, myself, and the heads of every department. We used to have to chase people down to talk to them, but now we can communicate instantaneously at all times. Mr. Dimmerling has saved us so much time over the years. Our special friends have grown to such great numbers that now I have to refer to lists to remember everyone's name. But Mr. Dimmerling was one of the very first CEOs to commit to our dream.

"When Mr. Dimmerling brought the transmitters here, Santa tried an experiment. He went to his office and sent Mr. Dimmerling to his bedroom. Santa would say, 'What do you see?' Mr. Dimmerling replied, 'I see a painting of your wife, Susie, and another of the dogs with the parrots.' It was starting to sound like a mind-reading act. Santa said, 'That's right! What is on the bed?' Mr. Dimmerling answered, 'A piece of paper with notes on it.' 'Right again,' said Santa. 'Please bring those to me.' When they met up again a few minutes later, after playing with the new transmitters some more, Santa told Mr. Dimmerling that this new way of communicating would definitely save all of us a lot of time here at the Christmas Village. We thanked Mr. Dimmerling for being so kind. He certainly was, and is to this day, a wonderful lifesaver, in many ways. He is another great contributor to our foundation."

Susie said, "There is a precious couple I will never forget, and that is Mr. and Mrs. Mattox from Canberra, Austria. They own their own phone company, and they presented us with a phone system. Mr. Mattox ran wires throughout the castle and to all the homes while they were here. We now could stay in touch with everyone just by picking up a phone. This is so much easier on the elves, since they don't have to run all over the village to deliver messages anymore. It took Mr. Mattox a few weeks to get the project done, and Buddy was a huge help to him. During that time, Mrs. Mattox and I became good friends, and to this day we still keep in touch. It's astounding how many people's lives they have changed all over the world with phone technology. They also contribute many times a year to our foundation. They are a very generous couple.

"Lon, Mr. and Mrs. Mattox are extraordinary people, but I have to say that it is typical of our guests to have working vacations at the North Pole. Besides contributing freely to our foundation, so many of our friends give generously of their time, energy, and expertise while they are here. They find ways to save us time so we can have quality lives with our families, even while we build more and more toys for children. This is what we love to do, as you well know. And we are so fortunate to be able to do it.

"Another good friend is a very special lady, Miss France. She owns and operates an old-fashioned jukebox company. She presented us with one here at the castle, and four more for our clubs. Santa said, 'Out with the 45s and in with the new CDs.' Goober was flying by, and he kept screeching, 'Out with the old, in with the new,' giving us all a great laugh, as always. Santa likes to use the best of the new technology here at the North Pole. Still, they did keep an old jukebox at the Eagle Ridge. Nostalgia has value too. That was a fun year here. Miss France told us, 'One of the happiest times of the day is after school. A lot of the children stop in my company on the way home, to play the jukebox. I love to watch them dance and have fun. Sometimes, I even dance with them!' We will never forget this sweet lady, Miss France, from Tokyo, Japan. She is a very giving benefactor to our foundation.

"Let me look at my notes, Lon. Oh yeah, I see here Mr. and Mrs. James. Did they ever have style! They own a towel company in Moscow, Russia. They have supplied us with oversize towels, hand towels, and washcloths for the bath, plus dish towels, dishcloths—the list goes on. Out of thousands of styles, they chose for us a white towel with red embroidery that reads "The North Pole." To this day, they take care of all our towel needs. They are also big supporters of the Kris Kringle Foundation, every year without fail, and we're only one of their favorite charities. They contribute so much to so many good causes around the world. They both have really big hearts, and I know they would give you the shirt off their back, if you needed it. I admire their extraordinary character. I really miss them. They are both jewels, no doubt about that.

"Another quite exceptional couple is Mr. and Mrs. Hoober. I spoke to them in Chinese since they are from Lanzhou, China. They own a furnace manufacturing company. Mr. Hoober and some of his family members invented a new type of heater. It looks like a real burning fireplace but doesn't burn lumber. Right away, that caught our attention. The heater heats up to sixty-six degrees. If it accidentally gets any hotter, it shuts off automatically. If you touch this heater when it's on, or if you place anything within thirty inches of the heater, it will shut off.

"It turns out, this unit is powered by a magnetic power pack. You crank the heater three or four times, take the handle out of the unit, and place the handle in its holder. In just thirty seconds, the heater will run on its own, without electricity. This revolutionary heater is totally safe and completely quiet. To shut it off, you just stand within thirty inches of it and the safety shutoff takes over. Santa couldn't wait to tell Ivy about this invention, since no more wood would have to be burned for heat. What a boon to conservation! We use this heater today. This is our newest technology at the North Pole.

"Mr. and Mrs. Hoober were so generous. They not only supplied the whole castle with this heating system, but they installed it in all of the elves' homes too. Many are built into the old fireplaces so it looks like there's a fire burning. It's very cozy. Clean heat, no mess, no ashes, no electricity, absolute safety, and the atmosphere of a fire-place. It has changed our lives, Lon. Santa and I hope we can someday meet the rest of the Hoober family who helped invent these magnifi-cent heaters.

"Lon, that was the year we really started to have a lot of changes around here, all because of magnetic power. We were sad to see the Hoobers leave, because they are so precious to us. Their donations to the Kris Kringle Foundation have increased each year. They say they give because they can. Santa and I keep in close touch with them. They're really extended family.

"Lon, I'm going to share with you a few more stories, because I really want you to know it's not just Santa and I, Buddy, and the elves who help children every year. We honor, admire, thank, and are blessed with many Kris Kringle Foundation extra-special friends. Our dream would never have grown to such proportions if it weren't for everyone working together as a team. The impact is global and con-stantly amazing!

"Now I must tell you about a Mr. and Mrs. Shepler from San Rafael, Costa Rica. This family owns a compressor manufacturing company. They brought to us still another new technology. They pre-sented us with air compressors that run on the magnetic power source, and not on electricity. These compressors are a marvel. They produce the air to run all kinds of tools, power saws, woodcutting machines, automatic screwdrivers, and automatic hammers, to name a few, that speed up the process of putting a lot of the toys together. No more doing this work by hand. And they do all this with absolute quiet. Now, even more toys can go out to boys and girls on Christmas Eve. Santa told Mr. and Mrs. Shepler, 'You have no idea how much time you have saved our elves.' Our design staff has really moved forward, designing all kinds of tools and appliances and fun things around this magnetic power source. They are definitely tickled by the possibilities.

"Mr. Shepler runs the compressor company, and Mrs. Shepler teaches art in high school. In one of her classes, they use a compressor to spray-paint one-of-a-kind art projects. Her students love the professional results; many of them proudly display their artwork on their walls at home. Mr. Shepler is very proud of his wife. He told us what a great teacher she is. Having talked with her at length, I can certainly agree. Mr. and Mrs. Shepler also donate to the Kris Kringle Foundation a few times a year They both love children and are a big part of helping us make children's dreams come true.

"I now want to share with you the story of a very caring couple, Mr. and Mrs. McCarley from Jerusalem, Israel. They own a chair manufacturing company. When they came, they gave Santa and me our very own power chairs. They also gave many to the clubs and the library. These chairs draw on a magnetic power source to create a vibrating massage for your body, with or without heat. When Santa first tried one out, he fell asleep. The McCarleys and I tiptoed out of the room and left him to nap a bit. Santa works very hard, and he looked as peaceful as a baby. I didn't have the heart to wake him. Later on, Santa apologized to the McCarleys for dozing off. He said he couldn't help it because this new chair was so comfortable and he was so relaxed. Mrs. McCarley just laughed. She said the same thing happens to Mr. McCarley all the time. Obviously, we just fell in love with the chairs. They're so wonderful.

"At the end of the week, we were able to spend a few days with the McCarleys. We started a wonderful friendship, the four of us, that will last a lifetime. They are very special to us and always will be. Mr. and Mrs. McCarley also give to the Kris Kringle Foundation several times a year. Santa and I speak of them often, and we try to keep connected through email and by phone. Their friendship over the years has been a real treasure to us.

"Then we have Mr. and Mrs. Hamilton from Dublin, Ireland. They own their own clothing manufacturing company. They were kind enough to make robes for Santa and me—and for everyone in the entire village. We also have a huge stockpile of robes to serve many,

many guests for years to come. It's such a nice personal touch here at the village. Everyone takes one home as a souvenir. Let me explain the detail that is on them. They are all white, then on the back of the robe is an embroidered picture of the Lady Laverne Mountain, with the forest all around, and the words "The North Pole." We embroider the guest's name on the front pocket. They brought us the machine to do all the lettering—"

I interrupted Mrs. Claus. "Yes, I really love my robe, Mrs. Claus." "Oh, of course, Lon. I was forgetting. We hope every time you wear it back home, you will think of us, as we will be thinking of you." I replied, "Mrs. Claus, when I unpacked, I noticed how personalized everything was. I was really overwhelmed. Many thanks to you and Santa for being so generous to me. I am certain I will get many years of wear out of my robe too." Mrs. Claus smiled and said, "The Hamiltons still send us these long white robes to give to our many guests. Even though we give so many away each year, our stock never goes down. It makes them feel good to help out as much as they can. Our guests send them thank-you cards all the time. Remind me later and I'll get you their address." "I'd like that," I said. "The Hamiltons are very giving people, and we had a very special time with them while they were here.

"By now, Lon, I'm sure I have filled your ears with enough stories to last a month of Sundays, but let me tell you one more, and then you can move on to your next adventure. This couple I want to tell you about is Mr. and Mrs. Snell. They are from Houston, Texas. You're going to be really surprised, I'm sure, as we were, when I tell you what they did for us. They shipped a ten-lane bowling alley to the North Pole for us. They sure did. They told Santa and me about it when they first came and showed us photos, because the bowling alley hadn't arrived yet. Mr. and Mrs. Snell said it would use a little electricity, just to get the bowling alley going. When you push the big, red master button, it starts up the magnetic power motors, then the electricity shuts off and the magnetic power takes over. Santa knew our design staff would have fun with the magnetic power and that all the elves would enjoy the bowling alley. Mr. Snell designated two of the lanes for the little ones, and he added bumpers to keep the ball from rolling into the gutter. If a little elf's ball rolls only halfway down the lane, a 'poofer' automatically blows air and pushes the ball on down the lane to the pins. That made Santa smile. Mr. Snell had thought of the children.

"Once the bowling alley arrived, it took four weeks of hauling to move the materials to the site. What a job that was, but also a very exciting time. Buddy read the directions and gave instructions to his crew. It took a few weeks and many elves to help put it together, but they really had a lot of fun doing it. And now they get a real charge out of playing the game. Mr. and Mrs. Snell told us, 'We do everything big here in Texas.' These Texans are something.

"Lon, that year all of the elves were honored with a lot of unexpected pleasures. Santa said people were beginning to realize, if it weren't for all the elves doing all these jobs, they just wouldn't get done. And we continue to receive gifts from so many people around the world, for which we all are so grateful. Not only are all the children of the world getting gifts now, but we are really blessed too. It is all coming back to us many times over. Santa tells the children in the day care all the time, 'If you give, you will receive.' It is so true."

I commented that many of these gifts were technologically advanced. They aren't in stores or on the Internet. Mrs. Claus reminded me, "Most all these people own their own companies, so we get items that may still be in development. They send us prototypes, some of the first pieces made. We may even have some collector's items.

"We visit with so many people, Lon. It takes almost the full three months to get to everyone, but we do enjoy them so. Santa and I continue to spread the word, 'Do good for people, and it will always come back to you.' Lon, I am sure you have experienced this to be true." I said, "Yes, I have found that to be true over and over again, throughout my entire life. You're absolutely right! Mrs. Claus, Santa and you are true examples of giving, year after year after year. I am so moved by what you started many years ago. I can see that everyone here at the village gives their all, and for that, you have been rewarded continually with a host of blessings. What a grand and rare opportunity I have been given to meet you and see all this." Mrs. Claus said, "Thank you, Lon. We live our lives doing what we love to do. I'm so glad you found your way here to the North Pole and our village, where our whole life revolves around making children happy. It's been such a pleasure." Mrs. Claus took my hands in hers and gave me one of her genuinely warm smiles. "Lon, you are a kindred spirit. I will miss you."

Chapter Twenty-One
The Librarian and the Dairy Farmer

Britches feeds Molly, Polly, Dolly, Bullets, and the chickens.

I was in a reflective mood after speaking with Mrs. Claus, and I was thinking the Quiet Hallows Library might be a perfect stop right about now. The librarian met me at the door. "Welcome, Lon. I'm Trinket. How about a cup of coffee?" Trinket and I talked for the longest time about books. She knew where every book was shelved. Inside, "The Niemergs" was carved in wood above the door. Mrs. Claus told me earlier the Niemergs had donated books of all kinds to the Quiet Hallows Library, and here their family name was immortalized. Trinket said, "We never want to forget, Lon, about the people who have given to us in Santa's Christmas Village at the North Pole. The

Niemergs are good friends of ours. They were here only once, but we still receive books from that family."

Trinket's husband, Britches, came in to see her. He said hi and asked if I was enjoying the library. I replied, "It's a very beautiful library. Trinket keeps it looking great!" Britches looked around and said, "I remember when we were building this library. We worked hard and it came together quickly. We now have a coffee and tea area, thanks to Trinket. That was her idea." Britches gave Trinket a little squeeze and said, "I just came by to say hi. Come over to the dairy later, Lon." I replied, "Okay, I will." Then Britches was off. Trinket said, "Lon, have you ever heard of a library called the Quiet Hallows? 'Hallows' means shrine." "Wow, that really shows how much Santa and everyone here value books," I said.

We talked about a lot of things, including her family. I said, "I hear you have three daughters." Trinket said, "Yes, I do. They work over at the Sewing Department. Their names are Velvet, Petunia, and Touch. Today, they are sewing dolls' clothes for the many dolls that are made here. Those daughters of mine really have fun with all the other ladies in the department." I asked, "Do you ever go join them?" "Yes, especially in the fall." said Trinket. "That's our busy time around here, building up to Christmas, so I help out over at the Sewing Department or the Wrapping Department, wherever they need me." I asked her about her trip to the North Pole, and she said, "Do you have time?" "I sure do and I love stories." Trinket said, "Good. Let me start.

"My daughters saw the ad that Kris Kringle ran in the newspapers. Our girls just wouldn't stop talking about it. They'd say, 'Let's go there, Mom!' Their dad wanted to know all about it, so they filled him in, and he was all for it. Well, they finally convinced me, and we were off to the North Hills.

"We had quite a journey. We took a ship, then a train, then did lots of walking. Britches packed the carts plumb full. With four ladies in our family, the carts were bulging to overflowing. We were squashed like pickles in a pickle jar. Our cows pulled hard. We had our sewing gear, sewing machines, clothes, furniture, and many other items. We looked like a traveling flea market, just waiting for our load to burst.

To add to all that, Britches said, 'I must take the tools of my trade.' So he had one bull, three cows, and a flock of chickens with their little chicks and cages to keep them all in. We had cheese-making equipment, buckets, butter churns, so much stuff I can't remember it all.

"We sailed away from home, Guatemala, Central America. Then we took a train to Jemdaza. We traveled far and had some hardships, but we did it as a family. Britches refused to sell his prized dairy cows, so they made it to the North Pole with us. Buddy met us and he was such a help. We thought we'd have it a little easier living here at the North Pole, because we had money. But since we've been here, we've never even used money, ever. It's like having play money. No one uses money here at Santa's Christmas Village. It isn't necessary. Everyone here has a good life without it.

"We were so glad that we brought the animals. Now we had eggs, milk, yogurt, cheese, butter, cream—so many products. And Britches enjoys running the dairy business.

"Our girls, Velvet, Petunia, and Touch, were thrilled to be a help in the Sewing Department. Our very first day here, they fell in love with this place. Once we got settled in, we all knew this was the best move we ever made.

"Long story short, all three of our girls married three wonderful men here, all in the same year. We have such a precious family, and we're all together here at the North Pole. I couldn't want more. Velvet married Skooter, who runs the garden. Touch married Luigi, the lumberjack. Petunia married Lincoln, who is in charge of Santa's sleighs. We are all so happy here. We would never even think about leaving. And all of my grandsons work with their grandfather. So we're really one big happy family within the one big happy family that makes up Santa's Christmas Village.

"Britches was the only elf who walked all the way from Jemdaza with his cows and bull. The cows' names are Molly, Polly, and Dolly. The young bull's name is Bullets. Britches said he talked to the cows all the way to the North Pole. When the lumberjacks cut trees, Wisp and Jesse now use our carts to transport the small wood branches up to the Lumber Department. So everything we brought has been put to good use.

"Since we have been here and among our own people, we all get along so well. We knew this was the place for us. We felt honored when we arrived and everyone welcomed us. We knew people had to eat, and we could provide a service with our dairy products. However, we knew nothing about making toys. So, we went to work.

"Santa and Mrs. Claus greeted us, and everyone—most of all, the chefs—was excited to see our animals. The carpenters got to work on the barn right away. Our Jersey cows are some of the best. They produce lots of milk every day. Chef Ice started to make chocolate milk, cherry milk, strawberry milk, mint milk, orange-flavored milk, blueberry-flavored milk, and all kinds of milkshakes in any flavor you could possibly think of. We branched out into ice cream, cream for coffee, cottage cheese, yogurt, even yogurt ice cream, butters, cream cheese, and cheese of all kinds. Chef Diamond and Chef Ruby baked a divine buttermilk cake and all kinds of cheesecakes. These chefs were thrilled to get their hands on all of our products, especially the eggs. They stopped using powdered eggs as soon as we arrived, because they now had glorious fresh eggs and milk. All the elves really enjoyed eating all these foods again, thanks to Britches. And Britches was so moved to be such a big part of our wonderful new community. Let's go see Britches now, over at the dairy." Trinket and I left the library and took a walk over to the barn.

Britches saw us coming and said, "Hello, Mom." Trinket replied, "I am not your mother." We all laughed. "I love my girls, and they keep me in line," said Britches. Britches was a real kidder, I was finding out.

"Since we had the largest family here," said Britches, "Santa gave us his and Mrs. Claus's log home. And that's when they made their move to the castle. So we live in the big house." "Britches!" Trinket scolded. "Okay, Trinket. See, Lon, these ladies keep me in line." Britches was definitely a card.

"But seriously, Lon," said Britches, "at first we took over part of the raindeer stables. But in a few weeks, Santa and the other elves had built us a small barn for all of the cows and chickens. It was really neat. Over the years, we wound up with about ten cows and forty chickens. As soon as we worked out the elves' sleeping cycle, the design staff went to work on equipment that would milk the cows January through March. The machine they built automatically stored the milk right into holding tanks, and it made butter, buttermilk, cream, whipped cream for pies, cheese, everything.

"The automatic machinery was built into the floor, right where the cows ate their feed. While the cows ate, the machines milked. It was sheer genius. The machines were on timers. Twenty minutes and the job was done, then the machines would detach from the cows. The feed was stored up in the barn and ran on timers too." Britches showed me the barn and how it all worked. "Hey, Lon, do you see the egg collector over there? When the chicken lays an egg, it rolls down here. Then it ends up there and is placed in the basket by the placing machine. When the basket is full of eggs, it is picked up by the machine and another basket is placed here to collect more eggs. Our design staff is phenomenal."

I said, "Britches, how did you get your name?" Britches replied. "I was afraid you would ask that question. Well there wasn't much room for my stuff on the cart, so I packed the least. All my ladies took up most of the space. I love my old coveralls, so I brought those, and my girls called me Britches. The name just kind of stuck, I guess.

"When we arrived here, everyone was so kind to us. My girls met gentlemen they cared for. Trinket and I were so pleased. What a wedding they had! We were all family. My ladies were so happy. I'm just thrilled we came here. My animals had a long rest when we arrived. Then the raindeer were glad when we got out of their stables. But now I look back, and it's plain as the nose on your face that we're better off here. The animals are well taken care of, the girls are happy, and, you know, if Mamma is happy, everyone's happy. I'm teasing Mamma, but she's used to it by now. And Lon, my Jersey Cows are my life There are times I help out on the production line with the toys. But there is much to do at the barn. One thing I can say is that the chocolate at the candy store tastes better now—no more powdered milk like when we first arrived. Now, all of the chefs can make the real thing. The things those chefs come up with, Lon…you couldn't get us to move from here.

"I never dreamed we would live like this. I have so many friends here. Trinket and the girls just love it here. This year, Lon, I am going to be a grandfather again. Isn't that wonderful? I'm telling you, Lon, excitement abounds here. I am so beyond happy." "I think you and your family have the best life here, Britches," I said. "It's heartwarming to see. Thanks so much for sharing your stories with me." Talking about food had got my appetite up, so we hugged and I left the happy couple for some of that great Baker's Dozen pastry.

Buttons had a Danish pastry I'd been wanting to try. It was a raspberry torte Danish. Wow! Was it good! It wouldn't do for me to live here long. This food was too excellent for my waistline. I was leaving the bakery, munching on my pastry, when Goober and Sammie flew up and landed on my shoulder. "Hey Lon, what do you think?" I said, "Goober, this is spectacular. I've never seen anything like it." Sammie said, "What did you like the most?" "Wow, that's a tough question. Well, I truly enjoyed meeting all of the elves. They were the highlight of my trip. And, of course, Santa, Mrs. Claus, and Buddy. And I'll never forget you and your family and the dogs." Goober said, "Are you going to stay?" "No, I must leave. I have family back home, and I must return." Goober and Sammie fully understood. Goober said, "Do you plan on sharing some of that Danish?" I laughed and replied, "Sure." I broke off a piece for Goober and a piece for Sammie. I had to think, was this a dream or what? Lost at the North Pole and talking to parrots. Will anyone ever understand what happened to me? I went back to the bakery for another Danish, thanks to Goober and Sammie. While I was there, Santa stopped in to get a Danish pastry also. I guess they were pretty popular. He said, "Care to join me, Lon? I'm off to read to the day care children. All of the little elves are waiting for me." I said, "Let's go!" I loved being read to by Santa.

Santa entered the day care, walked over to the big chair, and settled in. All the little elves were anxiously waiting to get a hug from Santa, their great friend. He spent time with each elf. "Hello, Skip. How are you today? Can you jump-rope?" Skip was little, but she was good at it. "Hello, Buzz. How is that pet bee of yours doing?" "Fine, Santa." "Did you visit your bee this morning?" "Sure did, Santa, and thanks for asking me." I later found out that a little bee would meet Buzz every morning at his house and would follow him all the way to the day care. Then, his bee would fly back to work with the other bees. That's how Buzz got his name.

"Hello there, Skates." "Hello Santa." "Have you been skating slow?" "Yes, Santa." "My, how did you get those scraped knees?" "Well, my skates…oh it's a long story, Santa." I could tell she was just learning to skate, and she skated everywhere she went. Wheels were embedded in the soles of her shoes, and that's how she got her name, Skates. "How's my Wannabee doing?" Wannabee wanted to be anywhere but the day care, so they always tried to keep him occupied. "How's Sugar today?" Sugar loved lollipops. "I'm fine, Santa." "So, are you all ready for me to read?" All of the little elves gave an excited "Yes!" And Santa began to read the story of "The Lost Elf."

"Once upon a time, a young and bold elf came to live in Santa's Christmas Village. He was five years old and very brave. His name was Snap because he would always snap his fingers. He decided to take a day trip. 'Now, you know, Santa's Village is huge and there are lots of areas that we cannot go into,' said his mother. 'We don't want to get hurt.' Snap decided to check out the place anyway. He ran behind this tree and sneaked behind that bush until he made his way to the village. He walked through the village and found the garden. He sampled some strawberries and blueberries, and off he went. Well, he was so small that he was overlooked. He made his way to the raindeer stalls. His favorite raindeer was Veben, the smallest of the raindeer. He would pet Veben and talk to him. Today Veben was tired and was starting to lie down in the hay, and so did Snap.

"When Snap's mother went looking for him, Snap was nowhere to be found. The red alert sounded, and over the music speaker a voice said, 'This is Mrs. Claus. Please stop what you are doing. We need to find a missing elf, Snap.' Everyone started to search everywhere. Every room, every house, the stables were all checked; the storage room was checked, every home. No Snap. Just where could he be? They checked inside the sleighs; they checked the garden. Still no Snap. Snap was lost.

"Everyone was starting to get very concerned. Then someone said, 'Could Snap have gotten outside?' The lumberjacks, Stefano and Luigi, looked outside. No footprints were found in the snow. 'He's not out here.' Everyone was checking everywhere but Snap was nowhere to be found. I said, 'Everyone, calm down. As I said, let's search every room again. I will check the raindeer stables, since they need to be fed.'

"I entered the stables and checked each stall. When I arrived at Veben's stall, there was Veben, lying down and resting, and right beside him was Snap taking a nap. I gently placed my hand on Snap's shoulder to wake him up; I didn't want to alarm him. Then I said to him, 'Snap, you gave us a little scare. We didn't know where you were.' I scooped him up and took him outside. Everyone was happy to see Snap in my arms. After all the excitement calmed down, I spoke on the speaker system and said, 'Children, always remember to never go out alone. And always tell someone where you're going, because we don't want to lose any of you.' The End."

During Santa's story, all of the kids had big eyes at times, and gave a huge sigh of relief when Snap was found.

I noticed the children were all wearing a pin on their shirts. I asked Santa about it. He said, "Bubbles' staff came up with a great little invention, 'The Happy Pin.'" Santa gave one to each child to wear. That made the pins special, so they all liked to wear them. What the children didn't know was the Happy Pin had a chip built into it and the Wiz computer knew where each child was at all times. That way, no one would be lost. Every parent made sure their child wore their Happy Pin from Santa every day. The invention staff always had something up their sleeves, and this one was a keeper.

The day care at Santa's Christmas Village was a happening place. The children would go on field trips to the garden, to the candy store, to the bakery, to the stables, to the kitchen and dining room, and Santa would come visit and read a new story as often as he could. Santa's stories were written down in books, so the children could hear them again and again. They all learned a lot from Santa's stories, which were like sweet medicine—they went down easy. I thought how grand it would have been to grow up at the North Pole on Santa's knee.

Chapter Twenty-Two
The Fish Hatchery

The fish multiply, thanks to Bear, Sparkle, and Scars.

Bear, Scars, and Sparkle had a story for me about the fish hatchery. Here's how it went... One day, Bear, Scars, and Sparkle decided to have a talk with Santa. "You do it." "No, you do it." "Okay, I'll do it." "You push the doorbell." "No, you push the doorbell." "I'll push the doorbell." "Did you hear anything?" "No, did you hear anything?" "That was the new doorbell." "You don't hear it, it just buzzes inside the castle."

Sir King, Goober, and Sammie raced to the door. Mrs. Claus opened it, and there stood Bear, Scars, and Sparkle. Mrs. Claus said, "Can I help you with something?" "No ma'am, we need to speak to Santa," said Bear. "Okay, come on in and I will go get Santa." "Where is Lady Queen?" asked Sparkle. "She's not feeling well today," said Mrs. Claus. "She's lying down." "We're sorry to hear that, Mrs. Claus," said Bear. "Thank you, boys. Let me get my husband for you.…Santa, you have company!"

Santa was in the middle of a snack. He put down his sandwich and said, "I'll finish this later. These boys must have something very important to tell me. Hello, boys." "Hello, Santa," they said. "Step into my office. Let me pull up a few chairs. Should I get Mrs. Claus?" "No, you're who we want." Lady Queen was lying by the fireplace. Sir King was now near Santa, and Goober and Sammie were on their stands. There were extra stands throughout the castle so the parrots could land and rest, and of course, barge in on all of the conversations. Santa said, "Who would like to start?" Bear said, "I was chosen to speak." "Okay Bear, I will listen. I will save my questions for the very end. Okay, you may start, Bear."

Bear said, "Santa, us boys have noticed, it's taking us longer and longer to catch fish, so we need to correct this problem. Here is our idea. We'll catch a few fish and put them in a holding tank until they lay eggs. Once the eggs are fertilized, we will gather them up so the other fish don't eat them. Then we'll put those eggs in a special tank with aerators so the tank gets plenty of oxygen. When the baby fish hatch, we'll put them in the first tank until we have more eggs. Then we'll move the little fish to the second tank. The baby fish will be one-to-three inches long. Tank number three is for fish four-to-seven inches long. Tank number four is for eight-to-fourteen inches long. Number five is for fifteen-to-twenty-four inches long. When they get that big, we will release them into the river. We will keep moving the fish through the cycle until we have a fully stocked river.

"We will need to feed the fish pellets made from corn, sugar, and wheat. We feel in one to one-in-a-half years, we will have thousands of fish to put into the J'Yakaboo River. All we need is a room approximately twenty by forty feet to accomplish this. We'd need help building the tanks and also running the air pumps to all of the tanks. The engineers might help with moving water from these tanks to bring in fresh water so we can keep the fish clean and healthy. We could eventually use this system with shrimp and lobster. But we want to do only fish at first. All three of us are willing to do the work. We feel this would be a benefit to the community, since everyone would have plenty of fish to eat and fishing would be more fun this way. Scars and Sparkle, did I leave anything out?"

Bear, Scars, and Sparkle had gone over this plan till they were blue in the face. Bear had done a great job of explaining it and there was nothing to add. They were ready for the challenge. Bear said, "Do you have any questions, Santa?"

"Wow! Sounds like you have quite a plan," said Santa. "Who is going to feed these fish when all of the elves are asleep in the Sleeping Chamber, January through March? That's ninety days." Scars replied, "Well Santa, we thought the design staff could put automatic feeders in for us like they did for the raindeer." Santa said, "Okay, sounds great. Let me talk this over with the design engineers. I will get back with you three." "Well, Santa," said Sparkle. "We were thinking, could you talk to them tonight?" Santa just laughed. "Can I keep your drawings? Okay, I will speak to Bubbles and Shadow tonight." The three fishermen thanked Santa, shook his hand, and out the door they went.

Goober said, "Do those boys know what they're getting into? Sounds like work to me." "Goober, calm down," said Sammie. Goober replied, "I don't know. What if they drop the ball?" "Goober, give the boys a chance," said Sammie. Santa always gives everyone a chance. I think the boys have a great idea." Goober said, "I don't know." Santa had been listening to the parrots' conversation, and it seemed to help him make a decision.

Santa picked up the phone and called Bubbles. Bubbles answered, "Good evening, Santa. What can I do for you?" "Bubbles, could you and Shadow come and see me now at my office?" Bubbles grabbed Shadow and they went to see Santa. Santa didn't waste any time. He shared the fishermen's ideas and diagrams with his design people and said, "Well, what do you think?" Santa held his hand up toward Goober as if to say, "Don't say a word." Finally, Bubbles spoke, "Well, I think it is possible, but we will need to control the fish smell. That would be our first concern. The second concern is where can we do this without creating a mess?" Santa said, "It could turn out great. If everything goes as planned, eighteen months from now, catching fish will really be a lot of fun." Bubbles and Shadow looked at each other and nodded. Shadow said, "Why don't we give the boys a chance?" "Okay then." said Santa. "Let's make this happen. I will tell Bear, Sparkle, and Scars tomorrow." "Well, Santa, they were sitting on your steps when we came in." Santa smiled at their persistence. "Let me go talk to the boys now then."

Santa, Bubbles, and Shadow stepped out of the castle, and the boys stood up. "Well, we're going to use your ideas and make the fish hatchery work." Bear, Scars, and Sparkle burst into unbridled joy. When the noise quieted down, Santa continued, "Bubbles is going to make your first tank tomorrow, using the vita ore stone. He has a new process that will make this easier. You will have glass tanks that you can see through to follow the fish's progress. Also, go by and visit Buttons. Check to see if he has any leftover bread. Start saving it; the fish are going to love it."

The next day, Bubbles started on the glass tank for the eggs. He figured he had three months to build the next one. Bear, Scars, and Sparkle caught a few fish and put them in the holding tank until the new tank could be finished. Santa said, "Bubbles, do you remember the storage room over next to the river? Could we empty it out for the boys?" "Well Santa, maybe we can combine that stuff with the storage for the sleighs for a while." "Great idea, Bubbles." When Wrinkles saw the boys carting boxes into the sleigh storage room, he was curious. "What's going on, Bubbles?" "We're in the fish raising business." Wrinkles just shook his head. He figured all would come clear eventually.

Bubbles did get the tank all set up and ran air to it, then the boys filled it up with water and dropped in ten fish. Sure enough, in about ten days, the fish laid their eggs. Bear, Scars, and Sparkle moved the fish back to the holding tank. "Now we have our tankful of eggs!" said Sparkle. They were all so excited. What they didn't know was they had tens of thousands of eggs. The Design and Engineering Department worked on a filtration system to keep the tanks clean. The concept worked great, and they asked Bubbles for tank number two. "Easy now, we have time," said Bubbles. Meanwhile, the three fish hatchers kept gathering eggs out of the holding tanks so they always had eggs in the hatching tank, tank number one.

Always the marvel, Bubbles finished the number two tank ten weeks early. Three weeks later, the eggs started hatching, and Bear, Scars, and Sparkle started moving the little fish to tank number two. They fed the fish the tiniest crumbs they'd saved up from the bakery's day-old bread. Santa stopped by to see how the operation was going and sprinkled some crumbs on the water for the little fish. "Looks good, boys," he said.

Three months into it, the fish in tank number two were one to three inches long. Bubbles had tank three, four, and five already set up, and one back-up tank just in case. The boys kept shuttling the fish from one tank to the other. Six months into the project, they were awfully tired, but their idea was working. The automatic feeders were in place and all the tanks were in operation.

When Wrinkles woke up the elves after their long sleep, the boys were excited to see how their fish were doing. They were happy to see the fish hatchery was thriving. Santa had kept an eye on the operation. Once he had to move them all, and he said it took him all day. So, the Design Department came up with a brilliant solution. They added a wood base with wheels to each tank. Now you could roll the tank to the next hookup instead of moving all the fish. Rolling the tanks around made the job a lot easier. This proved to be an incredible improvement and a turning point. All of the elves were talking about it and stopping by the fish hatchery.

Santa had hooked up the spare tank. With eight to fourteen fish, he thought it might be needed. The engineers added a new vent to the outdoors so the room always smelled fresh. Everything was working great. Bear, Scars, and Sparkle took turns feeding the fish once a day, and before long they had fifteen to twenty-four fish. It was time to release the first fish. The boys rolled out the tank and captured the fish in a net. As they lowered them into the J'Yakaboo River, the whole village was clapping. The forward-thinking Bear, Scars, and Sparkle released their fish over the next five years, at which time the river became fully stocked. The fish didn't need their help anymore. The fish hatchery experiment was a resounding success.

"What an experience!" said Scars. "We became known as the 'great fishermen of Santa's Christmas Village.'" Sparkle said, "When Santa toasted us at the celebration, he said, 'Always give people a chance. Over the last fifty years we have been catching and eating fish from the J'Yakaboo River all because of three little elves who have proved themselves to be three great elves.'" Then Bear jumped in, "Yes! And then Santa said, 'Please help me in thanking them.' And everybody clapped and shook our hands and we all celebrated with a village fish fry. It was terrific!

"Over the years, Santa has often said, 'Follow your dream. Think, plan, and give back to the world just like Bear, Scars, and Sparkle. Working so closely with the fish, they've even become better fishermen, ho-ho!'" Scars said, "Santa is so jolly, Lon. Then Santa said something that touched all three of us deep in our hearts. He said, 'I am so proud and privileged to call them my friends.'" Bear added, "Lon, we are so glad we gathered up our courage and spoke to Santa that day. Imagine what we would have missed, what our whole village would have missed, if we hadn't followed our dream of a fish hatchery." Wow! Just imagine. I had to agree.

Chapter Twenty-Three
The Texas Cowboy Bowling Party

The North Pole ten-lane bowling alley.

Midweek, I joined everyone over at the ten-lane bowling alley. It was reopening especially for the annual Texas Cowboy Bowling Party. Mrs. Claus outfitted me for the occasion. I arrived wearing a white cowboy hat, blue jeans, a bright blue western shirt with white piping and fringe, and cowboy boots. Thanks to Mrs. Claus, I fit in mighty fine with all of the elves. I couldn't wait to see what this night would be like. As it turned out, I was anything but disappointed.

When I arrived, Hammer and Beauty were all decked out in their western gear and they gave me a big "Howdy!" I wrote my name down on a card and dropped it into a box. Later on, these cards would be used to choose the bowling teams. Along came Hammer and Beauty's three children, the fishermen Scars and Sparkle, and their daughter, Winter. I went to shake hands and got some hugs instead. These people loved to hug. To an elf, a hug meant "hi" or "hello," "glad to see you." It was still kind of new to me, but I was getting to like it. I have never seen so many people, before or since, who showed as much respect for each other. I never heard any fussing the entire time I was at the Christmas Village, or on the production floor. Everyone got along so well. I guess the hugs were working.

Chef Ice was at the counter mixing any kind of soft drink anybody wanted. Diamond and Munch, and Ruby and Crunch were working on snacks for the party. Tapper joined Ice to give him a hand. The jukebox next to the dance floor was pumping out western music. The bowling alley was energized. I got to see how lanes nine and ten worked. These were the special lanes for the little ones. They were equipped with bumpers and poofers that made a gutter ball impossible. The ball always knocked over some bowling pins, and the little elves always had fun. Each lane had automatic scoring. All you did was put your name into the computer, then you were ready to bowl. Santa was giving the little ones a high five and they were all giggling, including Santa.

Tapper helped Ice get caught up with the drinks, then she punched in a country-western song on the jukebox and organized a line dance. "Lon, come join us." she said. There must have been twenty people on the dance floor. One of my student guides, Dallas, was there. He kept trying to help. "Two up, two back. Lon, follow me." We all watched Tapper. She was a great teacher but I was getting stampeded anyway. My boots were toeing when they should be heeling, and heeling when they should be toeing. I was bumping into people on my turns and sliding left when I should be going right. I was a disaster. Still, everyone was having a good laugh on me, and I thought it was funny too. After a while, I even started to catch on. It was a really good time.

I noticed, in the middle of the dance floor, huge red lettering that said "The North Pole," and all of the bowling lanes had signs that read "The North Pole" too. What was unique about the alley signs was that Mr. and Mrs. Snell, who had donated the bowling alley, designed the signs to light up and flash when you bowled a strike. All of the lanes were occupied, lights were flashing, and everyone was yelling and having fun. All of a sudden, Dallas shouted, "The other way, Lon!" But it was too late. We bumped into each other and laughed some more.

Hammer and Beauty took care of the bowling alley. It seemed to have an irregular schedule, but it was always scrubbed and shiny. Mrs. Claus and Santa were also dressed up in matching red and black western duds. That was a hoot and a half. They joined us on the dance floor. By now I was getting a handle on this dance, and Santa looked at me and said, "Lon, you're fitting in well." I nodded and tipped my hat to him. "Thank you, pardner," I said. I was having a ball.

The favorite drink of the evening seemed to be Ice's royal blizzard. Lazer supplied Ice with gallons of his flavored maple syrups, and the royal blizzards kept coming. Whippersnapper and Lazer put down their drinks and jumped into the line dance. Santa said, "Follow me, Lon. We're about to change dances. Dallas, let's give Lon a hand." But I needed a break, so I gave my apologies and moseyed on up to the bar for a tall, cool one. Actually, I had to move pretty quick to weave my way through the dancers on the floor. My royal blizzard was light blue and very fruity, just what I needed.

Wannabee, Skip, and Buzz wanted me to join them at the little elves' lanes, so I did for a bit. These little ones were good bowlers. Hot Rod, Chaps, and Zoie from the Mail Room came in and yelled, "Don't start the party without us!" That evening I bowled a one-eighty-three, which I thought was pretty good. But the elves were wiping the lanes with me. Their scores were all in the two-hundreds. Mrs. Claus and the lady elves were over on lanes one and two. They'd all scream and yell when one of them bowled a strike. Wannabee, Skip, and Buzz would jump up and down whenever they knocked any pins down.

Then Hammer turned off the regular lights and switched on the black lights. Wow! The bowling balls and pins glowed in the dark. If you made a strike, the lights would flash and flash. I looked at Rawhide and Tacoma, one lane over, and said, "This is way too cool."

Rawhide said, "Mr. and Mrs. Snell thought of everything. They customized this bowling alley just for us. Wild, huh?" Tacoma said, "Did you notice how the name of the high bowler flashes red above the pins at the end of the game on each lane? Who wouldn't want their name in lights, huh, Lon? It's so much fun." I had to admit, I'd sure like it, but I didn't have a chance with all of the outstanding bowlers in the room.

Santa and Mrs. Claus made the rounds, speaking to everyone, as usual. No one was left out. Santa stopped at the table where Bubbles, Shadow, Snickers, Ish, and Shooter were. Diagrams covered the tabletop, and they were talking about new toy inventions. Santa looked at their drawings and said, "Okay, guys. This is a party. Now, I want to see all of you party animals on the dance floor." They smiled at Santa and kept doing what they were doing. Santa spotted Tapper, Quicken, Glow, Paris, and Yawn and had a brainstorm. "Hey, gals. See those design engineers over there? How would you like to get those stick-in-the-mud elves up and out on the dance floor?" Well, I guess the ladies were only too happy to oblige, because they went straight over to the table and started pulling the guys out of their seats.

Santa watched with glee as all five couples took the dance floor. Tapper said, "Bubbles, work on that stuff later. Our Texas Cowboy Bowling Party only happens once a year." Santa shook his head and chuckled as the guys tried to avoid stepping on their partners' feet while moving in time with the music. Now he knew why they'd been glued to the design plans—they just didn't know how to dance. Tapper intervened and was giving all of them a quick lesson. They were pretty brave to get out there in the first place, and the steps were starting to come to them.

Santa came up to me and said, "Hey there, Lon. Come join me," and we stepped outside. He said, "Buddy was going to give me a hand, but he was busy." "Anything you want, Santa," I said, and meant it. With a big grin, he handed me half of a horse costume. Santa was holding the head and I was to be the tail end. Me and my big mouth. "Just follow me," he said. We entered the bowling alley neighing and whinnying, and the doors slammed shut behind us. Mrs. Claus snatched up little Skates and placed her on "our" back, since the idea was to give all the little ones a ride around the bowling alley. Santa and I tromped around in a circle and the little buckaroos whooped and hollered like regular cowboys and cowgirls.

An hour later, all of the little ones had enjoyed a fun ride on a horse. When Santa and I cranked our bodies upright again, the sweat was just pouring off of us. Santa looked at me and said, "Quite a workout, huh?" "You got that right, Santa," I replied. Santa slapped me on the shoulder and said, "Let's get a fresh drink and cool off." No one said anything when we cut in and went to the head of the line. Instead, they congratulated us. The little elves were still excited, talking about their horse ride. They'd had so much fun. Santa looked at me and said, "Good work, Lon." No drink ever tasted better.

Mrs. Claus said, "It's our turn, dear." "Our turn?" replied Santa. "They're doing karaoke and it's our turn to sing a country song." Poor Santa. He'd just sat down, but apparently the fun never stopped at the Texas Cowboy Bowling Party. Santa got up off the chair and put on his cowboy hat, and the Clauses launched into a song. Everybody clapped in time to urge them on. As soon as they finished, Fern and Nimbus started to sing. They did some fine yodeling. Then it was Wisp and Jesse's turn. Everyone was having fun doing something: singing, dancing, or bowling.

Over in the corner was a huge mechanical bull surrounded by a pit filled with spongy foam for a soft fall. Sporty was at the controls. He'd make the bull go up and down and spin around, tossing off the rider really fast. It didn't hurt because the foam cushioned the landing. Roxy would give the rider a hand getting up. Sporty caught me going by and said, "Ready for a bull ride, Lon?" I was determined to be game for anything tonight. "Sure," I said and sat on the bull. It was equipped with a huge set of horns made out of foam and had a big soft ring in its nose. This bull was really a pussycat. Sporty flipped the switch and the bull started bucking. Well, I lasted four and a half seconds before I was tossed off onto the comfy foam. "Roxy, could you help me up out of the pit, please?" I said. Everyone was clapping for me and a line was forming. They all thought they could beat my time, and they did. I have many fond memories of that Texas Cowboy Bowling Party. I was sad to see it end.

Elf Red rides the mechanical bull.

The next day, I spotted Santa a little ways ahead of me, hobbling along a bit slowly. I could only think his limbs must be as sore as mine. Everyone was still talking about our horse rides. They were the hit of the party. All the elves were back at work filling requests and stocking shelves. The toys were stacking up. Everything was in full swing on the production floor. I followed Santa to the day care. He was dropping in to see the little ones. Peace always enjoyed Santa's visits as much as the children did.

Santa spoke many languages and he wanted the children to learn more than one language too. He figured the sooner, the better, so Peace taught several languages at the day care. Often, Santa would quiz the children with something like "Let's count to ten in English, German, and Spanish." He felt if anyone ever wanted to leave the Christmas Village, they needed to be well educated and prepared for the outside world. Everyone studied, but no one ever left, of course, because life at the North Pole was more than enough. The elves were family, they had everything they needed, and they truly wanted to fulfill Santa's dream. Whenever Santa visited, the young elves would say, "Santa, read us a story! Read us a story!" And today was no different. Santa came prepared. He sat in his chair with the children gathered around and said, "Today I want to read to you 'The Story of Petey and Whitey.'

"Once upon a time, there was a young boy named Petey. He was a quiet boy, very shy, and kept to himself. Petey enjoyed school and was very good at math. The teacher would always say, 'Petey, you got all of the questions correct. Your grade is 100 percent!' The other boys didn't like him because they thought he was smarter than they were. They could never get a higher grade than Petey. But what they didn't know was he was very slow in science class, and his classmates teased him about it. Science was a subject he just didn't get. Petey also looked different. He had a couple of scars on his chin, one from when he crashed his bicycle and the other from when he fell out of a tree. So, the boys made fun of him some more.

"One day, Petey made friends with a boy named Whitey. They would stick close since Whitey was bigger than Petey and wanted to protect him from the boys who were picking on him. He would tell all of the other boys not to tease him, that it wasn't polite.

"Whitey happened to mention to Petey that he was really behind in math. 'I just don't get it,' said Whitey. Petey said, 'Let me give you a hand; I'm very good at math. I just wish I knew someone good in science.' Whitey said, 'I'm great in science. I'll help you.' So, both boys helped each other out and received great grades in both classes. Whitey told the other boys, 'No one wants to be laughed at or teased or be made fun of. Let's try to get along, because you never know when you will need a helping hand and someone right in your own backyard will be there to help you out.'"

Santa leaned forward in his chair, looked around the room at all the eager little faces, and said, "What a smart boy that Whitey was. The End.

"I learned a lot from this story, didn't you? First, always help each other. Second, always show kindness. Third, never tease or talk bad about anyone. Fourth, always be polite. Fifth, remember, everyone has feelings. And last, make friends and be a friend."

The little children always practiced what Santa told them. These were lessons they would put to good use right away.

Chapter Twenty-Four
The Design and Engineering Department

I've tried to leave nothing out about everything I saw at Santa's Complex. Some of the inventions were indeed quite complex for me, but I included every detail that I could remember, no matter how small, because I want you to experience Christmas in operation, just as I witnessed it.

I had personal reasons for wanting to learn more about the Design and Engineering Department, so, after I left the day care, I went to talk with Bubbles again. Ish was busy at his desk working on the computer, and Shadow, Snickers, and Shooter had their heads together over what appeared to be some new invention. Bubbles was more than willing to fill me in. "Over the years, Lon, we have come up with so many ideas and concepts. Of course, you've seen many of these in action, such as, the Bubble Dome, the waterwheel for the garden, the twin prop electric wind tunnels, the windows for the homes, the little elves' Happy Pins, the laser package shrinking machine, the fish hatchery, the redesign of Santa's sleighs—the list just keeps growing. It is important, however, to remember that it takes everyone's ideas and input for us to start working on solutions. We always try to invent things that will make the job easier.

"Our Wiz computer—now, that has made our jobs so much easier. The system is so advanced. It tracks every child's gift request from all over the world, all of our supplies, our toy production, our food stores, even the whereabouts of our children. It's extremely helpful in working out new designs and ideas, which is a full-time job here at Santa's Village. Here, let's take a look at what the elves are working on today.

"Hey, Shadow. What are you and Snickers working on?" "Oh, hello, Lon. Well, Shooter, over there, is working on a new control to create a mist of water. I'm assisting Snickers on a timer to turn on the mist. Ish is working on a new computer program to run the entire system." I wondered how such a minor invention could be important enough to keep the whole design staff busy. I said, "What is the problem that's got you working on this?" Bubbles smiled and replied, "We sleep January through March, and Santa and Buddy have to make sure the garden is watered. What we want to do is make their job less hectic, since their time is very valuable. They have so much to do during those three months, and all the elves are unavailable to help. Santa's guests come to the North Pole during that time. We want to give Santa and Buddy a break so they have more time to take care of our visitors.

"Here's how it will work. The computer program will control when the spray mist starts throughout the garden. Then all of the plants will get the proper amount of water. Ish is also working on soil moisture gauges. Once the ground is moist, a reading will be sent to the computer and the gauges will be turned off. The mist will stop in that particular area so as not to overwater. We don't want the garden flooded; we want to protect our trees and plants. They are our nourishment and medicine and provide beauty in our homes. This is a very big project, Lon, and we want it in full operation by August 18th, so we can monitor the system for four months to make sure everything is working in a proper manner." How wrong I had been. This was an important project after all. It certainly taught me not to judge by appearances. Santa's design team was highly organized and very impressive indeed.

Bubbles continued. "Another project in the works is our winter air boots. Ish had an idea that will be a great help to anyone who works outdoors. It's a simple concept, but those make some of the best inventions. The basic design is a boot inside a boot. In between the boots, you blow air through a tube to keep your feet warm. They look bulky, but your feet never get cold, no matter what the temperature. We've discovered a new material that doesn't puncture easily and is very lightweight. You may see Luigi and Stefano wearing the boots around the village. They've been very helpful in trying out various versions. Wisp and Jesse tried some out last week. Fern and Nimbus have signed up for next week. We always work in teams, Lon. But it does help us get the project finished. Keeping our feet warm is a constant challenge here. The only thing the elves complain about is their cold feet.

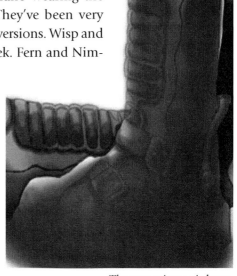

The new winter air boots.

"Our team is made up of some innovative engineers and design specialists. They have lots of great ideas, and we're working on all of them. Shooter came up with a whole new concept in solar panels that would warm the complex, provide light, and also heat all of our water. This would take some of the load off of our twin prop electric wind tunnels. Snickers is working on a new nontoxic paint that would emit just enough glow to light up a room using very little artificial lighting. Lon, when a problem is brought to our attention, we work on the solution right away until the problem is solved.

"Now, let me tell you what I'm working on. It's a new air exhaust fan that works in reverse to take stale air out of a building so we'll always have a balance of clean, fresh, warm air coming in. Shooter's solar panels come into play here too, since they would heat up the fresh air coming into our production floor, or any building for that matter. Right now, our system brings in colder air, so we're all working on this new idea. We always want to breathe good fresh air, Lon. Also, Shadow has lots of new toy ideas in development for next year. We're building prototypes to put to the test. The day care children will be very helpful there, using and abusing the toys to see how they like them and how well they hold up. After they're perfected, we'll put them into production. We want to make sure the children love the new toys."

Shadow had something to add. "Lon, I know how you like stories. Let me tell you one about Santa. He came into our office one day and said all the toys must be reworked. We couldn't imagine what he meant, so he explained. 'I want as many toys as possible to have moving parts. I want cement trucks to rotate the cement drum. I want dump trucks to actually dump dirt, rocks, and whatever else children want to put in them. I want dolls' arms, legs, and heads to move. I want fire trucks to spray water and ladders to move up and down. I want children to want to play with their toys, and I want toys to be functional. Gentlemen, let's get busy.' Well, Lon, we had been here for about ten years when Santa gave us this brand-new direction, and we rose to the challenge. It was so much fun redesigning the toys. Ever since that day, toys have been coming out of our Design Department every week. It did take longer to build toys, but they were functional, and children all over the world loved them. They sent us so many thank-you letters. It took a great effort on everyone's part. We had sketches all over the walls here at the design invention room. Computers came later, so all of this was done by hand. It was a bold move on Santa's part, but we pulled it off. Santa was so proud of the job we all did. That was such a busy year; we didn't have much private time. But the ideas just kept coming, and it was a huge success for Santa and all of us elves. We had a great time making another of Santa's dreams come true."

It was time for a break, so we took a vote and the Blue Water Club won. We went over for some veggie burgers, French fries, and root beers all around. It was good to connect with Smiles again in his soothing "underwater" environment. The Paint Department's snow-flake white paint invention for the Mail Room was a hot topic of conversation. Flip and Flop had done all of the painting and they had kept track of the results. Apparently, not one single child's letter had fallen off yet. Like anybody else, the elves loved to exchange information and catch up over lunch. They very graciously waited for me to finish up—I ate three times as much as any of them, and we headed back to the Design Department—rather, the Design and Engineering Department. We were all going to have to get used to the new name.

Bubbles, Shadow, Snickers, Ish, and Shooter all somehow sensed there was something troubling me. Bubbles spoke up. "Lon, what's on your mind?" I said, "I have a problem, Bubbles, and I'm wondering if maybe you and your team could help me with some answers. Out of all the twenty-two polar ice caps, only number twelve is getting smaller and smaller, and this is of great concern to my scientific team and our planet. The Earth needs the polar ice caps to maintain balance. If they start to shrink, there will be great changes in our climate. That's why my team of scientists is hard at work trying their best to find the answers. Polar Ice Cap No. 12 is located here, nearest the North Pole." Bubbles got very serious. He said, "Lon, we will work on some answers and get back with you as soon as possible." By now, I had perfect confidence in their abilities. I thanked them all and moved on to spend part of the day at the solarium greenhouse.

Petal, Orchid, Dreamer, and Pogo were deeply engrossed in their plants and trees when I arrived. They were always studying. I thought these scientists and their greenhouse were part of the garden, but Orchid informed me, "No, we're part of the Design and Engineering Department, even though our solarium is located next to the garden." Orchid tended scores of different kinds of orchids and the scientists made many innovations here. One was

A new breed of orchid, called the "winter orchid."

called the "winter orchid" because it wouldn't freeze. These scientists were developing a new line of orchids that grew in a variety of colors and shapes. The temperatures were carefully controlled for each plant. The winter orchid was hardy and had a frosted look. Orchid said, "Our goal is to plant these throughout the forest to give beautiful color throughout the woods even in the coldest temperatures." She showed me a tall, beautiful pink orchid she had developed. She called it the "flamingo orchid." Orchid had so many varieties of orchid and she started to take me on a tour, when Lavender, the herbologist, came in to get her input on something urgent. We said goodbye for now. The tour would have to wait. Work came first.

When I walked up to Dreamer, he was hunched over a microscope. "Hi, Lon. Come here. Let me show you what I'm doing. I'm in the middle of developing a faster growing pine tree that will reach full maturity in twenty-five years." Dreamer showed me how gene splicing works in plants. At the same time, Pogo was studying DNA in plants. Pogo said, "I love my work, Lon. It really intrigues me. The key to growing plants and trees in cold temperatures is to get good deep root structure for protection. That's the secret." Dreamer said, "I'm always dreaming up all kinds of new varieties of flowers. Creating dreamy new colors for flowers is so exciting." Petal agreed. "Santa has always said, 'Dream the dream, think about the dream, work on the dream, develop the dream, and you will see it come to pass.' That's the way we do things here at the North Pole, Lon."

Pogo said, "Lon, we've developed a new kind of wheat that has many advantages. Orchid and I combined the genes from a fast growing orchid with a wheat stalk. We found that the wheat became fuller and taller, and a little on the sweet side. The grain grows to maturity in twenty days and fills the animals up fast, so we always have enough feed for the cows, chickens, and raindeer. Also, the root keeps growing, so we don't need to continue to plant the wheat. The animals love the taste of this wheat, and they grow healthy and strong. It was a wonderful discovery."

Orchid and Petal showed me the winter orchids that were almost ready to be planted throughout the forest. Petal said, "The trees are so close together here in the forest that the branches keep a lot of the snow off the ground. The soil near the trees is warm enough to grow plants. Out in the open where there is just ice and snow, they won't make it." I remembered the plants growing in the dense forest when I first met Wrinkles. There were no plants around my igloo, just a raging blizzard. But when Wrinkles led me deep into the forest, there was only a light dusting of snow. I had seen firsthand how the forest gives protection.

Pogo and Dreamer showed me how to splice plants together to create a new variety of plant. They explained the process but it went over my head. Still, it was interesting to see some of their results. The work they were doing was much needed to develop the garden and the forest. I thanked Petal, Orchid, Dreamer, and Pogo and went for a relaxing walk through the garden and the village.

The garden was beautiful, a fresh surprise all over again. I said hi to Scooter. He was hoeing the dirt, loosening it around the base of the plants. Mrs. Claus stopped by to pick some fresh raspberries and blackberries and gave us a cheery wave. I crossed the little bridge over the J'Yakaboo River and entered the Christmas Village. I decided to check out the production facility. Hundreds of elves were moving about, and the toys were stacking up. Mrs. Claus poked her head in the door and called to me, "Lon, come join me for some berries and cream with vanilla bean ice cream, and some warm tea." She didn't have to ask twice. I was off for a sweet talk with Mrs. Claus.

Chapter Twenty-Five
Keeping Up With Mrs. Claus

The big red pine tree comes to life—thanks to the East Wind.

"Here, let me carry those for you," I said as I took the basket of raspberries and blackberries from Mrs. Claus. We went over to the River's Edge Club. Blue Eyes scooped out some vanilla bean ice cream and proceeded to make us a couple of luscious sundaes. She covered the ice cream with the fresh berries, added a slather of raspberry sauce, and topped them off with spoonfuls of whipped cream and nuts. Blue Eyes called this confection a blackberry twist, and it was one of Mrs. Claus's favorites. We drank warm herbal tea made with fresh spring water from the well beneath the polar ice caps.

I wanted to make the most of my time with Mrs. Claus. As we ate, I asked her for more details about the North Pole. "Mrs. Claus, can you tell me how Ivy started talking? He is a tree!" Just like Santa, she was always willing to answer my questions. "Here is what Ivy told Santa, and Santa told me. Years ago, before we came here, the East Wind was in control of the North Hills. He was the bad boy of this territory. The East Wind made it snow all the time and created freezing havoc for anyone who might come here. The year-round winter caused the polar ice caps to grow large.

"Ivy told Santa the East Wind had a special weapon called 'white lightning.' Whatever it hit would come to life, so the East Wind never dared to use it. But this one time, the East Wind was blowing snow and ice for days and days, watching the people and animals suffer, and having a grand old time. Well, apparently he got a bit carried away and accidentally shot out a bolt of white lightning that happened to strike a pine tree smack in its center. The tree was a tall red pine as big around as a sequoia. The lightning bolt shot off the tree and went in two directions at once, toward the north and the south, bringing the North Wind and the South Wind to life just as it had the big red pine tree.

"The North Wind and South Wind blew the East Wind totally out of the area. Ever since, the skies have been controlled by the North and South winds. The North Wind—also called Blow—controls the cold, and the South Wind—also called Heat—controls the warmth. And Ivy helps keep everything together. Because of this incident, Ivy, Blow, and Heat are best friends. Heat and Blow will only talk to Ivy. When Santa wants to communicate with them, he tells Ivy, and Ivy talks to the North and South winds. All three protect the North Pole. I think Blow and Heat are shy around people, but they are our friends. The engineers wanted me to tell you, Lon, that's why Polar Ice Cap No. 12 is not enlarging The East Wind is no longer in control, and

Blow and Heat try to make it a bit more comfortable for us. However, now that Santa knows about the climatic effects, he is taking some action to remedy the situation. He talked to Ivy, who will ask the North Wind to blow in a few blizzards to enlarge Polar Ice Cap No. 12. Santa is very excited that we will be able to help protect the fragile climate of the Earth. So I can reassure you, Lon, that over the next few years Polar Ice Cap No. 12 will be getting bigger again." I told Mrs. Claus how thrilled and grateful I was, how excited my team of scientists would be, and what a wonderful thing Santa, Blow, and Ivy were doing for the planet. What a happy conclusion. I couldn't wait to tell my team, but for now I would have to.

We finished up our blackberry twists at the River's Edge Club and headed over to the day care. It was Mrs. Claus's day to read to the little elves. My feet hardly hit the pavement after the wonderful news she had just given me. But as I thought more about what I would say to my fellow scientists, cold reality hit me like the East Wind. How in the world could I explain all this to scientific rational thinkers? They only understood what they could see with their own eyes and touch with their hands If I told them that I learned Polar Ice Cap No. 12 is going to enlarge, they'd want to know how and why. They'd ask for proof and measurements. After all, that ice cap has been shrinking for more than fifty years. If I said Mrs. Claus told me, they'd think I was crazy. I was going to have to work hard to figure this one out. But for now, it was time for Mrs. Claus to read a story to the little elves. We arrived at the day care, and all of the children gathered around. Their smiling faces were full of anticipation, and so was mine. Mrs. Claus sat down and opened a book with colorful illustrations. "Today's story is titled 'Grandma Marian.'

"Once upon a time, there was a senior elf named Marian. Everyone loved her and showed her great respect. In her younger days, Marian worked in our Sewing Department. And in her spare time, she enjoyed doing things for all of us. She was a great asset to Santa, Buddy, all of the elves, and me, and even to all the children of the world.

"Marian's hobby was quilt making. She had learned this craft in Three Oaks, Michigan, where she raised four wonderful children, three

Grandma Marian with one of her modern quilts.

girls and one boy. When she came to the North Pole, Marian's goal became making a quilt for every bed in her spare time. She would pick up all the leftover scraps in the Sewing Department and save old clothes that no one wanted. Then she would cut up all of this material and create bed coverings. She did this every day after work until she accomplished what she wanted to do. With help from her three daughters, she made a quilt for every home. She even made one for every bedroom in the castle. Marian knew in her heart that everyone would be warm at night and also during their long sleep after the Christmas holiday.

"Everyone appreciated Marian's beautiful craftsmanship and generous spirit. She was greatly respected in the community, and other elves started helping her turn out more and more quilts. Over the years, Marian and her quilters made thousands of quilts. Many children received them as Christmas presents.

"Marian's giving didn't stop with quilts either. She loved to do special things for everyone. She thought couples should spend good quality time together. So, she watched the little ones when their parents went out to eat at one of the many clubs. Marian would play games with the little elves and take them out for ice cream. Everyone started to call her 'Grandma Marian.' Well, Grandma Marian is no longer with us, but she taught us so many things. She would always say, 'First, always help your neighbors, especially if they are older. Second, always be kind and show respect to everyone. Third, take time to read to someone. Fourth, always spend time with someone. And last, be a giver.'

"These were Grandma Marian's five rules. She always encouraged others to live by them too. Grandma Marian taught the art of quilt making to Petunia, Velvet, Touch, Summer, Tender, and Joy, who all work over at the Sewing Department. To this day, in their spare time they still make quilts as taught by Grandma Marian. The End."

Mrs. Claus gave hugs to all of the little ones, and we were off to the garden to pick some fruit and vegetables for the chefs in the kitchen. Mrs. Claus said, "Lon, you fill the cart up with carrots for our carrot salad. I will get green Granny Smith apples for apple squares." All of the chefs were hard at work when we arrived with our bounty. Diamond, Ruby, Crunch, Munch, Quicken, Smitten, and Ice looked up, and Smitten said, "C'mon in, we're all having fun. Here are your hats. Lon, here's your apron." Mrs. Claus, of course, always wore an apron, just in case. We both donned our hats, and Mrs. Claus tied my apron for me. "Help us wrap up what we're doing," said Crunch. "Then we'll get started on the carrot salad and apple squares." Mrs. Claus and I chipped in. The chefs hovered around her. Everyone wanted to see what she was up to. She remained calm and quite at home. All of the chefs went out of their way to make me feel comfortable too.

Lavender came into the kitchen, looking to see what herbs and spices were needed. She was wearing the hat I'd seen her in earlier. It turned out to be functional as well as pretty. She said she always wore it in case of emergencies. Little Dallas came by. He had a stomach-ache. So, Lavender broke off an herb from her hat and handed it to him. "Here, Dallas, eat this." Sure enough, his stomachache went away. Lavender looked at Dallas and said, "Next time, have one scoop of ice cream." Lavender's house was always in bloom, and she grew every herb you could think of. She had herbs drying upside down in her house and even on her porch. The chefs would give her a heads-up when something was running low. "We're almost out of pepper," said Ruby, and Lavender made a note to grind up seeds to make pepper. She was always taking inventory. She never let the kitchen run out of spices. She used her wealth of information to help the village run smoothly.

Mrs. Claus was putting together the ingredients for the apple squares, and boy, was she fast. She rolled out the dough and buttered it. Then came cinnamon, apples, and a glaze on top of the dough. Now the apple squares were ready to bake. All without consulting a recipe.

Then we started on the carrot salad. Everyone participated, cleaning carrots, shredding them, adding raisins, tossing in pineapple—this was all making me hungry. When we were finished, we put the carrot salad in the mini-refrigerator to cool till the next day. Having done a great job, everybody washed up. Mrs. Claus and I next headed for the Sewing Department.

When we arrived, the lady elves were hard at work sewing dolls' clothes. Petunia was cutting out patterns and sliding the pieces over to Velvet. While Velvet sewed, Petunia would cut out the next pattern and slide those pieces over to Touch to sew. The sewing machines worked with a foot pedal system. Your foot would move the pedal back and forth, and that would cause the needle to go up and down to do the sewing. No electricity was needed. Kind of old-fashioned, but it got the job done.

Mrs. Claus said, "Hi, ladies," and everyone answered, "Hi, Susie. Hi, Lon." Mrs. Claus said, "Glow, what are you up to?" "I'm cutting out a shirt pattern," Glow replied. "Who's it for? asked Mrs. Claus. Summer spoke up, "It's for Pockets." "Ohhh." Tender was sewing the shirt together for Glow. Joy said, "If you want, I can take the shirt to Pockets and chat you up, Glow." "No, no, I will think of a way." Mrs. Claus said, "Maybe I can have you and Pockets over to our house, Glow." "No, no!" Glow objected. Mrs. Claus said, "When is his birthday?" "I don't know," said Glow. "Well, we'll have to work on that," said Mrs. Claus, and she made a mental note to find a way to get those two together.

All of the ladies jumped into the spirit of the conversation. Petunia said, "Should we plan a wedding?" Velvet said, "We can measure you for a wedding gown." Touch said, "I can work on flower arrangements." Tender said, "I can help too." Mrs. Claus said, "What can I do?" Glow said, "Easy, now. Easy, now. We haven't even had a date yet." "Well, get Hood to send over a message to Pockets," said Mrs. Claus. Glow tried to calm them all down. "Girls, girls! Please!"

I stayed quiet as a mouse, realizing I was in the middle of girl talk. Everyone was smiling and laughing. Velvet said, "We will have to plan." Mrs. Claus said, "Lon, when all the elves started to arrive, many of them were single and eager to marry. But things have changed. We came to realize what a long lifespan we have here at the North Pole. Nobody feels rushed to marry anymore. They take their time, think everything out, and move slowly—especially on the topic of marriage. Sometimes they need a little push." I was having a good time watching and listening to these lady elves. They were just as cunning as the carpenters! Glow was so flustered, she had to cut out a sleeve three times before she got it right. It seemed she might be falling in love with Pockets, but poor Pockets hadn't a clue. At this point, Mrs. Claus said her goodbyes and turned to me. "Lon, let's go over to the Mail Room to see if any letters have come in for me."

Mrs. Claus was excited to leave the Mail Room with an armful of mail. "I think I'll go straight to my office and answer these, Lon," she said. I thanked her for a fun, busy day, and she bustled out the door. Mrs. Claus was always in motion, and I was so happy to be able to tag along today.

I hadn't seen the Storage Room yet, and there was no time like the present. I knew the elves stored the gifts in this room. After the gifts left the wrapping room, they were placed on conveyer belts that took them to the Shrinking Room. Here there were huge bags designated for different parts of the world. As the gifts came through the shrinking machine, Charge would pick up one and read the address and country. If the country said Russia, for instance, he would put the gift into the bag under the Russia sign. If the package said Canada, it would be placed in the Canada bag, and so on. This went on throughout the day. K2 moved around easily on roller skates, dropping packages in their proper bags, which were then stacked up here in the Storage Room. At times, others would come in to give a hand. I realized, when your job was finished, or you were caught up, you went looking for another job. Everyone always helped each other out. That way, all the work got done, and everybody could have fun at a club, or bowling—whatever they wanted. The elves just never stopped. They would work, have fun, rest, go to work, eat, help each other, and have more fun. They loved their life.

I was feeling a little shabby, so I went over to the hairstyling shop for a wash, cut, and style. The barber's name was Hy-Rise. But we just called him Hy. His hair was thick and high, and he thought it made him look taller. At times, he wore a hat. But he didn't pull it down over his ears. Instead, he set it way atop his bushy hair. I guess it was another way to go. I walked in and said, "Hi, Hy. Could I get a trim?" "Sure. Have a seat, Lon," and he got to work on me. Fingers walked in. She worked on ladies' hair mostly. The lady elves loved the scalp massages she gave before she washed, cut, and dried their hair.

Then Pockets, of all people, walked in to get a haircut. Everyone was chatting. I said, "Pockets, when is your birthday?" "May thirteenth," he said. Fingers was working on Diamond's hair. I said, "Diamond, when is your birthday?" "January twenty-second," she said. I asked Hy-Rise and Fingers when their birthdays were, and they told me. I said, "Does anyone do anything special for birthdays?" "Sometimes, but usually we like to keep that quiet, Lon," said Diamond. Hy-Rise had finished with me, so I hightailed it out of there and headed straight for the Sewing Department.

I found Glow finishing up Pockets' shirt. I could hardly contain myself. I blurted out, "Pockets' birthday is May thirteenth." "How did you find out, Lon?" Glow was flabbergasted. "I was over at the hairstyling shop. And you know how everybody talks at the same time over there? Pockets came in, and I had this brilliant idea to ask everybody when their birthday was, and he told me." This cheered everybody up. The ladies went into high gear planning a wedding for Glow and Pockets. I had played cupid and I was feeling pretty good about it. After my haircut, I wasn't looking bad either.

I went to make a few notes about my day and take a nap. I had become very fond of the elves. They planned, they worked, they laughed, they played, and they did all of it together. And besides that, they really got things done. Plus, they respected each other and took care of one another. I could get tired just watching them all day. I really needed that nap.

Chapter Twenty-Six
The School

I woke up feeling refreshed and ready for some more elf activity. I wanted to see how the elves taught their children, so I went to visit the school. There were seventeen students in one room. Miss Needles and Mr. Pins met me at the door. "Hello, Lon," said Miss Needles. "We're just thrilled you're here. We've all been waiting for a visit from you." I remembered what Dallas and Turf told me when we toured the clubs for their report. They had said Miss Needles always pushed them to do better.

Mr. Pins was sharp and spoke many languages. He told me sometimes guest teachers would come into the classroom for the day. Bubbles had been in to talk about engineering and design, and Skooter had talked about botany and the garden. Lavender had a lot to share about herbs and nutrition. I observed how all the students respected their teachers. They called them "Mr.," "Miss," or "Mrs." Santa always encouraged it. He told them, "When you get older, you will want younger children to respect you. So practice courtesy and respect now, and they will do the same for you later." Today, I was Mr. Lon.

Some of the children spoke six languages. Dallas said, "It's easy if you learn at an early age, Mr. Lon." Miss Needles told me about the school rules. "Some can be bent a little. Years ago I was walking by the J'Yakaboo River and I observed Bear reading a book to Sparkle while Sparkle fished. When Bear fished, Sparkle read to him. They always worked as a team to get their assignments finished, and I never said a word. To this day those two are very smart and they still love to fish. All the elves like to quiz each other on languages. Teaching goes so much faster and easier when everyone helps each other. Santa

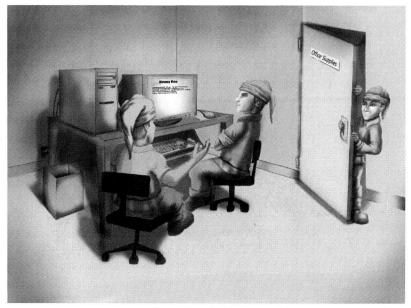

*Elf Dutch and Elf Spin work on a school project while
Elf Ish wonders, "What are these two up to?"*

always encourages the students to learn more and to make society
better."

Mr. Pins said, "Lon, let me tell you about two brothers, Dutch
and Spin. They were ahead of their time. They were always thinking
up ways to speed up their schoolwork. They hit upon a plan for a
voice-activated computer program and entered it into the Wiz. When
they had a report to do, Dutch would speak to the computer and the
computer recognized his voice and would talk back through its speak-
ers. As Dutch spoke, the Wiz put his story into sentences with proper
punctuation. When he was done, Dutch would tell the computer to
print, and his entire report would come out looking perfect. Then
Spin would repeat the process with his report. Each report took only
ten minutes from start to finish. All the other elves had to spend
hours on their homework and their reports never looked or sounded
half as good as Dutch's and Spin's. The computer did research too. It
didn't matter if the report was on the tristrom bird in Israel or the

pink flamingo in Africa. Dutch and Spin spoke to the computer, and in just two minutes it printed out the report. The rest of the elves were at the library still doing their research, and Spin and Dutch were over at the Whispering Pines playing games.

"While Dutch and Spin were having a good time beating the system, many of the senior elves were becoming suspicious. The two students played more than they studied, yet they always advanced in everything. What could they be up to? Then, one day, Ish just happened to be in the Design Department closet putting some supplies away, when he heard two voices in the office area. 'Hello, computer.' 'Hello, Dutch.' 'Hello, computer.' 'Hello, Spin.' Ish sensed something was up, so he stayed in the closet and watched through the crack in the door. 'I need a report on the yellow jacket wasp,' said Dutch. After a couple of minutes, the computer said, 'Your report is in the print box, Dutch.' Then Spin spoke. 'Give me everything you have on the bumblebee.' Another two minutes went by. 'Your report is in the print box, Spin.' Reports in hand, the boys thanked the computer and left the room. Ish came out of the closet, looked at the computer, and said hello. Nothing happened. 'Hello, Mr. Computer.' Still no answer. 'Hello, Miss Computer?' Again, no response.

"By now, Bubbles and Shadow were standing in the doorway, and they thought Ish had lost his mind. They burst into uncontrollable laughter. Shadow was rolling on the floor with glee, and Bubbles fell up against the wall in stitches. Ish just stood there. Bubbles and Shadow didn't mince words. Bubbles said, 'What are you doing?' Shadow said, 'Are you nuts?' Ish said, 'We'll see who's nuts. Come with me. I need to find Dutch and Spin—and Santa.'

"Well, poor Dutch and Spin were busted. Santa, Ish, Bubbles, Shadow, Dutch, and Spin were all in the Design Department. Shooter walked in unexpectedly and was invited to stay. 'Just shut the door, please, Shooter,' said Santa. Ish instructed Dutch to speak to the computer. 'Hello, Dutch,' the computer answered. Ish had Spin say hello to the computer, and the computer said hello back. 'Do you need a report today?' said the computer. They went through the whole demonstration. 'May I have a report on the red robin in the United States?' said Dutch. 'Your report is in the print box, Dutch.' Spin said 'Can I have a report on the fire ants of the Amazon?' 'Your report is in the print box, Spin.' The boys remained polite with 'Thank you, computer.'

"Ish said, 'See, I told you.' The boys explained they had written a voice-activated program for the computer to save time on their schoolwork. They figured their goose was cooked. Santa thought a minute and said, 'Boys, keep up the good work,' and Dutch and Spin were added to the Design Department. They were assigned to work with Bubbles' staff for two hours after school every day. The design team was speechless. 'What a great idea!' said Bubbles. That was the year we added voice activation to all the computers, and to the elevator at Santa's castle, as well. All you do is step onto the elevator, say the floor you want, and the elevator takes you there." "Yes, I've been on the elevator. It's fun, and a real technological marvel," I said.

"It sure is, Lon. Everybody is impressed by it. When Santa's guests arrived that year, Santa showed them the new voice-activated program. The presidents of major corporations took the new invention back to their company computers. These companies have earned millions and millions off of this invention, and many other inventions our elves have created too. The corporations always repay us with generous contributions to the Kris Kringle Foundation. The company presidents give gifts to the elves for their inventions and designs too. The talking computer put millions of dollars into the Kris Kringle Foundation. The last big gift we received for our village was the Miniature Jungle Safari Golf Course. Santa always says, 'Give, and it will come back to you.' This has been proven over and over again.

"We are deeply aware that this chain of events would never have happened without education. Year after year, students ask to work on the production floor. Santa's response is to visit the classroom and say, "Help us be more efficient. Figure out ways we can do things smarter." We have group competitions throughout the year. The students study English, foreign languages, art, chemistry, science, computer skills, math, algebra, trigonometry, history, finance, to name a few. Santa wants them to rely on their brains and intuition. That will give them creativity and the confidence to follow through on it. It works. No one has yet left our village for the outside world."

Miss Needles said, "All of our students have had cooking classes in our kitchen. They've all learned basic carpentry and painting. Santa says you just don't know when you'll be needed to help get a department caught up. Plus, when you're on the production floor, you might come up with an idea we can really use. Learning here is fun, Lon. We break for an hour during the school day. The students like to use this free time to drop in at a club or to bowl or maybe for a game of miniature golf. Then we head back for more schooling."

Miss Needles said, "Years ago we had a paint room competition. It illustrates our students' ability to work as a team and be innovative, Lon. Let me tell you all about it. The class broke up into four groups. Each group was instructed to invent something new and useful in the paint room. Everyone had four weeks to perfect their inventions. Group one decided to invent a paint that would glow if the sun hit it. It would be used to create designs on walls, t-shirts, clothes, and so on. Group two wanted to invent a spray paint robot, and its use was to spray designs on the toys or on clothing. Group three thought up a machine that would add pigment to paint. It would have the capability to create a hundred colors in small or large quantities for greater variety with less waste. Group four decided to invent a water-based paint to use for easy cleanup without harmful chemicals.

"The competition was on, and group one went to the school lab to start work. They experimented with all kinds of pigments and mixtures Group two went to the school design room to start on the layout of the robot. They would have to program the computer to control the robot, and they needed an air compressor, tables, and paint. They went searching for hardware to start building. Group three needed to use the computer for colors, pigments, and designs, so they started writing computer software too. I observed groups one, two, and three. Mr. Pins observed group four. They went to work in the chemistry lab, developing new products to dissolve paint.

"Four weeks later, the entire Paint Department and Santa were present to watch the competition. Giggles, the head of the Paint Department, tried very hard to keep a blank expression on his face. He didn't want to show partiality to any of the four groups. Group one really pulled it off. After studying how the lightning bug glows in the dark, they used these four different products in the paint: pigment 9274-3, pigment 173-2, pigment 86674, and pigment XOU7-4. The pigments had to be added precisely in this order to make the paint glow. The group one students were wearing shirts with pictures of Goober and Sammie. Whenever the sun hit the paint, the colors jumped out at you. Besides that, the paint stored up sunlight in light cells and at night the parrots glowed like a neon sign. The shirts were a big hit. Everybody wanted one. Santa whispered to Giggles, 'Can you get me one of those t-shirts?' They both laughed. 'I want one too,' said Giggles.

"Group two was also successful. Their robot had eight hands for spraying paint. It looked like an octopus with air lines for arms. The robot was hooked up to the computer and programmed to paint images of Sir King and Lady Queen. The paint was ready and sealed in cans. They hit the start button and the robot's arms swept in every direction with a "sch…sch…sch…sch" sound. After three minutes, the picture was finished. It showed the dogs standing with Goober and Sammie on their backs, all looking straight out at us. It was beautiful. The group presented Santa and Mrs. Claus with the painting and got a big thank-you. Santa was obviously impressed.

"Group three was ready to demonstrate their color mixer. Their invention started with white paint. They asked Giggles to choose a color. He went with fire-engine red, a highly saturated color that could be hard to produce. The students programmed the computer and the color mixer gave a "squirt…squirt…squirt" into the can of white paint. They sealed the lid and the machine shook the paint can. When the lid was removed, they had a brilliant, pure fire-engine red paint. Giggles said, 'No way. Let's try a different color. How about light blue?' Now they programmed light blue into the computer. "Squirt…squirt…squirt" went the machine into the can of white paint. The lid was sealed and the machine shook some more. This time the result was a lovely light blue. The students explained that by keeping a high concentrate of pigment in each of twelve tubes, they could make any color you wanted. All they needed was white paint to start Giggles said, 'Okay!' The entire paint staff was quite impressed. Each invention was as terrific as the one before. This could be the winning invention, but group four still needed to make their presentation.

"Group four held up the oil-based paint that was then in use. They pointed out how messy it was to use and how difficult it was to clean up. You had to use a paint thinner that contained harsh chemicals. Their invention was a water-based paint. When you're finished using the paint, you rinse the brushes in water and just wash your hands. You're done! Santa, Giggles, and the entire Paint Department were in awe. This contest was proving impossible to judge.

"Santa, Miss Needles, Mr. Pins, Giggles, and the whole paint staff all said what a great job everybody did. Santa said, 'Giggles, you and your staff will pick the winners.' There were four ribbons: first place, second place, third place, and fourth place. Giggles and his staff excused themselves and walked outside to confer. 'What are we going to do?' said Blitz. 'All of them are practical, useful, and can be further developed for different applications,' said Dance. 'I can't give out these ribbons. It's impossible,' said Giggles. Everybody agreed. 'I've got an idea,' said Sky, and they huddled as he explained. Giggles called out, 'Hey, Hood! Come here, please. Go tell Blue Eyes over at the River's Edge we need ice cream sundaes for seventeen people, and you stay there and help her. We'll stall for about fifteen minutes.'

"Hood went to tell Blue eyes what Giggles had said, and the two of them started scooping, pouring, sprinkling, dolloping, and dotting. All the tables were set up. In the meantime, Giggles and his staff solemnly walked back into the schoolroom. Giggles spoke. 'I'm sorry, but no first, second, third, and fourth place winners have been chosen. We agreed that all of the ideas are so imaginative yet practical, they can be put to use in our Paint Department right away. It would be doing you an injustice to pick one invention above all the others. Therefore, all of you will get a beautiful trophy that says "Dream the Dream." Now, let's go and get some ice cream sundaes and talk about all of these marvelous inventions.' Santa said, 'You handled that well, Giggles.' Giggles said, 'Thank you, Santa. I think I've learned a thing or two from you.'

"Blue Eyes served up the most incredible ice cream sundaes. She totally outdid herself. Everyone was laughing about all the mistakes they had made trying to get their inventions to work. This class had learned so much about problem solving, about calculations on the computer, and about mixtures. 'What a fine job, everyone!' said Santa.

Miss Needles and Mr. Pins kept me in stitches with more stories about their past students. Something funny happened the day I visited too. Miss Needles was teaching trigonometry, and one of the elves, named Hope, found an easier way to solve a problem. Miss Needles asked Hope to explain at the chalkboard. Hope was really smart and conveyed the information simply and clearly to the whole class. One hour into this trigonometry problem, and everyone was getting it. Not realizing it, the students started addressing Hope as Miss Hope. They were so used to calling whoever was standing in front of the class Mr., Miss, or Mrs. Everyone was helping everyone, and it turned out to be an exceptional class that day. But how funny! Miss Hope.

Miss Needles and Mr. Pins really made me feel welcome. They introduced me to the class as the scientist Lon, studying temperatures at Polar Ice Cap No. 12. All the students clapped, and since they welcomed a break from trigonometry, they were ready to listen to me. I spoke about why I was at Polar Ice Cap No. 12 and what I studied. Everyone was firing questions. They were just as intrigued with me as I was with them. I talked for two and a half hours and I felt like a real scientist again. Then school was over for the day so we all went to get a piece of candy over at the Knotty Pine. The students' minds were like sponges. They still had lots of questions about air quality and temperatures. I loved connecting with Miss Needles, Mr. Pins, and all of the students that day. And I have to admit I ate more than one piece of candy at the Knotty Pine.

Chapter Twenty-Seven
July 25th

Elf Blue Eyes and Elf Ice get married on July 25th.

I needed to stretch my legs and wet my whistle, so I walked over to the Eagle Ridge Club. I thought an ice cold root beer with lots of foam would taste good right about now. That was the club's favorite drink. S. T poured one for me and for himself. It was stronger than I was used to in a root beer. S. T., who ran the club, said it was an old-fashioned recipe, but it was cold and very good. Shots was sitting at a table having a sandwich with Pickles. Shots was the village doctor and I figured he probably had lots of great stories, so S. T. and I went over to join them.

Shots said, "You know, Lon, there really isn't much sickness here at the North Pole. I do give physicals and administer vaccine shots. Everyone has a chart, and I keep those updated. My nurse, Nikki, takes care of all the files. She is a tremendous help to me, also very knowledgeable and caring. We get all of our vaccines shipped in. Other than that, most of our medicine comes from my mother, Lavender. She uses all kinds of herbs to make natural medicines. She has a wealth of information. My mother and I are in charge of all new births, but normally it is pretty quiet here for me.

"My best patient is Scars. Usually all he needs are a few stitches here and there. I remember once when Scars went fishing. He was casting his line into the river when it caught the seat of his pants. Well, he came into my office holding the fishing pole with the hook still stuck in his bottom. The line went up and over his head, down his back, and the hook was stuck right in the seat of his pants. He had caught himself. I said, 'Scars, what did you do now?' Well, that cost him a few stitches. Bear was with him and we both stifled a laugh. We had a good guffaw later though, when Scars wasn't around. That boy just isn't a fisherman, but he sure does try. I'll give him that. I remember when he caught a really big fish. He reeled it in and when he pulled the fish out of the river, that fish flipped up and smacked Scars right on the head. Well, Scars was wearing his favorite fishing hat, with fishing hooks all over it. Scars said it made him look like a real fisherman. Well, it took me hours to delicately remove those hooks from his scalp. What a mess that was. But when Scars left my office, he was smiling because he had caught the largest fish ever out of that river. So, I guess he is some kind of fisherman after all.

"Scars' best friend is Bear. Bear cleaned that fish for him. They smoked it in a special smoker and added all kinds of enhancing flavors to the fish. The chefs made a nice presentation of it for Bear,

Scars, and Sparkle. What a real treat that was for those three boys. When they were younger, they were always into something. I could tell you stories about those boys all day, Lon. However, they are grown up now. The longer you're here, Lon, the more stories you're likely to hear.

"Most of my patients just have scrapes or bruises. I go through lots of ice and band-aids. Usually it's all minor things. You know, Lon, I've been with a lot of my patients all through their lives. Some are now married and have children. I have seen it all!

"My dad, Arch, is the pastor here. He holds services every Sunday morning from 9:00 to 10:00. I remember one of the longest services we had here at the North Pole. It started at 9 A.M., but it didn't end until late afternoon." I said to Shots, "Is that usual?" "Well, Lon, it's a long story, so I'd better get started telling it.

"Back when the elves started arriving here at the North Pole, we came from all over the world. We were strangers to each other. Many of us were single, and we had to learn languages so that we could communicate. Santa and Mrs. Claus know lots of languages and they helped us a bunch. But it took them five years to get us all straightened out. Santa acted as interpreter, and Mrs. Claus taught languages daily. That was a stressful time. We got through it though. Well, anyway, in the meantime, many of the single folks were dating, falling in love, and getting engaged.

"My Dad announced we would hold a day of weddings on July 25th. The idea has since caught on and become a tradition. It is the only day for weddings here at the North Pole, which means it's also the only day for celebrating anniversaries. We are so busy making toys, it just makes sense to devote one day to honor our relationships. So, once a year, we shut everything down to celebrate one of our biggest holidays, called 'July 25th.' But back in the beginning, this was a brand-new idea.

"Dad always held services in the village square. Now it was really decked out in anticipation of a wedding. Everyone was pitching in. There were white arches with red rose bushes intertwined, set out all the way down the street. A long white runner stretched from the first arch to the last. The far side of the village is still like that today. The bees love those flowers. Well, on July 25th everything was ready. Ellie played her harp for the occasion. What Dad didn't say was there were fourteen couples getting married. It was a surprise to everyone, including me. Incredibly, all the couples managed to keep it a secret. And that was Dad's longest service. To this day, we never know who is getting married on July 25th. All of us are always totally surprised. It's part of the fun.

"At that first wedding ceremony, the food was served at our banquet facility, and it was extravagant. The cake was a breathtaking twelve layers high and made of yellow cake with raspberry filling and a creamy white coconut frosting. All the tables were decorated with fresh-cut red and white flowers from the garden. Santa served as best man and Mrs. Claus was the matron of honor, for everyone. The guys wore black suits and the ladies were dressed in flowing white wedding gowns. The brides carried sprays of red roses that barely brushed the ground. Each groom sported a red rose in his lapel. Some of those getting married were musicians in the band, so everyone took turns playing at the reception that night.

"Sir King and Lady Queen stood to the left and right of Santa and Mrs. Claus. The parrots, Goober and Sammie, perched on Santa's shoulders, switching sides with each wedding. Sammie instructed Goober to be totally quiet until the ceremony was over. That was very hard for him, as you can imagine. The two white Great Pyrenees dogs sat very quietly. They are always so well behaved.

"Now for the surprise of who was getting married. Some had ideas, but nothing was certain till Dad called out their names. First there was Blue Eyes and Ice. Everyone just oohed and aahed. As they made their way through the arches, there was whistling and clapping. The parrots' wings would flutter, and Santa would say, 'Easy, Goober.' The dogs stood in honor of the couples. How regal they looked.

"The second couple to get married was Diamond and Munch. Third was Ruby and Crunch. Fourth was Tapper and Bubbles; fifth, Lady Whisper and Red; sixth, Petunia and Lincoln; seventh, Velvet and Skooter; eighth, Touch and Luigi—it went on all day. The ninth couple to get married was Summer and Wisp; the tenth couple was Tender and Giggles; the eleventh, Shy and Tank; the twelfth, Smiles and Speed; thirteenth, Fingers and Stefano; and last but not least, the fourteenth couple was Winter and Speed.

"All of us were stunned at the number of weddings that day. We never expected it, even though some of the couples had been dating for some time. We were so happy for them, and today they have wonderful families. I've assisted at all of their children's births, taken care of their scrapes and bruises, and now some of their children are married with babies of their own.

"It was the funniest thing when Goober said, 'You may kiss the bride.' Dad nodded his head and pronounced all the couples man and wife. We partied all night long. That day was a milestone and quite a night to remember."

I asked Shots when he was getting married. He said, "I was married, Lon, to my school sweetheart. Years after we married, she passed. I've just never had a desire to marry again. That's when I decided to become a doctor. I wanted to touch people's lives, and this is a great way to do that." I said, "I'm so sorry, Shots. I guess you've been around for some time." All he had to say was "Oh, yeah."

"Maybe you can answer some questions for me. I would really like to find out more information, if you don't mind." "Today is your lucky day, Lon. Fire away." "Do you know why Santa wears a red suit when he delivers gifts on December 24th and 25th?" "That's a great question, Lon. When Santa started delivering gifts with his dad many years ago, he wore a long coat, dark in color and trimmed in gold. His mom changed a few details on it over the years. She added fur around the collar, cuffs, and base of the coat. As time went on, there were more packages to deliver, and the long coat was getting in Santa's way, especially when he bent down to place gifts under the tree, and he was doing a lot of that. Eventually, Mrs. Claus experimented with a shorter coat and a pair of insulated black pants to keep Santa warm. They worked rather well, but there was room for improvement. So next year, the lady elves and Mrs. Claus got carried away and made Santa a really colorful coat. He used it that Christmas, but he said it was a little too much. Santa is most concerned about practicality; he leaves the creative wardrobe decisions up to the ladies. And every year they came up with a little bit different design.

"Then one day, Santa was working with the raindeer out in the woods. He was getting warm so he took off his coat, revealing a bright red shirt. When the raindeer saw his shirt, they froze in their tracks. They just stood there. Santa guessed that red must mean stop to the raindeer. He tested his theory again and again, and by golly he was right. That was the year Mrs. Claus made Santa a red suit with a black belt and black boots. She trimmed the collar, sleeves, and hem of the coat with white fur for extra warmth. The suit did its job. When the raindeer saw Santa, they stayed totally still until he stepped into the sleigh and snapped the reins. Then they took off like a shot. That year, delivering gifts became easier and more efficient. Santa didn't have to yell out the raindeer's names as much, he got in and out of the sleigh lickety-split, and the whole job took less time. Santa told his wife how well his new suit worked, and how much he loved it. Everybody was happy.

"Santa only wears his red suit on December 24th and 25th. And he never wears a red shirt around the raindeer anymore. He loves to talk to the raindeer so much, he doesn't want to ruin that relationship. The raindeer love to hear his voice too. But somehow they know they must stay as quiet as they can on December 24th and 25th to make Christmas a big surprise for children." Shots said he could tell the raindeer always love to see Santa and the elves. They like to be brushed down, and enjoy being talked to. They really are people-friendly animals.

"Lon, did I answer your question?" "Yes, you did, Shots. Thank you." Right then, Santa walked into the Eagle Ridge Club. He gave us all a hello, and S. T. said, "What can I get you, Santa?" "I'll have one of your famous root beers, please." S. T. brought Santa a frothy root beer and refilled our drinks too.

"Santa," I dared to ask, "I've got a question for you. Since I've been here at the Christmas Village, I've been surprised to see that elves don't have pointed ears and noses." Everyone broke into laughter. And I was laughing because they were. When everything quieted down, Santa said, "Let me address that rumor. Many, many years ago, we started Carnivale to kick off the start of our new work year. Our dentist, Dr. Allen Gerald Simpson III, better known as Beemer, had a bright idea. He said, 'Let's pull a huge joke on Santa.' Well, everyone got involved, even my wife, Susie. For Carnivale that year, all the elves, Susie, and Buddy wore stick-on noses and ears that came to a point. They all—and I mean all, even the little elves—wore a set of these things. Everyone jumped on the bandwagon to give me a huge laugh.

"The Sewing Department made green outfits for everyone, and the hats had bendy curls on top, like the ice cream in Blue Eyes' cones. Devere, our leathersmith and shoemaker, designed pointy shoes for all the elves, plus two pairs of bigger shoes for Buddy and Mrs. Claus. Everyone prepared for months and kept it a secret from me the whole time. Well, Wrinkles woke up the elves from their deep sleep, and soon the parade started. All of the elves appeared in their new costumes—so funny with hats, short coats, pointy toed shoes, pointy ears, pointy noses. Ho-ho! I was doubled over with laughter. I couldn't speak, I was laughing so hard. My tummy got a real workout. Then I saw Mrs. Claus and Buddy. Well, this time I nearly fell off my chair. They were two of the silliest, most gigantic elves you'd ever want to see. All the elves had a huge laugh at the sight of them.

"Swang, Dance, and JoJo painted a picture that used to hang in my office. It depicts all the elves in their elfin costumes, all green and pointy. It's expertly done and very funny. The following year, my friends who contribute to the Kris Kringle Foundation came to visit while the elves were deep asleep, as usual. As is our custom, we had long conversations in my office and I never thought anything about the new painting. No one ever said a word about it. But they must have taken it in, because after they went back home, the rumors started. Word quickly spread that Santa's elves dress in green and have pointy ears and noses, and pointy shoes and hats. Our guests have never seen the elves. They've always been curious, but when they visit, the elves are asleep in the Sleeping Chamber. I guess it was an honest mistake. Anyway, over the years, I've never corrected that rumor, because it was so funny and in a strange way it further protects my friends from intrusion. I still laugh every time I look at that painting. Ho-ho! It makes me laugh just to think about it. But I've moved it over to my bedroom, since I just couldn't get anything done with that picture in my office. Come with me, Lon. I'll show it to you."

That sounded like a great idea to me. So, Santa and I said goodbye to S. T., Shots, and Pickles, and left the Eagle Ridge Club behind. Well, Santa was right. His elf painting made us both laugh till we cried. When he got his breath back, Santa suggested we go get a snack over at the Echo Valley Club. "Mexican?" I said. "You're on, Santa." And off we went.

We were still laughing when we walked into the club. I think Cisco must be psychic, because he said, "Oh, you two must have been looking at the elf picture." We both nodded through our tears. I ordered two double tacos and two double burritos with extra sour cream. Santa said, "I'll have the same, Cisco. And add on a plate of nachos too, please." The excellent food immediately changed our focus and calmed us down. Santa said, "Lon, every once in a while the elves will put on their elfin gear for a lark, and that day becomes an unscheduled playday because we just cannot get anything done. Everyone laughs and all is lost. We sure have a great time here at the North Pole." I said, "Santa, I can see you do!"

Santa said, "One time, I made a pair of wooden teeth that fit right over my own teeth. They were dirty looking and pointing in every direction. I was scheduled to have my teeth cleaned by Dr. Gerald Allen Simpson III—uh, Beemer. I went into his office and covered my mouth as I said to him, 'I'm overdue for a cleaning.' I sat in the chair and opened my mouth, and Beemer started laughing like he'd been inhaling the laughing gas. He laughed so hard, he dropped his tools on the floor, and I was laughing right along with him. Ho-ho! Well, I don't have to tell you I had to reschedule my teeth cleaning. Poor Beemer gave up and closed his dental office for the rest of the day. Actually, it was a payback. It was Beemer's idea to have all the elves wear pointy ears and noses. He started the whole conspiracy then everyone else ran with it. I'm telling you Lon, we get so much accomplished here at the North Pole, but we have great fun along the way.

"You'll enjoy knowing that Swang, Dance, and JoJo did another painting just like my elfin painting, except this one shows all the elves smiling with dirty wooden teeth that go every which way. We gave that picture to Doctor Beemer. He hung it up at home, otherwise, he wouldn't be able to get much accomplished at work. Fun, fun, and more fun. Ho-ho!" I smiled and said, "Santa, you're a hoot!"

I changed the subject and asked Santa something else I'd been wondering about. "Have you ever given a piece of coal to a child for Christmas?" He replied, "Yes. Many years ago. I did put a note with it to do better next year, and the children have always improved. However, I don't do that anymore. I try to emphasize the positive. I give all the children a gift and a letter, if I think it could be helpful. If I can turn around a young person's attitude and direct them toward a life of love, sharing, and respect, I have fulfilled an important mission.

"I always tell the young elves here to respect their elders, Lon, especially their parents. Why? Because someday you will be a parent, at least you'll be older, and you will want respect also. Adults need to respect everybody too, old and young alike. I do feel that if children are taught properly, they will always be respectful. I also tell younger children that grown-ups have to live by rules too.

"For example, if a grown-up drives a car, you can't run a red light or a stop sign. You have to stop. If you have bills to pay, you have to go to work on time or you may get fired. That way you can pay your bills on time. We all have rules to live by. If you're a child, we have house rules also.

"I remember, Lon, my mom would always ask me where I was going and what I would be doing. As a child, this annoyed me, until I realized my mom just wanted to know in case she needed me for some reason, like an emergency. Then she would know how to find me. At first I thought she was being nosy. Not until I was older did I realize it was because she cared about me. She loved me, and that's why I came to understand her thinking. I always respected my parents, because I knew they loved me. They told me every day that they loved me. Even Dad. He was my dad 100 percent of the way. He always would give me a hug and say, 'Kris, I love you. Now, sleep fast so we can hang out together tomorrow.' Lon, I tell you, I would have done anything for my Mom and Dad, because I knew they loved me.

"Whenever I have a chance, Lon, I tell my guests, 'Never let children go to sleep without telling them you love them.' That goes for couples too. Susie and I say 'I love you' every night. I feel we should spread more love around. Soft words can mend broken hearts. We've never had children of our own, Lon, but I always try to show kindness. The last thing I will say on this topic is if you don't do these things—start now! It's never too late.

"Isn't it amazing how coal can get you talking about love and kindness?" said Santa. We both smiled, but I understood his meaning. I pondered everything he said. Right away, I knew this experience would change my life forever. Then and there, I started practicing being a nicer, gentler man. Santa had given me a gift. He opened my eyes and my heart.

Chapter Twenty-Eight
The Candlemaker

Beautiful candles made by Torch, Blade, and staff.

I strolled around the village, trying to hold on to everything I'd heard that day. Time spent at the North Pole was better than a spa for getting an attitude adjustment. I stopped in front of the candle shop, Big Bear Candle Barn. The candlemaker saw me and stepped outside to shake hands. "Hi, Lon. I've been hoping you'd stop by. Everyone calls me Torch. I guess it's because I like candles so much. I love how they warm the room and the atmosphere. I burn a lot of candles at home, all around the house, in every room. I love to make them too. Come on in." Torch was the master candlemaker. He showed me around his shop and introduced me to his assistants.

"Lon, meet Wick. He has a way of leaving candlewick everywhere he goes, but he's working on it. He's really a great help around here." I said hello to Wick, we shook hands, then he pulled a strand of wick from between his fingers and went back to work.

"Then there's Hats." "I like your hat, Hats," I said. "Thanks, Lon. I've got a different cap for every day of the year—baseball teams, U.S. states, different countries, you name it. I've got hats with all sorts of emblems and slogans, pro this, con that. I like 'em all." Hats was thin, but oh, my goodness, he did have style. "Just never, and I mean never, touch his hat, Lon," Torch warned. I guess he really loved his hats.

Torch continued the introductions. "Say hi to Tops, Lon." She was Torch's daughter and a real cutie. Torch said she and Hats were engaged. Tops liked to wear a different top every day to match Hats' hat. On this day, Hats was wearing a cap that said "Fighting Irish," and Tops' top said the same thing. Both were in bright green and white. "Nice top, Tops," I said. "Thank you, Lon." Apparently, wherever you saw Hats, you saw Tops, and vice versa. Those two were inseparable. "Tops and Hats started a fad here in the village," said Torch. "A lot of couples now show up at work with matching shirts and hats." I couldn't help think that Santa and Mrs. Claus might have had a little something to do with that too.

"This is my wife, Blade, concentrating over here. She makes perfect cuts every time." "Hi, Lon," said Blade. "We make all kinds of candles here and they're all handcrafted. See these glass squares? Bubbles created some frosted glass jars for us using the same concept as the Bubble Dome. We pour candles right into the jars. You can't see through them. The thin glass is opaque. Aren't they neat?" "Just beautiful," I said. The elves in the shop also made tapers for use in the homes. I looked around. On the shelves were intricately carved candles, votive candles, animal figures—all made out of wax, and all about the size of your fist. They even made soap. The elves loved that item. "We use a beeswax, Lon," said Torch. "Besides honey, the village bees produce this natural wax. Our colony of bees contributes so much to our life here." I had to agree.

"Our herbologist, Lavender, blends hundreds of combinations of scents for our candles. I can give you a candle to energize you and another to relax you. Some are spicy and others intoxicating as a heavy perfume. Lavender crushes the herbs, spices, and flower petals that give us all these fragrances. She's a genius at it." Torch held a candle close to my nostrils. "There. Doesn't that smell great?" The aroma was heavenly.

I was so happy to hear Torch say, "Let me tell you a story, Lon." "Please do," I said, and he began. "We all work as a team here, and we get the job done, but we have our funny moments too. One time, I was melting some beeswax in the wax tanks, and Hats was dipping some candles for Blade to carve. He was horsing around with Tops— those two are just so in love, when he dropped a huge candle into the wax vat. Wax splashed everywhere. On his hat, all over his beard and mustache, all up and down the front of his shirt and apron. Blade yelled, 'Don't move!' 'Why not?' said Hats. 'Because when the wax dries, we'll peel it off of you.' That took some time, and boy, did we laugh. That incident cost Hats some facial hair when we peeled his face. That was one day he was glad to be wearing his hat, since the wax didn't touch a hair on his head. Can't you just see poor Hats? It was a riot."

In the Big Bear Candle Barn, there were candles hanging everywhere. Torch said some children wanted candles for Christmas, and here the candlemakers created special candles just for them. "Blade and I were here for about six years before we got married," said Torch. Eventually, we had two wonderful daughters, Tops and Shades. Shades is still in school. I don't think she knows what she wants to do when she grows up yet, but I have a feeling wax is not in her plans." He smiled a daddy's smile.

Torch continued. "Miss Needles and Mr. Pins brought the school children over on a class trip yesterday. We had about twenty boys and girls, all wanting to get involved. So, we let them make candles. We lined them up and gave each a piece of wick. They dipped the wick into the wax and then moved to the end of the line. The air cooled the wax, so by the time they made it to the front of the line again, it would be cool enough for a another dip. This went on for twenty-four dips. That really wore the youngsters out. But when they finished, they had a nice-looking candle to take home to show their mom and dad. Then we made a mold of their hands. You dip the hand in cold water, then in very warm wax, and repeat this eight to ten times. Just like Blade pulled the wax off of Hats, we pulled the mold off of their hands, only without the pain. Now they had a wax copy of their own hand. They thought that was the coolest thing. They all wanted to be candlemakers when they finish school. However, I know they're taking a tour of Shots's doctor's office tomorrow, and then they will all want to be doctors. Children's enthusiasm is a wonderful thing."

Shots stopped by to see how the tour had gone. Torch told Shots all about it. "Well, tomorrow they are all coming to see me," said Shots. "I'm going to have them all listen to each other's hearts and check each other's ears and eyes, so I have a big day planned with those guys. I can't wait. One day this week Hy-Rise and Fingers get to have all the children over to the hairstyling shop. Fingers told me she was going to talk about hair and proper hygiene—not just shampooing your hair, but washing your face, and caring for your nails, hands, and feet also. They're going to style some hair too. At the end of the week, Dr. Beemer gets to clean their teeth and talk about brushing and flossing." Torch said, "Yes, I heard the kids talking, and they are getting excited about all the day trips planned for this week. It's a great idea. I like how they get to preview different careers too. It really broadens their education of the world outside the classroom."

While we were talking, the candlemaking team was hard at work. Tops and Hats were gathering candle orders together, and Blade was giving instructions to the computer. Then Tops and Hats delivered the packages to the Wrapping Department, getting everything ready for December 24th. Shades came in looking for her father. "Is Mr. Torch here?" she said. "He sure is, Shades," said Wick, and he yelled out, "Torch, it's for you!" Torch came out of the back room and said, "Hello, love." Shades gave her dad a severe look and replied, "Here is a package from Miss Needles that I am delivering to you, Mr. Torch." Torch took the package and gave a smart little bow. "Thank you, Miss

Shades." Shades smiled and left. I looked at Blade and said, "What was that all about?" But Blade addressed her husband. "Now Torch, your daughter is learning to be a secretary to Miss Needles, and she is very serious about it. She is just trying to be professional." Shades' daddy responded, "Okay, dear."

Torch opened the envelope and found thank-yous from the school children to Torch, Blade, Hats, Tops, and Wick. He read them one by one and slapped them up on the wall immediately, since the walls were painted with snowflake white and didn't need pushpins. What a wonderful gesture on the young elves' part. They were really learning Santa's lessons.

Lavender came by to drop off some different scents she'd just come up with: fresh peppermint twist, toasty creamy marshmallow, blossoming peach, tall evergreen, holly berry wreath, touch of Christmas, tempting blueberry muffin, fresh-cut flowers, and wild strawberry. They all smelled yummy, especially the tempting blueberry muffin. I was getting hungry again.

Hats said, "Wow, we can't wait to start pouring these new scents. They smell so wonderful." All the elves loved Lavender's fragrances. The production floor always smelled so nice when packages arrived from the Big Bear Candle Barn. Santa came by to say, "Heard about your class tour yesterday, Torch. Those children are still talking about it." Torch pointed out the students' thank-yous to Santa. "Ah, now that was nice. They're such good children. Your daughter, Shades…she's really looking like a secretary, working for Miss Needles." Torch said, "Yes, in fact, she just addressed me as 'Mr. Torch.'" Santa laughed, "Ho-ho, she's a real professional. Have a good one, gentlemen. I'm off to the day care. It's story time. They've been asking for me." As Santa jumped on his golf cart and started over to the day care, he said, "Hey, Lon, join me!" I replied, "Thanks, Santa, but I think I need to grab a snack to tide me over. I'll catch up with you a little later, if that's okay." Santa yelled over his shoulder, "That's fine, Lon. See you soon!"

Chapter Twenty-Nine
Sir King and Goober's Big Day

Goober and Sammie watch over their baby parrots,
Courtney, Brittany, Whitney, and Bloober.

My stomach had been growling for quite some time, and even though I would miss one of Santa's stories, I needed to get some food. I was overdue for a Danish at the Baker's Dozen. Buttons happily loaded a plate up with three enormous pastries and handed me a cup of delicious coffee. Business was slow for the moment, so he poured me seconds on the coffee and launched into a story.

"Let me tell you a story about the dogs and the parrots. It was around the time when Bear, Scars, and Sparkle came to Santa with their fish hatchery idea. Lady Queen hadn't been feeling very well for at least a few weeks. Everyone feared she could go at any time Shots had been there a couple of times, but she just wouldn't eat. They thought it might be a virus of some kind. On top of that, no one had seen Sammie for a while. We thought she might be sick as well or maybe just feeling bad about Lady Queen. Well, the search was on. We looked in every corner of the mansion. No Sammie. Where could she be? Then someone noticed some red feathers poking out of what could be a nest high up in the production facility, near the glass pylon that supported the ceiling. Sure enough, Sammie popped her head out over the edge of the nest.

"We all watched from a distance as she stayed up there for weeks. No one could get close, not even Goober. The elves would leave food out for her and Goober. Goober stayed as close as he could get during this time. He couldn't understand why she wouldn't let him near her. Ever since we knew them, they had been inseparable. 'What did you do, Goober?' we all wanted to know. But Goober was at a loss. 'I didn't do anything. I didn't do anything.' One day the carpenters had enough. They stopped work to build scaffolding to the high support beam. Everyone else stayed at their jobs while keeping an eye on the carpenters. Santa was there with Mrs. Claus and Sir King. They were all looking up. The room was abuzz with anticipation as Sammie was about to be rescued. Was she somehow stuck up there? Everyone had a theory.

"The carpenters continued their mission. Red and Speed were constructing the scaffolding, and Hype was climbing up it. When he made it to the top, Sammie took off like a rocket. Hype was so startled he almost fell. Thank goodness, he was wearing a harness attached to the beam. I can tell you, Lon, that took my breath away. There was nothing left for Hype but to start down again. Then he heard something. 'I need a smaller elf to climb up here,' said Hype. 'Where's Hood? Get me Hood.' Hood was not very happy about heights, and it looked like a skyscraper from down on the ground. But with encouragement from Santa and all the elves, Hood decided to be brave. He put on the harness and started the long climb.

"When Hood reached the top, Hype said, 'Don't look down.' That was good advice. In the meantime, Sir King had left the building. He was barking and running around toward the front of the castle. Several times Santa told him to calm down but it didn't seem to have any effect on him. Hype told Hood to stand on his shoulders and peek into Sammie's nest. 'And be careful!' said Hype. 'You don't have to tell me twice,' said Hood. Hood stepped up onto Hype's shoulders and his hat almost touched the ceiling of the Bubble Dome. Then he looked down. All we could see were the whites of his eyes as he almost passed out. But he managed to pull himself together and look into the nest. He reported to the crowd, 'There are four baby parrots up here!'

"Hype said, 'Careful, Hood. We don't want any of the little birds to fall out of their nest.' Santa said, 'Let's move them over to the castle. We'll turn up the heat so Sammie's new little babies can be warm and safe.' Everyone was so excited about the births. Poor Sammie was near exhaustion. Goober was flipping and fluttering, saying, 'I'm a dad! I'm a dad!' 'Yes, Goober,' Santa would say. 'Congratulations! Now, try to calm down. King, you calm down too. We know Sammie has four new babies. Take it easy, you guys!'

"Hype and Hood made it down the scaffolding with the new babies safely in the palms of their hands. Sammie had waited patiently for the rescue of her children. Santa, Mrs. Claus, Buddy, and the elves oohed and aahed and cooed over the adorable little birds. Mrs. Claus asked what their names were, and Sammie said, 'Goober and I will decide that together. Let's think about that, Goober. Right now I am very hungry.' Goober escorted Sammie to get some food, and Santa and Mrs. Claus carried the little parrots over to their new home at the castle.

"Sir King was still a whirlpool of activity. When Santa opened the front door to the castle, he raced toward Mrs. Claus's office. There, on Lady Queen's rug, were three new little puppies like furry snowballs. They were drinking milk from their mom. Mrs. Claus rushed to Lady Queen and sat down beside her. 'Oh, Lady Queen. Your babies are beautiful. We're so sorry we weren't here. We were trying to help Sammie. Sir King knew. He brought us to you. Oh, they are so cute!' Goober was flying in circles and saying, 'We're both dads, Sir King. We're both dads, Sir King.' Santa went to his office to fetch Sir King's rug. He placed it next to Lady Queen, and Sir King lay down beside her.

"Word of Lady Queen's new puppies spread to every corner of the village. Everyone spoke for days about the colorful new baby parrots and the fluffy white puppies. In a week or two, everyone would be able to meet the new puppies, but for now they needed to stay

Baby dogs Rosie, Sharon, and Runner with their mom Lady Queen.

close to their mom at all times. Sammie was a good mother. She would talk to little Courtney, Brittany, Whitney, and Bloober. Those were the names she and Goober had decided on, and Mrs. Claus made them known far and wide. Bloober was the only boy; the rest were girls. Goober was a proud papa; he loved all of his children so much. The carpenter elves made sure the parrots had homes in the castle and in the village so all the elves could spend time with them.

"Sammie and Goober were wonderful parents. Sammie showed her little family where their bathroom area was. They could make a mess there, but nowhere else. The baby parrots seemed to under-stand, even though they couldn't talk yet. They had begun to fly though. At first they were a little uncertain, but in a few days they had it all together. Goober would spread his wings and fly around the castle, and little Bloober would take off right behind him. And Sammie taught her daughters, Courtney, Brittany, and Whitney, to fly in a straight line behind her.

"The puppies were starting to crawl around. Lady Queen watched as Sir King would nudge them along. Mrs. Claus named the girls Rosie, like the fairest rose, and Sharon, after the rose of Sharon tree. The boy was a little scamp, always slipping out of your hands and shooting off in all directions, so she named him Runner. When they were ready, Mrs. Claus carried the puppies to the front door so everyone could meet them. Lady Queen didn't mind at all. Many of the elves brought gifts for the little pups. Ish and Shooter from the design and invention staff gave each a collar with a Happy Pin attached, so the computer could track the pups and they would never get lost. Rosie, Runner, and Sharon spent their days playing and running around, as puppies should.

"After these births of the parrots and puppies, life at the castle and village was never the same. The dog family and the parrot family became like one big happy family, and all of their children had the very same birthday. The little dogs played with the little parrots, and they all got along. That goes for all their parents too. There has been even more joy in the castle and village ever since." I said, "Wow! What a story, Buttons! You made me feel like I was right there. Thank you so much." Once again, I had been handed a piece of the puzzle that made up life at the North Pole. It was fantastic and real at the same time. I was warming up to this cold climate.

Chapter Thirty
Santa's Thumbprint

Santa helps all of us to become better people.

I went over to the Cozy Creek Club, which Phillipi and Ola operated. We exchanged hellos, then I ordered some seafood pizza, filled my personalized mug with flavored water, and sat down at a table. Just then, Santa walked in. I had become accustomed to the way he just showed up. Ola said, "It's good to see you, Santa. Can we make you something to eat?" Santa said, "Yes, thank you. I will have whatever Lon is having." Then he pulled up a chair and sat at the table with me. Ola said, "Coming right up!"

While Santa and I were waiting for our food, we got on the subject of the parrots and the Great Pyrenees dogs. Santa and Mrs. Claus called them their babies. They didn't have any children of their own, and these animals sure got a lot of loving from them. Matter of fact, everyone in the village seemed to spoil them, but it never went to their heads. They gave as much love as they got. Santa and I touched on a lot of topics. He filled me in on some of the new toys that were in production. They sounded amazing. Of course, I can't spoil the surprise, but if I was that excited, imagine how all those boys and girls will feel on Christmas morning.

I asked Santa to tell me more about the elves. He said, "Lon, I'll be glad to. As you know, I've been around for a long time, and I've seen so much in my life. I've observed how these little people were being treated so wrongly, just because they were small in stature. This really bothered me. If it was in my power, I wanted to do something about it. These little people were no different from other people, just shorter. How unfair it seemed. I observed how people who took advantage of them called them 'little,' and I thought that might be a good place to start. I decided it would sound better if they were referred to in some other way. That's when I came up with the name 'elves.' I wanted people to see them for who they really are: herself, himself, themselves. They really liked my idea. Wrinkles said, 'That's a great idea, Kris. Now we'll be seen not for how tall we aren't but for who we really are, ourselves." And that's what they've been called ever since.

"These elves are wonderful people, Lon. They're intelligent, and they're very friendly. In my younger years, when I lived close to them in Kaskinen, Finland, I was impressed by their strength of character and how giving and merciful they are. That's the main reason Mrs. Claus and I invited them to live here at the North Pole with us. Our hearts beat the same as theirs. We are simpatico.

"Since we've been at the North Pole, my wealthy friends have told me many stories about how our life here has changed them. Lon, you've been here only a short while, yet I can sense this environment has changed you too. Many people leave a mark on this world. We all want to make a difference. If I could leave a mark, Lon, this is what it would be. I would sit down and have a conversation with every parent to put my thumbprint on them forever. I would say, 'Show love.' I would tell the couples who don't have children to live a life of showing and telling your spouse that you love them, every day. Give each other at least one hug every day. These few words and actions don't take time so much as commitment. They can change lives forever. Lon, do you realize what this would do to an entire world?

"Let's take it one step further. Let's say you have children. Never, and I mean never, let your children go to bed without telling them you love them. Then embrace them with a genuine hug. This is something both parents should do I would tell the parents they should be involved in their children's lives. I would say that their children need them in a positive way, to help them build a solid foundation for life. Parents, be a help to them, and guide them through life!

"Of course, some children just have a mom or a dad, or are raised by a grandparent or guardian. In that case, the adult or adults of the household, whatever their relationship to the children, should spend good quality time with them. Real young children love gifts, but they also want your time. When they get older, that's when they realize the value of time spent together. Children who travel back and forth to live with divorced parents in different homes need both of their parents to keep in touch all the time. The absent parent needs to call the children, every day if possible, and let them know they care and love them very much while they're away from them.

"Also, as we grow older and don't see our children and grandchildren as much, an 'I love you' and a hug should be practiced whenever we see them. The same applies to children. Whenever they visit with their grandparents, they should always tell them they love them and be very generous with hugs. That is something money can't buy, and it means so much more than money. Children need to always give respect to parents and elders—especially to those they live with. They should be kind to them, hug them, and say 'I love you' to them every day. Love begins at home. Only then can it spread to the rest of the world.

"I would also urge children to be kind to their brothers, sisters, neighbors, and friends. I would say, 'Always be a gentleman, boys. Always be a lady, girls.' I would try to teach them good manners and also things like 'Never take anything that isn't yours.' Lon, if people as a whole would take this advice, the whole world would be changed for the better. There would be fewer fights and wars, less crime and hate." I could see that Santa was very moved about this topic. He felt it deeply in his heart.

Santa continued. "I tell children all the time, 'Treat people how you want to be treated.' I say to parents, 'When was the last time you and your kids made cookies or a cake for the neighbors?' Most people don't even know their neighbors, Lon. In general, people just need to keep a giving spirit alive within themselves. We need this in our lives.

"Over the years, I've seen people throw out toys that other children would love to have. Family members should refurbish the toys and make them like new again. Sometimes a paint touch-up is all that is needed, or maybe new batteries. Stuffed animals may only need a bath. These toys could be given a new life with children who aren't as fortunate. This alone would bring such happiness and so many smiles. I know this is a good idea—if people would just do it. What would we be teaching our children if families all over the world would do this? This is really powerful stuff, Lon! I honestly think we can change the world, even if it's only a few people at a time. This is a basic and important lesson.

"Some time ago, Lon, a certain family traveled here to be with us. The parents were a little short-tempered with their child. I met with this father and mother every night to help them work through their problem. I asked them, 'When was the last time you hugged your son?' They couldn't remember. I said, 'When was the last time you told him you love him?' They looked at each other and the father said, 'We hate to admit this, but it's been a long time, Santa.' I suggested we do an experiment.

"So that night, they asked their son to come into the living room. They looked him in the eye and nervously said, 'Son, we've made mistakes over the years, and we want to ask you for forgiveness.' To make a long story short, they told their son they were very proud of him. They told him that they failed him by not showing and telling him often that they loved him very much. They both gave their son a heartfelt kiss and long, tight hugs. Tears were in their eyes; it was a very emotional time. Lon, I want you to know their lives were changed from that moment on. Taking this one action caused them to start building a much more solid bond with their son. I took an action to talk with this mother and father, and they took an action to reach out to their child with love. It really worked. Their thinking has changed forever. Their whole family started treating each other with more respect, kindness, and love. And it still continues today."

Ola spoke up. "Lon, Santa's talking about us." I had completely forgotten that Santa and I weren't alone. Ola and Phillipi had been listening to our conversation, and they took the opportunity to back up Santa's story. "Our lives changed completely that day, when we told our son Louie 'I love you' and gave him hugs. We are so grateful to Santa for that, and we have never been the same since." Then Phillipi said, "Yes, Santa cares very much for people. That's why he delivers gifts to children's homes on Christmas Eve, because he loves them so much. We are all so blessed and thankful here at the North Pole. Our lives are so good, we want to pass it on to others. Santa practices what he preaches. He changes lives one by one."

Santa then said, "Yes, we are all very grateful for this grand opportunity in our lifetime. I tell many people on the phone, and in letters and emails, 'If you practice the art of giving, kindness will come back to you.' A return of kindness can be a gift from a store, or a gift of money, or a gift of a closer friendship with someone. Don't misunderstand me. There's nothing wrong with buying things for others or making gifts. Everyone likes gifts that are given from the heart. For when we give of ourselves and do things for other people in many different ways, then we are, in our own way, helping this world to be a better place. I tell children to give in any way they can, and it will return to them."

Santa bit into the last slice of pizza. Finally he said, "Lon, we've talked about so many things, but I'm passionate about this one. I show respect to all the elves. I remember Bear, Scars, and Sparkle who wanted to start a fish hatchery. I thought it was a little farfetched at first, but I respected them and listened to what they eagerly wanted to do. Now, because I let them try their idea, the J'Yakaboo River stays well stocked and everyone catches as many fish as they need.

"I get a lot of respect from people, Lon, but it is just as important that I give respect back…all the way up to my senior elves, Wrinkles and Joy. These elves know I love them, and I know they love me. They tell me, and I tell them, all the time."

I felt Santa's deep passion for this subject. His life was a shining example of how love can change lives. I said to him, "I know I will never be the same after hearing many of your truths today, Santa, and I am very grateful you have taken the time to share yourself with me. The short while I've been here has changed my life forever." I could hardly wait to get home, so I could tell my two girls, Tiffany and Stefanie, that I love them, and give them both big bear hugs and kisses.

Chapter Thirty-One
The Lost Letter

I needed one of Blue Eyes' deluxe sundaes with rich hot chocolate sauce, whipped cream, pecans, and cherries, so I walked on over to the River's Edge Club. I was enjoying the experience of cold ice cream slowly melting on my tongue, and I can't be sure, but my eyes may have been closed. Suddenly a poke in the arm brought me around. "Hi, Lon," said Mooksie. "Good, huh?" The only reply I could make was "Mmmm." Persona and Mooksie and their Mail Room staff joined me for some dessert. They were still wearing their name tags, which helped me out a lot. They were caught up with their work for the day and stopped in on their break. We put a few tables together and started to chat.

Persona's main job at the Mail Room was to read the letters sent to Santa. She also logged in and filed all the information on the children who sent the letters. They were from all over the world. For the most part, she kept records of their names, addresses, and their requests for the upcoming Christmas. Then, she would send the letters on to the sorters. Persona thought her job was the most fun you could have at the North Pole.

Mooksie said, "Let me share a story that happened a few years ago, Lon. It's all about a lost letter. I think you know what our number one rule is in the Mail Room." "Of course," I said. "'Don't lose a letter—not one, not ever.'" "That's right," said Mooksie. "Well, what a mess we had! This is what happened. When the mail arrived, we would all have piles dumped on our desks. We would rubber-band them in bundles and then go through one bundle at a time to answer them. Today we have a huge counter in the very center of the Mail Room, and it has a tall lip around the whole edge so the mail will never fall off. But at that time, we didn't. Well, one day, a letter fell between my desk and Glisten's desk. The letter was stuck there, and we just didn't see it.

"Christmas came and went, and we were cleaning up to get everything in shape so when we woke up we could just get to work. I was sweeping the floor and accidentally bumped the desk, and this letter fell down and hit the floor. All the elves standing near me also saw what had happened. We froze and stared at the letter. Finally, I bent down, picked it up, and held it gingerly. I looked at everybody and they nodded to me, so I opened it. It was from two boys in Michigan, in the United States, Germaine and Antowine. They requested two gifts each. Germaine asked for a dump truck and digging tools he could play with in the huge sandbox behind their house. His brother Antowine asked for a crane and a cement truck. These boys already had a history with Santa. Every December, they would take some of their favorite toys, clean them up, and paint them if needed to make them look new. Then they would wrap them up and give them to needy families in their town in Michigan. They knew if they did this, they would get new toys from Santa for Christmas. Santa really loved their attitude. And boy, this year the letter was lost.

"Well, that year Santa arrived at their house to deliver their gifts as usual. Their sister Princella had a simple list and asked for some clothes and a purse. After Santa placed Princella's gifts under the tree, he saw a note with 'To Santa' written in big letters across the envelope. So he opened it up and read:

Dear Santa,

On the kitchen counter we left you some double chocolate chip cookies and some oatmeal raisin cookies that we made. You can take them with you if you are in a hurry, or you can eat them now. Here's some carrots for the raindeer too. Oh, and a root beer for when you get thirsty. By the way, Santa, many thanks in advance for the gifts you brought us this year. Thanks for the dump truck, the sand-box digging tools, the crane, and the cement truck. Merry Christmas to you too.

Love,
Germaine and Antowine

"Santa said to himself, 'What am I going to do now? I can't go all the way back to the North Pole! I've got to be on my way across the United States. What a mess!' Santa realized something had happened to their letter, because it never got to him. Where did it go? Did it get mailed properly? Was it dropped? What happened? Luckily, Santa always packed extra gifts in his bag, just in case he ran into children who performed special kindnesses, like these two boys, Germaine and Antowine. He went out to his sleigh to see what might be in his Christmas bag marked 'extra toys.' He dug deep and pulled out two fire engines and two pairs of roller skates. The roller skates had an emblem with Germaine and Antowine's favorite sports team on them.

"That year, the boys didn't get what they asked for. But, on Christmas morning, they were happy with what they received anyway, because Santa left them gifts they didn't have already, and they were new toys. The boys were happy and thankful, as always. You see, Lon, this family was a poor family, but you would never have known that. Santa also left a few extra things for Germaine and Antowine, because he knew they gave some of their own toys to other children each year, and he wanted to reward them for giving freely and joyfully. Santa always wanted Christmas to be the best day of the year for presents for children, next only to their birthday. It is important for him to give them just the right gifts that will make them happy on this day.

"When Santa arrived back at the North Pole, Glisten and I were there to meet and greet him. We both felt so sad about the lost letter and the disappointed boys. We showed it to Santa, and he smiled and said, 'I want you to know that you two have always done a great job in the Mail Room. This lost letter was an honest mistake. Don't worry, boys. I took care of the situation on the spot.' Santa explained everything and put our minds at rest. He said, 'I know those two boys, and they will always be happy with whatever I choose for them, because they are thankful.' Santa told us, 'Children all over the world need to realize that I'm not God; I'm just Santa. All I can do is try my best to make some dreams come true at Christmas. All is well, boys.'

"Santa tells children, 'If you get something you don't ask for, just think that perhaps someone lost your letter by accident, or maybe it got sent to the wrong address. For unknown reasons, this sometimes happens. You might get something different from what you asked for, but please, always be thankful for whatever you do get.'" I looked at Mooksie and we both said, "That's the truth."

"Right after Christmas that year, the Mail Room was totally redesigned. The Design Department built that huge island with the ledge all the way around, so all the letters would stay on the table. So, at least one unknown reason for lost letters was eliminated."

Mooksie loved to tell stories about his job, and I was a willing victim. He said, "Let me tell you about the girl who sent her gift back to Santa. Her name was Tracy, and she lived in Koln, Germany. She wanted a real Shetland sheepdog for Christmas. Instead, Santa gave her a stuffed toy that looked like a Shetland sheepdog, and a doll. When she went to the tree and opened her gifts on Christmas Eve, there was no real dog. Lon, let me just insert this. Children need to understand that Santa doesn't have complete control of everything. Some things, like real animals, have to come from a parent, grandparent, or someone else who is a gift giver. This child didn't understand that. Well, Tracy rewrapped the stuffed Shetland sheepdog and sent it back to Santa. Santa said, 'Some children are spoiled and need to be taught to be thankful for whatever they receive, because it's a gift, not an obligation.' So, Santa sent Tracy a letter back to tell her that Santa has feelings too and she hurt his feelings. He said he counseled her a bit in his letter, but he never disclosed its full contents to us. Some things are private.

"After that Christmas, Santa saw many changes in Tracy. Santa kept us abreast of her situation, and told us that she turned over a new leaf and started giving gifts to less fortunate children during the year. All of us in the Mail Room were amazed at her turn-around. Wow! Santa's letter changed her, and to this day, she keeps giving throughout the year, and, I might add, she loves Santa. Santa said, 'Now she gives more than she receives, and it makes her even happier than when she was the only one receiving.'

"Santa always loves to give to givers. He says even a poor child can learn to give, since no gift is too small. They can make crafts, draw pictures, or perform a special chore for someone. Everyone can give something. Some of the greatest gifts are not bought with money.

"Tracy blossomed into a wonderful youth. Then years later, when she grew up, she became a professional handler and breeder of Shetland sheepdogs. Her love and passion for these dogs is such a wonderful thing. Santa said, 'Maybe the reason her life changed for the better was because she had a change of heart.' Tracy learned to give and she became blessed herself. She still writes Santa.

"Stories like Tracy's just melt Santa's heart. It pleases him that he can influence children to turn their lives around. Santa keeps those letters in a special place in his office and he reads them from time to time. He feels so blessed by these children. He loves to update us on their growth and progress when they become givers. Santa is thrilled that he has such an impact throughout the world."

Persona said, "Let's tell Lon about John from St. Thomas in the Virgin Islands. Lon, this child was really something. Does anyone remember his list?" Everyone from the Mail Room started speaking up. We ordered a round of hot cider and slowly sipped as Persona continued. "I'll take that as a yes. That letter, Lon, was known as the 'I want' letter. I'll try to remember how it went:

Dear Santa,

I want to instruct you to give me all my 'wants' listed here for Christmas, and then I will be happy. I want a matchbox car. I want a pair of tennis shoes. I want a basketball. I want a plane ticket to visit Hawaii. I want a baseball. I want a baseball glove. I want two tickets to see a baseball game. I want two baseball hats, one red and one blue. I want a chessboard. I want my own TV for my bedroom. I want a new bike. I want a four-wheeler.

John

"Wow, Lon. I just couldn't understand how someone could ask Santa for all this and expect to get it. I just had to read it to everyone in the Mail Room. When I finished, we looked at each other and started laughing. I said, 'What do we do with this letter, except show Santa?' Well, we couldn't wait to get this letter out of our hands and into Santa's. Santa said, 'That's okay. I have a special letter for children like this.' And Santa headed straight to his office for some stationery. He seemed to have every unusual situation already worked out, so this letter wasn't anything to get upset about. Santa showed us the letter he was sending John, and this is how it read:

Dear John,

1. *You cannot get a gift, John, if you're not a giver. In life, there are givers and there are takers. Always be a giver, John. When you give, whether it's your used toys or if you do something nice for someone, whatever you feel like giving, then you will receive back.*

2. *Never ask for numerous items, John. It's not polite and I cannot give them all to you. Your list puts a lot of pressure on me to decide which gift I should give you.*

3. *Always be thankful for what you get, no matter what it is. Remember, whatever you receive is free and given freely.*

4. *Always remember, John, I'm not God—I'm Santa.*

So John, enjoy the two baseball hats, one red and one blue, and here is a bat with two baseballs. I hope you get a lot of years out of them—sharing them with your friends.

"Santa also wrote some things that would help John become a more giving person. He gave him pointers on other matters that would be invaluable in John's life, and he told him that he loved him very much. John was another one who shocked us with his transformation. He changed over the years, for the better. He also became a giver, all because of Santa."

Persona continued. "Santa answers all of his letters from children, even—maybe especially—those like John's. He strives to help children in any way he can. If he can spark a positive change in a child, he is deeply happy. He wants to be a part of the hopes and dreams of making this world better. Santa not only wants our world to be a more friendly place, but he equally wants our actions to be more giving to each other." Mooksie said, "Over the years, we're seeing more children become better children, and they give more than they used to. Santa's dream really is working!"

Persona said, "If you have the time, Lon, I would like to tell you one of my favorite stories." I said, "I'm all ears for you, Persona." So, she continued. "It's a story about two sisters named Kaliani and Elka Patel. Their family was extremely poor. Kaliani wrote to Santa. Let me see if I can recall her letter:

> *Dear Santa,*
>
> *My name is Kaliani Patel, and I am from India. My sister Elka and I decided we just had to write to you. I know this is a hard thing, but I'm going to ask you for a home. My family works so hard. We've never asked for anything ever before, because we are taught to be humble. However, I feel very pressed this year, Santa, to ask you this. I promise I will never ask for anything else again. We are just so tired of getting rained on at nighttime, and my mother's health isn't good either. The mosquitoes bite us every night. It really gets very hot here in India too. I am so sorry to have to ask this, but thank you for even reading this letter.*
>
> *We love you,*
> *Kaliani and Elka Patel*

"What a letter, Lon. We shared it with all the Mail Room workers. We knew we needed to get this letter to Santa ASAP! Santa was at his desk. He read the letter right away and just wept. I did too. He wept for the little girls' situation, and because he knew he couldn't give her a home. He couldn't afford it. However, he took the letter straight to the Design Department and told Bubbles, 'This is an emergency letter. Please work on this right away. Figure out what we can make for this family to fix this dire problem. As soon as you have a solution, come find me immediately!'

"Bubbles filled in Shooter, Snickers, and Shadow on their new challenge. They knew Santa couldn't deliver a log home to India, and they were in deep thought over the problem. Their brainstorming hit nothing but dead ends. Then Hood entered wearing a new hat with water dripping off of it. Shooter said, 'Where's your hood, Hood? What are you doing with a hat?' 'Well,' said Hood, 'Petunia made this for me out of some special material at the Sewing Department. She poured water on my hood to show me how it doesn't get soaked and it doesn't leak. The water just runs right off.' Light bulbs went off over the heads of the whole design team. Well, not really, but you know what I mean. The same thought hit them all at the same time. They wasted no time getting over to the Sewing Department to see Petunia. They didn't even explain to Hood that he had handed them a monumental solution. He had no idea what was going on. Petunia told them that the material had been sent to the North Pole accidentally. It had been mis-shipped somehow.

"Well, undaunted, they left Petunia, and Shooter went straight to his design desk. He stayed there for hours, making drawing after drawing. By the next afternoon, he presented the team with the initial idea for a 'pop-up tent home' to sleep eight people. Petunia got to work on it right away, cutting sections and sewing them together. Only one day later, they set up the demonstration model in the middle of the village. We were all there to see the unveiling. It was a great event and a huge success.

"Santa watched as they put together the tent home in about twelve minutes, from box to completion. Most of it was easy, because the

Kaliani and Elka Patel's new home from Santa.

Design Department devised it in a way that it could, for the most part, pop up. It came with ropes and tie-downs too, and some metal posts meant to be pounded into the ground with any available rock, to hold it there. Easy instructions with pictures of every step were included. This tent home had a large zippered door and a few screened-in zippered windows. It was totally waterproof and insectproof; not a drop or bug could find its way in. And it was durable, with very heavy flex rods. It definitely fit the bill.

"Since this was one of our biggest gifts ever to be boxed up, we could barely get it to fit into the shrinking machine. Many of the elves helped. We pushed and squeezed and stuffed until we finally got it inside. We got into some pretty funny positions along the way. Our laughing probably slowed things down. But eventually we were victorious. Lon, this tent home not only sleeps eight, it also has mattresses that automatically fill up with air as soon as you unwrap them. They proved to be the biggest problem to handle in trying to get this wrapped. It took a lot of elf power to get all the air out of the mattresses and fold them up before they inflated again

"The innovative solution pleased Santa to no end. The Design and Sewing departments really pulled this one off in record time.

Now Santa could deliver a new home to Kaliani and Elka Patel's family in India. In fact, that year Santa gave a lot of poor people in India pop-up tent homes."

Persona finished her story just in time. She and the rest of the Mail Room staff had to get back to work. I thanked Mooksie and Persona for sharing their wonderful stories with me, and we hugged goodbye. I didn't have a schedule to keep, so I stayed awhile after they left and pondered Kaliani and Elka's letter. The speed with which the Design and the Sewing departments put the tent home together was truly inspirational. It made me feel I could accomplish just about anything I wanted. I could feel the possibilities. I made a vow to put that to the test as soon as I got home.

Chapter Thirty-Two
My Time With Wrinkles and Joy

Santa's first sleigh rests on the train in Jemdaza,
ready for its first trip to the North Hills.

Wrinkles and Joy had me over to their house for the afternoon. I was looking forward to visiting with them. My time here was drawing to a close, and very soon I would be returning to the Polar Ice

Cap No. 12 Base Camp. Joy wanted to tell me about their move to the North Pole from Kaskinen, Finland, before I left. She put out some homemade brownies and peppermint tea. Her eyes danced with excitement as she shared her story. I snacked while she talked.

"We took a train all the way to Jemdaza, with all our possessions, and loaded everything onto a sleigh bound for the North Hills On the sleigh were Santa, Mrs. Claus, Wrinkles, myself, and our two sons, Happy and Slim. Santa and Susie were great friends of ours, and we were committed to Santa's dream. All four of us had made the decision jointly to go looking for a way to make that dream a reality. The two parrots, Goober and Sammie, were also with us. The raindeer—Dancer, Prancer, Dasher, Flasher, Veben, and Vixen—pulled the sleigh. It was a sturdy, heavy-duty sleigh, very well built. But that was not surprising, for Santa and Wrinkles had made it. It had to be a strong sleigh to carry all of us and our belongings too. We had tools, furniture, food, seeds, plants, and some other essentials for setting up a new life in a vast, cold wilderness. As you can probably imagine, we were loaded down!

"The North Wind blew, but the raindeer didn't hesitate to pull the sleigh. Santa followed the map that Johnathan Andrew Witherspoon had given him. At times we were a little scared, but our minds were made up. Slim and Happy were very young at this point. As you can imagine, Lon, our sons thought they were off on a great adventure. They were just so excited to take off from school and go traveling. In fact, they didn't care where we were going. They just wanted to go 'somewhere.'"

Wrinkles jumped in. "Santa had a trick to make the raindeer go, Lon. He would say, 'Off—Dancer! Off—Prancer! Off—Dasher! Off—Flasher! Off—Veben! Off—Vixen' This would make the raindeer move forward. Riding in a sleigh drawn by raindeer was a thrill ride for the boys. We stopped only for brief rests and to eat. The boys eagerly asked Santa if they could feed the raindeer. Santa was always so kind to our boys. He said, 'Since you boys are so anxious to do this, yes, of course you can!' Joy and I were pleased to see this, Lon, because we knew it was the highlight of their trip. It seemed like we were making great time and perhaps would make it there before nightfall."

Joy picked up the story. "Santa felt right at home in the sleigh, since he loved the wintertime. As we approached the North Hills, he was the first one to spot a huge mountain in the distance. There were tall trees all around the mountain. Santa said, 'It looks like a huge pole in the middle of a forest. Ho-ho!' Happy yelled out, 'pole—North Pole!' And Santa said, 'Well of course, Happy! We will call this "The North Pole." We are home!'

"We continued on through the woods and right up to the opening in the mountain, where we arrived at the exact destination shown on Santa's map. We stopped at the opening to the cave, and Santa told us to wait in the sleigh while he checked it out to make sure it was safe. Santa yelled, 'Anyone here?' as loud as he could. No one answered, and he didn't see anything moving around. We certainly didn't want to run into any big bears roaming around inside the cave, or even sleeping. Santa got back into the sleigh and directed the raindeer to pull the sleigh into the cave. He unhooked the raindeer, and we all started the unloading process. We hoped we had packed enough food until we could grow our own. There were some signs of Johnathan Andrew Witherspoon's stay here. He had lived and worked inside this very mountain cave.

"At first, when we were unloading the sleigh, the parrots wouldn't budge. They preferred to stay warm in their cages with their blankets. They were snuggled together as if they were one. Santa made an announcement, mostly for the parrots' sake, that he and Wrinkles would soon get a nice hot fire going, to provide warmth in the cave. He was right. It wasn't long before we were all warm and toasty. Santa, Wrinkles, and the boys collected many long branches to put in front of the cave opening to keep the wind out—and the warmth in. Not only did the campfire keep us warm that evening, it also created enough light for us to see by. We were all rejoicing around our miniature bonfire, together with the children, Slim and Happy. The raindeer and the parrots were gathered around us too.

"All of a sudden, the boys started singing Christmas songs with the parrots. What a hoot! Most of the sounds were off-key, squeaky, and high-pitched, but Santa, Mrs. Claus, Wrinkles, and I cheerfully joined in. After all, we were celebrating arriving at the North Pole, and it was music to our ears. We had a great time bonding together that very first evening."

Wrinkles spoke again. "Singing Christmas songs around the campfire became an evening tradition until we moved into our own homes. We still talk about it to this day. When I look back on it, they were tough times, but we didn't see it that way at the time. We were happy pioneering in the north. Happy, because we knew we were living Santa's great dream—in its very first stages. How exciting it is to build a dream. And what great memories we all have now, along with the realization of that dream. It's almost too good to be true—but it is!"

"That's right, dear. We are very fortunate, aren't we?" said Joy. "Well, after getting some much needed sleep that first night, the next morning, after breakfast, Santa and Wrinkles started building a door for the cave opening, to keep heat inside and danger outside. Then we all went to work on building our homes, since we wanted out of the cave as soon as possible. Lon, we were grateful to arrive at the cave, but just as grateful to leave it. We owe the cave a debt of gratitude. It gave us shelter, and it sure put a desire in us to hurry and get things built. Most of the jobs that needed to be done we worked on as a team, which brought all of us even closer together, and we made the best of every situation. We all worked long days, because we knew if we did, it wouldn't be long before we would be in our own homes.

"You may wonder, Lon, how we could see inside the cave during the day. Well, thank goodness, there were enough cracks in the cave to provide a sufficient amount of light to do what we had to do. We were very thankful for that.

"Mrs. Claus and I had fun setting up our new cave home. There was a kitchen area, a sleeping area, and even a place we could use as a stable for the raindeer. A little stream ran through the cave and under some rocks, to somewhere outside. What a great advantage to have a natural water source inside the cave. A delightful waterfall was an added bonus.

"Just like the map said, there was a garden fairly close to the mouth of the cave. It was overgrown, but Susie and I went to work on it right away, planting our seeds and plants, and in a few days it was looking neat and hopeful. We found some tunnels throughout the cave. In one of them, we saw mushrooms growing. It was damp and dark, the perfect environment for mushrooms. There must have been thousands of them. No mushroom shortage here! Now, Lon, you can probably guess what we had to eat that first six months at the North Pole. Yep, mushrooms. We used them in everything. Good thing we all liked mushrooms. We had fried mushrooms, fried potatoes with mushrooms, batter-dipped mushrooms, mushroom soup, mushroom vegetable soup, mushroom pizza, stuffed mushrooms, mushroom gravy on biscuits, and all kinds of mushroom sauces. We got very creative. In a short time though, thank goodness, the garden started producing vegetables, because we were about 'mushroomed out.' We now had onions, radishes, lettuce, potatoes, carrots, tomatoes, cucumbers, and other vegetables. They were growing so quickly, but we didn't question it. We were so happy to have such a wonderful variety of fresh food to eat.

"Happy and Slim really gave it their all too. Even though they were young, they thought they could do anything, so we let them try. In their trying, they surprised us all and accomplished much, cutting down considerably on our workload and our time. The boys cut tree branches and hauled them in to keep the campfire going inside the cave. That was a tiring task for them, and at times it seemed like they were dragging—but they never complained. They took it upon themselves to keep us well stocked in firewood. I was so proud of my sons; they were such a big help.

"Whenever we could, Mrs. Claus and I helped carry the smaller logs for the log homes. The raindeer really pulled their load, in more ways than one. They hauled the bigger logs out of the forest and into the open area where we started to build the log homes. When our first homes were finished, trust me, it was like heaven. The same day the roofs were completed, Susie and I were digging in and getting settled, we wanted out of the cave and into our homes so bad.

"Our first home had a nice kitchen, dining room, living room, three bedrooms, and a bathroom. It was sheer luxury. Santa and Mrs. Claus's home was pretty much the same, except we built a loft above the living room, which served as a new home for Goober and Sammie. The great thing was that the heat from the fireplace would rise to the top of the loft and keep the parrots warm and comfy. They really loved that. It was perfect for them. Ha—it almost made me want to be a parrot too, Lon." Joy and I had a good chuckle over that one, and I said, "Me too, Joy! I wish I could have seen all of you in those days." Joy gave me an open smile and said, "That would have been lovely, Lon."

"Well, it wasn't long before Santa and Wrinkles and the boys had built a new stable area and a nice barn for the raindeer. The timing was perfect, since Dancer was about to give birth to another pair of twins. There was never a dull moment, I can tell you that."

Wrinkles said, "Santa kept his dream in front of us, so we always knew why we were working. While the boys and I helped bring in wood from the forest, Santa would share his ideas and plans for making gifts for children When I came back from a long hard day working with Santa, Joy awaited with excitement for every detail Santa had told us that day. He always sounded so excited about the future here. If you had heard him talk, Lon, you would have had faith also that this dream of his was really going to come to pass. He kept reassuring us that if we had enough faith, it would come true. He then told us that years from now we would look back on this beginning and know we had been an important part of making an awesome dream come true."

Joy spoke. "And that's how it's turned out. Amazing, isn't it? Where was I? Oh yes, it wasn't long before our North Pole was taking shape. We were protected by the mountain on one side and the forest all around us. This gave us security and shielded us from the weather. Our environment was becoming comfortable and safe, the perfect conditions for new growth.

"We had arrived at the North Pole in January, and now it was close to May. That was the time when a young man by the name of Lester Shreiner Zook I, whom we all know as Buddy, came to see us. He was just a teenager at the time. Buddy walked up with a newspaper clipping in his hand and said, 'I'm looking for Kris Kringle.' Wrinkles noticed him first and greeted him warmly, though he was a little taken aback by what he saw. Wrinkles introduced Buddy to Santa, and Santa said, 'I'm Kris Kringle. Can I help you?' Buddy said, 'I'm

Buddy,' and they shook hands. Susie took one look at the weary traveler and immediately invited him in for a nice hot bowl of soup with crusty bread and some chamomile tea. We all sat around the table and watched Buddy eat heartily. He won over Susie when he said, 'Mrs. Claus, you are the hostess with the mostest.'

We were all very eager to hear his story. He said, 'It was quite a journey. But I finally arrived to Jemdaza, and the folks there pointed me toward the North Hills. They tried hard to talk me out of coming, but my mind was made up.' Buddy said he was so elated when he saw the mountain and the surrounding forest. At the same time he could smell the faint aroma of burning wood. Then he spotted a thin stream of smoke rising from the direction of the mountain. He said he was so happy and relieved, because he knew at that point he was traveling in the right direction. Santa said, 'What do you want from us?' And Buddy replied, 'Here's your ad:

EMPLOYMENT: I WANT YOU!

Under 48 inches tall. Must relocate. Will give food and housing. Looking for great people willing to come dream a dream with me. Contact Kris Kringle at Jemdaza, North Hills. Directions to the North Hills: Upon arriving at Jemdaza, go north one hundred miles. Bring tools of your trade. Dress warm; it's cold here. Start the walk and we will meet you. Let's build together!—Kris.

"Before Santa could say anything, Buddy jumped in excitedly, 'Well, Kris, I'm seventeen years old, but I'm almost eighteen. I ran away from an orphanage because I was mistreated. By pure chance, I saw your ad in the paper. I cut it out and tucked it away. I put in a lot of thought about your dream, Kris, and I want so badly for it to be my dream too. You're probably wondering why I am even here, when the ad specifically says no taller than forty-eight inches. But I was determined. Somehow, with a burning desire in my heart, I just knew this would work out for me. So, I packed everything I owned and came here. I knew in my heart that no matter what, I was going to make it here! I wasn't going to let anything stop me.

"'My first obstacle was that I didn't have money for a train ticket. I was standing on the platform, wondering what to do, when the conductor came up to me. He asked if I was lost. I poured out my whole story to him, about the orphanage and your newspaper ad and how I was heading toward the promise of a better life. Somehow it touched him deeply. He had tears in his eyes and he told me that he wanted to be a part of helping me reach my dream. He was so kind. He paid for my trip out of his earnings. I think he got tired of me thanking him, but I was overwhelmed and so grateful. He smiled at me and said he knew I was thankful, and that was enough for him. This man had a really big heart.

"'I ran into some more good luck when I met a captain of a small ship that was headed in my direction. I told him all about my dream and what had happened to me so far, and he let me have a bunk for nothing. This man understood where I came from, because he had grown up in an orphanage too. At that point I really felt blessed and absolutely motivated to the point of no return. After my train ride and my boat ride, during the last leg of my journey I was on foot. I walked for a long time, but my desire to come to the North Hills and be part of a family was like a beacon that drew me forward. Somehow, I knew it was all going to work out for me.' Tears filled Buddy's eyes, and his voice broke for a second. 'I've never been part of a family before.'

"Suddenly, the weight of Buddy's journey fell hard on his slight body. He looked like he might collapse if he didn't get some rest soon. Susie got a pillow and some blankets and made a place for him on the couch. We were all moved by Buddy's determination to find a better life. He had never known family, yet he knew it was the very thing he needed to make his life complete. With tears in his eyes, Santa said, 'Welcome home, Buddy. You can live here with all of us, and be a part of our family here at the North Pole.' Now we all had tears in our eyes. And Buddy was on cloud nine. In fact, I don't think he has ever come down from that cloud yet. He says his life has been a series of miracles to be able to come here, and he will always have heartfelt thanks for Santa and Mrs. Claus and this chance-of-a-lifetime opportunity. By the way, Buddy doesn't mind at all being the only person over forty-eight inches tall to answer Santa's ad. He fits in just fine.

"Well, we insisted that Buddy rest for a few days to recover from his long journey. As soon as he felt revived again, Santa shared his dream with him. He told him how he wanted to help children in need and to respond to their requests for help. He said it was going to take a whole village of people to help make this dream come true. Santa explained how he had met Johnathan Andrew Witherspoon, about the map Johnathan had given him, and how Johnathan was participating in Santa's dream with his generous financial backing. He said he expected many elves to come, but there was no way of knowing how many or when. Buddy asked Santa if he could be his assistant. 'Whatever you want me to do, that is what I want to do,' said Buddy. He felt honored to be of help, and he has never, ever complained. Buddy knows what it's like to need help, and helping others fills him with joy. He is very respected here. He is a wonderful gentleman and a great asset to everyone. To Buddy, no one is a stranger. He has found the life he searched for.

"One of the first things Santa taught Buddy was how to pull a flat sled with the raindeer. The sled is mounted on skis so you could stack wood on top and pull it up to the cave and into the mountain. They had so much fun playing around with that sled. Buddy was a quick learner, and he did a great job."

Wrinkles said, "I remember the first time Santa asked Buddy to take the sleigh and raindeer to get supplies in Jemdaza. Ivy and the North Wind had helped Santa locate a family that was on their way to join us. Buddy was to pick them up and bring them to the North Pole. It was Buddy's first solo drive with the sleigh and he really enjoyed that job. Buddy came back loaded down with elves with their tools and possessions, plus the monthly supplies and the mail. He proved himself worthy of Santa's trust, and he won it from that day forward. Now Buddy always meets our guests on the way to the North Pole. Santa even gave him access to the savings account. Even though

Buddy is thoroughly capable of handling these trips by himself, Santa sometimes goes along so they can spend quality time together.

"We kept building one small log home after another, all in a row, because we expected lots of new arrivals would be joining us. One of the first families to arrive was Mr. and Mrs. Avanti Sebastiani Crimbottlesworth, wasn't it, dear?" Joy smiled and nodded. "When they saw a tall young man in a sleigh pulled by six raindeer coming toward them, they didn't know what to think. Knowing how hard our own journey had been at times, I can't say I blame them. Buddy expertly circled around and pulled up beside them, then said, 'I'm Buddy. Are you looking for Kris Kringle?' The answer was a surprised and delighted 'Yes!' 'Hop in,' said Buddy. 'Let's put your possessions on the flat sled, and I'll take you to him.'

"Mr. Crimbottlesworth is now our village candymaker. His wife's name is Joni. Ever since they arrived, she has served as assistant to Mrs. Claus. They share a close-knit friendship. You might say they're like two peas in a pod.

"The more people arrived, the more homes we needed, but the more help we had too, so construction was really booming. Everything was working out so smoothly We fit in with each other so easily, and we were becoming like family. Where we came from, we knew what it felt like to be looked down upon. So, in our minds, we all knew if we could live with other people our size, in the same area, we would live simply as equals. Size wouldn't be an issue. Of course, Santa, Mrs. Claus, and Buddy were the exception. They're not your typical tall persons. They're more like honorary elves and important members of our family. Family is key here at the North Pole, Lon. It felt like a family reunion every time another family arrived. We were all so glad to meet each other and start a new and wonderful life."

Joy said, "Wrinkles and I always made it a point to greet the new arrivals. We wanted to make everyone feel at home. Santa and Mrs. Claus extended a very warm welcome to everyone too. After they'd settled in, Santa would share his dream and figure out jobs for them. One way or another, most of them would be involved in making toys. This was exciting news indeed. What a great life's work! Everyone, without exception, felt special and useful. All of them wanted to be a big part of Santa's dream.

"Our population grew by leaps and bounds those first few years. More than two hundred and fifty elves arrived. The village was really taking shape. We had to enlarge the garden quite a bit, but everyone helped by growing plants in their homes. And still, little people kept coming. It was so interesting how everyone had a different story. We all had our struggles to get here, and I think all of us felt like turning back at some point. But we all knew 'home' wasn't really where we came from. It was where we were going. Somehow, we mustered the courage and determination to move on, and we all made it here to the North Pole. Then, when we arrived here, our sorrows fell away because we were with our own, and we felt like family. Thank goodness we didn't listen to the people in Jemdaza who tried to talk us out of hiking to the North Hills. They'd say how dangerous it was, just snow, mountains, and woods, and not a living soul. But we kept our eye on the prize. Kris Kringle had invited us to join him in building a better life, and we were going, no matter what.

"Oh my, look at the time. I didn't mean to talk your ear off, Lon." "Not at all, Joy," I said. "It's always a pleasure to visit with you and Wrinkles." Wrinkles said, "I hope we've filled in another piece of that North Pole puzzle you've talked about. I just want to say how glad I am I fell into your igloo that day. It's been a real pleasure having you stay with us. And you know, I think you would make a terrific honorary elf, Lon. Don't you think so, dear?" "Just terrific," said Joy, and she smiled her sweet smile. It was with some regret that I left them standing there in their doorway.

Chapter Thirty-Three
The Elves Honor Santa and Mrs. Claus

I walked over to one of my favorite haunts, the River's Edge Club, and sat out on the deck, drowning my sorrows in a double fudge banana split with sprinkles and cherries. I stared into the J'Yakaboo River thinking about all that had happened to me in the last week. I'd met so many wonderful elves who told me so many great stories. I had a lot of great memories to take back home with me. Goober and Bloober flew by, and I wondered what mischief they were up to now. The air was cool by the river, and the gurgling of the water was relaxing.

My eyes caught Britches trying to round up one of the Jersey cows. She had gotten loose and was having quite a happy-go-lucky time walking freely around the village. He finally caught up with her when she stopped for a drink at the river. Britches said, "Don't move, Molly." As he grabbed hold of her rope, he spotted two more cows, Jolly and Dolly, on the other side of the river. Britches walked Molly back to the barn and returned to spoil Jolly and Dolly's fun. "Here, Jolly. Here, Dolly." They looked up at him, resigned to their fate. I saw Sugar and Buzz peeking out around the corner and laughing the whole time, and I wondered…who let the cows out? I found myself laughing too. Something interesting or fun was always going on here, no matter where you were.

A lovely mature lady elf came out on the deck with two hot and steamy teas in her hand. She said, "I told Blue Eyes I would bring some hot flavored tea out to you, and if you don't mind, Lon, I'll have one with you." I pushed my chair back to get up and said, "I would love that. Please join me. I don't think we've met yet. What is your name?" She said, "My name is Lady Johannah." I said, "I'm very pleased to meet you, Lady Johannah, and thank you so much for the sweet hot tea." She said, "You're welcome. It's really relaxing out here, isn't it, Lon?" "Sure is," I replied. She said, "I see Britches caught all his cows and put them back in the barn. I think the little ones get a kick out of seeing Britches run after them." I replied, "Lady Johannah, that sure was a sight to see. It seems like these cows wander quite often. It makes me wonder if they get a little help." We shared a knowing laugh at that.

"So, Lady Johannah, what do you do here?" "I'm in charge of canning and freezing. I have many helpers who pick the fruit and vegetables. Then they help me prepare them for the canning or freezing process. We always stay busy, making sure the stockroom and big freezers stay full. That makes the chefs' work much easier. Whatever they need is always close at hand. My helpers and I replace items as they run out." I asked, "Do you make jams and jellies also?" "Oh sure. At the back of the dining room, off of the kitchen, is where the canning and freezing preparation room is. Those jams and jellies boiling in the pot make the whole room smell so heavenly. We never want to run out of them, so we keep close tabs on which ones are going the fastest and keep them stocked. Our top five are raspberry jam, blackberry jam, peach jam, cinnamon jelly, and plum jelly. Strawberry is a good one too. We make about thirty varieties total. The little elves really love the cinnamon jelly, especially on my homemade cinnamon rolls." I said, "Well, Lady Johannah, I would love to try one of your cinnamon rolls before I leave, if that's okay with you." She replied, "Oh, I know you'd enjoy them, Lon. I will be glad to make you some."

I asked her what she liked to can the most, and she said, "That would be peaches and blackberries. Santa and Mrs. Claus really like peach cobbler and blackberry cobbler. So I make sure we never run low on those two. In fact, Lon, I have always loved peaches also. So, how do you like our fruit here at the North Pole?" I said, "I think it is some of the best I've ever tasted. I like all kinds of fruit, and every piece of your fruit here is perfect and tasty. No complaints by me."

Lady Johannah continued. "Most everyone likes apples here, and I get a lot of requests for my famous apple pie on my days off from work. My helpers in the kitchen help me make applesauce too. As for vegetables, we blanch them before freezing. We also have huge vacuum-packing machines. They take all the air out of the bag prior to freezing, so no preservatives are needed in our fruit and vegetables. That's why they taste like we just picked them. We eat a lot of fresh vegetables and fresh fruit too. But when we cook our soups, the chefs use the freezer packs. One thing we have here, Lon, is plenty of food. We stay so well stocked that sometimes I think we will never use all of it up." We both smiled.

I said, "Lady Johannah, it sounds like you really enjoy what you do." "Yes, I really do, Lon. I came with my family from Germany, and all of us just love it here. It is so peaceful to be among our own." I said, "All the elves have told me a story about the North Pole. Won't you tell me one?" "Yes, I would like that, but let's get another tea first." We settled in with a fresh hot cup of tea, and Lady Johannah began to tell me the story of when the elves honored Santa and Mrs. Claus.

"The story goes like this, Lon. It was again time for the Cajun River Festival, our annual banquet. The chefs, Munch, Crunch, Ruby, Diamond, Ice, Quicken, and Smitten, all used their talents to prepare Cajun recipes. They had all kinds of Cajun fish dishes: shrimp creole, lobster Cajun style, trout, smoked salmon, lobster bisque, and a variety of fish salads that were very tasty too. Elaborate ice sculptures in the shape of fish that stood about four feet tall decorated the serving table. It was very impressive work.

"The dining facility was decked out and the tables were filled with so many entrées, you couldn't see a speck of tablecloth. Everyone was already seated when Wrinkles entered with Santa and Mrs. Claus, who had no idea what we had in store for them that night. Sir King, Lady Queen, and their pups, and Goober, Sammie, and all the young parrots were there too.

"Wrinkles seated Santa and Mrs. Claus, walked up to the microphone, and gave it a few taps. Then he announced, 'Santa and Mrs. Claus, we're here to honor you this evening.' Everyone clapped and cheered. The Clauses' jaws dropped open in shock. 'Santa and Susie, we could all write a book about how much we love and appreciate you two, but tonight, because the time will swiftly go by, we want to give everyone a chance to say something in appreciation of what you mean to them. I will start. Santa, Susie, I thank you both for being my true friends.' People were already lining up. Joy said, 'Thank you, Susie, for always taking time to listen to me when I need someone to talk to.' Slim said, 'Thank you, Santa, for being a second dad to me.' Happy said, 'Thank you for making me happy.'

"Joni said, 'Thank you for allowing us to share your dream.' Chuckles said, 'Thank you for running those ads in the newspapers.' Lavender said, 'Thank you for being there for me.' Pockets said, 'Thank you for sharing with us.' Diamond said, 'Thank you for giving to us.' Ruby said, 'Thank you for teaching us great character by the way you live.' Crunch said, 'Thank you for my wife. It's because of this Christmas wonderland that I met her.' Munch said, 'Thank you for my wife too. It's because of this Christmas wonderland that I met her also.' Ice said, 'Thank you for giving me your time.' Quicken said, 'Thank you for your council.' Lady Whisper said, 'Thank you for giving me space to do my art.' Bear said, 'Thank you for giving me and my family a new life.' Scars said, 'Thank you for giving me a chance.' Sparkle said, 'Thank you for helping with the fish.' Grandma Marian said, 'Thank you for your wisdom, sweet spirit, and your genuine love.'

"This went on for hours. At times, Santa and Mrs. Claus had tears in their eyes as so much gratitude landed softly on their hearts. Goober said, 'I thank you because you're my owners.' You could count on Goober to lighten the mood. When the last elf had spoken, Mrs. Claus went up to the microphone and very quietly said, 'Thank you for being our friends. All of you mean so much to us. We just can't thank you enough for wanting to be a big part of our lives and our dreams. You are all so genuine and I feel so blessed. Thank you, my dear friends.'

"Santa stepped up to the microphone, choked up, and with a tear streaming down his cheek said, 'I want to thank each and every one of you for helping make our dream here at the North Pole come true!' Then his voice got caught in his throat, he was so overwhelmed with thankfulness. Santa smiled and waved to everyone with both hands and managed to say, 'Mrs. Claus and I love you all very much, and always will.'

The Hand Fountain in honor of Santa and Mrs. Claus.

"A sea of children flowed around Santa and Mrs. Claus, locking them in. The youngsters presented them with matching white jackets with red and black lettering. On the front of Santa's jacket, 'Dream' was embroidered on the left side and 'Santa' on the right side. Mrs. Claus's jacket read 'Dream' and 'Mrs. Claus.' On the back of both jackets was a picture of all the raindeer, the beautiful white Great Pyrenees dogs, and the whole parrot family on the sleigh. Santa and Mrs. Claus thanked us again and again for their special gifts and our heartfelt sentiments.

"Now Bubbles stepped up to the microphone to announce a very special presentation for the evening. He said, 'Santa and Mrs. Claus, we want to honor you also by presenting you with something you will have forever. It's a fountain in the shape of a big hand. We call it the "Hand Fountain." Everyone in the village voted on what we should make, and our design staff made it happen. It's a monument to their engineering skills. We've placed it in the entrance hall of the castle. When you walk in, it's the first thing you will see. Please accept it from all of us with love and appreciation for inviting us into your lives.' Santa and Mrs. Claus just couldn't wait. Santa said, 'Let's all go look at it right now!'

"They stood up and everyone followed them out the door. As they walked toward the castle, Bubbles described the fountain. 'It is a clear piece of glass six feet high and eight inches thick. A unique feature is the tube through which the water runs. It's clear so it disappears in the glass and the water. The water flows down from the top and over the whole glass. At the top it is inscribed with the words, "Never Stop Dreaming." Then beneath that, all the elves names are etched into the glass. Everyone has seen it work and we're so excited to give it to you.'

"We arrived at the castle and hurried up the steps with Santa and Mrs. Claus in the lead. Santa and Bubbles opened the doors, and Mrs. Claus exclaimed, 'What a spectacular centerpiece!' She and Santa stared at its beauty. Santa walked up to it and ran his fingers over the names. Finally, Mrs. Claus said, "This is such a beautiful piece, worth much more than money. This entryway is just the perfect place for it too. Everyone who visits will see it when they first arrive. Then they will know it takes everyone working together as a team to make our dream come true.' Santa said, " Mrs. Claus and I will definitely look at this piece every day, and it will always remind us that you elves are what made our dreams a reality. It will serve as a constant reminder of the love we all share and our commitment to the same dream. Mrs. Claus and I thank you from the bottom of our hearts. We love you all so very much. Don't we, dear?' Mrs. Claus managed an emotional nod.

"Goober, Bloober, Sammie, Brittany, Courtney, and Whitney had landed on the glass hand with a splash and were drinking from it as Santa was talking. When Goober could get a word in he said, 'Is this my new bath? Is this my new bath?' We all laughed. Then Santa said with a twinkle, 'I'm sure the parrots are thankful too, since they're already enjoying the fountain. Ho-ho!'" Lady Johannah said that more names are added to the fountain every few years. When the younger elves get old enough to work in the facility, they get a place on the glass hand.

"After the presentation of the fountain, it was party time. The Cajun River Festival was in full swing. The band played Cajun, creole, and zydeco music all night. There was dancing in the streets, and paper fireworks for the little elves. They would pop them up in the air and colored streamers would shoot everywhere.

"Santa opened up the pool and Buddy took his post in the lifeguard chair. A pool party is one of our favorite pastimes. That night, Buddy had to help out a couple of rambunctious young elves who got into some trouble in the deep end of the pool. I think that was the day Buddy was first called 'lifeguard.' So, now you know where the term comes from, Lon. Our visiting benefactors brought it back home with them. Santa was so grateful to Buddy that night, he was moved to tears. Who knows what would have happened if he hadn't been there! Santa honored Buddy with a wooden figure of a dog, a precious memento his father had carved for him when he was a small child. He wanted to give Buddy something special, to honor his heroism and quick thinking. After all, saving a child's life is maybe the most important thing a person can do.

"I'm sure you've noticed, Lon, how wonderful and humble Santa and Mrs. Claus are. I guess it's not hard to tell that all of us here at the village cherish them very much. We would do most anything for them. One thing we do is leave them alone during their daily walks. Santa enjoys his private time with Mrs. Claus. No one, and I mean no one, not even the dogs or parrots, bother them at this time. Santa says we all need private time to reflect on our past and to plan for the future. So, we leave them be, and we've learned to take private time for ourselves too."

I thanked Lady Johannah for her fascinating story and asked, "Lady Johannah, could you answer a question for me?" She replied, "Yes, of course. I will try, Lon." "Do you know if Mrs. Claus has ever gone with Santa to deliver gifts on Christmas Eve?" Lady Johannah replied, "I know Susie well. That is another story, and I will share it with you if you want me to." I said, "I would really like that."

She started. "When Santa and Susie got married, she would walk with him all over Kaskinen, Finland, to deliver gifts on December 24th and 25th However, when they came to the North Pole, she stopped delivering gifts with Santa. We don't talk about it, but she is afraid of heights. She said she likes to keep her feet on the ground. She'll ride in the sleigh with Santa to pick up supplies or mail in Jemdaza. That she enjoys. She loves hearing Santa say, 'Let's go, Dancer! Let's go, Prancer!" as he snaps the reins. She loves the wind in her face and the soft whoosh the runners make as the sleigh speeds through the fresh snow. But flying is not for her. Susie decided she can best support Santa's dream with her sewing, her cooking, by caring for her community, and by being a loving life partner.

"During the year, Buddy actually uses the raindeer more than Santa. Buddy is a dear man, and he really has the respect of Santa, Mrs. Claus, and all of the elves. He is permitted to use the command 'Let's go!' with each raindeer, but never 'Up!' We'll hear him saying, 'Let's go, Dancer! Let's go, Prancer! Let's go, Comet!' and so on, with a snap of the reins. But 'Up—Prancer! Up—Dancer! Up—Comet!' are reserved for Santa on December 24th and 25th. That's the raindeer's signal to unfold their wings and fly. Did you know that the raindeer can fly only at night, Lon?" I replied, "Yes, Santa told me."

"Lady Johannah, are you off for the rest of the day?" I asked. "Well, no, I plan on canning some dill pickles later, and tomorrow is going to be a busy day also. We're going to freeze some okra and corn. We've also got to get ahead on canning some tomato juice since the chefs use that as a base for a lot of soups." "You are indeed busy!" I said. "I think I will leave you to your important work. Thank you again for the time you spent with me and the many stories you shared. You are such an asset to your community, Lady Johannah. You take such care to keep the food tasty and plentiful. You must know that Santa and Mrs. Claus and all the elves appreciate it. Look at how much they love their food! I'm sure your helpers, who are very funny by the way, are grateful for the knowledge you share with them too. You have so many wonderful talents, Lady Johannah. It's been a pleasure." She took my hand gently and said, "Thank you, Lon. The pleasure was all mine. I'll get those homemade cinnamon rolls to you!" One quick hug and she was gone.

I sat down and resumed my reverie by the river. I reflected on how I would often hear one elf say to another, "Great job today!" or "You had a great idea!" or "Thank you for your help!" No wonder they get so much done here at the North Pole, I thought. I promised myself to work as a team at my house when I got home and to get more accomplished. I wanted to teach my family the art of having fun while helping each other. But now more than anything I needed some rest.

Chapter Thirty-Four
Are the Sleighs Ready?

I woke up from a sound sleep in the middle of the night. I guess there was just too much excitement going on in my life. There was no getting back to sleep, so I took a walk through the village at 2:00 A.M. I noticed the production facility was still in full swing. I knew the elves required only a few hours of rest, but boy, did they ever keep busy! Some of the elves were working on the production line, some were on breaks, some were visiting friends, and some were putting toys into storage, where they would wait to be chosen, boxed, and wrapped up for the Christmas season. Elves were coming and going. A regular work shift was in progress.

And that wasn't all. A whole nightlife was happening out here while I had been sleeping. I strolled through the village to the accompaniment of Christmas tunes. An elf was sitting on his front porch with a bright lamp shining over his shoulder. He was making wooden whistles. I stopped to chat. Scraps of wood in different stages of completion were scattered at his feet. When he saw me, he said, "I know you. You're Lon." I said, "Yes, I am, and you must be Bamboo, the one who makes the whistles, including the train whistle. Have we met?" Bamboo said, "Yes, but I was dressed up in costume for Carnivale at the time, so I doubt you'd know me. Let's have a hug."

Bamboo lived in a quaint log cabin and asked me to join him on his porch. He was very friendly and showed me different kinds of whistles to try. No two sounded alike. Some were high pitched and some were low pitched. Some were large and some were small. The most fascinating one to me was, of course, his famous train whistle. He made it out of pinewood. "Toot, toot." It sounded like a real train coming down the tracks. Bamboo said he got his nickname when he first started making whistles because he worked with bamboo wood. He said, "My real name is Ronald Silvo Ciaccia Santoro. Now you know why everyone calls me Bamboo." I laughed. "I fill requests for all kinds of whistles." I told Bamboo, "You sure do stay busy." He said, "Yes, but I also have another important job. Let me tell you about it.

Santa's three sleighs in storage—ready to go.

"At my other job, Lincoln and I are in charge of the three sleighs that Santa uses to deliver Christmas gifts on December 24th and 25th We are the mechanical team. We make sure the sleighs are ready to go. Last year the three sleighs were totally refurbished by the design and invention staff. There used to be a bench seat up front that went all the way across from one side to the other. We took that out and put one pretty large seat in the middle for Santa, and a smaller seat on either side. We also added more safety precautions for Santa and the elves who ride with him on Christmas Eve. The backseat is for Santa's huge toy bag. All the new seats have armrests and seat belts and are nicely customized. They are so comfortable, with real soft leather to sink into. Santa thinks they're just perfect.

"We changed some mechanical parts too. We added shocks to give it a smoother, gliding landing. Now the sleigh also has lightweight fiberglass runners instead of the old heavy-duty skis on the bottom. The sides are made of fiberglass too. Lincoln and I ripped those sleighs totally apart and started from scratch. They are all a bright and shiny red. They're looking good—and what a liftoff. The Design and Engineering Department also added a new type of brake, so when the skis touch the ground, the brakes work automatically and ease the sleigh to a stop. There's a windshield that automatically slips into place to protect Santa from the wind when he makes a landing. It's a safety measure; it allows him to see better. Lincoln and I are pretty happy with all of our technological improvements. I know what you're thinking though, Lon. You're wondering, 'Why three sleighs?' Well, to deliver Christmas gifts to all the children of the world, Santa has to make many trips back and forth to the North Pole. We load up all of the sleighs, so when he comes back home for the next trip, there's no wasted time. The raindeer are always very cooperative. We hook them up to the next sleigh, Santa hops in, and off he goes again. Also, it doesn't hurt to have some back-ups, just in case anything goes wrong, which it usually doesn't. But we want to make sure no child is disappointed at Christmas.

"We installed a home map navigator system in Santa's sleigh. And, we designed a computer chip that tells him which toys go to which home. Once Santa leaves here, the computer directs him to the right house. It's a great system. It actually cuts Santa's delivery time to a fraction of what it used to be. Santa loves technology when it helps his cause.

"When Santa gets done with a trip, if his sleigh needs any maintenance or repair, we take care of it while he is off on his next run. We brush off the snow and ice then clean and polish it up. We oil the brakes, if necessary. We check and double-check everything on the sleigh. Santa doesn't leave until we're sure everything's in tip-top shape. And we do this for each trip.

"These new lightweight sleighs are easy on the raindeer too. Dasher, Dancer, Prancer, Vixen, Comet, Cupid, Donner, and Blitzen appreciate them, I'm sure. And now with the shrinking machine, the loads are lighter than ever and Santa is able to take so many more packages in fewer trips. It really works great!

"The year Hood discovered the secret of enlarging the tiny packages that come out of the shrinking machine, Santa took him along on his Christmas Eve ride. He even let him bring a friend. Since Santa makes several trips, Hood had the great idea to let some other little elves ride in the sleigh with Santa too. It was nice how Hood shared this opportunity, wasn't it?" I certainly agreed. "All the children wrote their names on a piece of paper and placed them in one of Hood's hoods. Then Hood pulled out two names to see who would go next. Hood felt this was the fairest way to do it. All the children were hopeful that they would be chosen. Imagine hearing Santa say, 'Up—Dasher! Up—Dancer! Up—Prancer! Up—Vixen! Up—Comet! Up—Cupid! Up—Donner! Up—Blitzen!' and then flying up to the clouds to make so many children happy. It was quite a fun time for them. Santa made sure they fastened their safety belts, of course. It was mind-boggling.

"As Santa delivers packages to all the children, we make sure he stays ahead of the time zones so he can get in and out before the children wake up. It seems like a spectacular event, but we really do plan down to the last detail. The raindeer, the sleighs, the elves, the smaller packages, the time zones, the home map navigator system— all of these help make the spectacular event happen. Then children all over the world awake to see Christmas gifts signed by Santa under their tree. It really does take everyone to make Santa say, 'It's another successful year!'

"Bubbles and his design team developed a highly magnetic glove. Santa loves it. In the houses where the fireplaces are being used, Santa has to find another way in. Of course, most of the time the front door is locked. In cases like these, Santa waves his hand over the doorknob and the lock unlocks. Then he enters and places the gifts under the tree. When he leaves, he waves his hand back over the lock and the magnetic glove locks up the house again. It works great.

"Some children think of all kinds of things to do so they can wake up when Santa comes. I could tell you a million stories, but for now I will tell you this one. At one house, Santa was going to enter through the front door because there wasn't a fireplace. Luckily, he could see through some cracks at the bottom of the door that the kids had boobytrapped it with empty cans. The door was supposed to knock all the cans over when he opened it so the children would wake up. Well, Santa had to think quick because he had a schedule to keep. What do you think he did, Lon?" I didn't have an answer.

"It was genius. He used his magnetic glove on one of the windows. Buzz, another little elf, was traveling with Santa that year. Santa helped him climb through the window so he could put the gifts under the tree. Unfortunately, Buzz fell and all the packages went every which way. As if that wasn't enough noise to wake up everyone in the house, when he fell Buzz accidentally touched the scattered packages with the pine branch Santa had handed him, and pop, pop, pop, pop, pop, all the gifts started opening up to normal size before he could get them under the tree! God only knows how Buzz got done and out of there without waking anyone. Whew! That was a close call! Santa said that family must have wondered where all the pine needles came from. And besides, since they had an artificial tree, why did the room smell like pine? Anyway, Santa was glad to get back to the sleigh and fly to the next stop."

I asked Bamboo to tell me more if he had the time. He was more than obliging. He said, "Santa told us about this one house. It might have been the Baker family. He put the packages under the tree and pulled out the branch to wave them back to size. When he was finished, he sat the branch down and accidentally left it there. He didn't realize what he had done until he was at the Thomas home. In a flash, he remembered where his branch was. Well, Santa now had to go to plan B. He was trying to break a branch off of one of the Thomases' evergreen trees, and it wouldn't cooperate. Co-Co was along with him this time, and he calmly said, 'Santa, would you like to use my little pocket knife?' From the mouths of babes!

"Once Santa laid out a few small packages so he could make sure he had the right gifts at the Johnsons' home. When he took the branch out to wave it over the packages, he came too close to his toy bag and all of a sudden, pop, pop, pop, pop! What a mess! He shoved the branch deep down in his coat pocket right away. Santa was coming out of the Johnsons' home with packages that were already full size again. Wannabee was riding along with Santa on that trip and he ended up holding all those packages until Santa got them delivered. That must have been an exciting time, Lon, watching them try to juggle those packages until Santa got done with that bunch! For the most part though, the deliveries are a great success and everybody has fun, including the raindeer. I can hardly wait till next year. Maybe I will get a chance to go with Santa one of these years." Bamboo sighed.

All the time Bamboo was talking, he was whittling. He finished up work on one of his famous train whistles, signed it, and handed it to me. It read, "Ronald Silvo Ciaccia Santoro, better known as 'Bamboo.'" "Very nice, Bamboo," I said. "It's yours, Lon." I was flabbergasted. "Thank you so much, Bamboo." I tried it out and heard a piercing "toot, toot." "It's a wonderful whistle," I said. "I will keep it forever. If I have grandchildren someday, I will play it for them, share with them the many stories you have told me, and we'll laugh together. What a great time that will be for me. Thank you for sharing your time and your great hospitality with me." Bamboo said, "I'm so glad I had the chance to do so. I was honored, Lon."

I was finally wearing out and ready to go to sleep, so we hugged goodnight and I went back to the castle to get some more sleep. That night I dreamed of raindeer flying and packages popping.

Chapter Thirty-Five
The Last Party—
End-of-the-Year Ball

Even though I hadn't slept very long, I woke refreshed and raring to shoot some miniature golf at the Miniature Jungle Safari Golf Course. Buddy had asked me to join him. As we were putting golf balls, Buddy began to tell me about the last party of the year, held at the castle on December 30th. He said that when Santa returns on December 25th, the raindeer are put in the stables and the sleighs are put into the storage garage. Then Santa takes a few days to rest while the elves clean and tidy up the place. They always start on their homes first. All the elves know that January 1st will be here sooner than you can say "Happy New Year."

"Lon, the beginning stages for this end-of-the-year party and ball event start with the ladies planning all the food dishes. Let me tell you, they really pull out all the stops! Each time, they make a meal that is better and even more memorable than the year before. Needless to say, the men love it

"Now, let me tell you what the castle looks like for the big party. Mrs. Claus chooses the colors to be used then all the lady elves go to town decorating. Throughout the entire castle there's an assortment of Christmas wreaths, bows, Christmas trinkets on shelves, all kinds of decorative bows and ribbon streamers, candelabras, and a variety of Christmas scented candles that give a wonderful holiday aroma throughout. All the while, dreamy Christmas music plays in the background. The lady elves take special pride in making sure the castle is decorated in a fun and elegant way, and they're mighty good at it.

"Several live Christmas trees are set up throughout the castle. Some are small and some are large, and we decorate them all. The tallest, most elegant tree stands in the main entryway. It takes us quite a while to decorate this one. We leave the bottom portion of the tree for the little elves to decorate. We all enjoy looking at what their little hands have done, since they use ornaments they have made early in December at the day care.

"Everyone makes it a point to dress up for the ball, and no one would dare miss it. Let me tell you about last year's end-of-the-year party and ball. Santa's shirt and Mrs. Claus's apron were covered with white-on-blue icicles. They always look quite smashing together when they dress for a party. They do it up right. The Golden Wiskers band were set up and playing great music. You remember them from Carnivale, Lon. Everyone danced, since it was the last dance of the year. I opened the pool for the elves and stood watch until the last elf was out of the pool. The entire castle was jumping. The game room was in full swing. Movies played nonstop. We really get a kick out of Christmas movies. They have no idea how we operate here at the North Pole. All the elves laugh themselves silly when they show the raindeer flying without wings. Lon, I've watched lots of those movies and they are really funny. The poor elves in those movies, all they do is work. They never have fun." I said, "You're right, Buddy. Now when I watch those movies, after I've seen what I've seen here, I'll be laughing right along with you."

"The elves have more fun than ever playing pool, since Bubbles devised a way to make the pool table go up and down. Before, they always had to stand on step stools. Now it's so much easier for them. Santa plays a few games on party night too. He raises the table, and the elves lower it again."

Crunch had been playing golf too and suddenly he got excited. "Hey Buddy, did you see that hole in one?" "Yes I did," replied Buddy. "However, you're still behind seven strokes." "Yeah, I know. I've been having too much fun with Goober, Sammie, and the young parrots." Buddy smiled and said, "All the elves enjoy talking to the parrots. But, to get back to my story…

Crunch and Munch play a round of miniature golf.

"Everyone is really happiest during this time. The big push for toys is over, every last one has been delivered, and the elves have earned their rest. Another great year is gone. There's a lot of hugging and kissing since we all know the year is coming to an end. At the party, Santa has all the glasses filled with punch and he toasts everyone for another great job just before the year comes to a close. He always makes the same toast. He says, 'If you make the children of the world happy, you make me happy.' And Mrs. Claus always says, 'I love you all. Sleep fast.' With glasses held high, they toast everyone at the North Pole. Then we all exchange gifts that have been placed under the many trees at the castle. The gifts are always piled high. Mrs. Claus usually does some pretty cross-stitching for all the lady elves. The lady elves make more aprons and dresses for Mrs. Claus. The parrots receive birdseed, bells, and popcorn, and it makes them feel special. One year, Santa gave all the men a wooden mug with their name on it, like yours, Lon. The men gave Santa new shirts to match Mrs. Claus's aprons, and also new suspenders. Sir King and Lady Queen and the pups always get special dog biscuits. They play with the elves until they are near exhaustion. The elves know they won't see the dogs until their ninety-day sleep is over.

"Did you know the dogs were a gift to Santa and Mrs. Claus from the elves and me? It's true. That was some years back. We figured we're all family, so it was appropriate. They are so wonderful to have around. Santa was as happy as a little kid at Christmas that year. He never had animals as a child. And now he had a pair of dogs. Santa's the one who named them. Sir King followed Santa everywhere. They were great pals. To this day, Sir King sticks with Santa and Lady Queen stays close to Mrs. Claus. The pups hang with all the elves.

"Santa's music system plays throughout the castle, so we can hear the Golden Wiskers no matter where we are. Santa loves dancing with Mrs. Claus. It's a great party." I told Buddy, "I love the stories everyone has shared with me. But sometimes I wish I could have been here to see some of the things I've only heard about." But Buddy had his head into the game. He was concentrating hard because he knew I was really trying to win. He said, "We're on the last two holes of miniature golf, and you're behind three strokes. Yea!" We finished up our game and went over to the stables to check on the raindeer.

When we got there, Buzz and Dallas were feeding carrots to the raindeer. Buzz would say, "You're my favorite, Vixen." Then he would give a carrot to Veben and say, "You're my favorite, Veben." I think all the raindeer were his favorites. Buddy and I smiled as we watched. Dallas was feeding Bloober and trying to teach him to say "Hello, Dallas." Theoretically, the baby parrots were still too young to talk, so I was amazed when Bloober said, "Hello. Hello Dallas." Buzz said, "Did you hear that?" Dallas exclaimed, "Yeah!" Again, "Hello. Hello Dallas."

Dancer made a noise in her stall, as if to say, "Give me a carrot." That's when Buddy came from behind the door and said in a high-pitched voice, "Hello. Hello, Dallas." Bloober hadn't spoken at all. It was Buddy pulling a joke on Dallas. Dallas said, "Buddy, you fooled me." Buddy said, "You keep working with Bloober. He'll be talking soon enough." Then all of a sudden, Bloober nodded his head up and down and said, "Hello Dallas." We burst out laughing at Bloober's timing. It was perfect.

I grabbed a handful of carrots to feed some of the raindeer, who could smell the luscious treats hidden in our pockets. Dallas and Buzz went to show Santa that Bloober could talk. Buzz's pet bee was following him around as usual. He would land on Buzz's shoulder and Buzz would say, "You're my friend, Buzz." He had named the bee after himself. He said, "This is my pet bee, Buzz." We all smiled and they were off. Buddy got some apples to feed the raindeer, one each. We marked on the door how many carrots and apples we'd given them, since we didn't want to overfeed them. If somebody came in after us, they'd know.

We went over to the Whispering Pines Club to have a snack and a drink. It was packed with elves playing every game imaginable. Whippersnapper said, "Lon, how about one game of pinball?" I said, "Sure." We started playing and drew an audience. Whippersnapper gave me a good whipping. He was a really good player. Some of the elves felt bad for me, but I said, "Hey, somebody has to lose." Hood was next in line to play, and I left Whippersnapper to him.

Our food was ready by now, so we brought it over to the River's Edge Club, one of my favorite hangouts. This time of day there wasn't much noise there, and Buddy and I could have a nice quiet talk. We sat at a table overlooking the J'Yakaboo River. Bear, Scars, and Santa were fishing. We watched as Dallas and Buzz ran up to tell Santa Bloober's first words, "Hello Dallas." Bloober was chatty. Santa watched as Bloober said, "Hello. Hello Dallas." Santa gave a good "Ho-ho!" and Dallas was off to show everyone in the village. He was so excited that he could hardly talk himself.

Sitting on the deck overlooking the river always relaxed me. I said, "Buddy, how do you like it here?" He said, "I like it just fine. Everyone accepted me the very first moment I met them. I've learned so much here. Santa taught all of us many things—to have character, be honest, be kind, be loving, be a giver, be useful, always be a help. Santa always tells us, Lon, 'I would rather have these traits than anything else in my life.' I feel the same way. All of us have learned the more we give, the more is given to us. We have experienced this again and again. Santa has told me over the years, 'If I could give everyone one thing, it would be to show love and kindness to everyone.' And this is what we do here at the North Pole. Santa has changed so many people's lives. But Santa is very stern about two things that I have never forgotten from the first time I met him. He likes to say, 'First, there is a God; and, second, I am not Him.'

"Lon, Santa has changed the thinking of so many CEOs, businesspeople, and wealthy people. He has made them genuine givers. Anyone you talk to here has tried to answer any question you've had. Have you wondered why? It's because we don't want to lose a single opportunity to help someone discover what life is all about.

"Lon, you have had an opportunity of a lifetime to be here. The storm will be over soon. We all know you will be leaving, that you must return to your family. If you take anything back with you, take the memories and, as Santa would say, change lives for the better. Start with your own family. It will grow from there. We all are in this life-changing business. All of us here at the village know that if we carry all these traits Santa talks about, and shows us by example, it is better than having wealth." I completely agreed with Buddy.

We exchanged email addresses, since I wanted to stay in touch with him. Our friendship had grown into a very strong bond. Buddy said, "Lon, I do want you to understand many people think Santa is God. But this just isn't true. Santa and the elves and I just fulfill children's dreams and wishes as best we can. That's all." I smiled deep in my soul because I fully understood that now.

Chapter Thirty-Six
Cleanup Under the Dome

Ce-Ce and Spring get ready to clean under the dome.

Buddy's words had gotten to me. I was already feeling sad about leaving the North Pole. I wanted to look at the production facility again and I bumped into Hype. "Hey, Hype! Give me a hug. Tell me, what's it like here after Christmas, Hype?" He said, "Let me tell you, Lon, we really button up this place. All we do for two days is clean. All the trash is recycled or burned. Lumber is stacked up in the Carpenter Department. All the machines are cleaned, oiled, and covered in a thick plastic wrap to keep dust and debris out. All the computers other than at the castle are shut down, cleaned, and covered too. The entire floor is swept and mopped so you can see your face in it.

"All the senior elves are in charge of their divisions. Everything is put in its proper location and dusted. All the fireplaces are brushed inside and out. Santa takes care of the cows, chickens, and raindeer during the three months we're asleep, and Buddy is a huge help to him. So, everything is stocked for Santa and Buddy, such as hay, straw, grain, and corn for the animals. We always stock up Mrs. Claus's pantry too. She still has access to the freezers and the storage pantry. The fish, lobster, and shrimp tanks are stocked. We basically get as much as possible ready for the upcoming work season, so when we wake up on March 31st we can go right to work on the toys. All supervisors in charge of their division get their supply lists together. Buddy collects the lists and puts all future supplies together for Santa. Santa also is a huge help to Buddy in compiling the supplies for the next work season. They make a great team.

"All the letters that were filed throughout the year are boxed and stored. The thank-you notes are put into scrapbooks for Santa and Mrs. Claus to read and enjoy. Everything that won't be used is sealed up tight. Santa's three sleighs are put into storage. We keep the winter sleigh out for Buddy. That sleigh is totally different from Santa's Christmas gift delivery sleighs. The winter sleigh is used to bring in our guests January through March, and for supplies and the mail. It will hold fourteen to sixteen people when pulled by six raindeer.

"Let's see. What else? We get the garden area all trimmed, everything from small plants to tall trees, and the bushes in between. New seeds are planted so that the garden will be in full bloom for us when we awake. Even though we call this our 'annual cleanup,' a lot of organizing goes on too. Everything is left tidy. It all sparkles from top to bottom. We get all of this done before our End-of-the-Year Ball at the castle.

"I know this all sounds like a lot of work, Lon, but it really isn't. We keep things neat, clean, and shipshape all year long, so it doesn't take long to do a touch-up. And the line between work and play is blurred here; we have fun no matter what we're doing. We still have lots of free time to spend with our families. The recreation room is full around the clock. All the little elves enjoy this time together too.

"The last big thing we do is make sure all inventions are covered for Santa. We always want to make his job easier. 'Less stress for Santa' is our motto. Then we're ready to sleep." I looked at Hype and heaved a sigh. "Boy," I said, "by that time, you sure do deserve a good rest."

Chapter Thirty-Seven
Letters to Santa

Santa felt it was important to share some letters from children with me. So, we sat down together while he sorted through his pile marked "special" and picked out some favorites. Here is a letter he received from Kaliani from India. It read:

Dear Santa,

I want to thank you and the elves, Bubbles, Shadow, Snickers, Ish, and Shooter. All the elves that worked on our home my family and I received from you, the pop-up home with a front door and windows with screens. Well, we followed the instructions and in about ten or fifteen minutes our home was up. Everyone in our community was totally amazed. There is so much to thank you for. First, we all slept without being bit by bugs. We all slept for the first time ever throughout the entire night. But that's not all. When it rained, we were kept dry. We might have awakened from sleep because of the rain, but we were dry. Some of my family cried as I did. But they were tears of joy. We were dry. That's not all. All of our clothes would stay dry and when it was hot, real hot, air would come through the windows. Well Santa, our family has never asked for anything else, but I do want you to know we all were overwhelmed and we thank you all.

Love,
Kaliani from India

Santa said, "That is what we are here for. To be a blessing and a joy to as many people in the world that we can be. Here's another one." Santa handed me a letter from John in St. Thomas, Virgin Islands. He wrote:

Santa,

Thank you for the letter you sent me with the two baseball hats, one red and one blue. I did get those two items that were on my list. But this year, Santa, I want you to know I did what you said. For my elderly neighbor, Miss Victoria Blooms, I have mowed her yard for free. I refused payment. My mom and dad even helped me make cookies, not for just one neighbor, but all six homes on our block. We met our neighbors. Some of them for the first time now. We're going to have a block party every July and October. That is really cool. I want you to know I started all that, Santa. I also am changing. I'm starting to be a giver and asking for less. My dad keeps asking my mom, "Is John okay? He's changing." I want to say thank you once again. Oh yeah, people really like being around me now. I also get more gifts and I don't even ask for them. Thank you so much.

John from St. Thomas,
Virgin Islands

"Some of the letters I've moved over to the castle," said Santa. "I like to look at them every day. They really encourage me. I relax in my electronic chair and read. Many times some just say thank-you. But others tell me more and are so inspiring. I read many of the letters to Mrs. Claus at dinner. I remember there was a disaster in the United States. Some areas were flooded by rains and the retaining walls gave out. This really was devastating. Well, I received a letter from a child in that area." Here is that letter:

Dear Santa,

I'm Patricia from Portland, Oregon. Thank you for the gifts this year. I also read your letter on helping other people in need. This year I want to give you a report. During a national disaster here in America, I knew people were in need, so I went through our entire city and collected new and clean used blankets. My dad is a trucker. He saw what I was doing, so he turned the garage into a storage facility. Mom works at a radio station and she talked about a girl who was collecting blankets for this disaster—me. People were coming to the rescue. Well, Mom never said it was her daughter, but we collected lots of blankets. People would call for me to pick them up. My neighbors helped with this. We had a team going. After two weeks the program finished. Well, Dad and the guys from the neighborhood loaded up all those blankets and Dad and his friend delivered the blankets to Louisiana. Another friend of mine collected canned food to fill up the rest of the truck. A car dealership gave Dad a check to pay for the fuel. So all Dad gave up was his time. Santa, I enclosed an article from the newspaper. I think you might like it. It brought our community together. Our little city decided to be givers. Thank you, Santa, for your encouraging letter, and could you get me a dollhouse this year for Christmas?

Patricia

"This letter just touched my life," said Santa. "There was another child, Travis. He was a real thinker. He sent an ad from his local grocery store." It read:

Every one thousand dollars spent, you will get one turkey weighing seventeen to twenty-five pounds. This offer good October 1st through November 20th only.

Santa continued. "Travis lived in Holland. Well, this kid was sharp. He stood outside the grocery store and asked for receipts as people came out of the store. He would stand out there every Friday and

Travis picks up 400 turkeys to give to families in need.

Saturday, all day. His parents wondered what he was doing, so they followed him to the store and watched as he approached everyone for their receipts. Eventually, he brought them over to his way of thinking." Here is part of Travis's letter:

> *Mom and Dad asked me what I was doing. We weren't poor and they couldn't figure it out. Well, I showed them your letter about being a giver, Santa. I said, "Mom and Dad, this store is giving away free food. I'm here collecting receipts to get those free turkeys to give to poor families that really need a turkey." Mom and Dad were amazed and they decided to join me. Every Friday and Saturday night for six weeks, all three of us were out there collecting receipts. On November 20th, we picked up 400 turkeys from the grocery store, and all of Dad's buddies helped load them into their pickup trucks to give away. We had turned in $400,000 in receipts. Well, the store said they'd never run that ad again, but that year 400 families had turkey to eat for the holidays. Thank you for teaching us to be givers, Santa.*
>
> *Travis, Mom, and Dad*
>
> *P.S. The local bike store heard what I did and for Christmas and I received a new 14-speed bicycle. I didn't even ask. Wow! Wait till I tell you about my future plans. I'm using my brain to help people, Santa.*
>
> *Love,*
> *Travis*

Santa said, "I tell you, when you give, it really will come back to you in ways you would never imagine, Lon. I remember a girl from Ukraine. Her name was Michelle. She collected coats for children. Her grandmother and mother would knit little sweaters and give them to all the babies in their town, for the weather gets very cold in Ukraine. They wanted all the children to have warm coats. Winter came early that year and stores didn't have their winter gear in yet. But Michelle had been collecting all kinds of winter clothing during the summer, so she could give warm coats to lots of children that year.

"I get letters like this all the time. I do know the world can change. People are good. People want to do better. I tell people all the time, in person and in letters, to be givers and make life better for others And I really love to hear from kids about some of the things they are doing to help people. One young man would give a gift to strangers at Christmas and sign the card: 'One of the Elves.' I loved that one. In a funny way, anyone can be one of Santa's elves. I really enjoy it when elves get a thank-you. It makes them want to do more for children. That's what it's all about.

"I'm always excited when children write me and tell me what they've done for someone, no matter how small. I want to hear their stories. Maybe they were kind to someone. Well, I want to hear about it. I urge them to tell their parents what they're up to, because maybe they'll want to help too. 'Dream!' I say. I love it when children write me about what they're doing, and ask me for what they want too. I will try my utmost to fill their requests on December 24th or 25th—with a little help from my friends, Mrs. Claus, Buddy, and the elves!

"Oh, here's one from Christopher and Berry. They were two boys from Maine. These two were creative." Here is the letter from Chris and Berry:

Santa,

We would like a train set, a race car set, two kites for the summer, two new suits for spring, four pair of jeans, four new shirts, one basketball, and could you get us one bike each? Thank you.

Chris and Berry

"Well," said Santa, "that year the boys received one pair of jeans each, one shirt each, one basketball, one race car set, and a letter from me. It ended with 'Give, and you will receive. Santa.'

"You'll be happy to know, Lon, that those boys made big changes. They decided to spend time reading books to the elderly in their town. They would make their rounds for the seniors at the Chestnut Grove Home for the Aged. The elderly men and women always enjoyed it when the boys came by to read to them. Sometimes they even got tips. They refused them, but when somebody was insistent, they put the money in a jar to use for repairing old toys. All summer, they collected old toys around the neighborhood. Their mom Connie helped with the repairs. They sanded, painted, and gave them a total overhaul. Like magic, the toys became new again. Then their mom wrapped them up and put a small 'g' or a small 'b' on the package for 'girl' or 'boy.' And at Christmastime, they went all over the city delivering gifts. These were changed boys.

"That year, they received a $100 gift certificate from a local clothing store. They also received two new bikes from their local hardware store. I brought them a thank-you letter along with the train set they wanted, and a nice radio. They shared everything together.

"Some of these stories are burned into my memory, Lon. There are young men and women, boys and girls, and grown-ups all over the world who help me make dreams come true. Give, and you will receive. That's our motto."

Chapter Thirty-Eight
The Butler and the Maid

Mr. and Mrs. Brinkley arrive at the castle to assist Santa and Mrs. Claus.

During my week at the North Pole, I had many conversations with Buddy. He and I were at the spa one day when I asked him, "How do Mrs. Claus and Santa take care of the castle during the three months while the elves are sleeping, especially with guests coming and going all the time? You're busy picking up supplies and visitors, Buddy. How in the world do all of you keep up?"

Buddy told me, "Grandma and Grandpa Brinkley are still young, in their 50s, and they arrive on January 2nd every year. They stay until March 28th, just missing the elves' reawakening. They have been huge supporters of the Kris Kringle Foundation for many years. They are the third generation of Brinkleys who have come to the North Pole to assist Santa and Mrs. Claus. The first Brinkleys were invited here after they sent a letter asking them to let them be their butler and maid. Santa and Mrs. Claus were touched and very grateful for the offer.

"The first and foremost duty of the butler and maid is to make sure Santa and Mrs. Claus get their rest. They wait on them hand and foot. At night, they lay out their clothes, making sure everything matches correctly. Although Santa and Mrs. Claus are served breakfast in bed every morning, nobody can keep Mrs. Claus out of the kitchen. She just loves cooking and baking all kinds of dishes, so we gave up trying long ago. She helps to make lunch and dinner whenever she wants. Of course, as the years go by, she doesn't want to as often as before. Today, she accepts help from the butler and maid more than she used to.

"The butler and maid definitely have their work cut out for them. They dust, clean floors, clean windows, and tend to all the guests' rooms as needed. They also do all of the laundry for Santa and Mrs. Claus and their guests. They keep the kitchen in tip-top shape all the time by making sure all the dishes are washed and put away. And, of course, for the most part they prepare the meals, whenever Mrs. Claus isn't inspired to take over the chore. Santa and Mrs. Claus enjoy variety, but they have their favorite foods too, so the chefs leave recipes and meal plans for the butler and maid.

"You can see what lifesavers the butler and maid really are, Lon. They are a tremendous help during the sleeping months. And they actually enjoy their jobs here at Santa's castle. They make sure all the trees and plants inside the castle are watered. The maid even helps Mrs. Claus with her hair. These two are very versatile.

"At first, Mrs. Claus was a bit resistant to accepting help. It was only a natural response…bringing a strange couple into her home to have the run of the place. But she quickly changed her mind. The Brinkleys won her over right away. Now she's always thrilled when they arrive. We all look forward to having them here. And Santa and Mrs. Claus are freed up to tend to their office duties and spend quality time with all of their guests. Santa still likes to spend time with the raindeer, and I help him feed them and brush them down.

"There was a time when we had thirty to forty construction workers come to work on the castle every year. This went on for many years. The Brinkleys were invaluable during this time. Now that the castle is complete, things have slowed down in that regard. But guests still arrive every year, and we've been able to step up activities for them only because the Brinkleys are here. It's always a sad time to see those two leave. Santa always says what an asset they are.

"I can tell you my personal experience, Lon. The butler and maid are always tidying up my room, picking up my towels and the towels at the pool. And I've noticed that many of our distinguished guests are acquainted with them. The Brinkleys are highly respected by all of the professional people who come here. The fact is the Brinkleys own a real estate empire. They just enjoy contributing to our efforts in this way. A funny thing is that most of our guests pick up after themselves anyway, because they know the Brinkleys and they also respect their decision to give by directly assisting Santa and Mrs. Claus."

I looked at Buddy and said, "You're a huge help, Buddy. You're probably one of the greatest assets Santa and Mrs. Claus have." Buddy just smiled and said, "I just want to do my part, Lon, like the butler and the maid."

Chapter Thirty-Nine
Back to the Science Compound

I woke up the next morning and Blow had stopped blowing. The blizzard was over. The stranded mountain climbers would now be able to pack up and go home. Sure enough, Blow told Ivy, Ivy told Santa, and Santa told me that the climbers had struck camp, loaded up their backpacks, and headed back to Jemdaza. Word started to spread fast in the village, thanks to Goober and Sammie.

"Lon, the storm is over," said Santa. "I know you will want to be returning to the Polar Ice Cap No. 12 Base Camp. I'm sure everyone is looking for you." "Yes and no," I said. Santa laid his hand on my shoulder and gave me a knowing smile. It was a sad moment for me, because I had made so many new friends. I had seen so many wonders, heard so many incredible stories, tried so many different kinds of food, and learned so many enlightening lessons that I would bring back with me to use and share with my family and in my work.

Every time I would speak to Buddy, Wrinkles, Santa, Mrs. Claus, the many elves, even the parrots, I would remember even more. In my journal I had written down many notes and recipes. I didn't want to forget anything I had encountered during my week in Santa's world. I would never forget the many hardships that so many of these elves and Buddy had endured. The stories were burnt into my memory. I now had incredible but true answers to questions about Santa and the North Pole that I never dreamed existed. I knew some day I would share it all with someone special, when the time was right.

Everyone was there to see me off. I was wearing the clothes I'd arrived in. My backpack was filled with food, extra clothes, and the mug with my name carved on it. Lady Johannah had packed me some of her homemade cinnamon rolls. I also had my chef's hat and a few other gifts. Buddy agreed to take me back on the everyday sleigh. I thought to myself, one more memorable experience...being pulled by Santa's raindeer. I asked Buddy if I could hold onto the reins during the ride. He said, "Sure." Nobody here ever refused me anything. It took some time to say goodbye. Santa said, "Lon, one more thing. Will you promise to come back to visit all of us?" I tried to made a sound but couldn't. I was too choked up. So I just nodded. I know Santa understood. Mrs. Claus hugged me dearly, I jumped up on the sleigh, and Buddy gave the "let's go" commands to the raindeer. I was returning to the tracking machine at the Twin Peaks.

As Buddy urged the raindeer on, a thousand memories of the past week flooded my mind. I also had a nagging feeling that something might be wrong at the North Pole. I said to Buddy, "Did Santa seem preoccupied to you this morning?" Buddy said, "You noticed that, huh, Lon? Santa does have something weighing on his mind. This morning Dancer gave birth to a new little raindeer, only one. This was the first time she hasn't had twins. And her baby was born four weeks early. Only a couple of us know about it. Santa asked us to keep it quiet, but since you're leaving today I figured it couldn't hurt to tell you, Lon." I asked Buddy if he'd seen the newborn himself. "Yes, and he's so cute. But he looked weak and very small. He also had a strange glow about him. That's all I can say. But that's why Santa was so distracted. He's very concerned about the little guy. We're all pulling for him." "Me too, Buddy," I said.

After we came out of the woods, I turned to look back at the castle. I had never seen it from the outside, because of the storm. It was magnificent! Buddy let me hold onto the reins, as he had promised. In a short while we arrived where the tracking machine should be. I was surprised I could see it. "It's not covered with snow at all," I said. Buddy said, "You can thank Heat for that. He's been blowing a warm wind on the tracking machine to save us the trouble of shoveling it out." I yelled out, "Thanks, Heat!" Buddy gave me a big hug and said, "Lon, it was a real treat to have you here. Please remember to email me." With a tear in his eye, he turned and got back in the sleigh, and with a wave, home he went. I watched Buddy and the

Lon sees the castle for the first time, on his way back to the base camp.

sleigh and raindeer until all I could see was the little cloud of snow they'd kicked up. I stood there feeling deeply sad.

The only cure was work, so I took some air and temperature readings on the spot. I packed them away and hopped onto the tracking machine. It started up right away and I was off. Upon arriving at Polar Ice Cap No. 12, the other scientist ran out to meet me. Sonny, Sim, Pat, Marie, Fred, Arlie, Tom, and Leo—they were all so excited to see me alive. Where were you? How did you survive? Where did you go? What did you do? The questions were coming at me left and right. Are you hungry? Let's get you warm. "Some hot soup would be perfect," I said.

They took me to the base camp building, got me a warm blanket, and fed me. As scientists, my friends were still clamoring for answers. I said, "I got stranded. I built an igloo and ate the food I'd stored in my backpack. When the storm finely stopped so I had good visibility, I found the tracking machine and made my way back. I'm just happy to be here." Leo said, "What did you do for a whole week in an igloo?" I told him I wrote in my journal and took some air readings. Tom said, "Lon, we looked for you the best way we could, but the storm…" I said, "Guys, I'm back, and I'm safe. Now, let's finish our job and get out of here."

We wrapped up our research. It had been a productive project. We were positive our superiors would be pleased. I was glad, but at this moment I had mixed feelings about going home so soon. I was already missing everyone at Santa's Christmas Village. Still, I knew they would somehow always be with me. I had learned so much in the last week, and I was taking home with me a whole new meaning of what family and giving are all about.

With that, Grandfather Lon finished telling me the most amazing story I had ever heard. I had stayed awake the whole time, curled up in his lap. He gently brushed the hair from my forehead and said, "Time for bed, Tony." Something was left unsaid. A question lingered in his smile. I looked up at him and answered, "Grandfather, I believe."

Chapter Forty
North Pole Recipes

Tempting foods from the North Pole.

Cooking in the kitchen with the elves gave me some of my best times at Santa's Christmas Village. Mixing, measuring, stirring, baking, bumping, sharing, laughing, tasting, spilling, and cleaning up. I enjoyed it all just as much as sitting down and appreciating our results. Mealtime also gave us a chance to catch up with each other. Some of the best stories I heard were told over a delicious meal at the castle and at the clubs.

Before I left the North Pole, the adult elves wanted to give me something to take back home, so they presented me with their favorite recipes to remind me of our good times together. Not to be left out, the children were also excited to pass along their special recipes. Everyone got into the act. I wound up with hundreds and hundreds of recipes. Well, I knew I couldn't include them all here. What was I to do? Then I hit upon a wonderful solution. I put all the recipes in a big box and pulled out fifty at random. I couldn't miss because every dish is a surefire winner. Now I want to share them with you. And look for a special note at the end of each recipe.

We all know how important it is to share. Santa, Mrs. Claus, Buddy, and all the elves at the North Pole practice it many times every day. Santa always says it's the best way to have fun. That is why you'll see that all of the recipes allow for generous servings. That way you can eat some and also take some to your family members, friends, neighbors, classmates, teachers, or co-workers. I hope you enjoy the cooking, eating, and sharing just as much as I do!

Elf Joy's Breakfast Spirals

4 tsp. granulated sugar
2-8 oz. packages cream cheese
2 cups softened butter (4 sticks)
4 cups flour
2 eggs beaten with 2 tbsp. water, for glaze
$1/8$ cup granulated sugar, to sprinkle on top

Filling: 2 tsp. ground cinnamon
           1 cup light brown sugar, packed firmly
           2 cups pecans, finely chopped

Preheat oven to 375 degrees. Grease two cookie sheets or layer them with parchment paper.

Beat sugar, cream cheese, and butter with electric mixer until smooth. Sift in flour and mix to form a dough. Roll into a ball and divide in half. Flatten each piece, wrap in plastic wrap, and refrigerate for 30 minutes. Meanwhile, mix cinnamon, brown sugar, and pecans and set aside.

After 30 minutes, roll out each piece of dough into a thin circle about 10 inches across (a dinner plate can be used to trim the outer edge of the circle). Brush the top of each circle with egg glaze. Divide the filling in half and sprinkle evenly over both circles. Cut the dough circles into quarters, then cut each quarter into four wedges. Starting at the pointed tip, roll to form a spiral. Place each piece on cookie sheet and brush remaining glaze on top of spirals. Sprinkle with granulated sugar. Bake 15 minutes or until golden brown. Cool.

Joy says, "Remember to share with others. This would be a great treat to hand out to co-workers after lunch!"

Elf Touch's Chocolate Gravy Over Biscuits

3 cups milk
2 tsp. flour
¼ cup granulated sugar
¼ cup cocoa
¼ cup butter (½ stick)
breakfast biscuits of your choice

Combine all ingredients except biscuits and bring to a boil. Continue to boil, stirring until mixture thickens. Remove from heat and stir while pouring over biscuits.

Touch says, "When your little ones have friends staying overnight, try this. They will love it for breakfast!"

Chef Munch's Lemon Poppy Seed Bread

4 cups granulated sugar
4 tbsp. poppy seeds
6 cups all-purpose flour
1½ tbsp. baking powder
1½ tbsp. salt
3 cups milk
2 cups vegetable oil
6 eggs
2 tbsp. vanilla
1 tbsp. lemon extract

Preheat oven to 350 degrees. Grease and lightly flour two loaf pans.

Combine the first five ingredients and set aside. In a large mixing bowl, mix milk, oil, eggs, vanilla, and lemon extract. Stir in the dry ingredients and use an electric mixer to blend until smooth. Pour batter equally into prepared loaf pans. Bake 1 hour. The bread is done when a toothpick inserted in the center comes out nearly clean.

Chef Munch says, "I drizzle a different icing over the Lemon Poppy Seed Bread slices every time I serve it. This is great to eat at the kitchen table and share stories over. Yum!"

Elf Crunch's
Favorite Pumpkin Bread

3 cups all-purpose flour
1½ tbsp. baking soda
2 cups granulated sugar
1 tbsp. nutmeg
1 tbsp. cinnamon
2-15oz. cans of pumpkin
4 eggs
1 cup vegetable oil
1 tbsp. vanilla
1 tbsp. orange flavoring

Preheat oven to 350 degrees. Grease and flour two loaf pans.

Combine flour, baking soda, sugar, nutmeg, and cinnamon and set aside. In separate bowl, mix pumpkin, eggs, vegetable oil, vanilla, and orange flavoring. Add dry ingredients to pumpkin mixture. Blend thoroughly and pour into prepared loaf pans. Bake 1 hour. Cool.

Crunch says, "Personally serve each one of your family members a slice and show them how much you care. They will love it!"

Elf Snickers' Zucchini Bread

3 eggs
1¾ cups granulated sugar
1 cup vegetable oil
2 cups cake flour
¼ tsp. baking powder
2 tsp. baking soda
2 tsp. cinnamon
1 tsp. salt
2 tsp. vanilla
1 cup chopped walnuts
4 cups shredded raw zucchini

Preheat oven to 350 degrees. Grease and flour two loaf pans.

Beat eggs, sugar, and oil. In a separate bowl, combine cake flour, baking powder, baking soda, cinnamon, salt, vanilla, and walnuts. Add to egg mixture, stirring with a large fork until all ingredients are blended well. Add zucchini and mix well again. Pour into pans and bake for 1 hour or until toothpick inserted comes out nearly clean.

Elf Snickers took a survey to see which was more popular—the zucchini bread or my carrot cake. They tied! Snickers says, "Pass around slices of both to your loved ones and take your own survey!"

Elf Pockets' Maple Walnut Muffins

1 cup softened butter (2 sticks)
1 cup brown sugar, packed firmly
1 cup maple syrup
4 eggs
4 cups all-purpose flour
2 tbsp. baking powder
2 tsp. salt
1½ cups milk
1 cup chopped walnuts

Preheat oven to 375 degrees. Grease muffin pan or line with muffin paper cups.

Cream butter and sugar. Add maple syrup and eggs and beat well. In separate small bowl, combine flour, baking powder, and salt. Add flour mixture to creamed butter mixture alternately with milk until blended well. Stir in walnuts. Fill muffin cups three-quarters full. Bake for 15 to 20 minutes. Repeat and bake until batter is all gone. Muffins are done when toothpick inserted comes out clean. Cool.

Pockets says, "My friend Flash really loves it when I bring along an extra muffin for him. That's what friends are for!"

Elf Shadow's Pumpkin Apple Streusel Muffins

1 tsp. salt
2 tsp. baking soda
2 tbsp. pumpkin pie spice
4 cups granulated sugar
5 cups all-purpose flour
4 eggs, lightly beaten
2-15oz. cans of pumpkin
1 cup vegetable oil
4 cups apples, cored, peeled, and chopped

Topping: 4 tbsp. all-purpose flour
           ½ cup granulated sugar
           1 tsp. ground cinnamon
           2 tbsp. butter

Preheat oven to 350 degrees. Lightly grease muffin pan or use paper liners.

In large bowl, sift together salt, baking soda, pumpkin pie spice, sugar, and flour. In a separate bowl, mix eggs, pumpkin, and oil. Add dry ingredients and mix just enough to blend. Add apples. Set aside. In a small bowl, mix muffin topping ingredients. Set aside. Spoon batter into muffin cups three-quarters full, then sprinkle muffin topping on top of batter. Bake 30 minutes or until toothpick comes out clean. Repeat spooning batter into muffin cups, adding topping, and baking until all the batter is used. Cool.

Shadow says, "People's ideas deserve a chance—and so do these muffins! Bring some to your neighbors. They will thank you for it!"

Elf Slim's
Pecan Peach Muffins

3 cups all-purpose flour
1 cup granulated sugar
4 tsp. baking powder
2 tsp. ground cinnamon
$\frac{1}{2}$ tsp. salt
1 cup melted butter (2 sticks)
$\frac{1}{2}$ cup milk
2 eggs
4 medium peaches, peeled and diced (may substitute frozen-thawed or canned)

Topping: 1 cup chopped pecans
$\frac{2}{3}$ cup brown sugar, packed firmly
$\frac{1}{2}$ cup all-purpose flour
2 tsp. ground cinnamon
4 tbsp. melted butter

Preheat oven to 400 degrees. Grease muffin pan or line with paper muffin liners.

Combine flour, sugar, baking powder, cinnamon, and salt in a bowl. In a separate bowl, mix butter, milk, and eggs. Blend both mixtures together, but do not overmix. Stir in diced peaches just until blended. Spoon into muffin cups. Mix topping and sprinkle over muffin batter. Bake for 20 minutes or until toothpick inserted comes out clean. Remove from pan and set aside to cool. Repeat until batter is all used up.

Slim says, "If there's a person in your life who's like a second mom or dad to you, bake them some Pecan Peach Muffins and tell them how much they mean to you. Santa's like a second dad to me, and he loves them!"

Elf Slowpoke's Pineapple Muffins

2 cups buttermilk
1 cup melted butter (2 sticks)
2 large eggs
$2^2/_3$ cups all-purpose flour
1 cup granulated sugar
$^2/_3$ light brown sugar, packed firmly
2 tsp. baking powder
1 tsp. baking soda
1 cup chopped pecans
$1^1/_3$ cups rolled oats
2-15 oz. cans crushed pineapple
    drained well
1 cup shredded sweetened coconut

Topping:
$^1/_2$ cup all-purpose flour
$^2/_3$ cup light brown
    sugar, packed firmly
4 tbsp. rolled oats
6 tbsp. cold butter, cut
    into small pieces

Preheat oven to 400 degrees. Grease muffin pan or use muffin cup liners.

In a bowl, whisk together buttermilk, melted butter, and eggs. Set aside. In another bowl, mix flour, sugar, brown sugar, baking powder, baking soda, pecans, and oats. Pour buttermilk mixture into center of flour mixture; stir to blend but do not overmix. Gently fold in drained pineapple and coconut. Spoon batter into greased muffin pans, filling two-thirds full.

Mix all topping ingredients together, except the butter. Then cut in butter with a pastry blender or two forks until coarse crumbs form. Sprinkle topping over muffin batter.

Bake about 20 minutes or until toothpick inserted comes out clean. Remove muffins and cool. Wait 5 minutes before placing next batch of batter in pan.

Slowpoke says, "Bake these with friends and you'll all be the hit of the party!"

Elf Tapper's Pumpkin Muffins

1½ cups raisins
6 eggs
2-15oz. cans of pumpkin
1 cup unsweetened applesauce
4¾ cups all-purpose flour
4 cups granulated sugar
1½ tsp. baking powder
1½ tsp. baking soda
1½ tsp. salt
1½ tsp. nutmeg
1½ tsp. cinnamon
1½ tsp. ground cloves
1 cup chopped walnuts

Preheat oven to 350 degrees. Grease two muffin pans or line with paper muffin liners.

Cover raisins with hot water and soak for 5 minutes to plump. Drain. In a large bowl, mix the eggs, pumpkin, and applesauce until smooth. In a medium bowl, combine the flour, sugar, baking powder, baking soda, salt, nutmeg, cinnamon, and ground cloves. Add dry ingredients to pumpkin mixture and blend until smooth. Stir in raisins and walnuts. Fill each muffin cup halfway. Bake 30 to 35 minutes or until a toothpick inserted comes out clean. Repeat until all the batter is used up.

Tapper says, "Dance and sing in the kitchen as you bake. Life isn't meant to be a chore. Work goes better when you're having fun!"

Elf Wrinkles'
Blueberry Muffins

2 tsp. finely grated lemon peel
1 1/3 cups granulated sugar
1/2 cup softened butter (1 stick)
2 eggs
1 tsp. vanilla
1/2 cup blueberries, mashed
1/2 tsp. salt
2 tsp. baking powder
2 cups plus 4 tbsp. cake flour, sifted
2/3 cup milk
2 cups whole blueberries
1/2 cup chopped pecans

Topping:
2 tsp. granulated sugar
1/4 tsp. ground cinnamon

Preheat oven to 375 degrees. Grease and lightly flour muffin pan or use paper muffin cups.

In a large mixing bowl, add lemon peel, sugar, and butter. Beat for about 2 minutes until light, then add eggs and vanilla. Blend in the mashed blueberries. Set aside.

In a small bowl, use wire whisk to mix salt, baking powder, and cake flour together. Add milk and dry ingredients to creamed mixture, alternating. Stir in whole blueberries and pecans. Spoon mixture into muffin pan three-quarters full. Mix sugar and cinnamon for topping and sprinkle on muffin batter. Bake 20 to 25 minutes or until toothpick inserted comes out clean. Repeat until batter is used up.

Wrinkles says, "These muffins taste like home. Spread them around and see how much joy follows!"

Lon's Broccoli and Cauliflower Salad

2 heads broccoli
2 heads cauliflower
1 large sweet onion
1 cup mayonnaise
1 cup Miracle Whip
½ cup granulated sugar
½ cup vinegar
1 cup chopped pecans
½ cup dried cranraisins

Cut broccoli and cauliflower into small florets. Set aside. Cut onion into small pieces and set aside. In a bowl, blend mayonnaise, Miracle Whip, sugar, and vinegar. Stir in pecans, cranraisins, and onions to mix. Add broccoli and cauliflower to mixture. Chill 2 hours and serve.

I just want to second what the elves have said. It's a hoot to cook with and for people!

Lon's Sweet Potato Casserole

2 large cans sweet potatoes, drained
1½ cups light brown sugar, packed firmly
1 large can pineapple tidbits, drained
½ cup chopped pecans

Preheat oven to 300 degrees.

Layer bottom of 9" x 12" pan with small chunks of sweet potatoes. Sprinkle light brown sugar evenly on top. Layer pineapple evenly across top of brown sugar. Top with pecans. Bake for 40 minutes.

This is sure a sweet way to get your veggies!

Elf Bear's
Blackberry Cobbler

2 cups all-purpose flour
2 cups granulated sugar
2 cups milk
4 tsp. baking powder
1 cup salted butter (2 sticks)
2-21 oz. cans blackberry pie filling
vanilla ice cream

Preheat oven to 350 degrees.

Mix flour, sugar, milk, and baking powder in a bowl. Set aside. Place one stick of butter in each of two 9" x 9" glass baking dishes. After oven has been preheated, place pans in oven until butter is melted and bubbly. Remove from oven. Dump half of flour-sugar mixture in the center of one pan. Do not mix! Repeat with the other pan. Next, divide and distribute blackberry pie filling over batter mixture in each pan. Bake 1 hour or until crust is golden brown and top is fully baked. Serve with vanilla ice cream.

Bear says, "Scars and Sparkle almost forget all about fishing when I make this dessert!"

Elf Britches' Pumpkin Cake With Browned Butter Icing

4 cups all-purpose flour
2 tbsp. baking powder
2 tsp. baking soda
1 tsp. salt
4 tsp. ground cinnamon
1 tsp. ground allspice
2 cups granulated sugar

1 cup light brown sugar, packed firmly
2 cups vegetable oil
8 large eggs
2 tsp. vanilla
2-15oz. cans pumpkin

Icing: 10 tbsp. unsalted butter
5 cups confectioners' sugar, sifted
2 tsp. vanilla
4–6 tbsp. milk (a little more if necessary)

Preheat oven to 350 degrees. Grease and lightly flour two 9" x 13" baking pans.

In a large bowl, combine flour, baking powder, baking soda, salt, cinnamon, and allspice. Set aside. In another large mixing bowl, beat granulated sugar, brown sugar, oil, eggs, vanilla, and pumpkin with electric mixer until very well blended. Slowly add dry ingredients and beat until batter is smooth. Pour into pans. Bake 30 minutes or until cake springs back when touched lightly in center. Cool.

Icing: *Melt butter in saucepan over medium heat until melted. Continue cooking just until butter begins to turn brown. Remove from heat and cool. After butter is cooled completely, add sifted confectioners' sugar, vanilla, and 2 tablespoons milk. Slowly beat, adding 2 to 4 tablespoons milk, or more if necessary, for a smooth texture. Apply icing when cake is cooled.*

Britches says, "I'd walk all the way from Jemdaza for a piece of Pumpkin Cake With Browned Butter Icing! Seriously though, it is a great hit at family gatherings. My wife Trinket and my daughters and their husbands all say it is out of this world. What a great use of butter, milk, and eggs!"

Elf Coco's Stuffed Brownie Bites

³/₄ cup unsweetened cocoa
²/₃ cup vegetable oil
2 cups granulated sugar
4 eggs
2 tsp. vanilla
1¹/₄ cups all-purpose flour
1 tsp. baking powder
¹/₂ tsp. salt
1¹/₃ cups white chocolate chips
²/₃ cup semi-sweet chocolate chips

Preheat oven to 350 degrees. Grease muffin pan or line with paper muffin liners.

Mix cocoa and oil together until blended. Add sugar and mix again. Then add eggs and vanilla and mix well. In another bowl, use a large fork to blend flour, baking powder, and salt. Add this to cocoa mixture and stir well to mix. Add 1 cup of the white chocolate chips to mixture and stir until combined, keeping ¹/₃ cup in reserve. Fill each muffin cup with 2 rounded tablespoons of batter.

Bake 11 to 15 minutes or until you see small cracks on top of the brownies. Take the pan out of the oven and place six semi-sweet chocolate chips in the center of each brownie. Wait one minute then swirl melted chips to frost tops of brownies. Place one white chocolate chip in the center of each brownie. Cool before eating.

Coco says, "These are a great hit in the production facility at break time. I can't seem to make enough of them!"

Elf Giggles'
Banana Cupcakes

2¹/₂ cups all-purpose flour
2 tsp. baking powder
¹/₂ tsp. salt
2 cups granulated sugar
¹/₂ cup butter (1 stick)
2 eggs
2 cups mashed bananas
2 tsp. vanilla

Preheat oven to 350 degrees.

Combine flour, baking powder, salt, and sugar in a bowl. Set aside. Mix remaining ingredients in another bowl. Add dry ingredients to banana mixture. Pour batter into cupcake pan until half full. Bake 20 minutes or until toothpick inserted comes out clean. Cool and eat.

Giggles says, "If you follow the directions, baking Banana Cupcakes is even easier than painting fire engines. My paint staff thinks they're dreamy!"

Elf Shy's Chocolate Chip Cream Cheese Cupcakes

2-8 oz. packages cream cheese, softened
$2^2/_3$ cups granulated sugar (used in two different places)
$1^1/_4$ tsp. salt (used in two different places)
2 eggs
2 cups chocolate chips   2 tbsp. vinegar
3 cups sifted flour   2 tsp. vanilla
$^1/_2$ cup cocoa   2 tsp. baking soda
2 cups water   36–40 cupcake liners
$^2/_3$ cup vegetable oil

Topping: 1 cup granulated sugar
           $^1/_2$ cup chopped pecans

Preheat oven to 350 degrees. Place cupcake liners in cupcake pan.

In a bowl beat cream cheese, $^2/_3$ cup sugar, $^1/_4$ teaspoon salt, and the eggs with an electric mixer until creamy. Add chocolate chips. Set aside. In another bowl, beat flour, 2 cups sugar, cocoa, 1 teaspoon salt, water, oil, vinegar, vanilla, and baking soda until smooth. Fill each cupcake liner with $^1/_3$ cup of this mixture. Then place 1 heaping teaspoon of the cream cheese mixture on top. For topping, combine sugar with pecans and sprinkle on top. Bake 25 minutes or until toothpick inserted comes out clean. The heaviness of the cream cheese will make the cupcake centers fall a bit but they are still delicious. Cool and enjoy.

Shy says, "If you give, you will receive. That's what Santa always tells everyone—the elves, Buddy, and our guests who give so generously to the Kris Kringle Foundation. Give these cupcakes and see what happens!"

Elf Grandma Marian's Red Velvet Cake

3 cups granulated sugar
5 cups cake flour
4 tsp. cocoa
2 tsp. baking soda
4 eggs
2 cups buttermilk

2 bottles red food coloring
   (total ½ oz.)
3 cups Wesson oil
2 tsp. vinegar

Cream Cheese Frosting:

2-8 oz. packages cream cheese
1 cup butter (2 sticks)
2 boxes confectioner's sugar

2 tsp. vanilla
2 cups chopped pecans

Preheat oven to 350 degrees. Grease six 9-inch round cake pans. Line with cut-out rounds of waxed paper to fit.

Combine first four ingredients. Set aside. Mix remaining ingredients. Add dry ingredients to moist ingredients and mix until creamy. Distribute evenly in cake pans. Bake for 25 minutes or until toothpick inserted comes out clean. (Recipe will fill six round cake pans to make two 3-layer or three 2-layer cakes.)

For frosting, mix cream cheese and butter until smooth. Add sugar slowly and blend well. Stir in vanilla and nuts. Frost cake when cooled.

Grandma Marian is no longer with us, but she passed this recipe on to her quilters, Petunia, Velvet, Touch, Summer, Tender, and Joy. Velvet says, "Grandma Marian left us so many wonderful memories. She was as elegant as this recipe—a true lady who taught us to share our talents with our community. We will always love her dearly."

Elf Scars' Simply Delicious Cherry Cobbler

2 cups all-purpose flour
2 cups granulated sugar
2 cups milk
4 tsp. baking powder
1 cup salted butter (2 sticks)
2-21 oz. cans cherry pie filling
vanilla ice cream

Preheat oven to 350 degrees.

In a mixing bowl, combine flour, sugar, milk, and baking powder. Set aside. Place one stick of butter in each of two 9" x 9" glass baking dishes. After oven has been preheated, place pans in oven until butter is melted and bubbly. Remove from oven. Dump half of flour-sugar mixture in center of one pan. Do not mix! Repeat with other pan. Next, divide and distribute cherry pie filling over batter mixture in each pan. Bake 1 hour or until crust is golden brown and top is fully baked. Serve with vanilla ice cream.

Scars says, "Always have the courage to speak up, or the world might miss out on the wonderful things you have to offer. And remember, everything goes better with cherries!"

Elf Sparkle's
Peach Cobbler

2 cups all-purpose flour
2 cups granulated sugar
2 cups milk
4 tsp. baking powder
1 cup salted butter (2 sticks)
2-21 oz. cans peach pie filling
vanilla ice cream

Preheat oven to 350 degrees. Mix flour, sugar, milk, and baking powder. Set aside. Place one stick of butter in each of two 9" x 9" glass baking dishes. After oven has been preheated, place pans in the oven until butter is melted and bubbly. Remove from oven. Dump half of flour-sugar mixture in the center of one pan. Do not mix! Repeat with other pan. Next, divide and distribute pie filling over batter mixture in each pan. Bake 1 hour or until crust is golden brown and top is fully baked. Serve with vanilla ice cream.

Sparkle says, "Bear and I love to fish and study together. Miss Needles says we're very smart. She also says teaching goes so much faster and easier when everyone helps each other. An after-school treat helps with homework too!"

Lon's Golden Carrot Cake

4 cups granulated sugar
2 cups vegetable oil
8 eggs
4 cups finely grated carrots
4 cups flour

3 tsp. baking soda
3 tsp. baking powder
2 tbsp. ground allspice
2 tbsp. ground cinnamon

Crème de la Cream Cheese Frosting:

2-8 oz. packages cream cheese, softened
¾ cup softened butter (1½ sticks)
2 tbsp. vanilla
4 cups confectioners' sugar
1 cup chopped pecans or walnuts

Preheat oven to 375 degrees. Grease and lightly flour two bundt cake pans.

In a large mixing bowl, blend sugar, oil, eggs, and carrots. Set aside. In a medium mixing bowl, combine flour, baking soda, baking powder, allspice, and cinnamon. Gradually add dry ingredients to carrot mixture and stir until blended well. Divide mixture into two equal parts and pour into bundt cake pans. Bake 1 hour or until toothpick inserted in center comes out clean. Cool completely and pop out of pan.

Frosting: *Mix ingredients and beat until smooth. Lather frosting onto the cake after it has cooled.*

Santa shares better than anybody else I know, but he loved my Golden Carrot Cake so much he ate the last piece. If you make this recipe, save some for Santa!

Elf Blue Eyes'
Gingerbread Cookies

1½ cups shortening
2 cups granulated sugar
2 eggs
½ cup molasses
4 cups all-purpose flour
1 tbsp. baking soda
1 tbsp. salt
1 tbsp. cinnamon
1 tbsp. cloves
1 tbsp. ginger

Preheat oven to 350 degrees.

Mix shortening, sugar, eggs, and molasses. Gradually add all remaining ingredients until mixed well. Refrigerate for 1 hour. Roll out cookie dough onto lightly floured cutting board to ¼-inch thickness. Use cookie cutters (gingerbread cookie cutter, if desired) to stamp out cookies. Place dough pieces on lightly greased cookie sheet and bake for 8 to10 minutes. Repeat until dough is all used up.

Blue Eyes says, "When cookies are done, surprise someone with warm gingerbread men just out of the oven."

Elf Diamond's Mouthwatering Sugar Cookies

2 cups butter (4 sticks)　　　3 cups confectioners' sugar
2 eggs　　　　　　　　　　　5 cups all-purpose flour
2 tbsp. vanilla　　　　　　　　1 tbsp. baking soda
1 tbsp. almond extract　　　　1 tbsp. cream of tartar

Diamond's Favorite Icing:

2 cups confectioners' sugar　　dash of salt
3 tbsp. butter　　　　　　　　1 tsp. almond extract
1 egg white

Preheat oven to 350 degrees.

Place butter, eggs, vanilla, and almond extract in a bowl and mix well. Add dry ingredients and mix again until blended. Chill for 2 hours. Roll out dough on a lightly floured surface to $1/8$-inch thickness. Cut into rounds or other shapes with cookie cutters. Lightly grease cookie sheet or line with parchment paper. Bake for 8 to10 minutes. Cool. Repeat until batter is gone.

Icing: *Mix all ingredients well. Add food coloring of your choice— a few drops at a time for desired color. Add colored sugar sprinkles on top.*

Diamond says, "My husband Munch swoons for these cookies. Try making them for your sweetie too!"

Elf Happy's
Thumbprint Cookies

1 cup softened butter (2 sticks)
1 cup granulated sugar
2 large eggs
1 tsp. vanilla
1 tsp. salt
2 cups all-purpose flour

Preheat oven to 350 degrees.

Mix all ingredients until smooth. Drop by rounded tablespoonfuls onto a nonstick cookie sheet. Press your thumbprint into center of each. Bake for 11 to13 minutes.

Optional: *Add 2 cups finely chopped pecans.*

Happy says, "Santa tells everybody to show love. I'll bet your neighbors would love to receive a tin of your super-duper Thumbprint Cookies!"

Elf Lady Whisper's Cranberry Crunch Bars

2 cups light brown sugar, packed firmly
2 cups softened butter (4 sticks)
3 cups all-purpose flour
2 tsp. baking soda
4 cups quick oats

Filling:

2 eggs
1½ cups granulated sugar
2 tbsp. grated lemon peel
2 tsp. vanilla extract

2 cups sour cream
4 cups dried cranberries
4 tbsp. all-purpose flour

Preheat oven to 350 degrees.

With a fork, mix brown sugar and butter in a large mixing bowl until blended well. Stir in the flour, baking soda, and oats until mixture looks crumbly. Place half of the crumble mixture in an ungreased 9" x 13" x 2" pan. Put the other half aside until later. Bake for 10 minutes or until light golden brown in color.

Filling: In a large bowl, mix the filling ingredients and pour on top of baked crust.

Take the remaining half of the crumble mixture you put aside earlier and sprinkle it over the filling. Place pan in oven and bake for 25 minutes or until top is a light golden color. Cool completely and cut into squares.

Lady Whisper says, "This dessert is a work of art. It's a great treat to share with your local fire department!"

Elf Ruby's No-Bake Chocolate Oatmeal Cookies

5 cups granulated sugar
½ cup cocoa
1 cup milk
1 cup butter (2 sticks)
½ cup peanut butter
4 cups Quaker whole grain oats

Combine sugar, cocoa, and milk in large saucepan. Bring to a small boil for 2½ minutes. Stir in butter until melted. Add peanut butter and mix until blended well. Mix in oats. Remove from heat and drop spoonfuls onto waxed paper to cool.

Ruby says, "Remember to share these with your neighbors and friends—perhaps as an afternoon snack!"

Elf Skates' Double Brownie Cookies

6 tbsp. butter
1-16 oz. bar bittersweet chocolate
1 cup all-purpose flour
½ tsp. baking powder
½ tsp. salt
4 eggs
1½ cups granulated sugar
1 tbsp. vanilla
4 cups semi-sweet chocolate chips

Preheat oven to 350 degrees.

In a double boiler, melt butter and bittersweet chocolate until smooth. Set aside until room temperature. Combine flour, baking powder, and salt and set aside. In a medium mixing bowl, beat eggs, sugar, and vanilla till fluffy (about 3 minutes). Add cooled chocolate mixture to egg mixture until combined. Then add flour mixture, stirring by hand until smooth. Fold in chocolate chips. Chill for 1 hour. Use ice cream scooper to place dollops on nonstick cookie sheet. Bake for 10 to12 minutes.

Skates says, "These cookies will make you want to skate figure eights. Share them with a new acquaintance!"

Elf Snap's
Ginger Snaps

4 cups all-purpose flour
1 tbsp. ground ginger
1 tbsp. ground cinnamon
2 tbsp. baking soda
1 tsp. salt
1½ cups vegetable oil
2 cups granulated sugar
2 large eggs
½ cup light molasses
granulated sugar for coating

Preheat oven to 350 degrees.

Combine flour, ginger, cinnamon, baking soda, and salt. Set aside. Beat together oil, sugar, and eggs until fluffy, then add molasses and stir until blended. Add dry ingredients. Shape dough into ¾-inch balls and roll in sugar. Place 2 inches apart on ungreased cookie sheet and bake for 8 to 10 minutes. Cool.

Snap says, "When you eat these cookies they will make you want to snap your fingers. As a friendly gesture, share half with someone who would least expect you to."

Santa's
Oatmeal Cookies

1½ cups vegetable shortening
2 cups brown sugar, packed firmly
1 cup granulated sugar
2 eggs
½ cup water
2 tsp. vanilla
2 tsp. salt
1 tsp. baking soda
2 cups all-purpose flour
6 cups uncooked quick oats

Preheat oven at 350 degrees.

Combine all ingredients except oats and blend well. Then add the oats. Drop by rounded tablespoonfuls onto a nonstick cookie sheet. Keep cookies about 2 inches apart from each other. Bake for 12 to 16 minutes or until lightly golden brown.

Variations: *Take it a notch up—add dried cranberries, dried cherries, or raisins.*

Santa says, "You don't have to save these for Christmas Eve. You can be a giver anytime of the year!"

Susie Claus's
Peanut Butter Cookies

1 cup softened butter (2 sticks)
1½ cups peanut butter
1 cup granulated sugar
1 tsp. vanilla
1 cup brown sugar, packed firmly
2 large eggs
2½ cups all-purpose flour
1 tsp. baking powder
1½ baking soda
½ tsp. salt

Preheat oven to 375 degrees. Lightly grease cookie sheet.

Mix all ingredients until smooth. Use one tablespoon of batter for each cookie and shape into balls. Place on cookie sheet about 2 inches apart. Flatten with fork in crisscross fashion, pressing to ½-inch thickness. Bake 10 to12 minutes or until golden brown.

Variation: *For a twist add 1 cup of mini chocolate chips.*

Mrs. Claus says, "Remember to give half of your cookies to the principal and secretaries at your school."

Elf Whippersnapper's Chocolate Pretzels

1 cup butter (2 sticks)
2 eggs
2 cups confectioners' sugar
3 tsp. vanilla

1 cup shortening
1 cup cocoa
5 cups all-purpose flour
2 tsp. salt

Whippersnapper's Chocolate Topping Glaze:

4 oz. unsweetened chocolate
4 tbsp. butter
4 cups confectioners' sugar
6–8 tbsp. water

Preheat oven to 375 degrees.

Mix butter, eggs, confectioners' sugar, vanilla, and shortening. Then add cocoa, flour, and salt and blend well. Take a level teaspoonful of dough and knead to a moldable consistency. Roll dough out into a pencil-size rope 8 inches long. Twist dough rope into pretzel shape and place on cookie sheet. Keep cookies about 2 inches apart. Bake 8 minutes or until set. Take cookie sheet from oven and let sit for 2 minutes before removing pretzels. Cool before glazing.

Glaze: *Slowly cook chocolate and butter over low heat until melted. Remove from heat. Blend in confectioners' sugar and water to a smooth consistency. Dip top of pretzels in the chocolate glaze. Makes about 8 dozen pretzels.*

Variation: *For the Christmas holidays, sprinkle crushed peppermint pieces on top of the chocolate glaze.*

Whippersnapper says, "Enjoy sharing half of these fun treats with a day care in your area. The little ones will love it!"

Buddy's
Pecan Rolls

2 cups granulated sugar
2 cups light brown sugar, packed firmly
4 tbsp. corn syrup
$^1/_2$ tsp. salt
1$^1/_3$ cup milk
4 tbsp. butter
2 tsp. vanilla
1 cup chopped pecans

Heat sugars, corn syrup, salt, milk, and butter in a 6-quart sauce-pan over medium heat, stirring constantly until all the sugar is dissolved. Cook till temperature reaches 234° F on a candy ther-mometer (soft-ball stage). When you put a drop of the mixture into ice-cold water it should turn into a small ball that flattens when taken out of the water. Remove from heat and add butter.

Cool until bottom of pan is lukewarm. Then add the vanilla and beat until no longer glossy, about 8 to12 minutes. Mixture will hold shape when dropped from a spoon. Place mixture onto waxed paper and shape into two 12-inch rolls; roll over pecan pieces. Cover tightly with plastic wrap and refrigerate until firm. Cut into ¼- to ½-inch slices. Makes about 8-dozen pieces.

Buddy says, "Be giving and take half of this recipe to a one-parent family. Short or tall, Santa loves us all!"

Elf Lavender's Lemon Raspberry Parfaits

4 tsp. cornstarch
2 tbsp. granulated sugar
2 tsp. grated orange peel
2 tbsp. orange juice
2-10 oz. packages frozen raspberries, partially thawed
1 lemon
2 quarts lemon sherbet
1 can whipped cream

In a 3- or 4-quart saucepan mix cornstarch and sugar. Add orange peel, orange juice, and raspberries. Squeeze lemon and add the juice to the pan. Cook over medium heat, stirring constantly until mixture boils and thickens. Boil one minute longer. Refrigerate for 15 minutes. Spoon mixture into parfait glasses, alternating with sherbet. You'll want two or three layers of each. Refrigerate for another hour, then top with whipped cream and serve.

Lavender says, "This makes a very colorful ending to a meal. Invite your aunts, uncles, and cousins for dinner and serve them these luscious parfaits. They will feel very special!"

Elf Ice's Pink Flamingo

4 oz. chilled pineapple juice
1 oz. chilled lemon juice
4 oz. chilled cranberry juice
2 chilled lime wedges
1 bottle chilled club soda

Chill all ingredients in refrigerator for at least 1 hour. In a small pitcher, combine everything except soda. Fill glasses three-quarters full with mixture. Top with club soda.

Ice says, "Invite your friends over for a dance party and get every-body in the kitchen to mix up some cold drinks. This one is sure to hit the spot!"

❄ ❄ ❄ ❄ ❄

Elf Jasper's Christmas Punch

2 qts. chilled apple juice
2 qts. chilled cranberry juice
1 cup granulated sugar
1 cup chilled lemon juice
ice cubes
2 bottles chilled ginger ale

Combine first four ingredients in a large punch bowl. Add plenty of ice, then the ginger ale.

Jasper says, "Always remember, fabulous solutions—like snowflake white paint—start with difficult problems. So never give up!"

Elf Wannabee's Blue River

1-6 oz. can chilled orange juice
2 chilled bananas, peeled
1 cup chilled blueberries
ice cubes

Mix first three ingredients in blender until smooth. Serve over ice.

Wannabee says, "I love blue drinks. Santa told the day care to always tell someone where we're going, because he doesn't want to lose any of us. It makes me really happy that we are loved so much!"

❄ ❄ ❄ ❄ ❄

Elf Skip's Fuzzy Peach

6 medium chilled peaches, pitted, peeled, and sliced
6 oz. chilled pineapple juice
½ cup frozen lemonade concentrate
1 bottle chilled club soda

Puree first three ingredients in blender until smooth. Fill glasses three-quarters full and top with club soda.

Skip says, "My friends, Wannabee and Buzz, and I make these whenever an adult will run the blender for us. Mmmm, we love 'em. It's always more fun to do things together!"

Elf Buzz's Watermelon Splash

4 cups chopped chilled watermelon, seedless
1 cup lemonade
4 cups ice
strawberries for garnish

Ask an adult to help with the blender. Blend first three ingredients until smooth. Add a few strawberries to garnish.

Buzz says, "This is totally refreshing after bowling with friends. Santa always says to make friends and be a friend!"

✳ ✳ ✳ ✳ ✳

Elf Skates' Tropical Wiz

2 cups chilled pineapple with juice
1 cup canned coconut milk
½ cup chilled fresh orange juice
12 large ice cubes

Mix in blender until slushy.

Skates says, "Lon, this does go down real smooth. Come visit again and we'll make some!"

Elf Hot Rod's
North Pole Breeze

2 chilled mangos, peeled and seeded
2 chilled papayas, peeled and seeded
1 cup chilled fresh strawberries
$^2/_3$ cup chilled orange juice
15 ice cubes

Process in blender until smooth.

Hot Rod says, "You will think you're here with me at the North Pole when you try this chilly drink!"

❄ ❄ ❄ ❄ ❄

Elf Turf's Slippery Icicle

2 chilled bananas, peeled
12 chilled strawberries
2 chilled kiwis, peeled
1 cup frozen vanilla yogurt
¾ cup chilled pineapple juice
¾ cup chilled orange juice

Blend all ingredients until smooth.

Turf says, "Santa tells us to be polite and social, and this drink sure helps. It's a real icebreaker!"

Elf Dallas's Wake Up

16 oz. chilled orange juice
2 chilled bananas, peeled
1 cup chilled strawberries

Blend in blender until smooth.

Dallas says, "This is a great tasting drink. But Lavender taught me to have only one helping at a time if I don't want to get a stomach-ache!"

❄ ❄ ❄ ❄ ❄

Elf JoJo's Raspberry Splash

16 oz. chilled orange juice
2 chilled bananas, peeled
1 cup chilled raspberries

Blend all together until smooth.

JoJo says, "This drink is a rosy thing of beauty, and beauty is meant to be shared. So, whip up a batch and enjoy with friends and family!"

Elf Patches' Banana Splash

1 cup chilled pineapple juice
3 chilled bananas, peeled
1 tbsp. honey
2 cups ice

Blend everything until smooth.

Patches says, "The honey from our North Pole bees makes this drink incredible. Try it with your honey and see what you think. Invite your co-workers to do a taste test!"

✳   ✳   ✳   ✳   ✳

Elf Stitches' Subzero Chiller

6 cups water	12 oz. chilled orange juice
4 cups granulated sugar	5 chilled bananas, peeled
6 oz. can frozen lemonade	42 oz. chilled pineapple juice
¾ cup cold water	3 quarts chilled ginger ale

Boil 6 cups of water and the sugar until boiling. Set aside and cool 3 minutes. Blend the lemonade, ¾ cup of water, orange juice, and bananas in a blender. Add pineapple juice and the sugar water mixture. Freeze overnight. Remove from freezer one hour prior to serving and place in a punch bowl. Add the ginger ale.

Stitches says, "We never tease or talk bad about anyone at the North Pole. Invite friends of yours who've never met each other for a get-together and let the party begin!"

Elf Shots's Cherry Jubilee

2 cups chilled cherry juice
8 oz. cold water
8 oz. chilled orange juice

Mix well and serve over ice.

Shots says, "Always show kindness to people—and animals too. Feed and walk your pets, groom them, talk sweetly to them, and play together. They will become some of your best friends!"

❄ ❄ ❄ ❄ ❄

Elf Spin's Lost Pineapple

$^1/_2$ cup chilled pineapple
$^1/_2$ cup vanilla bean ice cream
$^1/_8$ cup coconut cream
1 cup ice
pineapple slices

Blend first four ingredients until smooth and pour into glasses. Add a slice of pineapple to each.

Spin says, "Drink up and you will say, 'The lost pineapple—I found it!' Santa says to have fun every day—before, during, and after work. There's always time for fun!"

Elf Bottles' Orange River

8 oz. orange sherbet
4 oz. chilled pineapple juice
2 oz. coconut cream
1½ cups ice

Blend all ingredients until smooth.

Bottles says, "Treat a buddy to a tall glass of Orange River. Santa taught me that you never know when you will need a helping hand and someone right in your own backyard will be there to help you out. That's the buddy system!"

❄ ❄ ❄ ❄ ❄

Elves Flip and Flop's Fantasy

6 oz. chilled orange juice
4 oz. chilled pineapple juice
1 oz. kiwi syrup
8 to 10 chilled strawberries
2 cups ice
2 small pieces chilled musk melon (optional)

Blend everything together until smooth.

Flip says, "Sometimes a letter gets lost. Just know it was an honest mistake and Santa loves you." Flop adds, "Don't be upset if you get something different from what you asked for. Always be thankful for whatever you do get. It's all good! And always be a giver, then you will receive back."

Give the Gift of

I Believe
Lost at the North Pole

to Your Friends and Colleagues

CHECK YOUR LEADING BOOKSTORE
OR ORDER HERE

❑ **YES**, I want _____ copies of *I Believe* at $29.95 each, plus $6.00 shipping per book (Pennsylvania residents please add $1.80 sales tax per book). Canadian orders must be accompanied by a postal money order in U.S. funds. Allow 15 days for delivery.

❑ **YES**, I am interested in having Lonnie R. Brinkley speak or give a seminar to my company, association, school, or organization. Please send information.

My check or money order for $_____ is enclosed.

Please charge my: ❑ Visa   ❑ MasterCard
                      ❑ Discover   ❑ American Express

Name _____

Organization _____

Address _____

City/State/Zip _____

Phone_____ Email _____

Card # _____

Exp. Date_____ Signature _____

Please make your check payable and return to:
Big Bear Publishing US
P.O. Box 191, Ronks, PA 17572

Call your credit card order to: **717-768-4644**

www.ibelievesanta.com